PASSION PLAY

"The Kosinski hero is unique in literature . . . as
recognizable as the Hemingway hero used to be."
—*Washington Post*

"His descriptions of equestrian combat belong
on the same shelf with Hemingway and Tolstoy."
—*Time*

"Few will be able to put it down."
—*New York Daily News*

"A sharply controlled talent."
—*St. Louis Post-Dispatch*

JERZY KOSINSKI

JERZY KOSINSKI

PASSION PLAY

PASSION PLAY

*A Bantam Book | published by arrangement with
the author*

PRINTING HISTORY

*St. Martin's edition published September 1979
Bantam edition | October 1980*

ISBN 0-553-13656-9

Published simultaneously in the United States and Canada

Bantam Books are published by Bantam Books, Inc. Its trademark, consisting of the words "Bantam Books" and the por-
trayal of a bantam, is Registered in U.S. Patent and Trademark
Office and in other countries. Marca Registrada. Bantam
Books, Inc., 666 Fifth Avenue, New York, New York 10103.

PRINTED IN THE UNITED STATES OF AMERICA

0 9 8 7 6 5 4 3 2 1

For Katherina, a gift of life,
so much above life's allowance

All this I have said, mistress, to prove to you the difference there is between some knights and others. It is only right, then, for every prince to think more highly of this last, or rather of this first species of knight errant. For, as we read in their histories, there have been some amongst them who have been the salvation, not only of one kingdom but of many.

CERVANTES, *Don Quixote*

How can the prisoner reach outside except by thrusting through the wall? To me, the white whale is that wall, shoved near to me. Sometimes I think there's naught beyond.

MELVILLE, *Moby Dick*

Fabian decided to get a haircut. He parked his VanHome at the curb, across from the first barbershop he saw. Only when he went through the door did he realize that the place was a salon, catering to a young, fashionable clientele. There was a note of mod in the décor and in the men and women being pampered by female barbers.

A woman in her early twenties, her hair a curly, cherubic mop, gave him a shampoo. Dressed in jeans, a sleeveless silk vest hardly restraining her breasts, she chewed gum with the monotony of a tired mare chomping on its food, oblivious of the movement of her jaws and the sound of the chewing. Fabian, his head bent backward over the sink, staring at the ceiling, felt her hands massaging his scalp, the pressure of her breast against his shoulder as she leaned forward.

"How are you today?" It was a routine opening.

"Fine," said Fabian.

"You still have a lot of good hair," she said, rinsing off the soap. "Not too much gray for a man your age!"

"Thank you," Fabian replied. As he spoke, he regretted the poverty of language and feeling that so casually dismissed gratitude and obliterated one's true state of being with the soiled currency of "thank you" and the worn coinage of "fine."

"You live nearby?" the young woman asked when he was settled in the barber chair.

1

"Across the street," said Fabian.

"No kidding!" The girl was surprised. "Amazing how many people live right next to you in this city and you never know it." She began to cut his hair, her vest shifting with her every move, disclosing the curve of her neck, the pockets under her arms, glimpses of her breasts. He watched her in the mirror; their eyes met casually, then passed on to something else.

The sight of her put Fabian's sexual instinct on alert. He felt that he would pursue her in thought until, unable to dismiss her, but unwilling to contemplate her apart from that original impulse, he would enter again into sexual foray.

Yet he was alert to the workings of his mind and, after a moment, regarded the first onslaught of feeling as a momentary languor of the senses, a substitute for desire, not strong enough to propel him into the world, again in quest.

"What do you do?" she asked.

"I play polo," Fabian said.

"Polo! For a living?"

"For a living."

"In this city?"

"No, not here. I go places," he explained.

"I've never seen polo," said the girl, "just a TV show about this guy, a polo player, who fell off his horse, got crippled for life; then he had to play from a wheelchair. Have you ever seen it?"

"I don't think so."

"What kind of a game is polo?" the girl asked.

"Fast."

"What else do you do?"

"I write."

"For movies or TV?" She was still hopeful.

"Neither. Just books. Books on horsemanship."

"You mean a 'how-to'?"

"Not quite. More about what it means to be a rider."

"What does it mean?"

"If you really want to know, you could read a book or two about it."

After a moment of silence, she made a final attempt. "Most guys who come in for a haircut just sit and look at themselves in the mirror," she said. "You keep looking around. Why?"

"I already know the guy in the mirror," said Fabian, "but I don't know this place."

She was certain by now that there was nothing in him that could interest her, and she returned to her original state of boredom, drying his hair hastily, in her rush scalding his scalp with hot gusts from the hair drier.

He paid the cashier, then returned and gave her a tip. She pocketed the money without a glance.

"See you around, polo player," she said, a joyless smile barely breaking the line of her lips.

It was warm outside. Fabian decided to find a park to walk in. Before he set out, he attached to each side of his vehicle a brightly lettered sign that read INTERSTATE WILDLIFE CRUISER. In this fashion, while Fabian attended to business and other affairs, his Van-Home and his horses remained stationary and secure, unmolested by traffic police.

The park was crowded. An outdoor restaurant overlooked a meadow where men and women strolled or lounged on the grass, while children and dogs darted among them, playing. At a small corner of the terrace was a table, obligatory consumption its price. Reluctantly, he ordered a sandwich and a drink. Dotted about the terrace, old, solitary women, poodles coiling between their feet, and old men, discarded, leaning on their canes, sat warming themselves in the afternoon sun. Several dogs chased each other among the chairs. Next to Fabian, a group of roistering, young men joined forces with a cluster of college girls.

There were many of them, and they tried to force Fabian to leave. One of them asked him to relinquish the table and find another seat. When he politely refused, they turned ugly and jostled their chairs against his table, laughing at and whispering snidely about his Western-cut jeans and jacket, his high-heeled riding boots. They mocked his manner and speech; he

heard one of the more pretentious girls refer to him as
"that existential cowboy." Fabian remained indifferent;
he would not allow them to provoke him. Soon, tiring
of their futile game, they turned to the more obvious
targets of food and liquor, the sensuous weather, the
tension they had worked up.

After an appropriate interval, Fabian got up and
casually, as if searching for a dropped object, bent to
the ground. There, leaning toward an adjacent table,
he dipped a corner of a paper napkin into the yellow-
ish puddle freshly released by one of the poodles.
Then, the napkin concealed in his fist, he moved between the packed chairs, still pretending to look for
some lost article. As he negotiated his passage, Fabian
managed to brush the corner of the napkin along the
bottom of the young men's jackets, draped over their
chairs. He was not noticed and, throwing the napkin
away, he returned to his table and ordered another
drink while he settled back to wait.

The poodles that, up to now, had confined themselves to scouting the ground and the undersides of
chairs and tables found a new enticement in the unmis-
takable scent. Sniffing in expectation, with that grace
proper to their breed, one after another of the poodles
started to nose the jackets, each male dog fastidiously
raising its rear leg to shoot with the precision of a
galloping polo player striking a ball.

The sun was warm, and the men, leaning back,
turned their faces to it. The dogs sported about, returning on occasion to leave their particular calling cards,
unnoticed. But soon, one man reached behind him for
cigarettes in the lower side pocket of his jacket. He
quickly recoiled, snatching back his hand. Some remote affiliation with the animal kingdom prompted
him warily to sniff it.

Having identified the odor, the man looked around
for its source. He found it in the dogs joyously running
around. Fabian watched the man glance about furtive-
ly, to assure himself that no one had witnessed what
had befallen him. He seemed resigned to the futility of
any action against the dogs and surreptitiously dried

his hand with the edge of the tablecloth; then he pulled his jacket from the back of the chair and laid it on his lap to dry.

It was not long before the other men discovered the convenience their jackets had provided to man's best friend. In mounting fury, they summoned the manager and, pointing to their soiled jackets and the contents of their pockets, they demanded restitution. The terrace, so peaceful moments before, became a noisy arena of accusations, demands, confusion. The manager refused to submit his nose to the laboratory of odors the men thrust at him, shouting he was not a dog, as they insisted he smell their jackets. The men fell to snarling at each other; the college girls, giggling, drifted away. One by one, the aged lords and ladies reclaimed their hounds, leashing them again, reluctantly leaving behind the sweetness of a summer day, in search of a less turbulent watering place. Fabian watched the parade departing.

In his travels, Fabian kept himself a nomad of the highway, shunning the communities of vans where so many other owners of motor homes gathered to exchange tall tales of engine trouble, of sewage vaporizers, of water tanks. Like a Bedouin's tent, his VanHome went with him, and he with it, across whatever shifting landscape or mutable desert he might choose or chance upon, a place in which to bivouac or pitch camp when an unexpected oasis detained him, a companion when he bore down on the receding horizon, his thirst for what it promised never appeased, his voyage without destination.

Powered by its smooth diesel, Fabian's VanHome, an ingenious hybrid of truck and trailer, immense on its nine pairs of wheels, seemed to glide over the highway like a Hovercraft.

Shielded by large windows opaque to the world outside but transparent to the traveler within, a man could proceed from its spacious driving cabin to a sitting lounge, a versatile and carefully equipped studio for work, to an alcove above the studio, with a full-sized bed—a double bed, under a sliding transparent Plexiglas dome. Next came the galley, nautically precise, from which a narrow passage led to the bathroom; finally, passing between flanking storage compartments on both sides, he would arrive at his ministable, which housed his two horses. What Fabian's VanHome announced was the dignity and economy of a free man who cared about moving fast and about his own well-being and that of those creatures under his will. The VanHome was a veritable mobile showplace, and the delight it afforded strangers confirmed Fabian's taste, enhanced his own sense of reality. Its beauty was like the charm of a woman passed on the street, her image crystallizing a desire for something one had not before imagined.

In his VanHome Fabian could go anywhere but to the top of a business or profession that demanded the predictability of a permanent address. Any point on the country's map was his potential address, and any community his place of rest. He carried the *who's who* of the country's polo players, horse breeders and stable owners, many of whom he had met in the past, as well as directories of city, community and private stables, of public and private parks that allowed riding, of garages high enough for his VanHome, and of motor-home recreational areas.

Fabian, who could afford only a second-hand motor home, had kept an anxious eye out for it, alerted by an advertisement cut from one of the horse and polo magazines. He kept calling the dealer, offering payment, but he was able to raise only half the price.

The VanHome had been built to order in Oklahoma, commissioned by a young Texan who resisted his family's plan to make him settle down. Instead he decided to stay on the road, taking with him his girlfriend and two of his favorite horses. With the girl he played all the while; at polo, whenever he could find a field and a willing team.

Perhaps what set the young Texan originally in motion was that legend of Cortez's conquest of the

Aztecs, who, having never before seen horses, took mounted men to be invincible gods and yielded up their kingdom to them; but, immured in his metal-plated VanHome, the young Texan could not quite see himself as a new conquistador of America's highways: boredom set in. After three years of living in and driving his mobile home, he put it up for sale. For a while, there were no buyers. But finally, with a bank loan, Fabian was able to meet the price. The Van-Home belonged to him at last.

Just as he prized his VanHome for its compact and economical mobility, so also he admired the horse, a creature superbly engineered for stamina and utility. In the odyssey of landlocked man, the horse had been the oldest craft of voyage, the most prophetic ship through space. Man astride his mount—even that first man, his horse at a full run, its hoofs cleaving soil and space—had been the original passenger through air, the travel-er borne by winds. To the horse, man had always entrusted the foundation of his support, his legs and his seat, permitting only that animal such intimate access, allowing the horse to intercede between himself and solid ground. The horse carried him and his tools to work; it charged with him in battle; it permitted him his games of racing, hunting, jumping; it performed for him in a riding school, a show ring or a circus arena. And in polo, the horse shared equally with man in his oldest recorded ball game.

A professional polo player, as fascinated by the animal as he was by the game, Fabian reasoned that, if once man had traveled on a horse, or his horse had pulled him in a carriage, then now, in the era of the automobile, it was time for man to carry his horse with him—in a motor home.

Fabian reached the outskirts of a city. Acre on acre of cemeteries seemed to surround it; the dead watched the city like massed troops waiting for a fortress to submit. Against a smudged horizon, behind the giant ant hills of the city dumps, skyscrapers were strewn without pattern. He fixed to each side of his VanHome a sign that read QUARANTINED. The signs had proved useful: thieves kept away, and so did pedestrians and other drivers; but if he needed help sometimes, the signs let him more readily muster it.

Nature opened between men the chasm of forest and river, but a city offered that solitude which was not only freedom but refuge. To Fabian, a city was always a place of deliverance. Here, in this enclosure of touch, of sidewalks, subways, buses, theaters, hospitals, morgues, cemeteries, where flesh was always only feet away from flesh, all streets led to his psychic home.

The city was a habitat of sex. Fabian speculated that if nature had given humans, in proportion to their size, the largest and most developed organs of sex, it had done so because, of all mammals, only they could keep themselves in a state of perpetual heat. Sexuality thus became the most human of instincts. Life gave humans the fullness of time, to think and to do, to lust and to act. Because those powers were suspended in sleep and were to be retrieved in sex, Fabian divided his life into the sphere of sleep and the sphere of sex.

In sleep Fabian was time's hostage, in a prison which muted action, now inviting dreams, now forbidding them entry. Sex liberated him, giving language to an urgent vocabulary of need, mood, signal, gesture, glance, a language truly human, universally available. Sleep was the expression of his life's inner design, sex its outward manifestation. In sleep, he existed for himself; in sex, for others. Thus, sleep imposed; sex proposed. He refused to think of "sleeping with somebody" as synonymous with having sex, the bed in which sleep and sex took place being often their only point of communion.

Sleep came easily to him, and it was deep; his sexual urges beckoned often, their span very brief; he went about their fulfillment as in the crafting of an artwork, ultimately independent of the artist's own life. He did not see himself as sexually desirable; to be given sex was a favor, and he was always ready to return one favor for another—the gift of a meal in his VanHome or in a restaurant, a ride on his pony in some park, advice or money.

Recently, Fabian had noticed blood in his stool. Though he felt no pain or discomfort, he went to a hospital to be examined.

He parked his VanHome in the parking lot reserved for hospital personnel and suppliers, and replaced the signs on the sides of his vehicle. They now read AMBULATORY. Fabian's experience had demonstrated that the word, even though meaning "itinerant, capable of walking or moving," evoked in the collective mind of street and highway the image of an ambulance, contributing in his absence to the safety of his Van-Home.

In the examination room, a young black nurse told Fabian to prepare for the enema he required before the examination. She asked him to take off his boots, jeans and underwear. Half-naked, he felt old and inept, his shame fused with self-pity. She asked him to lie down on his side on a cot as she inserted a nozzle. He could barely hold the fluid rapidly entering him. About to finish, unconcerned, the nurse told him to retain the fluid for five minutes. He turned around and saw her shapely calves and knees, her thighs firm under the uniform. He wondered whether, in approaching her outside the hospital, he would do so as an obscurely humiliated patient, as the invulnerable man he felt himself to be in his VanHome, or as a potent athlete sitting on his horse in a polo game.

Alone in the brightly lighted bathroom, he noticed that his pubic hair had begun to go gray. This surprised him: the last time he had consciously examined himself—how long ago, he could not recall—the hair was all black.

Back in the examination room, he found the doctor, young, unusually good-looking, exuding the self-confidence and strength of a winning player. Fabian, naked except for his loose and dangling shirt, crawled clumsi-

ly onto the examination table. His thighs spread wide
by the pedal-like traps clamping his feet, his braced
knees and elbows exposing his buttocks below the
doctor's face, Fabian thought of himself as a woman
explored by her gynecologist, then as a man entered in
sodomy by his lover.

The doctor put on rubber gloves. Applying lubricant
to a pipelike instrument, he noticed his patient's uncertain glance. "Afraid of the sigmoidoscope?" he asked.

"Of pain," said Fabian.

As the sigmoidoscope entered him slowly, his muscles offering little resistance, he felt discomfort, then
pain. The doctor moved out of Fabian's view.

"Does it feel sensitive?" he asked.

"It doesn't. I do," replied Fabian.

The mascot Fabian always kept on the dashboard of
his VanHome resembled a heavy-duty letter opener. It
was an aluminum blade, long, tapering and curved,
dull, but crowned by a large knob of shining chrome.
No visitor had ever guessed that the mascot was an
artificial hip joint, used to replace an irreparably shattered or deteriorated one. It was there to remind Fabian of his fear of surgery. He recalled one of his
uncles, a celebrated scholar and writer, whose lectures
Fabian often had attended as a student. In the course
of surgery for a minor growth in the ear, the surgeon's
hand slipped and injured a nerve. Fabian's uncle came
out of the operation with one side of his face drooping,
unable to close one eye tightly, his mouth drawn down
to the side, so that food and saliva dribbled from its
loose corner when he ate and his words slurred when
he spoke. When corrective surgery failed to remedy his
deformity, Fabian's uncle resigned from the academy,
then volunteered for the war. He never returned.

When Fabian had to have his tonsils removed, his
parents, whose only child he was, insisted that the
operation be performed by a famous surgeon, an eminent professor in the medical school. Then seventy
years old, he operated only on serious cases and had

not performed a simple tonsillectomy in decades. But he agreed to operate on Fabian for the benefit of medical students who would observe his performance.

A large auditorium was transformed into an operating theater. Fabian sat bound in the operating chair, his head extended backward, his mouth fixed open. Under local anesthetic, he felt no pain, only fear and discomfort. The surgeon began the operation, with a microphone under his chin, describing to his students each step of the process, his choice of move and instrument.

Suddenly, Fabian coughed. Taken aback, the professor dislodged and dropped to the floor a clamp that tied off a blood vessel. From the open vein, blood flooded Fabian's throat. He began to choke. Reaching for a spare clamp on a portable tray, the nervous assistant knocked the tray down. Another assistant ran out to bring clamps from another operating room.

The students gasped in shock, then watched in silence. The surgeon grabbed Fabian's tongue between the thumb and forefinger of one hand and pulled on it; with the fingers of the other, he palpated under Fabian's throat, as if readying for an incision there. Mindless of his students, he alternately screamed at Fabian to keep on breathing and shouted instructions to his assistants.

The surgeon's sweaty face and trembling hands were now only inches away; Fabian, his throat swollen with blood, finally caught his breath. In that moment, streaming through the auditorium like an Olympic torch bearer, the assistant appeared, spare clamp in hand; the simple surgery resumed.

At the wheel of his VanHome, Fabian tracked in the mirror above the dashboard—the mirror no longer ready to be bribed by vanity—the changes nature had worked in his face. With probing fingertips, he worried the beady transparent eruptions around his nose and in the wrinkles of his forehead. Minuscule globules of fat, faintly visible threads of sallow grease jetted out from their wells, spiraling, reluctant to leave. He rolled the waxy substance between thumb and forefinger until it turned pasty. Then, with precision, he plucked the random gray hairs from his scalp. Some refused to submit; the broken top discarded, the lower half curled defiantly backward as though to root itself doubly in his scalp.

In the midst of an eyebrow, there was one hair longer, thicker, darker than the other hairs. Fabian hesitated before pulling it out. The defiant hair might have grown from a particular cell that had rebelled against the pervading rhythm of his body. If the hair were plucked, would the aberrant cell revolt, and a cancer metastasize? He pulled the hair out; for a moment the eyebrow itched as if the cell, annoyed by his intervention, communicated its resentment at violation.

He did the same with the hair that had chanced to grow on his chest. When he pulled it out, he wondered whether the growth of a single hair was an occurrence as unique as the onset of a cancer—or of a thought, of emotion? With all its formidable array of impersonal power and technology, science was able to explain only occurrences that formed a whole class, the genesis of whose origins and behavior—universal, uniform—could be determined and predicted in advance. But science could not explain, or explain away, the unique. What if the single hair he had pulled out was just such a one-time occurrence?

Frame by frame, the documentary of aging unreeled in his imagination: the bad faith of the balding patch, the descent of graying hair, the betrayal of the lashless eye, the juiceless eyeball, the waxless ear, the dry, freckling skin; the snares of pus in sputum, of bile in urine, of mucus in feces; the reflection that debauched the spirit.

Even though he combed his hair to mask the bald planes that flanked both sides of the widow's peak at his forehead, the receding hair diminished the impact of his face and emphasized the shape of his skull. In each hair lost, in the unannounced arrival of each wrinkle or swollen pore, in sagging flesh, he saw nature cut close to the bone.

Fabian puzzled over whether he resented going bald because it was so obvious an announcement of the process of aging within. As his looks had never done much for him one way or another, he believed that the fewer people he attracted, the deeper the hold he had on those he did attract. What if now, because of time and loss, he might attract none? He continued his scrutiny of decay. In the mirror, he caught a glimpse of lusterless teeth, now yellow or shot with blue-black mottling, a few tarnished silver fillings against a flare of gold. His gums were pale; like old chewing gum, they had lost elasticity, hardened, receding to bare more and more of each tooth's eroding root. Struck with the precariousness of his mouth, he pressed the lower front teeth with his thumb; no longer firm, they shifted slightly, almost imperceptibly. One day, without warning, when he collided at polo with another rider or was unseated by him, they might simply fall out. He kept a log of the steady remolding of his face, particularly when fatigue set in, the folds in the eyelids thickening, the overpliant chin sagging with flesh.

At such moments, Fabian saw his spirit as remote from his body. His attempts at mechanical perfection, his horsemanship, his polo were acts of violence committed by the spirit against an unwilling, submissive body. But now, his body, once only the expression of his spirit, had become a form for aging, nature's own expression.

Like any other creation, he was also to be changed according to nature's own timetable; like a ruin, any ruin whose walls crumbled away from life, he might be the setting for a striking drama.

Fabian was about to enter his VanHome when a middle-aged man came up to him briskly, one arm raised in salute. He was Hispanic, lithe and wiry. A sweeping hat, its brim cocked at an extravagant angle,

crowned his eager, vigilant eyes as he read the sign
INTERSTATE WILDLIFE CRUISER.

"Hey, wildlife man," the man called out jauntily,
"you need a farmhand? Body servant? Wet nurse?
Meat for the lions? Anyone, or anything?"

"What if I do?" Fabian replied. "Are you, sir, meat
for my lion?"

The man's hand shot out. "I'm Rubens Batista, once
of Santiago de Cuba, now of these here freedom-loving
United States." Fabian took the hand, its fingers a riot
of ornate rings.

"That's some fancy rig, Mr. Wildlife," Batista said,
surveying the VanHome with admiration. "Never seen
anything like it. A real palace on wheels," he declared,
stroking the VanHome's aluminum siding.

"I'm glad you like it," Fabian said.

"So am I. And those mustangs in there must sure
like it."

"How do you know about my horses?"

"I heard them horsing around inside. And I smelled
them."

"Smelled them?"

"I smell a lot of things."

"What else do you smell, Mr. Batista?"

"I smell a rich *caballero,* all alone in his big bed on
wheels, who might be able to take advantage of my
services." Batista jogged in place as if about to dance.
"Those I horse around with call me Latin Hustle."

"Latin Hustle?"

"The fastest footwork you'll ever see, Mr. Wildlife."

"And where can I see your footwork, Mr. Batista?"

At once, Latin Hustle was all business. "At a place
where you can find yourself some household help."

"What kind of help?"

"A man, a woman, even a whole family. People
from voodoo land," he said, "just fresh from Haiti, just
aching to work for you here."

"And you're hired to get that work for them?"

"I am. By people who brought these voodoos here,"

Latin Hustle explained. "I take a finder's fee, of course!" His teeth gleamed.

"Why can't these Haitians get a job by themselves?"

"The voodoos can't get anything by themselves. They don't speak English, Mr. Wildlife. They're not—" he paused—"strictly legal. Strictly speaking, they're illegal aliens," he announced briskly. "And there is no way back for them, no way. Get it?"

"I get it. I was once an alien myself," Fabian said. "Where are these people—and where's the sale?"

"A couple of miles away. A different place each time a new shipload comes in, on the fishing boats, by way of Florida. That's two or three times a month, if the sea cooperates."

"Let's go," Fabian said.

"At your service, Mr. Wildlife. Just follow me." Latin Hustle tipped his hat rakishly to Fabian. He swaggered across the street to where a silver Buick Wildcat was parked, then slipped behind the wheel. Fabian climbed into his VanHome and waved that he was ready.

With Latin Hustle in the lead, he picked his way first through the city's dense and rushing heart, frantic with business, then swept by rows of theaters and chic movie houses punctuated by some of the city's most stately hotels.

It was not far, less than three miles, before Fabian, guided by Latin Hustle, turned abruptly into a wasteland of sprawling decay. Burnt-out houses, their windows smashed and gaping, tottered on the fringes of vacant parking lots, strewn with the rusting shells of cars.

Latin Hustle signaled Fabian to stop in front of the dilapidated fortress of a scarred old apartment house, the entry to its courtyard garlanded with a ring of battered garbage cans flowering with an overflow of stinking refuse.

In the sullen light of the courtyard, Fabian confronted a herd of people, perhaps a hundred, mostly dark-skinned, the men in clusters, smoking, some of the women nursing babies, the children silent or playing dully. The atmosphere was somber, the clothes drab, patched, hanging and bulging oddly.

The appearance of Fabian's VanHome had caused a stir. A white man in a crisp gray business suit greeted Fabian. Even before Latin Hustle was able to introduce his prize catch, the white man made it clear that he was one of the entrepreneurs.

"My name is Coolidge," he began, sizing up Fabian and his VanHome. "That's the biggest motel on wheels I've ever seen. I'll bet it takes lots of horsepower to keep it running."

"I bet it takes a lot of manpower, too," Latin Hustle interjected.

"Well, manpower is what we deal in here," Coolidge said, taking Fabian's arm as he turned to assess the crowd.

He steered Fabian through the mute herd parting to make way for them, as well as for several buyers coolly appraising the Haitians.

"How does the law feel about all this?" Fabian asked.

Coolidge looked at him. "What was that you said?"

"All this," Fabian said. "Isn't selling people against the law?"

"Nobody sells *people*," Coolidge stressed with a touch of pedantry. "We sell opportunities. To people who need work or to people who need people."

"But these Haitians are here illegally," Fabian insisted politely.

"What's legal or not legal is for the law to decide," Coolidge declared, unshaken. "The law couldn't stop hundreds of thousands of these Chicanos, voodoos, Dominicans—you name them—at the border. Now it's too late for the law."

"You mean to say that the police, the Immigration people, the unions, the welfare agencies, the press, that they all don't know what's going on right here in plain daylight?" Fabian asked.

"To know is one thing, to do something about it is another," Coolidge came back smoothly. "The law doesn't have enough men and means to round up all these people, all over the country, to get them a lawyer, to put them one by one on trial for breaking a law they don't even know exists, to translate into English what they say and into voodoo what the law says, to prove them guilty, to hear their appeals, to try them again, to deport every one of them all the way back to Haiti or Mexico or Colombia. It's just too big a job. The law would rather chase after marijuana. That's easier to catch."

"These voodoos, all they can say in English is 'Give me a job,'" Latin Hustle intoned.

"We help them find food, shelter and work," Coolidge went on. "After all, somebody has to help them."

Fabian looked at him directly. "How much does such help sell for?"

"If you take one person, that costs more than, say, a couple. Taking a whole family, particularly with young kids—well, there's a real bargain for you."

"How much would it be for these two, for instance?" Fabian asked. He pointed at a couple, dark-skinned, the man short and aging, in his fifties, the woman, probably his wife, a bit younger, yet wrinkled, her eyes tired. The couple caught his look and sign; they shuffled with animation, eagerly ogling him, showing their broken and decaying teeth in forced smiles.

Coolidge threw a brisk professional glance at the two. "Now, a couple like that can still work miracles on a farm or an estate."

"Voodoo workers, miracle workers," Latin Hustle echoed.

"What would happen if I took them?" Fabian asked intently.

"They know they're yours for keeps. Signed, sealed, delivered, Mr. Wildlife," Latin Hustle explained.

"You mean that's all there is to it?" Fabian asked.

Coolidge shrugged his shoulders. "What else is necessary?"

"Do I need work permits for them? Social Security, insurance, some kind of official certificate?"

Coolidge patted him on the shoulder. "Relax, my

friend, you worry too much. Our voodoos aren't after your welfare."

"It's jobfare they're after," Latin Hustle crooned.

Coolidge nodded in agreement. "Remember, only a week ago they were starving in Port-au-Prince."

"Now *you* could be the prince of their port, Mr. Wildlife," Latin Hustle went on.

"You give them work—you own them." Coolidge was catching Latin Hustle's fever.

"What if I change my mind later—and won't need them or want them anymore?" Fabian asked.

"Then it's all up to you. You might pass them on to a good neighbor," Coolidge said slyly, "or call the police and have them deported. Or ask us to get rid of them for you."

"Call me, and I will do it for you," Latin Hustle volunteered.

Fabian looked at the couple again. The ingratiating smiles faded from their faces as they sensed that they had been passed over. They seemed suddenly impassive, numb with indifference.

"Let me sit on it," Fabian said quietly.

"Don't sit too long," Coolidge warned him brusquely. "When the sea gets rough, a lot of them just go down on the way."

"And as they go down, the price goes up," Latin Hustle chimed in.

Coolidge walked away, waving his hand in dismissal. Fabian saw him moving on to another potential buyer, a powerfully built man. Several airline tickets bulged out of the pocket of his jacket.

Latin Hustle looked speculatively at the man and at the tickets.

"*There's* a cat who knows why he's here. Even before he buys his voodoos, he gets the tickets to put them on the plane. I bet they'll be fixing up his farm tonight."

Fabian began to wander through the crowd again, Latin Hustle at his heels, though with diminished interest.

"But there are no young women here," Fabian said casually.

"Would you be interested in a young woman?" Latin Hustle asked nonchalantly.

"What man wouldn't be?" said Fabian, drifting toward his VanHome.

"How young?" Latin Hustle was still at his side.

They were on the street. A black woman passed by them with her children in tow—a boy and an older girl. Latin Hustle caught Fabian glancing at the girl. "That's one pretty girl," he announced.

"Hardly a girl, almost a young lady," Fabian countered.

"I know what you mean." Latin Hustle shifted into a thoughtful mood. "Would you like to father one like that?"

Fabian laughed. "Father her? Isn't it a bit late? She already has a father."

"But what if she doesn't? Would you want to become her foster father?"

"Let's say I wouldn't mind having her for a stepdaughter," Fabian said warily. "Why?"

"I can take you to a place where kids like her are given to foster parents like you every day."

"How legal is that?" Fabian asked.

"As legal as the sky," Latin Hustle declared grandly. "These kids are orphans. Abandoned. Thrown out by a mom and pop who can't or won't support them or who starve and beat them up."

"What's in it for you?"

"My usual, a finder's fee—that's all."

"From the kids?"

"Are you kidding, Mr. Wildlife? These kids own nothing. The foster pop pays. But it's worth it—it's fun to have a kid."

"Let's go," Fabian said abruptly.

"Be my guest," Latin Hustle replied.

They took again to the teeming city streets, Latin Hustle slowing his car to a pace that would allow the VanHome to keep up. He signaled Fabian to stop in front of a sprawling building, shabby but with the air of once having been an official structure. They climbed to the top floor, where Fabian found himself with four other men in a large, anonymous waiting room. Latin Hustle disappeared into one of the two cubicles separated from the room by makeshift plywood walls. The other men were in their forties and fifties. Their faces, pale and sagging, wore an identical enigmatic expression.

No one broke the silence. Latin Hustle reappeared and gestured to Fabian to follow him.

In the cubicle, a short, balding man with glasses sat behind a desk. He stood up and introduced himself to Fabian as a lawyer, pointing to the neatly framed diplomas in Latin and Spanish.

Fabian sat down across from him, while Latin Hustle pulled up a chair beside the desk, like a mediator.

The lawyer looked Fabian in the eye. His formality softened in a polite smile.

"Rubens tells me you're the owner of a horse stable from out of town."

"I am," Fabian said.

"And that you travel with some of your own horses in a custom-made rig."

"Yes, I do."

The lawyer leaned across the desk. His smile deepened. "You are, then, a man of certain means."

Fabian nodded.

"Excellent," the lawyer said with satisfaction. "And Rubens has suggested that, as a man of means, you might be in the market for—" he broke off at the phrase to correct himself—"you might be considered as a foster parent for a child of a certain age, a child with no means to support itself."

"To support *her*self," Latin Hustle threw in.

The lawyer reprimanded him with a glare, then picked up a pencil and a sheet of paper. He turned to Fabian.

"Are you married, sir?" he asked, suddenly a census taker.

"I am not."

"Divorced?"

"A widower," Fabian said.

"Excellent," the lawyer said. "So sorry to hear that," he added quickly. "And your wife died of—?"

"Cancer," Fabian said. "She died in a hospital."

"Cancer," the lawyer noted. "In the hospital. And how many children of your own do you have?" he continued.

"No children," Fabian said.

"Lucky lady, your wife," the lawyer said philosophically. "Leaving no orphans, no one but her husband to mourn her, alone." He paused. "Do you plan to marry again?" The question was an afterthought.

"Not now," Fabian replied.

The lawyer sighed as if the most exacting phase of his ordeal had passed. "And a girl—" Again he hesitated, correcting himself. "A child of what age would interest you most?" The pencil hovered. "For foster parenthood," he added pointedly.

Fabian hesitated.

"School age. Almost a young lady," Latin Hustle said.

The lawyer made a note. "And would you prefer to send the child to school or to have her reared at home?"

"To have her reared." Latin Hustle grinned.

"I would provide for her to be schooled," Fabian said.

The lawyer seemed to want to stress what he was about to say. He took off his glasses and laid them in front of him.

"Let me be candid with you," he said formally. "Do you prefer to be the original foster parent, the first adopter—or would you consider being a consecutive one?"

"I don't understand," Fabian said.

"The original foster parent is the one who adopts the child for the first time," he explained.

"Like original sin," Latin Hustle interposed.

The lawyer ignored him. "A consecutive adopter is one who replaces—or succeeds—a previous one."

The lawyer waited for it to sink in. "Most young ladies of the age you require have already been foster children—with several different foster parents in their history." He tapped the desk with his pencil. "Some gentlemen, married or not, with their own children or without them, like to offer a home to a foster child of a certain age and keep her only for a certain period of time, two years, let's say, even three. When she gets too old for them—hardly a girl now, if you know what I mean," he interjected with a slight smirk, the first Fabian had noticed, "the young lady again needs a foster home. Her last adopter now starts looking for another child—girl—of the age he is most at home with—if you know what I mean?" His smirk glided into a leer.

"I think I know what you mean," Fabian said.

"There is, of course, a greater demand for white girls," the lawyer said, his official manner returning. "Finding a girl up for her first adoption is usually more expensive," he added in a cautionary tone.

"Not yet a lady," Latin Hustle crooned half to himself.

"But after two or three adoptions, the welfare people get more cooperative, and the girl gets cheaper," the lawyer reassured Fabian.

"Not a lady anymore," Latin Hustle cut in.

"And what is the cost of adopting an average foster child?" Fabian asked.

"That would depend, of course, on the child, her color, her background, her looks, et cetera," the lawyer said speculatively, making some calculations.

"The et cetera adds to the price," said Latin Hustle.

"But I daresay a little girl could fulfill all your expectations for no more than you might pay for a pleasure-riding pony," the lawyer concluded.

"Pleasure-riding it is!" Latin Hustle erupted.

As if the matter were settled, the lawyer quickly placed in front of Fabian a large portfolio of neatly mounted photographs of boys and girls. "They're all here," he said. "Unfortunately, some pictures are of inferior quality."

"But fortunately, the girls are not." Latin Hustle winked.

"Vital statistics—age, body size, height, weight, et cetera—are noted under each picture," the lawyer said briskly. "The initials refer to the file we keep on each child—family records, church, school and foster-care agency affiliations, prior accidents. . . ."

"Arrests for vagrancy." Latin Hustle was growing bolder.

The lawyer tried hopelessly to wither him with a stare. "Vagrancy is a hazard with adventurous children," he said coldly. Then, anxious to regain lost ground with Fabian, he hastened to add: "To protect the adopter from unwarranted legal surveillance, we never fail to provide him with statements from certain welfare caseworkers, among others, who certify that the foster child has had a history of insinuating—even inventing—that her new father has shown her the wrong kind of affection. In other words, we try to make it legally clear that she is susceptible to flights of fancy."

"Is there a lot of paperwork involved in such an adoption?" Fabian asked.

The lawyer waved his hand. "There is. But, as I said, those we do business with are most enlightened, and they're our friends."

"What if the girl turns out to be a disappointment?" Fabian asked.

"She might be helped to run away," Latin Hustle suggested.

"As I said, we can put her up for adoption again," the lawyer said, a shade testily. "You might then want to adopt another child, older, or perhaps younger," he went on.

"A real professional father." Delight could be heard in Latin Hustle's voice.

The lawyer stood up, his business at an end. "Please feel free to take your time with this," he said, deposit-

ing the heavy album in his client's trust. Latin Hustle
ushered Fabian ceremoniously out of the cubicle, settled him on a bench in the waiting room and again
disappeared behind one of the plywood walls. Three
men remained in the room. No flicker of curiosity
disturbed them as Fabian turned the thick, glossy
pages of the portfolio; the book held no surprises for
them.

Most of the photographs had been taken with a
Polaroid camera or in an automatic booth at some
amusement park or bus station. Several bore traces of
having been torn out of a family album, or from a
newspaper or magazine illustrating the more blatant or
lurid cases of child abuse. Every photograph pictured a
girl or boy of school age, some smiling with naive
seduction, some staring blandly, others frowning, as if
annoyed, frightened or suspicious.

Fabian's eyes stopped at the photograph of a girl,
perhaps fourteen, frail, her eyes expressive, her lips full
in a face of Latin intensity. Her black hair, long and
gleaming, hung loosely draped over her shoulders; an
oversized robe, cinched like a monk's habit around her
boyish waist, shrouded her; a towel dangled over one
arm.

For a moment, Fabian felt the impulse to write
down the number and the initials underneath the photograph, and to embark on the road of fatherhood.

In that moment, he acknowledged he had neither the
energy nor the means to follow through. He weighed
the page, then reluctantly turned it over. Sliding, it
joined the ones that had gone before.

He drove through the city's financial district, almost
deserted at the close of business, until he found a large,
empty parking lot wedged in between skyscrapers mir-
roring, in the neat rows of spaces, the buildings' in-
finity of identical windows. Fabian parked his Van-
Home so as to block entirely the entrance to the lot.
He had now created a field for his horses and his polo.

Lowering the rear platform of the VanHome, he drew the two mares out, Gaited Amble briskly sniffing the air, Big Lick capering and prancing, eager for movement.

Gaited Amble was an American Saddle horse, creamy white with a flat face and small, slender ears. It stood something over five feet at the crest of the base of the neck, or sixteen hands, as horsemen like to put it, the neck arching gracefully at a curve not common to any other breed. When Gaited Amble stood motionless, its short back gave the impression of having been abandoned by a heedless or impatient sculptor. Big Lick, a Tennessee Walking horse, was a sharp contrast, just under fifteen hands and jet black, with a patrician muzzle and short, round ears well set on a thick, sturdy neck, its ribs well sprung, giving way to broad, muscular hindquarters.

Professional polo players, who rode swifter, bolder and more agile Thoroughbreds, were open in their ridicule of Fabian's ponies. They pointed out that the long curving neck of Gaited Amble obstructed its rider's view and made hitting the ball, particularly underneath the horse's neck, difficult. And occasionally when Big Lick broke into a canter or gallop, its old show habits recurred, and it bobbed up and down or swayed to and fro like a wooden horse on a carousel. Fabian took his critics' disdainful ridicule as casually as did his ponies.

He had acquired each for a third of their market value only because they repeatedly had failed as show horses. He had retrained them for polo himself and, to keep them accustomed to the speed and rough-and-tumble of the game, rode them whenever he was invited to play.

But he continued to school them in the gaits they had learned, omitting only the excesses to which they had been subjected in training for show. Gaited Amble, for example, like most other American Saddle horses, had been drilled repeatedly in performing the gaits its breed was celebrated for—a fancy caper, a distinguished trot and its famous amble, that broken, slow pace in which the hoofs hit the ground at predetermined intervals.

The elegant carriage of the mare had been contrived by cutting the depressor muscles at the base of its tail. The horse had been fitted with a harness that forced the tail to be erect and would not permit the severed muscles to heal; before each show or display the harness was removed and, to enhance even further the pluming jet of the tail, a galling powder was inserted into the anus of the animal. The tail rose to still more exalted height.

Even after Fabian had come into possession of Gaited Amble and had abandoned the harness, the tail did not soon return to its normal mobility. To protect the horse from flies each time it was let out, Fabian had had to spray it with insect repellent.

In its poised, harmoniously composed stance and the taut slimness of its body, Big Lick, like Gaited Amble, was a triumph of the labor and persistence of its previous owner. As with most Tennessee Walkers, the three special gaits that were its trademark had been cultivated by a unique regimen. The horse had been shod with elevated pads and heavy wedges, unevenly angled, that strained its muscles and ligaments into an altered stride. Its forelimbs had been smeared just above the hoofs with a potent chemical lubricant, then cinched with chains near the joint and encased in weighted boots. The chemical, together with habitual movement of the chains and boots, had created sores so inflamed that they often ate two or three inches into the flesh. Precariously balanced in its altered gait, the horse, to relieve the burning lesions, would resort to the exaggerated prancing for which it was prized. Foremost among these was the running walk, a gait crowned by the "big lick," in which the horse's foreleg was raised to its peak. At the same time the hind leg would cleave the air, overstepping the track of the front leg by as much as fifty inches.

To slim the line of its belly, Big Lick had been fed a special diet; to trim the neck and shoulders, it had been forced to sweat for months under a plastic hood. Even the exaggerated arch of the mare's neck was the result of years of pressure from a gradually tightened checkrein.

In the parking lot, Fabian put rubber boots on his horses' hoofs for protection against the asphalt, then rode each horse around and across the lot, allowing it to sense the unfamiliar air, explore the unknown landscape.

He began to feel the grip of that peculiar elation that came over him when he was about to challenge a horse's might with the precision and command of his own performance. Fabian knew that the beauty, allure and menace of the horse rested solely in its anatomy and not in a complex intelligence: the union of rider and mount was, at base, a duel of human brain and animal physiology. He had a repertoire of images for this elusive and mysterious essence of the horse. Sometimes he thought of it as a self-propelled crane, with the animal's back as the cab and its arching neck as the boom, now raising and lowering the bucket which was its head. Then a horse would seem to him a mobile suspension bridge, its legs the pylons, its muscles the cables; or as a kind of autonomous spring mechanism that would catapult itself up and forward through space, then return to earth unshaken, ready to rebound.

But just as those sophisticated devices were vulnerable to misuse, so, too, any horse, however skillfully trained, might, when pushed beyond the limits of its physiology by a rider's will, collapse without a flutter of warning; the most bitter penalty for any polo player was to have his pony violently give way under him during a game.

Fabian had once heard, perhaps at one of those fire-and-brimstone revival meetings he sometimes came upon in his travels, that if God wished truly to lay a man low, he would take from him the sacred flame. Fabian knew that his only fire was polo, his only art the power, mounted and in motion, to strike a moving ball, his only craft the guile to place that ball where he would within the field, undaunted by the presence of other players—he astride the horse at full gallop, his polo stick a lance at the ready, his brain a compressor of present, past, future in a single act, matchless, without flaw. Within the compass of this briefest, most incandescent of life's occasions, he was possessed by bliss, surprised by joy, a pioneer beyond the realm of known condition and circumstance, a god in a perfect moment of existence.

After moving both horses at a brisk trot around the empty lot, Fabian picked up a mallet, threw a ball out into the darkening silence and mounted Gaited Amble. He used occasions such as this to practice what professional polo players called stick-and-ball—riding out to strike the ball over and over again, in solitude, away from the heady turbulence of the game, where, unexpectedly, from any quarter, the ball might come rushing at one headlong.

Besides maintaining his aim and coordination, stick-and-ball kept his ponies accustomed to the swing of the mallet and alert to the game's jostling and collision. He had constructed a rig which harnessed them together in a combination of bridle and surcingle. Now, astride Gaited Amble, he was still able to lead both horses with his left hand. With his right he was free to strike the ball from either side of the horse; sometimes his mallet inadvertently flew out and harshly whipped Big Lick, dragged about haphazardly by the rig. Slipping and stumbling on the lot's pitted, uneven surface, the horses sometimes crashed brutally into each other, rearing up, bucking, their shoulders and flanks in a steady, nervous scrimmage.

With Gaited Amble primed and ready, it was Big Lick's turn, and, mallet in hand, without losing momentum, Fabian vaulted onto the saddle.

At once, free of his weight, Gaited Amble picked up speed, sprinting and trotting as much as the harness would allow. The mare now became the target for some of Fabian's flaring strokes, but still did not shy from them, keeping its pace. Once again, Fabian reflected, his ponies had demonstrated their acquiescence to his will, had justified his reliance on them in the game.

In short spurts of trot, canter and gallop, grasping the reins and a whip in his left hand, the mallet in his right hand, Fabian entered upon the ritual of stick-and-ball. He began to drive the ball forward across the lot with a relentless volley of forehand shots; as it bounced and veered off course, he caught it in a steady flow of backhand strokes. Then, describing another pattern in the crisscross intersection of parking lot transmuted into polo field, he reversed his strategy, angling to the left over the horse's withers and propelling the ball backhand; as the ball rushed back, he followed it and lofted it with a forehand shot.

The intense running exhausted Big Lick; the mare stumbled and lost its footing. Fabian tied the animal, foaming, to the back of the VanHome. Sensing its turn, Gaited Amble began to prance and sidestep eagerly, ears twitching in nervous expectation. Now Fabian placed an array of empty wine bottles upright at the far end of the lot, scattering several balls in the space between. Mounting the pony, he prodded its sides sharply. From its easy standstill Gaited Amble shot out in full racing mettle, legs stretched, hoofs pounding.

Fabian kept the mare in tight check, in a sequence of pivot, half-turn, gallop, with the ball always near the horse's forelegs. Shuttling his eyes between the ball and a bottle, he accelerated for the fury of a strike, wielding an erect mallet, his right arm arched up and back, his elbow and wrist locked. Rising with the spring of his taut knees and feet, thighs clutching Gaited Amble, he thrust his left shoulder forward and, with a scythe-like movement, swung his upraised mallet in a mighty blow at the scampering ball, sending it fifty yards in a graceful jet before it shattered one of the bottles, splintering the afternoon's silence.

Suddenly a shower of flying glass fell away in the

distance to disclose the figure of a derelict huddling, as if fixed to one of the grimy walls that enclosed the lot.

Fabian slowed Gaited Amble and rode it toward the wall where the man cowered. The mare whinnied and shied uneasily, reluctant to inch closer to the vagrant. The man, his pants smeared and caked with dirt, was wrapped in a tattered raincoat, one of its sleeves half torn off at a jagged angle.

"What's the riding for, captain?" he asked, revealing his missing teeth.

"To make a living," said Fabian, prodding his horse closer.

"In that Big Top?" asked the man, pointing to the VanHome.

"It's my home."

The man raised one hand—its swollen wrist a feverish, scaly red, ending in fingers that were stumpy and clubbed—to pat the horse, but when Gaited Amble snorted nervously, he withdrew it quickly.

"Would you have some soup left, captain?" His glance pleaded.

Fabian backed off Gaited Amble, turning as if to leave. "Come and see me at home," he said.

The man followed Fabian and his horse unsteadily across the lot, sweating as he tried to keep up with them. He hesitated at the door of the VanHome as Fabian tied Gaited Amble alongside Big Lick.

"I don't visit often," he said, peering suspiciously through the door. "You won't kidnap me, captain?"

"Kidnap you? What for?"

"To experiment," he whispered. "To try things on me: drugs, a beating, a torching. Guys do things like that to people like me, you know."

"I don't deliberately hurt people," said Fabian. "I like them. I play with them."

They were now inside the VanHome. The man looked about curiously. "Mind if I see the rest, captain?"

Clutching his raincoat, deference mingled with caution, he followed Fabian to the galley, where he carefully examined the power generator and the microwave oven, jumped back in alarm as Fabian set in motion the compactor, and smiled with faint puzzlement as Fabian explained to him the self-timing, automatic trouser-press. He was fascinated by the bathroom, a Fiberglas module containing a sink, toilet and built-in whirlpool bathtub. He nodded with approval at the medicine chest. Trotting in Fabian's footsteps, he peeked into rooms stored with polo gear and tack and equipment for the schooling of horses. The saddle and boot racks as well as Fabian's clothes and riding apparel did not interest him at all, but he was taken aback by the sight of the fully rigged practice horse. Made of wood and set on springs, the fifteen-hands-high horse was enclosed within a vaulting cage of chicken wire; astride its immobile bulk, Fabian would stick-and-ball, his shots recoiling from the wire mesh of the cage.

In the galley, as the man slurped the soup Fabian had heated and served him, his eyes kept darting to the row of bottles at the bar. When he finished, he asked for a drink, and Fabian fixed it for him. They moved into the lounge.

"Some home to have," the man exclaimed. "Some have no home," he mused, looking around. "In a pawnshop, any gizmo like this could keep my kind for a whole year," he muttered, his eyes fixed on the TV console. "It's a nice home, captain," he said finally. "Really nice. How do you keep it?"

"I fight for it," said Fabian.

"You fight for it?"

Fabian nodded.

The man moved closer. "Dangerous? Can you be killed?"

Fabian nodded again.

"Why do you fight like that?"

"Because of you," said Fabian, pouring him another drink.

The man reached for it eagerly, his hand trembling.

"Because of me? How come, captain?" A sudden glint in his eyes showed that he sniffed some reward.

"I fight for this home so I won't become what you are," said Fabian.

The man lowered his head. Without a word, as if absorbed in solitary thought, he slowly sipped his drink.

Fabian had a fear of inordinate skill. He felt awed and troubled by his aim—that elusive interplay of muscle, vision, brain, that rippling fusion of reflexes, that constellation and apparatus of impulse, knowledge and will which enabled him, while mounted on a horse at swiftest gallop, to hit a polo ball, lying seven feet from his shoulder, so precisely that it would reach a target no larger than a player's helmet and forty yards or more away. What's more, he could maintain that precision for at least sixty strikes out of a hundred. He knew that such skill carried with it a state of uncertainty, a mood of apprehension: the possibility of failure. The man who attained a pitch of skill in sport or trade, in some profession or in his intimate relations with other men and women, had undoubtedly found the most direct path to his goal. Yet, confusing progress toward that goal with progress through life, he believed that he had simplified the maze of life. He would, however, soon lose himself in one of the traps which composed that maze, many of them unavoidable, even inevitable, and so become the prey of his own facility, a parody of prowess and of technique.

Fabian had discovered his aim as a boy, playing a peasant game, astride a farm horse at full gallop: with a rake handle, he had sent a ball, the size of an apple, twenty yards across a meadow, hitting a target no larger than a pumpkin. It had been his first strike; he hit the target a second time, then a third, finally a fourth. Since that time, his aim had not failed him: it was not he who had shaped his faultless stroke, but the faultless stroke that had shaped him. To that wisdom of his body he submitted himself implicitly. He wondered often if an advance agent of conscious choice had determined so early that polo would be the landscape of his potency.

Fabian imagined the components of each strike: the plane of the field and the level of his shoulder, the pliancy of his mallet shaft and the hardwood of its head, the resistance of grass and air to the trajectory of the ball, his body's shifts and changes, his pony's speed; in this plenitude of variables and circumstances, he saw his counters to chance. Whether he was alone or in collision with other players, whether he swung at the ball from the horse's side or under its neck or tail, the ball Fabian hit sped to its target.

Polo was a team game, the roles of its four players clearly delineated: always forward, number one set up the shots; number two was a driving force of attack; number three, the pivot man, often captain of his team, linked attack with defense; number four stood guard at the team's back. No one of those roles fully consumed Fabian's ability to strike and to score—and to do this unaided. Most players were content to outmaneuver their opponents in reaching the ball, wrestling it from them, driving it in the direction of the goal posts. The confrontation of opposing teams, each attempting to score a higher number of goals, was the core of polo, but for Fabian the game was essentially a one-on-one contest between two players fighting for possession of the ball during any moment of the game. From the outset of his career, his disregard of the other three players on his team—many of them standing in the foremost international ranks—antagonized and humiliated them.

Whenever he played on a team, to preserve a sense of the team's unity, Fabian was forced gradually to restrain his attempts at scoring goals on his own; he scored them only when team expectations justified it. His self-imposed impotence thwarted him. Whenever an opponent infringed upon Fabian's legitimate right to strike the ball, when fouls were committed against him, Fabian seemed to repay the breach by striking the ball, hitting the guilty player's shoulders or thighs, or the shoulders or flanks of his pony.

In polo, a sport of solitary valor and collective assault, with horses at full gallop and the ball in motion through the air most of the time, Fabian's retaliations against players had been called accidental, unfortunate consequences of the loss of precision any player might encounter in the rush of the game. But in time, some players began to discern a disquieting equation between Fabian's strokes and the men and ponies that were the targets of his shots. Somewhere, someone voiced a concern; elsewhere, another seconded it. Unaware, Fabian was watched now by the referee, his shots monitored by members of his own team, as well as by his opponents. Penalties were imposed on the team that sheltered him, for the personal penalties he levied against certain riders and their mounts. He had become a menace to the collective soul of the game.

Polo players often shift team allegiances. Those whom Fabian punished one day were on his team the next day. Many refused to play with him, and soon Fabian, dropped relentlessly from one team after another, slipped gradually into the notoriety of isolation, a maverick.

Polo, the fastest, boldest team game played today, was also among the oldest organized sports in the country. Its cowboy-like horsemanship so close to trick racing, its daring use of stick and ball, the roughness of clashing teams, made the sport, in Fabian's eyes, ultimately American. Still, in the entire country, there were only about two dozen polo patrons wealthy enough to sponsor their own team. By now none of them would consider employing Fabian. For a while he was polo coach at one of the Ivy League colleges, but it was not long before some of the school's older alumni, considerable polo players themselves at one time and now on the board of trustees at their alma mater, denounced his presence in their collegiate athletics, citing what they called his inability to play in concert with polo teams of Europe, England or the Americas.

As a student, Fabian had thought that his distrust of team play was simply the fear of being trampled to death by a massed tonnage of horses and men, each player, no less than his pony, driven by a momentum that did not spring from the solitary force of his own will to live, from his unique instinct to survive, but stemmed, rather, from a collective strategy in which an individual destiny mattered little.

Later in life, he decided that the spirit of the collective and the team bore for him another implication less ominous but equally disturbing: collective responsibility diluted one's faults, but it also diminished one's achievements, took away from them stature and consequence. One could no longer distinguish what was due to oneself and what to one's team; the boundaries of success and failure, victory and defeat were blurred in a tangle of humility and pride. Even further, the collective mood was insidious: after an impressive score, applause for the group left players heady with a sense of invincibility; then a player, racing his pony too fast at a turn or jostling an opponent too impetuously, would find his mount suddenly losing its balance and falling, burying him under it, just at the moment he was most confident of his prowess. The loss of a player in a crippling accident often devastated the team's morale, impairing each player's sense of security, leaving him prone to accident and easy panic.

Fabian's polo—polo as Fabian played it—was the ground of his being in the world, the only uniqueness at his command. Shunned by most teams, he resigned himself to traveling around the country in search of work as a polo referee or as a player in one-on-one polo games with wealthy opponents. Since these engagements were infrequent, he explored almost desperately the avenues of other talents, but found none.

At times he worked as a riding instructor or lecturer, but, as he acknowledged with chagrin, by many of the formal standards of horsemanship, he was not thought to be a faultless rider. According to these standards, the goal of horseback riding was to achieve that utmost security of a good seat, the calves, thighs, knees, hands, voice deployed gently by the rider to communicate his will to the horse without submitting it to unwarranted checks or restraints or violating its natural instinct toward self-preservation, its harmony of balance and sudden reflex.

Polo, however, was a game of surging takeoffs, of abrupt halts and sudden veers and pivots. It demanded a rapid displacement of the weight of a horse and its rider; it called for the strategy of reins insistently pulling on a horse's mouth and bearing on its neck, the ceaseless prod of the spurs and the nip of the whip, the smiting heat and clash of one horse evading collision, colliding, seeking collision with another. Years of playing polo, practicing for it, riding ponies bred and schooled exclusively for that game had evolved in Fabian habits contrary to the safety, decorum and propriety of dressage, a hunt or a jump. Practicing at a stable, arena or paddock, he would often exhibit a demeanor in his horsemanship that disturbed, sometimes even shocked, other instructors, whether beginning or advanced. Worse yet, the incorrigibility of his mistakes, and their vehemence, frequently tended to unnerve even the most pliant and submissive mounts.

To write about horses and horsemanship became, for Fabian, one way to make a living, but he seemed to lack something of the zeal and verve of others who worked that territory. In twenty years, he had published only a meager handful of books, each of them including a few sections on polo. But polo was still an exotic sport, evoking in the popular imagination phantoms of Britain and India at the Victorian high noon of empire, of Theodore Roosevelt, the last polo-playing American president, of gentry and military alike chasing the ball and one another across the trim and decorous turf of a Long Island country estate. And most riding instructors and people who had a special feeling for horses showed little interest in polo or sympathy with it, in angry dissent from what they took to be its violence against animal and rider alike.

Friends advised him to enter the world of state and national horse shows, not in the role of judge, which he frequently accepted, but as a competing entrant. They pointed out that from Vermont to Oregon, from Georgia to Hawaii, the horse show had progressed from the local pleasure of the entry of the family back-garden horse to the big business of keen international competition, the winning horses commanding staggering prizes, their value increasing with every championship they won. His friends tried to persuade him that his prestige as a polo player, coupled with the distinction he now commanded as a writer on equestrian art, would compensate for his defects in horsemanship and would persuade some of the better-known stables and individual owners or breeders to hire him and exploit his minor celebrity to win attention for their horses at major shows and events.

But competition of this order was foreign to Fabian. In one-on-one meets, he fought another man for supremacy in the short span of their play, submitting to rules that both contestants obeyed, without an umpire, away from the fickleness of a public that might choose favorites. Horse shows rated men and animals according to an order of excellence and accomplishment that did not interest Fabian. The essence of competition, for him, lay not in the challenge offered by others but always in the challenge posed by oneself.

F abian lay in wait for fall in Massachusetts or Vermont, sometimes along the shallows, pleasant dunes and stretches of the coast, but mostly in the northern reaches of the East, where summer put up its fiercest resistance, until the last, to break with life.

There the leaves still clung to the trees, and the mantling shrubbery, misted by the mild noon of autumn, bristled at the frosting chill of night.

Fabian's thirst for this spectacle, for its prick and stir, the immolation of odor and hectic bloom that only autumn offered, would come as suddenly as any other, ignited by a whiff of bark or mealy oats, the supple aroma of leather or hide, the musk of roots trailing a wind along the highway. He took it as a longing for something apart from thought, different from memory, beyond them, something to which one could stake no claim of one's own, a realm outside the deed of charter or possession.

When, in that season, Fabian would find his road approaching some grand estate, a frontier of thickly wooded land dense about it, acre on virgin acre, he would drive off the highway into a clearing nearby and park his VanHome, the signs PERISHABLE clearly fixed to its sides. Avidly, like a boy on the scent of play, he would saddle his ponies quickly and, in a white polo helmet and padded knee guards that protected him from branches and underbrush, he would cut into the wood, astride one horse, the other, also saddled, on a lead rein, the ponies snorting, jostling in the promise of the run, plunging through the wiry brambles, thrusting forward, great plows scything the earth, tearing the ligaments and arteries of the stubborn thistles, the prickly shrubs, leaves in their clustering.

Picking his way through the thicket, he would wade through layers of leaves, stalks, roots and stumps heaped in profusion, their dry, crackling billows making a sea music, soughing, the tidal lap rising about his ears, muting even the drum of the horses' hoofs. The woods folded before him in silence: pine and fir, oak and beech sentinels of his transit.

Perched on shoots of burdock, humiliated by the brawl of color that framed them, a flock of blackbirds, motionless, would watch Fabian's caravan sailing along channels and freshets of hazel and hornbeam, blackberry and sumac. Like a skiff bringing up the rear, a solitary leaf, its fretted veins a lair for the sun, would scud in his wake. At a pond, its surface brackish, mantled with mottled leaves, random patches of turbid fluid between brownish clumps reflected the yellow leaves of an overhanging tree.

Breaking into an open path, his chest thrust out as if to take the crest of the wind, Fabian would sink into the saddle, his knees and calves firm about the horse as he threw it into a canter; then, rising in the saddle, his weight full in the heels, he would prod it into a gallop, his eyes taut as bowstrings, reaching ahead, his hands on the reins alerting the horse to every shape, every color, the animal swift in its leap over a branch bent across the path or a fallen log. The other horse galloped directly behind, or, in the unexpected spaciousness of a clearing, alongside; in another stretch, he would goad them again into a canter, then slow abruptly, huddling in the saddle, and pick his way through pits and claws of broken branches, pools of stagnant water. Roots and clusters of stones, cradled like nuts beneath the dead leaves, peeled out from under the horses' assault, then shards of sundered rock, clumps of soil; he breasted the barricades of old dislodged tree trunks, their bark gone leprous, bald, dangling in strips, naked stumps like beggars guarding the dark corners of the wood.

Sometimes Fabian would chance upon others: a troop of boys wandering from the usual ruts, playing at scout and pioneer; a family encamped in a clearing, knapsacks and sleeping bags strewn about, children idling with heaps of cones or stalking the fleet, scattering life of the underbrush.

Erupting from a brake in the woods, Fabian's convoy could stir alarm and a flush of panic; people would halt at a distance far enough to take flight, yet near enough to see the figure of a rider framed against the trees, helmeted in white, booted in long sheaths of black and brown rising from the crested gleam of spurs to the armor of his knee guards, a black-gloved hand curved about the poised lance of his long whip. A child, even one six or eight years old, would often break into howls of fear. Boys would scamper in yelps of confusion at this sudden apparition from a realm of fantasy and early memory. A man and woman, paling, agape, would draw children close, uncertain of what they were looking at, puzzling out its incongruity, calculating how to make a truce. Fabian's easy greeting would calm them. Stammering, they would explain that there were no stables where they came from, that horses were too expensive for people like them to have anything to do with; they might even admit, embarrassed, a little hesitant, that not only their children but even they themselves had not seen a horse and rider so near to them, except on television. Most children stayed wary, distant, sneaking glances at Fabian and his ponies from behind the secure wall of their parents. Typically, a girl would ask her father why the horses were so much bigger than they looked on television, or a boy would wonder if the man on the horse was going to shoot him and his family down. Fabian would declare that his ponies were as tame as kittens and ask the boy to touch the horse or to see what it was like to sit with him in the saddle for a moment; the boy, silent, pondering, would almost always refuse.

Fabian's path would at times take him onto a narrow bridge, a concrete wedge suspended above the highway that knifed across the forest. Lingering at its brink, returned again to the hurtling clamor of men and the machines they had contrived, he would look down at cars streaking in whatever freedom the highway allowed, each blur a rider buckled in his plastic-covered saddle, in command of his solitary mount, his energy and surge a fusion of oil and flame, his tack and harness a cocoon of glass and steel. On impulse, Fabian might raise an arm in greeting; as metal, rubber and flesh hurtled below him, he was aware of heads turned for an instant from the asphalt belt to a man on a horse, a bizarre sentry standing guard on the overpass. Eager again for the woods, lost to everything but his senses, Fabian would turn the horse on its haunches and trot back into the thicket, cutting through huge stalks of hornbeam, sumac and boxwood.

Toward dusk, he would ride easily back to his VanHome, relishing the promise of the meal he would soon prepare. From the refrigerator in his galley he would take a thick slab of beef, glistening and marbled, its bone doubling its weight, a ribbon of fat hemming the piece like lace. Studding it with spikes of garlic, dusting it with pepper and salt and herbs, he would place it between layers of onion and leave it to marinate, the meat now a pungent sandwich of bathing scent, before he sallied forth to ready his forest banquet.

Taking a canvas bag or a sack, he would gather scraps and strips of bark, the season's maple and birch, chestnut, oak, sheaves of the narrow-leaved branches of spruce and fir and pine, then a variety of cones, the springy pliant ones, young and full, as well as the desiccated, withered husks. The sack swelled with great clumps of weeds and damp grass mingling with batches of common fern, ribbons of liverwort, some moss, a heap of quillworts, whatever plants and herbs he chanced upon in trampling the brush.

Quiet evenings were best for the rites of forest, food and solitude, and he would make a shelter for himself secured by the barrier of his VanHome, cloistered from the gusting invasion of the breeze. Scooping out a shallow hollow of earth for his fireplace, he would bolster it with shoals of stone, then bridge the stones with an old iron bar from a stable. He would first set a match to a layer of coarse bark, then feed the fire with dried-out clusters of pine cones and perhaps a branch or two of spruce or larch; but when the flames spread to swamp the wood, he tamped them down with splashes of water he brought from his galley, until the hollow was only a dull amber glow. He heaped the embers then with the verdant plunder he had gathered in the forest, shuffling the heap until smoke appeared.

He would put the meat on the bars, suspended high enough above the smoking fire to escape searing by a stray raw flame erupting through the layers of leaves and moss, fern and pine. The smoke clotted, its tang more acrid, the meat starting to sweat, then recoiling and shriveling, the fat a trickling dribble prodding the fire to yet another volley of blue and orange flame. When Fabian turned it over the first time, the steak had already changed color; soon it was time for more salt and pepper, the herbs anointing its gleaming surface, then more heat, a fresh slew of the greenery that would mute the flames, and again the cycle of rotation.

The process was long; twilight dissolved into night. Fabian would settle down to his meal, the banked embers flickering out, the smoke a trailing funnel above him, his hands and clothes and the forest enclave liquid with the aroma of cooked flesh, the steak as docile and comforting in his mouth, without taint of char or scorch, as it had been in the mouth of the boy, a farmhand, long ago, when he had had to smoke chunks of horseflesh for the farmer's family, making certain that the cherished meat, hoarded for months, would be spared the open flame, the essence of its life preserved, its tender substance sheltered by the gentle smoke long after the heat was gone from it.

The country's major polo resorts at which Fabian could have played, whether those in the Midwest, where polo was a game of summer and early fall, or the lavish, sunny retreats of Florida's Sunshine Belt, where it was a winter pastime, were closed to him for a variety of reasons. They offered accommodations and their sumptuous facilities of fields, stables and other quarters only to those who, first, bought and maintained the extravagant villas and condominiums that fell within their purview, and second, could meet the rigid, exclusive social and financial conditions that governed admission to the ruling country clubs.

Even those qualifying for membership in the clubs, should they or their guests actually wish to play polo, were required to furnish and maintain at least one string of five or six ponies, together with the grooms to tend them. On those rare occasions when friendship or chance brought him into the recesses of one of these prodigal polo resorts, Fabian was not at all surprised to learn that the purchase and annual maintenance of a modest string of ponies and gear, and the expense of transporting them, could easily amount to a sum comparable to the salary of the head of a flourishing corporate enterprise.

Denied access to the central circuits of the game, unable to meet on common ground those who would be open to playing with him, Fabian was forced into his nomadic existence as much by necessity as by choice. The irony did not escape him that, of all the sports in which he might have excelled, polo was the one in which only a very rich man could still afford to indulge, and at that, so few of them did.

The closing and decisive game of the Third International Eugene Stanhope Polo Tournament, played annually at Stanhope Estates, one of the country's major polo and golf centers, near Chicago, for the Grail Industries Trophy and, not incidentally, a purse of a quarter-million dollars, was delayed by a downpour. In the stands and around the field, more than three thousand polo fans shuffled their umbrellas and raincoats, wondering noisily whether the South American Centauros and New Zealand's Hybrids would be able to play on a marshy field. But the rain stopped as abruptly as it had begun. Near Fabian, a silver-haired woman in a tweed suit folded an umbrella that she had been holding over a young man. Fabian saw that the young man's head, neck and torso were trapped by tightly fitted aluminum railing and knobs. His face— pale, pure features, oddly serene within that cage— seemed familiar; Fabian recognized him as an American polo player who a few months earlier had broken his neck in a game in the Midwest. At a sound coming over the loudspeakers, the young man twirled a knob at his hip; the contraption rotated him in the direction of a loge in the front row.

There Commodore Ernest Tenet Stanhope, once an eminent polo player himself and now the family's ninety-year-old patriarch, had risen to speak into the microphone. Wearing the customary white polo breeches and British helmet, he announced that, as honorary chairman of the tournament named in memory of his late son, Eugene, he had just been informed that his other and only surviving son, Patrick Stanhope, would regrettably not be able to attend; his obligations as president and executive director of Grail Industries, the Stanhope family enterprise and the nation's largest electronics manufacturer, detained him. He had, however, generously made available the helicopters which would help to dry the field, so as to permit the tournament to take place. A roar went up from the stands, and then the patriarch passed the microphone to Lucretia Stanhope, his daughter-in-law, a stately widow of forty. Serene in her position as chief organizer, she apologized briefly for the delay.

Having taken occasion to remind the spectators that only two years before her husband, Eugene Stanhope, had been killed tragically in a freak accident while preparing for this very tournament, she paused, then closed by announcing that the Eugene Stanhope Stables, breeders and traders of some of the country's finest horses, would be open after the game as a courtesy to visitors, free of charge.

Barely had Lucretia Stanhope finished when four turbopowered Grail Industries helicopters, hovering in formation above the field, descended slowly, wafting through the air to a point a few feet above the ground, the powerful downdraft of their blades blasting the puddles out of the sodden turf, hastening evaporation.

At the far end of the field the drivers and owners of perhaps seventy vintage cars and about half as many antique planes—museum pieces rolled out annually for the parade that always started the polo tournament—began gently to swab down the gleaming waxed surfaces of their machines. Television crews settled into their perches on the aluminum towers that had been erected for the match.

Several photographers, burdened with camera gear, scurried about, quick to spot star players who had begun to emerge from tents around the field. Some were already snapping the better-known polo ponies as their owners' grooms started to saddle them up at hitching rails next to trailers and motor homes. Still other reporters prowled through the stands, on the lookout for personalities from the local and international jet and polo sets always drawn to the tournament.

A motorcade of two dozen open convertibles sporting balloons, flowers and American flags began to circle the field. They carried officials of the various U.S. polo associations and officers of the corporations that supported the tournament and contributed to the purse. The antique cars inaugurated the parade, proceeding slowly in sequence, each braking carefully to avoid collision. They were followed by high school marching bands, with bouncing cheerleaders in miniskirts. Behind them floated a large flower bed nestled on a moving platform from which Miss Polo Cup, a vivacious brunette in a bikini and polo helmet, pelted the crowd with flowers. Bringing up the rear of the parade, four stunt riders encased in medieval armor, lent by one of the local museums, conducted a mock jousting tournament. Pivoting their mounts, they bore down on each other at full gallop, lances outthrust, horses straining beneath the unaccustomed weight of metal-clad riders, and with spectacular showmanship averted by inches the brutal jar of body and armor.

A middle-aged man, his gaunt features marked only by a thin mustache, turned toward Fabian. The man was dressed in a faultlessly tailored safari jacket, white breeches and two-tone shoes, a brier burl pipe in his manicured hand.

"I say, this is quite a show they're putting on here," he said with an exaggerated English accent. "These copters alone could take over my whole country, you know." He laughed, showing uneven yellowed teeth. "Who do you suppose that rabble could be?" He pointed his pipe with disdain at the stands.

"Polo fans. Stable owners. Farmers. Breeders. College polo teams, plain folks like you and me."

The man twitched his shoulders. "Plain folks? I flew first-class to this tournament."

"Where from?"

"From Brunei, my home, by way of London, of course."

"Brunei? That's exciting," said Fabian, not certain he had ever heard of the place before.

"Exciting? Not really." The man puffed another cloud of smoke. "Our only natural resources are squash and badminton—and the breeze of the China Sea."

"Squash, badminton and the breeze?"

"Well, yes. And, I'll be damned, polo, of course."

"And polo?"

"Polo. Recently introduced by our gracious government."

"By your government?"

"Yes. By His Highness the Sultan and his brothers. It will be played by the Royal Brunei Regiment, as well as by the police force and our air wing, of course."

"But of course," said Fabian.

Sweeping slowly back and forth, the helicopters completed their task. To a storm of cheering from the stands, they gradually rose, hovered for a moment, and then wheeled out of sight. The field was suddenly quiet. It was still a bit soggy and steaming in the sun, but the shiny pools of water had all gone.

Fabian divided the world of sport into games played with a ball and games played without one. Among those in which the ball was pivotal, polo was, for him, matchless. In the mesh of two opposing teams, each composed of four players, he saw the equation of man and horse, the duel of man with man, as defining poles on a field of tension. The space was compact, encompassing both the solitary drama of the player, isolated in the display of his own singularity and that of his mount, and the massed ritual of group combat exhibited in the contradictions and fusions of the team's collective will.

"Pony quick and polo stick," Fabian would often muse, distilling the essence of polo, the game of six or eight chukkers, each chukker a maximum of seven and a half minutes long. Its constants were the pony—four to six horses, usually Thoroughbreds, all balanced and short-strided, expertly schooled in polo, needed by each player in the course of a game—and the mallet, a sixteen-ounce stick more than four feet long, its shaft a bamboo shoot, a rubber-bound handle at one end, and at the other end a nine-inch-long cigar- or cylinder-shaped head of solid bamboo, maple or mulberry, its hitting surface less than two inches wide, its toe tapered, its heel squared off.

The polo pony had to be steadily trained for two or three years to become speedy in takeoff, fleet in running, agile in turning and pivoting, quick to stop dead and just as quick to take off again from a standstill. Mounted on such a pony galloping across a green about the size of nine football fields, a polo player might drive the ball with a ferocious blow of his mallet across hundreds of feet. In that flight toward the goal posts, twenty-four feet apart, the ball—a wooden globe three and a quarter inches in diameter and not more than four and a half ounces in weight—often speeding at a hundred miles an hour, could gather momentum sufficient to shatter a horse's bone, smash pony or rider into insensibility or even death.

The armored medieval knights, still jousting in mock combat, finally moved off the turf. The two field umpires scuffed and prodded the ground, testing it before they waved their arms to the referee, in the grandstand, to signal that the field was dry enough for the game to begin.

Fabian took in the babble of fans rustling about him, odds, stakes, small-time betting. The Hybrids, the New Zealand team, seemed to be a favorite. Each of their players was rated at nine out of a possible ten points; many in the crowd were convinced that the Hybrids' mounts were among the best in the world, so valuable that, unlike the Centauros, the Hybrids bore the expense of taking their ponies home with them after the tournament. The polo fans felt that such prized ponies guaranteed supremacy. They liked the New Zealanders' link to an Anglo-Saxon legacy of respecting the horse, a heritage which, while refining and perfecting the caliber of horsemanship, invariably brought out the best in the mount.

Fabian, on the contrary, threw in his lot with the South American Centauros. He knew the common objection to them—that since they sold their ponies at auction after the tournament, they must have left their best breeds at home—but he knew, too, that their team claimed two of the six foremost international polo players, each assigned a top rating of ten, and two more rated at eight. Moreover, they were players well into the second and third generation, bred in a climate where the polo pony filled a need not unlike that of the automobile in the United States. Just as a mechanic here took pleasure in tuning, revving up or tinkering with a car left in his trust, a skilled South American groom took a comparable freedom in schooling a polo pony to his will. Since South American players never staked winning on one horse, changing ponies several times during a game, and kept equally skilled mounts in reserve, to them training a pony meant, above all, making it a fast runner. To prolong endurance and accelerate pace, they might inject the horse with stimulants rousing it to a pitch of heady charge. They knew how to liquefy its blood to speed circulation and how to numb its legs to pain by local anesthetic or by a procedure called nerving, which deadened feeling in the animal's legs.

From opposite ends of the field, the Hybrids and the Centauros now entered the arena, proceeding toward a point before the grandstand. The players wore cotton T-shirts in their team colors, sleek-fitting white breeches and high leather boots capped by thick-ribbed knee guards. Wide-rimmed pith helmets or the newer plastic helmets enclosed their heads; their eyes and faces were shielded by narrow guards. Their ponies were trussed with cheekpieces, throatlatches, bands across the nose and brow; they were harnessed with lip straps, snaffles that gagged, curb bits and chains, breastplates, stirrup irons with broad footplates. Tightly coiled bandages blazing with team colors cushioned their legs against the mallets, the ball, the flying hoofs of other horses. Marshaled in formation, mallets held upright like flags on parade, players on mounts reined tautly, they suggested fleetingly a moving frieze of man and horse approaching ceremonial combat.

An antique biplane, trailing the banner of Grail Industries, circled the field, startling the mounted horses; when it flew away, one of the umpires tossed the ball into their midst. The game began. In an explosive melee, players and ponies took off at full pace, mallets threshing the air, clumps of the still-damp turf flying at the impact of hoofs scrambling, braking to a dead stop, pivoting.

Within moments of takeoff, each team revealed its distinctive style. The Hybrids adhered to their familiar strategy of playing the man rather than the ball. Each player worked on showing off his pony's secure and easy grace. He held the reins, either single or double, in the English fashion, one finger between each curb and snaffle, the hand clenched in a fist around the whip, knuckles up. Even at the game's hottest pitch, he spurred his pony more by the pressure of knees and calves than by punishing it with a whip, bridling the mouth only in short spurts, his mount balanced, one foreleg always leading on the side of the turn. In taking out after the ball, the player rose, balancing with his knees, shoulders tilting over the pony's ears, his suppleness in the hips and waist a visual pleasure. As he jockeyed the reins with his left hand, his use of the mallet with the right was invariably correct: its handle in the palm of his hand, between thumb and forefinger, the mallet wheeling in a swing—a forehand always to the front of the pony's forelegs, a backhand near its hind legs.

Mounted on fast and bold, superbly trained Argentinean Thoroughbreds, the Centauros were celebrated for their speed and audacity, for turning a polo field into a chessboard where team strategy dictated each team mate's tireless search for the goal. With a peculiar vehemence of temperament, each player kept his pony under relentless check—the snaffle reins bunched together between the thumb and first finger, the curb reins between the first and second fingers, the whip held by the thumb against the palm, the knuckles of the fist sideways—the bit and spur steady pressures in a sequence of changing pace, fierce stops and deft turns. His eyes on his opponents, on the line of attack and on the ball, each Centauro, an image of perfection, drove and whipped his pony, flanks already bloodied, into a frenzied gallop. The Centauro was unique in his habit of momentarily transferring the reins to his right hand, next to the mallet handle, thus freeing his left hand to use the whip with full force. His grip on the mallet firm, wrist supple, elbow close to the ribs, arm and shoulder in harmonious alignment with the mallet as it struck—he scooped the ball smoothly off the ground, propelling it in an arc into the air.

Fabian remembered an incident in a game that called up echoes of a memory beyond time. A South American player had violently accelerated his mount; it responded by raising its foreleg in a propulsive drive well ahead of its forward weight just as its rear leg hit the ground. By instinct, the pony stretched out in a buoyant spring, its ears sleekly flattened to counter the drag of wind. In a single frozen shaft of movement and force, millennia fell away, and Fabian saw the streaming flight of a horse from its flesh-tearing foes. The speed pounded. Suddenly, trying to bump an opponent off the ball at full gallop, then to hook his mallet from immediately behind, just when he was about to hit the ball, the player pulled brutally on the reins, gagging the pony. The animal abruptly lost momentum, its natural rhythm snapping with the retracted foreleg. As the rider spurred his mount to push off, its foreleg tripped, then crashed on the turf, shattering the bone just below the knee. The pony, foaming in its frenzy, kept at the gallop, its splintered leg buckling, a bare bone protruding at every footfall, until, staggering, the animal pitched and stumbled. Only then did the rider, as frenzied and possessed as his mount, become aware of what had taken place.

The gala to celebrate the tournament, sponsored by the residents of Stanhope Estates, was given at the Polo and Golf Club for members of the competing teams, other polo players and visiting international personalities in sport and society. Fabian arrived without an invitation and wandered uneasily among the formally dressed crowd.

In one of the rooms, he heard his name. A middle-aged man in a blue suit was heading for him, his silver tie pierced by a stickpin in the shape of a polo ball of pearl being struck by a gold mallet. The man's eyes settled on Fabian with a bird's rapacity.

"I know who you are," he announced, closing in with an air of mock conspiracy.

"So do I," Fabian replied.

"There you are, the famous Fabian," the man exclaimed, dragging Fabian by his upper arm to a corner. "Michael Stockey," he introduced himself. "I kept looking for you among the polo mercenaries here," he said, "but I was told you hadn't sold to anyone. True?"

"I hadn't sold because there weren't any buyers," said Fabian.

Stockey edged closer. "Come to think of it," he said in a cheerful voice, "you and I met once before. At the polo tournament at Los Lemures, in the Caribbean."

Fabian apologized for failing to remember their meeting. Stockey was undeterred.

"In any case, your name came up recently," said Stockey. "At Grail Industries, we feel that polo is the game of the future—the fastest and most dangerous sport in the world. Half a ton of man and horse smashing into seven other horses and players on a thirty-five-mile-an-hour collision course—and all chasing a billiard-sized ball! Every second the player risks his life for a competitive edge! What a blitz of a game that is!" He began to warm to his vision. "Polo, the supersport: the hazards of steeplechase, the speed of racing, the violence of ice hockey, the tension of football, the precision of baseball, the challenge of golf, the teamwork of roller derby. Polo—the ultimate action sport." He paused, pleased with himself, then continued. "The game of kings is still the king of games. Grail Industries might even underwrite a One-On-One Polo World Championship to open either in Wellington, Retama or Boca Raton, with each of the hundreds of American and foreign polo clubs selecting players—high-rated professionals as well as amateurs—to compete one-on-one for the title of the World's Best Polo Player. Think how such modern jousting will revitalize polo's image on television! It will be a real winner! What do you say, Fabian?"

"It's like no other sport," Fabian said.

Stockey shifted his weight from one leg to the other. "Then that's where you fit in, Fabian: a host for our series. Who could be better? You wrote books about polo. You helped write the amendments to the Horse Protection Act. You've lived half your life abroad, played polo all over the world. You personally know some of the best polo players." He stopped, anxious for Fabian's reaction.

"Whose idea was I?" Fabian asked guardedly.

"Patrick Stanhope himself asked me to track you down and sound you out about it. He's very grateful for all the attention you gave their little Vanessa, teaching her to ride and jump so well; she's never had a fall. Of course, not everyone was on your side." Stockey paused. "Some polo association people—well, privately, they say that no team will have you. That you're the ball hawk who plays solitary, that you seldom miss a goal—and never another player."

"I know what they say," Fabian said.

"There's a story." Stockey coughed nervously, then went on. "They say you learned those trick shots as a kid, during the War in Europe, when you were forced to work on a horse in some peasant bullring, that you belong in a circus, not on a polo field. They don't even want you as an umpire or a referee."

"I know."

"And I suppose you also know that some people say that what happened—well, that Eugene's accident was no accident—that the two of you were fighting a kind of duel."

As Fabian maintained his silence, Stockey folded his hands into a steeple, wagging them pensively. "Mind you, though, a duel—even when there's death—well, the law doesn't call it murder." His voice was trailing off slyly. "You know what I mean."

Fabian gave no sign.

Stockey released his clasp, throwing his hands wide with a deep gusty sigh of confirmation. "The groom who was there that morning said you both played fast and rough, but that Eugene rode straight into the ball that smashed his face. What's more, you rode with a hand badly hurt the day before!"

"I cut off my finger," Fabian corrected him.

Stockey twitched anxiously. His teeth crept into view as he forced another smile. "Mind you, Patrick Stanhope knows his brother's death was a plain accident. Is there any serious player who was never injured at polo?"

"I was never injured at polo," said Fabian.

"Good for you!" Stockey exclaimed. "Although most experts are supposed to have gone through many accidents."

"If you have many accidents, you're not an expert," Fabian said.

"That's a pretty extreme view," Stockey said cautiously. "You sound like your books, Fabian. People like to think they're pros even when they fail." His voice dropped. "Your books spoil the sport for them."

"Accidents spoil the sport, not books about accidents," Fabian said.

Stockey gave him a long reflective look. "But come to think of it, your books make you a spokesman for polo safety—and even a better prospect for our TV show. What d'you say, Fabian?"

"I'll have to think about it," Fabian said.

Stockey clapped him on the shoulder. "We can help to set you up in Florida—say, in the Palm Beach Polo and Country Club—and think what fun you're going to have then! The best players from all over the world, great crowd, all the celebrities you can handle!" He handed Fabian an engraved card. "Call me sometime soon and say yes, will you?" He walked away, toward the bar.

At the center of the room, a group of women in rippling flowered dresses spooned mounds of ice cream into long-stemmed silver bowls from a raspberry-and-vanilla polo player on a chocolate-mocha pony: a mock Stanhope Tournament polo trophy. The rain that had gone in the afternoon had come back for its revenge, trickling along the glass walls of the club room, one flash of lightning pursuing another.

Unwilling to be recognized again after the conversation with Stockey, Fabian sat down at an empty table in the room's dimmest corner. Two waiters rearranged chairs and changed the cloth.

A woman approached his table, the sheath of her gown yielding to every movement of her body. He recognized Alexandra Stahlberg.

"How are you, Fabian?" she asked with a faint smile. Her large oval eyes took on a mischievous glint as she smiled, her slightly parted lips revealing the milky perfection of her teeth.

Fabian rose. She extended her hand and he took it—smooth and narrow, firm, cool.

Memory summoned at once the pressure of her hands on him, the recollection of fingers probing, opening the way for lips and tongue. He glanced at her hands.

She caught his look. "Are you still fascinated by a ring finger, Fabian?" she purred coyly, stirring and shifting toward her escort.

"I am—by you," Fabian said, as he pondered this second entry of Alexandra Stahlberg into his life.

In the time since Eugene's death, Fabian had seen Alexandra many times, but only in advertisements—tempting him in an airport waiting room, enticing him from the ranks of glossy magazine covers arrayed under the harsh lights of an all-night newsstand. Once, standing in line at a public telephone, he glanced up to find himself the target of her seduction. She loomed, demanding, on a billboard that announced some new lip gloss, her chin resting on those intricately twining fingers, one of them erect, brushing the provocation of her lips, as if to signal, to silence, to alert, her eyes locked in a duel with those who gazed up at her.

Fabian and Eugene Stanhope had been friends. Eugene often hired Fabian as his partner in polo practice or matches, and they traveled in Eugene's private

plane to various clubs and tournaments around the
country and abroad. Together they played against the
Central Romana team of Maharaja Jabar Singh, the
legendary Indian polo player, at La Romana, the resort in the Dominican Republic. On one flight to La
Romana, Eugene introduced Alexandra, a young fashion model, to Fabian. She was an old friend, Eugene
said easily, not troubling to conceal what Fabian could
recognize at once—that Eugene and Alexandra were
lovers. Later during the trip, to dispel gossip and to
distract the vigilant eye of his wife, Lucretia, he asked
Fabian to pretend that Alexandra was Fabian's girl.
Fabian agreed. From then on, he was frequently Eugene's guest at Stanhope Estates; Alexandra would
usually show up a day or two after his arrival for her
trysts with Eugene.

About a year after Fabian met Alexandra, Eugene
again hired him as a practice partner before a tournament and invited him to stay at Stanhope Estates.

A few weeks before he was to see Eugene, Fabian
ran into Alexandra. She was with a French film producer; although only a casual polo acquaintance of
Fabian's, the Frenchman pretended intimacy, expressing a lively pleasure that Fabian and Alexandra, whom
he apparently had known for a long time, also knew
each other. Alexandra maintained a sullen silence, but
the Frenchman revealed freely that he and Alexandra
often traveled together, and that, with an eye to her
obvious allure, he was planning to build one of his
sexually explicit films around her. When with a kiss he
sent her off to go shopping, Fabian, who had been
attracted to Alexandra from the moment of Eugene's
introduction, caught her anxious stare.

Alone with Fabian, the producer boasted with elaborate detail and relish about his affair with Alexandra.
What he said fueled Fabian's fantasy, replacing old
images with new, spurring his initial attraction. Fabian
felt he should make a determined effort to know Alexandra.

He arrived at Stanhope Estates eager to reassure her

that she could trust his discretion; he would not betray to either man the critical presence of another in her life.

Eugene had been called away on a short business trip, leaving orders that a comfortable old house on the grounds should be put at the disposal of Alexandra and Fabian. Alexandra took an upstairs bedroom; Fabian moved into a room on the ground floor. He released his ponies to be groomed and exercised at the Stanhope Stables, then parked his VanHome near the house.

After dinner at the Polo and Golf Club with several players and their wives, Alexandra suggested that she and Fabian walk across the deer park sloping gently between the club and their house.

Overhead, wind ruffled the treetops, but on the sandy path, where moonlight hung like smoke, the quiet was broken only by a steady whir of grasshoppers beckoning them from the ground. Fabian's awareness that he was alone with Alexandra for the first time caused his thoughts to flow in strands, shifting with the slightest pulse of the uncertain moment.

Alexandra broke the stillness. "I have always supported myself." She spoke, as if to herself, in a cool, detached voice. "And as long as I am not abused by the men I live with, I choose to live with those I do."

Fabian was quick to reassure her. "I won't tell—"

"I know you won't," she broke in, "although even if one day you do, neither of them would mind. They know what they want."

"What do they want?" Fabian asked.

The forest was dry, the air sultry, the clatter of grasshoppers incessant. A lightning bolt, swift and thunderless, carved the sky. As Fabian strained his eyes to fill in the contours of the night, another flash of lightning revealed Alexandra, standing near him.

"I promise better than any woman in the world," she said, "and they want to follow through on what I promise."

They were close to their house now, about to pass his VanHome. As if she were leaving a mark in ghostly dust, Alexandra drew one finger across its surface.

"Can I see the inside?" she asked.

Fabian looked at the mesh of shadows on her face and bare shoulders. "Could it wait for another time?" he asked, confessing the impotence of reason.

"It could. But should you?"

He entered the cab of the VanHome and turned on the lights in the lounge. She stepped in behind him.

"So this is where you hide out?" She looked around the lounge, then peeked up at the alcove.

"This is where I live and work," Fabian said.

Alexandra asked for red wine. Relieved to be able to conceal his anxiety, Fabian went to the wine rack, where he pulled out the last bottle and uncorked it, pouring her a glass. She sipped the wine slowly. Her eyes rested briefly on a boxed collection of Fabian's polo books, but she did not reach out to touch them. She was amused by the writing chair he had made by setting a polo saddle on a wooden tripod. Lifting the hem of her evening dress, she slid astride the saddle; the movement pushed her dress up, above her thighs. She leaned back, and her mane of copper-colored hair, trembling with a sheen of light, rippled in waves over her neck and shoulders. In her shimmering dress, straddling the chair, the front of the saddle between her exposed thighs, her feet nude in their high-heeled sandals, leather straps binding her ankles, she tantalized.

With the knowingness that made her so proficient a model, Alexandra splayed her fingers over her ankles, coiling and unraveling her hands, showing the red stain of her nails, molded for exhibition, then interlocking her fingertips with her enamel-glazed toes.

Fabian watched the complicity of hands and feet, fingers and toes: all elongated, tensile, nervous, they seemed at moments like the fragile plaster features on a religious figurine, in perpetual danger of snapping off.

She raked her fingers through her hair, cosseting it

as if gathering the silence of the room, then glanced into a mirror on the wall: twins, one arrested in glass, one flesh, each chary of the other. The woman in the mirror caught his stare; he could no longer watch, unobserved, the bare shoulders of her twin. Alexandra smiled.

"At work, they call me the centipede," she said.

"Centipede?"

"Yes. Legs, feet and hands."

She shifted to one side of the saddle, her hands on her lap, her legs drifting apart, the dress snaking even higher. She knew he could see the insides of her thighs.

"What are you thinking, Fabian?"

"I wonder who inhabits such a perfect being."

"Take a look, then." Alexandra slipped off the saddle, her dress slithering down her legs. She walked to the bar and picked up the bottle of wine Fabian had opened for her. Bottle in one hand, glass in the other, she leaned against a wall and looked at him. She was waiting.

Fabian felt himself at a crossroads, forced by the will of another to unsettle the harmony he had achieved between his codes and inclinations.

He liked Eugene and was comfortable in his company. Even when Fabian was in a low mood, he never resented or envied Eugene's sturdy health, good looks and fortune. Possibly because Eugene recognized that Fabian was living his life precisely as he wanted, Eugene returned that steadiness by never belittling his own money, power and position, or by pretending that he chafed at the confinements of being rich. His wealth was like a toy he had chosen to share with Fabian; they would play with it together. It was Eugene's co-signing of the loan that had permitted Fabian to acquire the VanHome; then a cash gift from Eugene on Fabian's birthday had helped to pay for Big Lick and Gaited Amble. Now, by asking that Fabian be on call for him to hire, Eugene had become the chief source of Fabian's income. Eugene was aware of the complex tangle of friendship and debt and, as if to put

Fabian on a more independent footing, had mentioned
the possibility of underwriting a series of manuals on
horsemanship, with Fabian as the editor.

Fabian felt Alexandra's gaze steady on him. She was
still waiting. He knew she was Eugene's emotional
property, another facet of his measureless wealth, but
was that sufficient to impose a check on Fabian, to
bridle his desire for her? Did her affair with the French
film producer not intimate her availability, a sexual
field on which many could sport? Finally, did Alexandra herself, intent on ensuring Fabian's connivance,
now choose to invest her body in that silence?

To decline Alexandra's challenge, to thwart his instinct toward her, would ratify an indolence or lapse in
value. Either would subvert his trust in himself. Without looking at Alexandra, the balance of his mind
restored, Fabian abruptly turned off the overhead light
in the lounge. A single blue bulb lighted the narrow
staircase to the sleeping alcove.

For reasons of mental economy, Fabian chose to
think of certain people as polarized, their unity sundered into compatible or antagonistic hemispheres.
There were the symmetrics and the asymmetrics. In the
symmetric, the halves, the face, the body and the soul
were harmonious; the symmetric rested in calm, a
stranger to compulsion, seldom bent to the extremities
of life. In the asymmetric, the halves were at variance,
constrained by no uniformity; undulant, the asymmetric gave way to spasmodic eruptions of play. Character
defined the symmetric, personality the asymmetric. The
symmetric was driven, the asymmetric enacted. To a
casual eye, the symmetric was comely, the asymmetric
interesting.

Alexandra had seemed to Fabian a classical symmetric; during their night together, however, in lovemaking that was unrestrained, even obsessive, she divulged
that chasm between her external poise and her inward
turbulence. Fabian responded with fascination.

In this freedom to make love to her, in his awareness of that gift of herself as an incarnation of his need, he scanned the waxing of his own excitement, revealed himself naked before her, to signal to her that there was nothing in him that was not hers. She accelerated the mounting spiral of his pleasure with a deliberate rhythm.

In the haze of morning, he watched her sleeping. He had scheduled stick-and-ball practice for early that day, and when he rose, leaving her in his bed, longing and doubt streaked through him, intermittent, unruly, leaving him numb and uncertain.

At lunch, he was told that Eugene, who had not been expected back for two or three days, had returned and wished to see him in the old house.

He went directly to the drawing room. Eugene and Alexandra were waiting for him. Eugene, formal in a gray business suit and white shirt, sat in a heavy leather armchair guarded by the sweep of an ornate hunt table. Alexandra was perched on the thick arm of his chair, one of her legs swaying slightly. Her breasts showed through the sheer halter of her jumpsuit. Fabian started to hold out his hand, but something in Eugene's expression arrested him midway. He looked at Alexandra, and she turned her head. He pulled a chair up to the hunt table and sat down.

Eugene scrutinized him. "I thought you were my friend," he said, measuring the words.

"I *am* your friend," Fabian replied quietly.

Eugene circled Alexandra with his arm and brought her closer. She let her weight rest on him. Both of them looked at Fabian as if he were a schoolboy called to account.

"Alexandra tells me that, last night, under the pretext of showing her your trailer, you tried to force her to make love to you," Eugene said.

Fabian felt out of his element, alien and solitary. "Alexandra is lying," he said. His eyes turned to Alexandra. She sat calm and indifferent, regarding him with an expression that remained long after the emotion that formed it seemed to have dissolved.

"Alexandra admitted that the wine you forced on

her made her a bit drunk." Eugene paused. He looked up at Alexandra, and she nodded as if to prompt him in what he was about to say. He turned back to Fabian.

"She also told me," he went on in a harsh voice, "that, even though she remained fully dressed, she spent a few minutes next to you, on top of your bed, before she felt safe enough to run out on you." He paused again. Alexandra pressed his shoulder and, as if ashamed of herself, lowered her head.

"I know everything there is to know, Fabian, and I know it from Alexandra," Eugene said. "Alexandra and I have no secrets from each other—that's the secret of our love. Did you think you could destroy that with one bottle of wine?"

Fabian looked at Alexandra, a soft glow on her cheeks, her lips parted. She wore a look of an obedient daughter submitting to the wisdom of Eugene, her all-knowing father.

Fabian's memory had not yet edited out her presence when she lay next to him. As he watched her now, the memory of what had happened between them brought her words back to him: "I've been stuck, Fabian. Stuck waiting on men and what they want, always what they want, their weary flesh in search of an easy hole. All that sweating, their clumsy kisses and useless embraces, and moaning and humping—that constant in-and-out missionary commuting. They leak into me, then off to sleep they go, and then on to the office."

He had glided closer to her, one hand under her waist, rising, the other lingering on her neck, her shoulders, hesitant to descend onto her breasts, to know again the sensation of their firmness, their sculpted shapes. He kissed her on the mouth, and it came back to him, pressing, a response vigilant and insistent. She watched him, commanding his gaze, not allowing him to lose or deny the expression in his eyes, or for a moment, even in thought, to withdraw to another world, one that might be entirely his own—or one that he might share, in recollection or fantasy, with another woman.

He thought of her legs upon his chest, her calves girdled round his ribs. Her skin lapped him with a smoothness that Fabian imagined to gleam in the darkness. She sought him with her feet, her narrow ankles, her soles supple against his cheeks. He was conscious of the high arch of her instep, the roundness of the heel grazing his jaw, her toes, lithe and fragile, prodding his lips, splitting the furrow of his mouth, prying open the clenched gate of his teeth, plying his tongue. Her hand deep within him, her foot mastering his mouth, he labored as if to summon life, but each time she brought him to the brink of orgasm, her hand refused to allow him to yield to it: consenting to submit to passion, he was denied the thrust of the gift.

Now he stared across the hunt table at her hands, their slender, carved fingers linked in her lap. He thought of those hands, in the night: how they had summoned the muscles of his body to their collusion, kneading him at will, exploring him with boldness, her cool nails tracing the taut membranes of his depth, ignoring his resistance, unlocking him to her mouth, inciting him to submit to her tongue.

In her eagerness to have him open to her, her refusal to permit him to retain some region of his body as inviolate, the license she extended to her mouth and tongue to venture where her hand and fingers had gone before, there was an unmasked avidity of possession. But he also sensed her conviction that what she was doing, although offered to him as pleasure, was exacted as proof that—in whatever manner she invoked—he would be hers.

She was able, finally, to abolish his last thin awareness of her will. He no longer cared what impulses she submitted to in her commitment to his need: whether they were stages in a drama, ordered by her and enacted by him, that would permit the revelation of his own nature, his pleasure at the discovery a tribute to her zeal; or whether, provoked by her, he was the one who would disclose what lay hidden in her, what she could not otherwise release, the pleasure she sought most.

The pensiveness of her voice returned to him now, musing: "I've always been turned on by a man's rear, Fabian. Always. Doing it to a man's rear, with my fingers, my hand, my mouth, my tongue, that's the only sex that sends me up. But Eugene hates it. One time he got really upset. He screamed at me that it was a sick and savage thing; no other woman had ever done such a sick and savage thing, trying to make a fag out of him."

As she spoke, Fabian reflected that her lawlessness in seizing her pleasure, bending him to her will, that very lack of constraint might have arisen from a vanity and terror at abandoning herself to the play of sex, to the risk that she might, in the presence of her lover, lose the carriage and control that her profession imposed. Knowing that, with his orgasm, her power over her lover waned, she would violate any taboo to prolong his craving, break any bond, penetrate any boundary.

Eugene let go of Alexandra and leaned forward across the table, his finger pointing at Fabian, his voice thick with menace. "Alexandra says you tried to force her to do a sick and savage thing, but she pushed you away and ran out."

"Alexandra is lying," Fabian said.

"You're the one who's lying!" Eugene shouted. "You're the liar."

In their time together, Fabian had seen Eugene defeated, his pride wounded. He had seen him in physical pain, seen him knocked unconscious. He had witnessed his control and easy bearing among simple horse breeders or trainers who had no idea of his position, had observed his tactful restraint among foreign polo players, some of them abusive, to whom the Stanhope name meant nothing. He had felt Eugene's commanding presence in his offices, the fount of his corporate power. Yet nothing he thought he knew of his friend could have prepared Fabian for the flood of rage that now confronted him. Under that abuse, face to face with the contortions of fury, Fabian understood what a poor judge of character he had been.

"Alexandra is lying," he said. "Last night I took her straight home."

In the telling, Fabian regretted his own lie. Desperate only in his attempt to thwart Alexandra's assault on the bond between him and Eugene, his mind denied her entry to his VanHome. The words betrayed his despair, and he realized it was futile to retract his lie.

"You're a liar," Eugene said. "The minute she saw you, Alexandra warned me to stay away from you. She said you wouldn't lift a finger for me. Now I know how right she was. Get out of here!" His face still contorted, he leaned back in the chair, pulling Alexandra toward him again.

Fabian's rage was now as uncurbed as Eugene's. Reaching across the table swiftly with his right hand, he seized an Indian dagger that lay anchoring some papers. At the same moment, he smashed the table with the palm of his left hand, fingers splayed. In one urgent arc, he brought the dagger down and sliced off the tip of his ring finger. Blood spurted from the stump as the severed piece skidded across the surface.

As Alexandra recoiled, turning away from the table, Fabian picked up the fingertip and thrust it at Eugene.

"Here it is," he said, dropping it and the dagger in front of him. "Alexandra was wrong: I have lifted it for you."

Eugene shoved the bloody tip back across the table with the dagger. "You're still a liar, Fabian!" he shouted. "Alexandra told me that, to make her drunk, you gave her your strongest wine. She told me she almost finished off the bottle. This morning, after you left for stick-and-ball practice, I went to that stagecoach of yours and, just as she said, I found the bottle where Alexandra said it was." He caught his breath only to shout louder. "I ought to teach you a lesson in decent conduct. Get out!"

They were all standing now. The fingertip lay on the table between them, and for a moment Fabian had a wild urge to leave it there. Choking back his dread, his fury an anesthetic against pain, he reached out and picked the fingertip up, held it reluctantly between his thumb and forefinger. He almost expected it to respond to his touch, but the gobbet of flesh felt like bloodied rubber, the nail plastic. He quickly joined the fingertip to the throbbing stump and, grasping both firmly in his right hand, turned to go. Blood dribbled down his trousers and across the floor.

"You hired me to play polo with you," he said to Eugene. "Play it tomorrow, six in the morning, and teach me to stick-and-ball any way you can. Training field. No witnesses."

"I'll be there!" Eugene was still shouting as Fabian left.

Back in his room, Fabian poured antiseptic over the mutilated finger, attempting to seal the amputated tip to the raw bleeding stump with a winding bandage. Pain dazed him in the car as a stable boy drove him at full speed to the hospital. In the emergency room, a surgeon stitched together the parts of the severed finger and, wrapping a bandage around the wound, reassured Fabian that there was a good chance the coupling would take and that in time the finger would be restored to use.

Fabian returned to his VanHome and lay down on the bed he had last shared with Alexandra. Later that day, feverish and a bit groggy from the injections the doctor had given him, he felt his pain yield to a mastering sense of defeat.

He slept poorly that night, waking each time his weight pressed on the wounded finger. At dawn, he walked through the misted woods to the Stanhope Stables. The morning air lifted from him the traces of narcotic stupor from the day before.

He then attended to his ponies. Gaited Amble and

Big Lick were usually easy when about to be bridled, but this morning they were skittish, pawing the ground, sniffing the air. Fabian knew that they were responding to his wound: the dread of sundered flesh was a remaining link between man and beast. Anguish without ground, guilt without motive, the vice of scruples were the province of man alone.

Careful not to jar the bandage on his finger, he proceeded to select with precision the polo tack for the encounter with Eugene, almost as if every piece were an amulet of circumstance, an agent in shaping destiny—incapacitation, death or painless triumph—which could be influenced before it was brought to pass. He harnessed each pony with its double-reined bridle—tightening the noseband, checking the tautness of the bit, the curb chain and lip strap, the length of the martingale—then adjusted the slack of the girth under the animal's belly, cinching the saddle to an exact fit, checking and rechecking the stirrup leathers, and fastening bandages on the horse's legs. When all was in place, he brought Big Lick and Gaited Amble back to his VanHome. The smell of the stable they knew animated both ponies, and as they frisked, he checked again the snugness and fit of each saddle.

Drenched from labor and dull pain, he went inside the VanHome, undressed, and ran the water for a lukewarm bath. He sat in the tub, his bandaged hand wrapped in plastic, eyes closed, his sensations wayward, his pain the tocsin of conscience.

What he faced now was not of his choosing. He had no prior quarrel with Eugene, none with Alexandra. He had initiated no breach, sought no conspiracy. He did not see himself as a victim, bested by their hostility; neither was he impelled by an image of valor or gallantry, the avenger requiting his humiliation, the hero asserting his potency. He bore his own standard within.

The imminence of peril always evoked in him a peculiar fastidiousness. Like a dandy of combat, he surveyed his polo wardrobe, the assortment of his gear, refining his choices meticulously. He and Eugene would be alone on the field, but Fabian prepared for their contest as though they were going to play in the presence of spectators, under the scrutiny of judges, press, television. He pulled a fresh shirt over his head and sheathed his legs in new white breeches and his best polo boots, their stiff leather bracing each curve of his muscles; the resulting splendor appeared to him a conscious rebuttal to the clamor, the foaming sweat and whipping dirt of the game that was about to ensue.

He locked in place the zippers on his boots, tightened the supple leather thongs that fastened his spurs at the correct angle. Even though, quite likely, he would use only one mallet, it was his custom to take several with him, and he did so now, selecting each after he had thoughtfully tested its pliancy and springiness.

To Fabian, the intensity of his acts was always knowable; he seldom had a comparable knowledge of his motive. To track the source of his present act would be no easier than to unravel the tangle within which Eugene and Alexandra acted. He saw the meaning of an act emerging with its consequences, a train of causality hinting ultimately at the impulse that had initially prompted it. He conceived of acute self-awareness as vitiating instinct, and meditative self-analysis as digging a grave for action. Living implied the necessity of maintaining his will, even without a motive, with memory fostering remorse for what he had or had not done. Was remorse over a contest, perhaps won, perhaps lost, but fought to the end, less gnawing than regret over a challenge one had refused? And how could he determine this without discerning what his motive was for entering upon the duel he had provoked?

Leaving the door of his VanHome like a crusader compelled to abandon the fastness of his citadel, he turned for a last look at it. His gaze swept the world of objects fashioned by other men; serene, untouched, invulnerable, they were indifferent to whatever fate might come upon the one who had lately bent them to his use. The events that drove him from this world had been abrupt and inescapable, but he was not yet their victim, not their prisoner; he was still in command. Soon enough, in battle, the pores of his skin would open to the sweaty, viscous reek of his own fear, the pungency of leather and tarnished brass on his tongue.

It was time to go. He put on his newest polo helmet, the face guard an internal part of it. He swung heavily into the saddle on Big Lick. Pain pounded in his hand. He held it high above the mare's mane, the reins girdling his wrist. At a slow trot he moved away from the VanHome, Gaited Amble following behind on a lead rein.

Eugene was waiting in the middle of the training field. Fabian disengaged Gaited Amble, loosely hitching it to the bars of a crude post at the end of the field. As he approached Eugene, he recognized his mount, one of the swiftest and most powerful Thoroughbreds, its ears pricking with excitement. Fabian looked at Eugene; from beneath his polo helmet with no face guard, Eugene stared back at him. Without a word, Eugene threw the ball on the ground between them.

They bore down on the ball, Eugene hitting it first in a long forehand stroke. Mallet upright in his unmarred right hand, Fabian tightened his grip on the handle. Locking his calves and knees against Big Lick's withers, thrusting his left shoulder forward over its neck, Fabian cut his spurs into the pony's flanks, prompting it to break into its fastest pace.

Eugene reached the ball at a full gallop, his mallet erect. He pitched it far back above his shoulder, then brought it down toward the ball in a scything arc. Just then Fabian's mallet sliced the air; its head snared Eugene's mallet. Eugene, jabbing and twisting, unhooked it, but instead of tracking the ball, he sheered his mount, still at taut rein, sideways toward Big Lick, bruising and jostling the mare as both horses plunged on. With a snorting roar, Big Lick tugged cruelly at the reins bound about Fabian's wounded hand.

Eugene kept pricking Big Lick with the tip of his boot, his knee guards ripping and tearing at Fabian's calves. Wild with agitation, glistening with patches of foaming sweat, Big Lick charged. Rearing, gouging the air with its forelegs, the mare fought Fabian, its neck distended and thrust out. Fabian wrenched at the reins, and the horse, obeying, plunged forward. The sudden movement scorched Fabian's arm and shoulder with a torch of pain. Eugene's eyes brimmed with contempt as he again swerved his Thoroughbred into Big Lick; Fabian averted a side collision only by fiercely gagging his mare to an abrupt halt. Heaving in pain, the pony swerved on its haunches, then bolted away from Eugene at redoubled speed, kicking the grass in frenzied bounds.

As Fabian gained on the ball, striking it toward the edge of the field, he felt his skull girded with the cold despair of certainty. Instead of rushing ahead, hitting the ball toward Fabian's goal posts, Eugene was lagging behind. Fabian recognized the strategy: Eugene expected him to head off the ball with a back shot, sending it across the field, toward Eugene's goal posts. But each time Fabian accomplished the shot, he merely delivered the ball back into Eugene's arena, and, bolting forward, Eugene recouped the ball before Fabian could challenge him for possession.

With Fabian now in front of him, Eugene, in a forward shot, sent the ball smashing, not toward the goal posts, but into Big Lick, ominously close to the animal's head—and Fabian's.

Turning for the ball slowed Fabian down; unfaltering and much faster on his pony, Eugene again seized the ball. Fabian prompted Big Lick into a flat-out gallop and, looking back, caught sight of his opponent straining in a swing; in that moment, the ball soared, whistling by Fabian's neck as he bent sideways. It had missed him by an inch.

Now, as Fabian bore down on the ball, Eugene

behind him in close pursuit, the horses heaving and snorting, Fabian no longer allowed himself to think of his pain. Perception yielded to fear, and he knew his life was now at stake. Reluctantly he saw that Eugene was no longer playing to kill Fabian's inner conviction of his own mastery: Eugene was playing just to kill. Stick-and-ball offered a convenient guise in case he should succeed. So the pattern swiftly emerged: as Fabian went in pursuit of the ball, Eugene followed, riding him off to dodge the track of the ball, bumping him at full gallop, aware that Fabian's wound of the day before reduced his control and made him more vulnerable. Fabian, who had hardly slept during the last two nights, began to feel stamina seeping out of him.

Steadfastly refusing to be drawn into Eugene's fury, Fabian still hoped that their confrontation on the same field, which, in the past, had so often brought them together, would lessen his friend's conviction of betrayal.

He countered Eugene's assault by slowing down to an easy pace, then twisted abruptly across Eugene's path in a sinuous thrust, striking the ball at every chance. With the ceaseless leaching of his strength, his legs grew stolid, sweat clouded his vision. His only strength rested in his aim, and he wondered how long he would be able to maintain it. An image of himself lying dead on the field dominated his thoughts.

Polo, even when played under strict formality, barely managed to restrain the force of human flesh, the speed and mass of the horse. To Fabian, this had been the game's sheer beauty; it was now its ultimate terror. He recalled vividly one of the amateur polo games he had witnessed in Los Lemures. During the first two or three chukkers, the pace was leisurely, safe and slow, giving each player a chance to demonstrate his skills and to relish the accomplishment of the others.

One of the players was an old acquaintance of Fabian's, a recently retired American businessman who had arrived for the occasion only two days earlier. He was accompanied by his wife and his two sons, whose wives and children also were in the party, all enthusiastic not only about the holiday, but for the happy chance to see him resume polo, the sport he had been most fond of as a young man, and to which, after three decades of what he called executive golf and tennis, he was most eager to return.

During the last chukker, a substitute player was enlisted by one of the teams. He was a young ranchero, a local boy, not often given the chance to take part in a game reserved for visiting polo players. Eager to make his mark in front of his companions and other spectators, he promptly threw his pony into a reckless display of speed, performing at the same time with an uncanny mastery of the ball. By playing so much faster than others on the field, he engaged the spectators on his side; cheered for every strike, he forced the line of attack and defense to be extended across almost the entire length of the field. Even though the other players were tired and on the brink of ending the game, prompted by the applause of the spectators, they quickly surrendered to the rapidly increased pressure of the game, and Fabian saw how his friend, reluctantly and with effort, was compelled by the speed of his team to mobilize his pony, chasing the ball at the same headlong pace as the other, younger players.

With only three minutes left to the end of the game, the young ranchero scrambled for the ball in a frantic gallop that left his pony choking for air. The other players, challenged by his aggression, spurred their ponies downfield, jabbing, fighting for possession of the ball. Fabian saw the American suddenly pull out of the scrimmage and, wielding his mallet like a hockey stick, come at the ranchero, attempting to ride him off. As the tumult of hoofs pounded the ground, the crowds in the stands, responding to the beat and tremor of the earth, broke into volleys of shouting and applause, inciting the players to goad their sweat-sodden mounts to even more drastic speed. Heedless now of everything but possession of the ball, the ranchero pitched into a steep turn, the American hard on his heels. At that moment, in a blink of time, swift as a coiling wrist, the wave of horses and men swelled, then as quickly broke, spilling from its center, in a jet of fluid motion, the glimpse of a horse thrown sideways, then buckling, its neck a sculpture of terror, its rider, the American, frozen in air, a puppet suspended above the empty saddle.

Horse and rider went down in a rolling tide of flesh, human and animal, closing then unfolding before the other players, as if what lay on the ground were a prey they had run to earth.

One after another, the players began to dismount; from both ends of the field, the umpires, grooms and the man's family rushed to the fallen player. They dropped to their knees and bent over him. The setting sun stained the blood that spilled from his head and neck, brimmed into the helmet that his fall had knocked askew, oozed through his torn shirt; nose and jaw lay limply together, pulverized by hoofs; flesh and cloth blended, matted with grass, caked with mud. While the ambulance slowly crossed the field, the ponies sniffing blood and the odor of death, prancing in fear, strained at the reins the silent grooms held taut.

The inevitable intimidated him, but now, facing Eugene, Fabian felt his spirit draw back from the vision that had obstructed it—and from the fear of death and the seduction of survival. Awake to life, he was in a trance, in which perfection was the brain's unalloyed response, enacted by the body with the certainty of sleepwalking. With Eugene racing at Fabian's left, readying the assault to unseat him, Fabian slowed Big Lick to a canter, the ball at the pony's right side. In perfect obedience, bobbing its mane imperiously, Big Lick responded instantly. Slightly to the front, Eugene, assuming that Fabian was still dribbling the ball forward, gathered momentum to drive him off course.

Poised above the ball, his mallet erect, Fabian rose in his right stirrup and hunched over Big Lick's shoulder; he quickly drew his hand close to his chest. Then, swerving his body to the right, his left knee and thigh braced high against the saddle, he unleashed all his strength into his arm, uncoiling it in a long drive beneath the pony's shoulder. In one smooth, measured blow, Fabian's mallet struck the ball dead center; crossing under the pony's neck, it catapulted into the air just when Eugene slowed down his horse and turned to the side, his mallet vaulting. He arched to look back at his enemy, and in the second that the glance consumed, Fabian's ball smashed into Eugene's face, the impact cocking his helmet forward, over his forehead. Amid the din, Fabian caught the high, thin echo of cracking bone. Eugene slumped in the saddle; his body pitched forward, then tumbled to the ground.

Even before Fabian dismounted, he knew that his friend had been felled by a fluke hit.

M emory was a fraudulent bookkeeper and, with time, Eugene was little more than a recorded fact, but here, at the tournament named for him, Alexandra Stahlberg was not. Facing Fabian, she took the arm of her companion, a man in his early twenties, familiar to Fabian. He was powerfully built, his compact physique defined by the sleek cut of the tuxedo, his patrician head and features molded with a glowing Latin harmony.

"This is José-Manuel Costeiro." Alexandra pressed Costeiro's arm, but her eyes stayed fixed on Fabian. "And this is Fabian, my old friend I told you so much about."

Fabian remembered recent photographs of Alexandra in the society pages of polo and riding magazines; Costeiro, whom Fabian had once seen playing for the Centauros, was always at her side or somewhere in the background. He came from a distinguished Argentinean cattle-breeding family who were proud of his skill at polo, but who disapproved of his indulgence in women; with both, his talent was formidable.

As a waiter poured champagne, Fabian felt Alexandra and Costeiro staring at him. He looked quickly at Alexandra across the table. Her face shone with a soft luster, almost childlike, her broad, mobile mouth framing wide teeth. Only her green eyes pierced intensely.

75

"Do you still play polo one-on-one for stakes, Fabian?" she asked with that easy, ingenuous smile.

"It depends on what stakes and against whom," Fabian replied.

"Against me, Señor Fabian," Costeiro interjected, leaning forward and smiling evenly. He paused, his eyes bright and hard; then, when Fabian remained silent, he continued. "Two ponies, and first to score five goals—with no time limit." He fingered his glass; then he proposed a sum.

"That's about three times as much as I can afford, Mr. Costeiro," Fabian said.

"I know you write books about horsemanship and appear on television talk shows; you can't be a poor man, Señor Fabian," Costeiro said.

"In this country, writing books and appearing on television are vanity sports. I make my living on a horse."

Costeiro's eyes softened as they rested on Alexandra. Then, as if the sight spurred him, he turned back to Fabian.

"How about this: If I lose, you take the full sum. If you lose, I take one-third. Agreed?" He waited, full of force, eager.

Alexandra cocked her head, observing Fabian. No expression betrayed her thoughts.

"Agreed," Fabian said.

"Tomorrow morning, then." Costeiro sat back pensively. "Nine o'clock in the practice field closest to Brook Forest and the Hunter Paces trails. No spectators—just my grooms, don't you think?"

"Gentlemen, gentlemen." Alexandra broke her silence vivaciously. "Since I arranged this game, do I get my agent's cut?"

"You'll get your cut from me," Costeiro said, all smiles.

He looked at his watch. Alexandra interpreted the signal and stood up languidly. Both men rose with her.

"Can't I even watch the game?" she asked, pouting, draped against Costeiro's shoulder.

Costeiro embraced her amorously. "Of course you can. But only if Señor Fabian doesn't mind your being there."

"Fabian is my friend. He wouldn't lift his finger against me. Would you, Fabian?"

Fabian raised the ring finger of his left hand. Since the severing, the wound had healed, but the finger remained slightly crooked. "For you, Alexandra—not even a finger," he said with mock courtesy.

He watched Alexandra and Costeiro cross the room, then slowly left the club and returned to his VanHome. He climbed the stairs to the alcove and slid the dome open to the night sky. As he shed his party clothes, he contemplated the easy guile with which Alexandra had arranged this match. What was she hoping for? In the coming game, Costeiro would have advantages over Fabian: he was younger and stronger, with superbly schooled Argentinean ponies at his command. What if, to unleash Costeiro, Alexandra had told him that she and Fabian were once lovers? Wrapping himself in a warm blanket, still unknowing, he lay down to unquiet sleep.

The sun woke him at dawn, moist air cool on his face. Shivering, he looked out through the open dome. Aimless patches of fog roamed the woods, then slipped away, baring a grove of elms. Rising from the thick carpet of underbrush, the trees stood bare, inexplicably stripped of their foliage.

He slipped coming down the steps from the alcove, bruising his shoulder against the door. An accident, he wondered, or was he losing his coordination under stress? In a game, a blur, a smudge, a single break in the chain of coordination might bring him to earth.

He knew that his own apprehension and fear were hazards that might, at any moment before or during his fight with Costeiro, bend him to the humiliation of gagging, vomit or the wrenching flood and waste of the body.

As a precaution, he began his preparations for the match by quickly forcing his stomach and bowels to rid themselves of food and waste, a cleansing evacuation without pain or any other unpleasant side effects. He had learned to do this during his travels in countries where the practice of voiding one's stomach, intestines and bladder was done at will, a recourse when people wished to pleasure themselves at table without distraction or where a failure or reluctance to continue partaking of the largesse of one's host would be construed as an insult.

Fabian then turned on a tape recorder, raising the volume until it consumed the space around him with random songs and melodies he had recorded from his VanHome radio, the music reminding him of an evening with a lover, an afternoon of ease among friends, a day of writing, the whiling away of a forest noon, no menace to cloud the enclosure of his thought.

He had listened to this music often, the current of his memory moving toward those interludes of harmony and light. Now, as always when he played it before a game, the music came at him like a rallying cry, a call to arms, the bugle that would alert the line of emotional defense he needed to stave off fear.

He let the heat of a bath invade him, unraveling the knot at his center. Then he lathered and rinsed his hair until it slipped between his fingers. He was careful not to burn his scalp with the hair drier, and he brushed his hair as if he were polishing it, arranging it by habit on both sides of the widow's peak, a gesture that had become mere reflex by now, a shadow of an atavistic belief that his vigor depended on how much pelt covered his scalp.

He brushed his teeth with the firmest brush he had and the powder to which he was accustomed, then he massaged his gums with yet another brush, soaked in a solution that scaled the tissue, a prelude to the jet of water he finally shot into his mouth, laving his teeth and gums, until he felt vivified, without stain.

Then, with precision, almost surgically, he shaved, planing his skin to the polish he would bring to a night of love. There was still time to kill, and he trimmed his fingernails and cuticles, vigilant not to cut himself; he proceeded then to his feet, trimming his toenails, dislodging the dead skin that had formed around them and under the toes. Next he swabbed his ears with wads of cotton, scrutinizing the film of yellow wax, the dirty smudge that soiled the cotton, scouring the channels that curved behind the lobes.

Fabian performed all this in earnest, with diligent objectivity, as he had prepared for earlier sieges and combat, much as if his power was determined by the amount of clogging food, fat, wax, husks of dead skin and nail or decay he could strip from the apparatus of his body: a rite of purification, of priming, for the unsullied summons of the encounter.

The slight wrench of pain in his back was by now a familiar companion; he went to sleep with its pressure and awoke at its prod. He had devised a routine to subdue and mitigate it: sleeping with a pillow under his knees, avoiding sharp or abrupt movements, saddling his ponies only when he was squarely balanced on both feet. Still, at polo or on the practice field, each time he stood up in the stirrups—a mallet in his hand, his shoulders and trunk parallel to the line of the ball, whether veering to the right, poised to strike, or swiveling at his hips, then tilting sharply across the horse to hit on the left—each torsion of his body was as adamant as the swinging of an iron gate, pushing the joints and ligaments of his back beyond the point of tolerance, risking a spasm that could immobilize him not only for the instant but for days to come.

To support his back now, he wound an elastic brace around his hips, tightening the fabric like a corset until he felt the middle of his body as an unassailable sheath. He took pleasure in that sensation of tautness and inner compression, curiously relishing the knowledge that even though he had to enlist an external instrument, he could still affect the involuntary mechanism of his body.

Ready at last, he left his alcove and released Big Lick and Gaited Amble from their stalls in the rear of the VanHome. He saddled them meticulously, strapping a bundle of polo mallets to the rig on Gaited Amble, who would follow on a lead rein, then mounted

Big Lick. The practice field was about a mile away, and, relishing what time remained to him before thought must yield to habit, he began to advance on it slowly, the sun like a vast ball in the distance.

He slid back in the saddle, without will, his gaze sweeping the shallow meadows, the redolence of thyme and the tart fragrance of damp weeds pricking his nostrils. A surge of longing for the city rose within him, the anonymous lure of its streets, the vortex of men and women, of shape, feature, color making a discordant frenzy in which he could immerse himself— a mortal forest, uprooted, divested of its past, of all that bound it to earth.

He had acted always in the conviction that to master his life, to assert dominion over that indifferent span, what he must do was to shape it into drama, each scene so charged, so unrepeatable, that no interval could be permitted to divert him from the spectacle of which he was both protagonist and solitary witness.

Now it broke on him savagely that in the theater of his life he had contrived to make of himself a grotesque figure, a Don Quixote of the turnpike, a Captain Ahab, moorless in his big ship of a VanHome, and from the void at his center, a hideous, soundless laughter spilled out, derisive, racking him, buckled, polished, poised astride the horse.

Contempt for himself, for Alexandra and Costeiro, for deeds of this world and its ways assailed him like an unbearable stench, a wave of vileness he could not breach. In his imagining, the film of Alexandra in his VanHome began again to unwind, the images unrelenting, a whip of vicious poignancy, goading him to desolation, spiking and bloodying a depth of anguish in which he drifted as the reel revolved.

He shriveled at the thought of what kind of figure he cut in their arena, baffled at what distorting mirror in his vision and character had seduced him into that image of himself as the gallant knight in a tournament of passion, rather than as the paltry clown in a carnival play. The gall of life, a fever of contempt for the part he had consented to enact, fell on him with all its futile weight.

He thrust back in a panic of survival, panting, hot with sudden thirst for the drama before him, tugging at the horse's bit, goading his spurs deep into its flanks. He punished it with the snaffle and the curb, and the animal reared as if scorched with a hot iron. Fabian began to lash at its neck and belly and flanks until Big Lick, a captive of the bit, whip and spur, hurtled forward, the heave of its bulk parrying the wind, the space ahead a promise of blows that would cease, pain that would end. Gaited Amble, behind, snorting and squealing, careened at the end of the lead rein.

Fabian arrived at the field shaken. He lifted his eyes only to halt, numb with astonishment. The field was broken up with posts and rails, oxers, parallel and triple bars, hedges and fences—the kinds of obstacles used for jumping competitions—perhaps a dozen of them placed at various angles, strewn about without any seeming order of progression.

Instantly it dawned on him what Costeiro had done, and with that rush of awareness, a throttling sense of entrapment stormed over him, provoking a spasm of nausea, brief and intense; he steadied himself on Big Lick, swallowing in quick, deep gusts. In the distance, parked at the far edge of the field, a sports car, gleaming, its top down, caught his eye. Alexandra, her helmeted head a white dazzle in the sun, sat at the wheel. Costeiro, spruce in his riding gear, lounged against the convertible, toying with his mallet, his head hovering over Alexandra. To the right, at the viewing stands, two grooms were adjusting the saddles of the Argentinean's ponies.

Fabian rode across the field to the stands, where he hitched Big Lick and Gaited Amble, the ponies calm again after the turbulence of their ride in the field.

He began to stride deliberately toward Alexandra and Costeiro, trying to tug off his riding gloves, sharply aware, as his fingers fumbled with the supple leather, of how cold his hands had gone, gelid sticks, almost rigid. The air was hot on his face and shoulders; sweat brimmed under his helmet. He looked at his hands, marble with chill pallor. Their cold seemed to him a frost of premonition.

He could not tell whether his fear was a response of his flesh, in revolt against a threat to the dominion of character and will; or whether fear had usurped the very province of that character and will, exposing further some critical lesion in their authority.

What he drew strength from was a consciousness of the fitness of his presence, the note of readiness for combat that he gave off in his taut shirt and breeches, the padded leather knee guards, his thick leather boots, the blade of brass zipper that split each of them, glistening.

Coming at Costeiro in the full blaze of morning, watching the springy power of Costeiro's shoulders and thighs, the gleam and luster of his face, how fluent with a molten grace his gestures were, Fabian had to acknowledge, envy twitching within him, what a worthy rival the Argentinean was. He remembered Alexandra telling him that what she found most alluring during her Latin American tour was the sight of the native Indian men, their bodies smooth and muscular, always hairless, flesh moving toward sculpture, sculpture mobile as flesh. The thought of Costeiro molded with Alexandra, the two of them at night together, one sculpture in love with another, rankled, yet he knew that his envy of Costeiro was at root an adolescent urge to escape his own shape, to become, if only in transient fantasy, someone else, another being.

Costeiro's wealth, too, was an insolent rebuke to him, and the humiliation of his own last few hundred dollars hidden in a box inside his wooden practice horse galled him. He knew he could still cancel the bout with Costeiro, return to his VanHome, stable his ponies, and wait until he was restored. There was time still to retreat to the turret of the cab, switch on the ignition, take up his own rhythm from the surge of the engine, and move ahead, slipping onto the vacant ribbon of the highway.

He knew, also, how brief was the time before he could no longer afford to buy fuel for his VanHome, feed his ponies or himself. He might soon have to put his whole way of life up for auction. Interest in his books had been dwindling for years; now there might be no serious clients to bid on his VanHome, his ponies, his gear and tack. He could live for months on the money that he might win—had to win—from the Argentinean.

The sight of Costeiro, with his youth, security and easy command, reminded Fabian that he could claim no constant place as home, summon no assistance as he sought to make his way again, a way uncertain in its prospect and goal. Poverty was a blackmailer with amiable manners: it left all choices to its victim.

He thought of the city and remembered the old, tattered vagrant, trudging and cadging, the yellowing crown of scabs on his head, his feeble hands and lips twitching at the soup, the mumbling mouth.

"Good morning, Fabian," Alexandra called out, a movie camera and a tripod in her hands, her smile flashing with the provocation that never deserted her. She wore a scarred polo helmet; a moonlight sheen parka, thrown open enough to show the cleavage of her breasts, contrasted with sleek leather pants, tapered down, her ankles wreathed in the golden straps of her sandals.

Nodding coolly to Alexandra, Fabian shook the hand of the smiling Costeiro, then pointed at the field. "What's this obstacle course for?" he asked.

"It's for us, Señor Fabian," Costeiro replied. "When my ponies were schooled, they were also taught to jump. It should come as no surprise. Alexandra tells me she has seen your horses jumping—quite well, too."

"I thought our game was polo," Fabian said, "not jumping."

"The game is what sportsmen make it," Costeiro said easily, speaking with that patient condescension reserved for calming the overwrought.

"Just as love is how lovers make it," Alexandra broke in lightly.

"What do you make of this, then, Mr. Costeiro?" Fabian asked evenly, still civil.

"I make of this our game. One-on-one polo, with a handicap—a few jumping obstacles to even things up between us," Costeiro replied. "Surely you didn't expect that I, always a volunteer on a team of amateurs, was going to let you, a hippodrome sharpshooter, just shoot all the goals, take the money and run?" There was a veiled insolence in his tone, but Fabian did not rise to it. "Of course, you don't have to play," Costeiro went on.

Fabian looked at Alexandra. Her helmet was bent toward the camera, and she pretended not to be listening, her face hidden while she played with the knobs and adjusted the various dials.

"What other handicaps have you thought up for me, Mr. Costeiro?" Fabian asked, still evenly.

"Nothing but these." The insolence gave way to charm. "Today I'm not in the best form. Last night I taught Alexandra to dance the *milonga*, the stepmother of the tango. She looked so ravishing, so sexy—and, as a result, this morning—" He broke off, implying no explanation was necessary.

"Looking sexy is Alexandra's handicap," Fabian said.

"Indeed it is!" Costeiro agreed. "And so this morning I'm suffering from a terrible *resaca*, what you here call a hangover. And to play polo with a hangover, I need a lot of what we in Argentina call *garra*—the will to fight on a bad day." He turned to Alexandra for confirmation.

"The hangover and *garra* even things up further," Alexandra agreed, looking up, her eyes unreadable behind the shield of her sunglasses.

"I suppose I should be grateful to Mr. Costeiro for

not having tossed in a bull or a steer so we could also have a rodeo," Fabian said.

Costeiro rose to the spur with a genial smile. "Indeed you should, Señor Fabian. The *cuchilleros,* the knife fighters of the pampas, are, like myself, more fond of the bull and the steer than are you, the cowboys of the baseball field."

"What are the penalties for knocking down an obstacle?" Fabian asked abruptly.

"None, of course. An obstacle is already a penalty." Costeiro's smile was tinged with challenge now. "Each time one is knocked down, my grooms will set it up again. That's all."

Sensing Fabian's apprehension, Costeiro leaned back against the car with an amused expression, his hand stroking his mallet. "Of course, no one can force you to jump, Señor Fabian. You can just circle the obstacles."

"While you go straight over them," Fabian replied, managing a smile.

Costeiro broke into laughter. "While I score the goals."

Alexandra switched from her mimicry of absorption to a mimicry of film-making. "Lights! Camera! Action!" she called out brightly, lifting the camera to her sunglasses, pointing the lens first at Costeiro, then at Fabian, then back at Costeiro.

"I'm ready!" Costeiro announced, slapping his polo gloves against his breeches. "But let's not coerce Señor Fabian into playing in our film."

"Fabian can't be coerced," Alexandra said, bright still. "Corrupted, yes, but only by vanity. But not coerced. He's too proud for that." She pointed the lens directly at Fabian. "I've never been able to tell whether Fabian is too proud to be vain or too vain to be proud."

"I'm ready," said Fabian, his mouth dry with the tension of what had just passed, what was just about to begin.

"Let's start, then," Costeiro said briskly. He took

the helmet from Alexandra's head and set it on his own, adjusting the chin strap, then put on his gloves. He reached into the sports car for a container of polo balls and handed it to Alexandra. "After we've ridden across the field to get acquainted with the obstacles, Alexandra will throw out the ball for us," he announced.

Alexandra took a ball from the container and juggled it eagerly. The promise of competition stimulated her. "First a ball to the players, then a kiss to the winner," she said. "Or should the loser be kissed first?" She took off her sunglasses. "What would you say, Fabian?" She looked at him directly, but even without the sunglasses, Fabian could find no expression in her eyes.

"I suppose it depends on the needs of the one who is kissing," he said. Abruptly, he turned away from Costeiro and Alexandra, and started to walk toward his ponies. As the last drops of dew misted on the leather sheen of his boots, he was conscious of how indifferent he had been to the sun in its healing warmth.

Big Lick and Gaited Amble stood calm, submissive, tethered to their posts. Fabian quickly loosened each pony's martingale, the leather strap that ran from the bit down between the forelegs, circling the horse's girth; he also removed a noseband from above its muzzle that was used to prevent the animal from tossing its head about in defiance of pressure from the bit.

For his first encounter with Costeiro, Fabian decided on Big Lick, although the pony flinched as he took the reins, neighing in apprehension from the remembered run to the field. He then selected a short, light mallet, its cane flexible, perfect for tricky shots.

He swung into the saddle and cantered toward the middle of the field, conscious of the peace, the fresh stains of paint on the obstacles a pleasant blur to his eyes. As Big Lick wove its way around the obstacles, he calculated their height and width, the space between them, the number of strides the horse must take before each jump. He kept imagining what soon might be a reality: his collision with Costeiro, the rebounding of horses and mallets against the barriers, falling on each other, thrusting, parrying for the ball when it lay between the obstacles or was caught under them.

Fabian knew that, by arranging for obstacles and jumps to impede their game, Costeiro hoped to diminish his opponent's ability to strike well, the very control he claimed he wanted to generate and exploit in their competition. In that strategy, in Costeiro's scheme to defeat Fabian by the random disordering of the field with barriers—thereby imposing on the rider an unnatural, disjointed movement—Fabian saw the Argentinean as an exponent of the team mentality, which stressed the passing of the ball from one player to the next to achieve an uninterrupted flow in the game.

The irony of the plan, not lost on Fabian, who savored it with a grim relish, was that by resorting to just such maneuvers and wily ruses, the Argentinean only confirmed Fabian's preeminence in the art that issued directly from what Fabian saw as the very essence of any game: the mind of the man who played it, his ambition to take each shot as an independent event, formally detached from what preceded it and from what might follow—the reverse of a group code.

He tested his speculation by surveying the several practice jumps that Costeiro, his mallet raised upright, took in rapid succession. From a distance, it seemed that his pony cleared each obstacle smoothly, cresting the gentle swell of an invisible wave, sloping fluently with it toward the ground, the jump completed with the animal unshaken, the rider secure in his seat, mallet curved in a hit at the ball. But as Fabian moved closer, intent in his scrutiny, he began to see defects in the Argentinean's technique.

He noticed that, without comprehending the basic realities of jumping, Costeiro exhibited a mannerism, common among polo players, shortening the reins, clipping the animal's reach, and, by stiffening its spine, cribbing its freedom of movement, forcing the pony to

slow down in the face of the obstacle. By slowing his
mount on the brink of a jump, so dangerously close to
a blind area of the animal's vision, the Argentinean
nullified its instinctual gift to calculate, from a proper
distance, the height and depth of an obstacle, and the
momentum and effort needed to clear it.

The heavy gear that Costeiro's grooms had laden on
their master's pony—as poorly schooled at jumping, in
Fabian's view, as the man who rode it—could easily
become an additional handicap. With the pony's martingale taut under its neck, the noseband dropped low,
ready to constrict the nostrils whenever pressure was
exerted on the reins, the neck confined, Costeiro's pony
could neither raise its head to see the obstacle at close
range nor stretch out its neck to achieve balance in
preparation for a jump. With so many restraints,
Costeiro had only reinforced the pony's habit, artifi-
cially cultivated for polo, of propelling itself on the
hock joints in its hind legs only, somewhat like a rabbit
or a kangaroo, instead of relying, in a jump, on the
freedom and momentum of its entire mass.

As Fabian threaded his way among the obstacles,
Big Lick intermittently shying and bucking at one or
another of them, he continued to contemplate Costeiro's strategy, to ponder his own. He concluded that
the Argentinean, like so many other polo players, valued teamwork and the urgency of the game, its incessant volley of pressure, danger, skill; solitary forms of
horsemanship—even jumping—presented themselves
as inferior in drama and thrill, and therefore were to
be carried out casually, as gentlemanly diversions that
called for no further authority, preparation or expertise.

He was distracted by a slight commotion at the
fringe of the field. Two of Costeiro's grooms helped
Alexandra set up the camera on its tripod, and Fabian
saw her in the distance, the sheen of her jacket a
luminous backdrop to the black metal. The Argentinean, still practicing, preened for her with several
fresh jumps, now hitting a ball one of the grooms
threw to him, radiating the conviction, as his mount

cleared the obstacles, that he was as accomplished a jumper as he was a polo player. Fabian observed that whenever Costeiro's pony was accelerating to clear the obstacle, the Argentinean, plying his mallet in anticipation of striking the ball, would tilt over the horse's mane, shifting his weight above its shoulders, burdening its forelegs before his horse had a chance to clear the obstacle. If he was about to attempt a back or side shot, he would bend back or sideways, shifting his weight onto the pony's rear, burdening its hind legs with further weight. In both instances, Costeiro carelessly tended to tip the pony off balance at the exact moment when, to hurdle the barrier, the animal most needed its balance.

It was time to practice. Fabian threw Big Lick into a leisurely trot and then steered the horse toward the first of the obstacles.

The mare took the jump smoothly, the hoofs of its forelegs higher than its belly, hind legs tucked in neatly behind the thighs, lifting its heaviest bulk in a clean sweep above the barrier. The pony's performance was a reward for the time and care Fabian had spent in maintaining Big Lick and Gaited Amble at jumping.

He repeated the maneuver, continuing to guide the horse solely with his legs, his hand gently holding the reins, his mallet at the ready. Each time he jumped, giving Big Lick its lead, the freedom to stretch out its neck, to balance its head, Fabian was careful to maintain a steady seat and not to shift his weight in a polo saddle that did not offer the support of one properly canted for jumping. To curb any association of jumping with pain, which could impel the mare to stop short in front of an obstacle and unseat him, he refrained from using the whip before a jump and was cautious not to rein in the horse too abruptly after it had cleared the obstacle.

A half-dozen of Costeiro's grooms moved into positions along the field and at the goal posts. Costeiro raised his arm, a signal that he was ready to start. Now he and Fabian began to ride toward the center of the field.

Alexandra, her hair a liquid fan about her neck, stepped from behind the camera as the two men advanced toward her. Fabian saw the white ball in her hand; he sensed the stir she created, a schoolgirl about to play, waiting avidly for the signal to toss the ball.

As Fabian and Costeiro came to a halt at the edge of the field, she threw the ball in, its lithe arc cleaving the morning light. Before it tumbled to a halt beside them, Costeiro, heaving in his zeal to get at it, already seized by the heat of the game, swerved his pony, his mallet scooping the ball gently into the air. As it scythed upward, he chased under it, his mallet a pendulum, his mount smoothly negotiating a parallel bar in pursuit of the ball. Just as his horse crested the bar, he caught the ball in flight, arrowing it toward the goal. Fabian, three lengths behind, unable to overtake him, watched the Argentinean's pony take three more obstacles with springy ease. About a hundred yards from the goal, Costeiro bore down on the ball. Once again his mallet made faultless contact with it, a clap of triumph. In vaulting catapult, the ball drove straight between the posts—making the goal.

Spurts of applause, yelps of Latin exultation and encouragement erupted from his grooms at the goal posts and the fringes of the field. Costeiro, slowing down, raised his hand to announce his scoring the first point. Tipping the brim of his helmet, the Argentinean, flushed with the pride of his performance, his habit of command unruffled, pranced his pony about in front of Alexandra's camera, responding to her wave of victory with the homage of his raised mallet. As Costeiro and Fabian moved across the grass toward her, again returning to the starting point, a groom handed her a fresh ball, and she burst out from behind the camera, glowing with excitement. Boldly she threw the ball down, like a challenge, between the two men.

This time, the ball rolled close to Fabian, yet he felt sluggish, torpid, uncertain whether he was able to muster the spirit to match Costeiro. Preoccupied with the attraction between Alexandra and Costeiro, with the Argentinean's mastery in hitting the ball, Fabian still missed the contour of his own will, the bent of his own strategy: whether to play the ball or to play Costeiro.

With the first few shots, the sweat began to bead under Fabian's helmet, trickling into his eyes, blurring his vision, forcing him to blink more often; soon its taste was salty on his lips, and it began dripping down his neck and chin. His left hand holding the whip and reins, his right gripping the mallet, he could not pause long enough to lift his face guard and blot the sweat. To shake it off, he lowered his head, looking straight down at the lush turf that glided, like a conveyor belt in perpetual, verdant motion, under his horse. The surface and depth of the grass were clear to him, every parched patch, every emerald strip. His eyes recorded mechanically the burnt-out blades of grass, mangled and flat, that smeared the head of his mallet at each strike, the dew that the ball, almost as if sweating, trailed like a fine mist in its course.

To ready himself for the challenge of a strike, Fabian drew on his fund of mental blueprints, envisioning the moment of the hit upon him: his mallet in a swing at the lowest point of the ellipse of his arm, now moving upward, toward the point of impact that lay slightly ahead of the line of his foot, the flipping arc of his wrist adding speed to the mallet just when its head met the ball below its dead center, lofting it into the air with the concentrated momentum of his own energy, the velocity of his horse, even the breeze that, cooling his neck, sped him onward.

He outflanked Costeiro and with an effortless stroke hit the ball, sending it swiftly on its way, to rest just inches from a triple bar. He had broken into a fast canter, clearing crossbars as he beat his way toward the white blur, when he realized that Big Lick had misread his command and was not slowing down enough for him to strike the ball. The mare plowed into the parallel bars with its chest, knocking the rails noisily askew, ribbons of color splintering beneath Fabian.

Just then, Costeiro, seizing the chance, jammed

through, goading the pony into a clever prance over the fallen bars, pushing Big Lick off balance. The ball his again, he launched a perfect backhand at it, and as it reeled into the distance, he curbed his mount; the pony, rearing, choked as Costeiro swiveled and took off after the ball. Breasting a pair of triple bars and two post-and-rails in swift progression, Costeiro overtook the ball and scooped it into the air again, catching it with a blow as it hurtled over the field. The ball, a thread of white, whistled toward the goal. Fabian, helpless, watched as Costeiro scored for the second time.

The two men took starting positions again, changing sides. Alexandra pitched in a ball, and Costeiro, alert to the challenge of Fabian coming at him from the side, took off at full gallop, steadying himself as he reached the ball. His mallet missed it by an inch, but before he could return to claim it, Fabian charged up from the other end of the field; his legs hard on Big Lick, hurdling the post-and-rails, he bumped into Costeiro, riding him off and taking the ball by swatting it under the pony's neck. Costeiro would not slacken his speed, and bore down as both riders simultaneously jumped a wall barrier. He could not pass Fabian, but uncoiling his mallet in a full swing, he propelled the ball into a tumbling roll that smashed it against a hedge-and-rail. Erect in his stirrups, Costeiro wheeled his foaming pony abruptly, circling back to snatch the ball from under the hedge, spoiling Fabian's chance for a shot at the goal.

Just as Fabian readied Big Lick to breast a double set of post-and-rails, to retaliate with a back shot, Costeiro came at him from the side. The Argentinean's mount jarred Fabian's pony into a skid that knocked both obstacles sprawling in front of Fabian before he could steady himself in the saddle and bring Big Lick to balance. Gagging his pony, Costeiro forced it into a veering side collision with Fabian. Big Lick, tossing in panic, reared. Fabian, the animal plunging beneath him, felt one boot slip from the iron clasp of the stirrup. He lurched to the side, on the brink of losing his seat.

At that moment, off balance, the security of his saddle awry, Fabian saw the ball. It was within reach, luring him, a summons he could not deny. His arm wheeling and winding with mounting velocity, one hand drawn close to his body, his eye stalking the ball, he stretched his arm, launching the mallet with a wrench of his shoulder, smashing at full tilt, the ball soaring into a high, liquid arc, steep above the barriers. As the ball spun against the air, the hand of the groom at the goal post was raised in announcement: Fabian had scored his first point.

There was a mild flurry of scattered applause. A rush of blood invaded Fabian's brain, and tides of breath pounded in his ears and throat. From a distance, he saw Costeiro's friendly salute as he wheeled and rode toward his grooms, apparently having decided to change his pony. Alexandra gave no sign of recognition, moving out quickly to meet the Argentinean, who embraced her after he dismounted. For a moment, they looked at Fabian, who was beginning to circle the field slowly on Big Lick; then they turned away, retreating into their intimate whispering.

As he watched them, Fabian was no longer torpid, without will. This morning, on this field, he knew his strategy.

He returned to the starting point, watching as Costeiro took his new pony over each obstacle, priming it, the grooms calling out in Spanish. Fabian chose to keep Big Lick, although the mare, lathered and foaming, shining with sweat, quivered and trembled still. He stroked and gentled the horse, readying it for the next bout.

He was aware of Alexandra ignoring his presence as she busied herself with the camera. When a groom scrambled toward her with a ball, she took it from him coolly and moved toward the rim of the field. Without a glance at Fabian, she tossed it before the Argentinean gently, almost an invitation.

Fabian and Costeiro collided in their rush to it. Attempting a long tail shot, the Argentinean coiled his mallet in a whipping stroke that lunged up to catch Fabian under the brim of his helmet. Dizzied, Fabian swayed in his saddle, Big Lick suddenly aimless beneath him, the painted jumps and bars a grid of random colors, the ground a smudged reel of green.

Costeiro circled back, pivoting his horse, smiling and gesturing a sportsman's apology. Fabian, the daze of the blow receding, Costeiro's blur of words drifting across the stir of the horses, met the Argentinean's eyes, gleaming, alert. He attempted the response of the field, but the answering smile would not come: he remembered his troubled thoughts of the night before.

Quickening to his instinct, Big Lick shot out, shoving Costeiro to the side and crowding his mount; Fabian and Costeiro locked and unlocked mallets in a melee over the ball. In the breach that opened between them, Fabian caught sight of the ball, directly in front of Big Lick's legs. Collecting the horse, thrusting himself well into the saddle, he drove the ball straight from under the pony's neck. It shot across the field, a white pellet winking in the sun, vaulting over two obstacles. Cutting off Costeiro, he took after it, clearing both jumps as he bore down on the ball. He reached it just as Big Lick was about to clear an oxer, the last obstacle before the goal posts, and pounded the ball high into the air. He could feel Big Lick gathering, bunching lithely to hurdle the obstacle. To keep his seat secure, Fabian forked his body tautly, tightening his legs around the horse's ribs. At the pitch and zenith of his flight, he closed in on the ball, infusing his mallet with the mass and momentum of the horse, with the surge of the leap, with his own energy and will, a radiant stream of force cresting at full flood on the very brink of its shuddering collapse. Wood cracking on wood, the head of his mallet overtook its quarry. He watched the ball's passage between the posts. He had scored his second goal. The game was at a draw.

Once again, Fabian and Costeiro returned to the starting point, passing each other with a cool formality

as they observed the ritual of changing sides of the
field.

The Argentinean's face was dark with concentration,
his eyes sullen. Alexandra, standing at the rim of the
field, ignored both players, calculated, then hurled the
ball out well over their heads, almost defiantly, mus-
tering a force she had not drawn upon before. With the
ball behind them, Costeiro and Fabian swiveled instantly, plunging their ponies over the first two obstacles, their jumps parallel lines of force, merging almost
in an alignment so close that it seemed they wanted to
ride each other off while still in flight. Big Lick's eyes
bulged in panic, skidding and shooting sideways, as the
mare breasted a barrier, measuring the space between
itself and a horse it did not know. The riders cleared
the brush-and-rails, but the savage competition went
on, a jostling duel as they bore down on the next
obstacle. Fabian found himself braking Big Lick as the
Argentinean snaffled his mount pitilessly at the approach to the parallel bars. Under strips of cheerful
color, nestling in the green turf, the ball lay, waiting.

A fight for possession broke out. Thwarting Fabian's
pursuit of the ball, Costeiro rammed his mount at Big
Lick's neck and haunches, butting and bunting, trapping the mare in the tangle of trampled rails. Canting
Big Lick against the other pony, Fabian struck back,
his knee guards ripping at Costeiro's, hooking, then
breaking loose, their mallets hissing as they whipped
the air, flogging the legs of their prancing ponies,
catching their hoofs, cramming the air with a staccato
rattle of wood barking on wood, wrenching, the cracking noise a tide about Fabian's ears, drowning the rush
of his breath, his pitching chest. The ponies, foaming
with panic and effort, their eyes wheeling in terror of
the turmoil and of each other, reared violently, bucking
and trampling. Its haunches pushed against the rails,
Big Lick bolted, as if seared by a bar of flame, dislodging the rails with a swift kick of its hind legs;
taking their flailing tumble as a springboard, the mare
now catapulted forward, shoving Costeiro and his
pony, bristling in frenzy, to one side, allowing Fabian

to come at the ball in a perfect side back shot. While Costeiro tried to calm his pony, Fabian turned Big Lick on its hocks and followed the ball, striking it again, sending it in a sleek skim over a fence well before he cleared that obstacle, then, after the jump, whipping the ball straight toward the goal. Only two obstacles, one post-and-rails and one triple bar, remained before him. He was standing in the stirrups, already coiling his arm, poised to launch the mallet in a stroke that would send the ball over both obstacles, arrowing to its target, when he saw Alexandra. Hovering over her camera, she was midway at the side of the field, only a few yards away from where the ball had come to rest. Following Fabian's run, waiting to catch his stroke, the camera an extension of her profile, Alexandra adjusted the aperture. In the lens of his thought, Fabian saw the face he would remember always, hovering over his body, a face he had touched, that had touched him; then he saw the ball pounding into Alexandra's head, leveling her ear, the ruptured veins spurting blood, her jaw fallen away, pulverized bone burying one eye, a slimy mussel in its splintered shell, her forehead an oozing fissure in a skull like a discarded visor, the jet of blood from her temple rising, bright crimson.

He was almost on the ball now, one part of his brain measuring the span between his mallet and the ball, the speed of the pony, the distance to the goal, another instantly denying the image of that bloodied face, imposing on it the black shield of the camera, its knobs and dials beacons in the sun, flickering only inches from the softness of her face, the tumult of her cascading hair.

As he bore down on the ball, he tightened his grip on the mallet. In one slope of unbroken impulse, his body canted to the plane of the ball, his arm raised, straightening, wheeling with impetus, his shoulder following, his wrist flexing back and up, he scythed the mallet forward, well ahead of Big Lick's trunk, swinging down, connecting the very center of the mallet's head to the equator of the ball in a clap of annihilating force.

The ball rose into the light, flying like a skeet target bolted from its trap. Fabian looked full into the sun, his eye on the ball, its faint whining above him. His eyes flickering for a second on the silver blur of Alexandra, he watched the ball. It descended, pounding into the camera, shattering against it, tumbling it and the tripod down. Alexandra was left standing, her hands to her head, her screaming spilling over the field, the jab of Costeiro's mallet on Fabian's arm, flogging, flailing, dragging him to a halt.

"What happened, what happened?" the Argentinean shouted, his face a storm of rage. Vaulting from his pony even before it stopped, he broke into a run toward Alexandra, his mallet a discarded toy. Three grooms rushed toward Alexandra apprehensively, one of them stopping, almost reverently, to pick up the mangled camera. Fabian got off Big Lick and followed Costeiro calmly to where Alexandra stood, her hands twisting her hair, damp with fright, the mask of her composure askew, tears brimming in her eyes focused in a dead stare.

"Alex, are you hurt?" Costeiro asked, taking her urgently, almost brutally, by the shoulders, searching her face, his hands plying her head and neck and throat, then thrusting her, limp in his grip, away from him. As she began to sob, he shuddered with relief, bringing her closer, his mouth on her forehead, whispering away her fear, brushing straw from her jacket, stroking her neck. Fabian watched the scene impassively; the grooms were openly excited and curious.

"I'm terribly sorry," Fabian said. "My pony slipped just as I was about to strike the ball—just as I hit it."

Costeiro turned to him, shouting. "You could have crippled Alexandra for life, you could have killed her."

Steadied by Costeiro's arm, Alexandra looked at Fabian. Her throat was still pulsing with terror, but the first wave had passed, leaving her listless.

"I know you didn't mean it, Fabian," she mumbled. Fabian could not decipher whether her incoherence was the result of the accident or a fresh resumption of the mask, as she went on, her voice a drifting trail. "I know that if you meant it, it wouldn't have been the camera." She slumped against Costeiro's shoulder.

"The man strikes but God carries the blow." Costeiro was suddenly formal with an impersonal wisdom. "Alex should be thankful to God she is still alive," he said gravely, one hand caressing her hair. He turned to look at Fabian evenly, coldly. "And you, that you didn't kill her."

"I am," Fabian said. "Do we continue our game, Mr. Costeiro?"

They went back to their ponies. As he picked up his mallet, Costeiro threw a last, anxious glance at Alexandra. Fitful, she sat hunched on the grass.

Costeiro touched the mallet to his helmet as a signal, and one of the grooms threw in the ball. The game continued. Costeiro's first moves were sluggish, and Fabian realized that the Argentinean's thoughts were with Alexandra. In the first scuffle, he lost the ball to Fabian, who tracked it easily, in free flight across the field, taking one obstacle after another without incident. Then Costeiro, his pony whinnying at the incessant use of the whip, the spurs bloodying its flanks, swerved to bear down, hard in the wake of Fabian, only inches behind Big Lick. Fabian knew that if Big Lick were to slow down, Costeiro might run into him; if the mare refused a jump, the slam could be dangerous. Instinct mobilized him again, every power alert, as he recognized that Costeiro's aim might now be to punish him for the incident with Alexandra. He slackened the reins and with his legs gently prodded Big Lick into a run, goading it toward the triple bar; but just as the mare was about to take it, he braced himself in the saddle, and threw all his weight and strength to one side, forcing Big Lick to sidetrack the jump. The maneuver was swift and, in the classic response of the polo man, Costeiro, desperate to bring his pony to heel, made the blunder of wrenching at the reins, locking the martingale and noseband in a vise that strangled his pony's nostrils and bridled it, momentarily choking the animal's breathing. Its sight of the barrier having been obstructed by Big Lick, Costeiro's pony confronted an obstacle it had not seen from afar and was now too close to see well. Punished by the reins, panicking at the looming presence of the triple bar, the horse refused violently, pitching Costeiro, bent forward in readiness to take the jump, over its head and into the barrier.

Seizing the moment, in a series of smooth forehand strokes, Fabian propelled the ball to its target. By the time Costeiro lurched to his feet, Fabian had scored his third goal.

Costeiro was shaken and disheveled by his fall. Flecks of blood from a gash in his arm spotted his shirt. Two grooms rushed toward him, one retrieving his pony, aimless without its rider. On impulse, the Argentinean said he would continue to play. But as he moved to pick up his mallet, his mouth twitched in pain.

"I think I've twisted my ankle," he said, his eyes reluctant to meet Fabian's. Then, feigning the nonchalance of the sportsman, he added, "It's your game, Señor Fabian."

"We could continue at some other time," Fabian said.

"Another time would be another game. I seem to have been thrown out of this one." Leaning heavily on the arm of a groom, Costeiro grimaced sharply and for a moment looked up, his eyes brisk with their earlier fire. He held out his hand as Fabian dismounted. Alexandra joined them, still pale and tentative, her mask restored. Costeiro released Fabian's hand.

"Your stakes will be at the club," Costeiro said indifferently, then reached toward Alexandra. "Let's go home, my love." He did not look back as she led him limping off the field.

Fabian often contemplated the vagaries of fortune, whose perverse whim it so often was either to grant the fulfillment of his deepest wishes when he had already ceased to entertain them or to exact as the penalty of that fulfillment a consequence that always lay concealed in the gift.

It was in this mood of chagrin that he would sometimes recall his time as a polo partner in the service of the once celebrated Fernando-Rafael Falsalfa, the unchallenged autocrat of the Latin American republic of Los Lemures, an island rich in much of the world's supply of tobacco and sugar. Then Fabian had known a feeling of permanence, his capacities and powers acknowledged and financially rewarded. Within that security, he was free to indulge whatever pleasure might invite him, the rhythm of his days broken by no event that could not be mastered.

Falsalfa, now dead, was known, sometimes with irony, as his country's El Benefactor. Already advanced in age at the time he engaged Fabian, he used an occasional polo playing to foster his image as an active, virile man, as much a macho sportsman as he was, at least in his own eyes, a master statesman. To retain that image, he could not have for a polo partner a local player, who might conceivably talk and so dispel one of the myths El Benefactor had so carefully nurtured. The translation of Fabian's books into Spanish and their publication in Latin America had first brought him to the attention of Falsalfa and prepared the way for his entry into the sealed world around El Benefactor. Fabian soon found himself installed, with a salary equal to that of a high public official, in one of the splendid bungalows facing the sea at Casa Bonita, Falsalfa's sumptuous private villa in La Hispaniola, the Caribbean resort which was his private property.

Only two hours by car from Ciudad Falsalfa, the island's capital, to which El Benefactor had bequeathed his name, La Hispaniola was a spectacular resort of lavish private homes and villas, immaculate polo fields, stables of hundreds of the choicest ponies, along with an array of seasoned grooms to tend them, and facilities for some of the best golf, tennis and boating in the hemisphere—an opulent monument to the art of conspicuous consumption. Rich and worldly travelers arrived at La Hispaniola by private jet each season to relish the resort's natural and man-made pleasures.

Casa Bonita, as well as the resort of which it was part, offered to El Benefactor a retreat from the demands of his responsibilities as head of state. It had also become a shelter from the claims of his aging wife and numerous children and grandchildren, all of whom were sequestered either in the presidential palace at Ciudad Falsalfa or in any number of princely resorts around the island. Casa Bonita, however, was reserved for El Benefactor alone, as well as for those members of his retinue who, like Fabian, in no way threatened his personal security or impinged on the intimacy of his private and social life while in La Hispaniola.

Fabian's sole duty at Casa Bonita was to be available whenever El Benefactor decided that he wanted to play polo: either stick-and-ball practice or a one-on-one game.

Team games were sometimes staged for the purpose of affording an opportunity to film Falsalfa in a few moments of play, sequences that would then be edited artfully to suggest that he had actually taken part in the game as a member of the victorious team. In all such instances, Falsalfa relied on Fabian for his counsel, company and discretion; it was Fabian's task to supervise preparations for the game, as well as to instruct the other players, already screened and approved by Falsalfa's secret service, in the strategies of the scenario that had been arranged for them.

Even though he had been hired by Falsalfa as a member of his staff, Fabian's position in his entourage was more that of an intermittent confederate, an acquaintance in residence, than it was that of an employee. Some of this he owed to a spontaneous, unpredictable liking the old man had taken to his new foreign-born partner at polo, the charm of a novelty and surprise. With time, Fabian, scrupulous never to overstep the bounds of his role, became a fixture in Falsalfa's household, invited to take advantage of the facilities of the house and resort.

Only the imminent arrival of El Benefactor and whatever nonofficial guests he would bring with him from the capital interrupted the luxury of Fabian's pleasures and days. Under the apprehensive eye of Casa Bonita's security chief, ever mindful of the fate of his predecessor, who had been stripped of rank and imprisoned as a punishment after the villa's lights had gone out during an evening cocktail party at which Falsalfa had been host, the villa now became a hive of frantic preparation. The usually phlegmatic servants were suddenly busy cleaning, polishing, disinfecting; nothing escaped their attention, from the vaulting dome of the main living room, giant tortoise shells adorning each column of the walls that supported it, to the needle of the record player in the adjacent sound studio. Gardeners prowled the lawns and bushes of the grounds, energetically deploying their electric cutters and clippers. Random debris of leaves, insects and other casualties of nature were skimmed off the pool, and its level of chlorine was meticulously checked. At the villa's marina and heliport, in its garages and the hangars of its airstrip, a squadron of mechanics and engineers systematically inspected and cleaned every piece of machinery and equipment, certifying its fitness, its ultimate safety.

Later in the afternoon, to the distant drum of paratroopers on drill in preparation for whatever chance inspection they might be put on by any one of the autocrat's military comrades, who often accompanied him to La Hispaniola, Falsalfa's presidential jet would land, gliding to a halt in front of a broad avenue that led directly to the gates of Casa Bonita. The weekend had begun.

As soon as El Benefactor stepped onto the runway, flanked by his bodyguards, followed by the entourage of guests who had been chosen to spend the weekend with him, a cascade of flowers, strewn by his household staff, spilled before him, while a formation of soldiers presented arms with martial precision, as if he had returned from months of exile, instead of the brief span of days that had elapsed since his last visit.

The roster of guests who drifted in and out of Casa Bonita during each of those weekends was formidable, some arriving only for drinks, others enlisted for fishing, water-skiing, sailing parties and occasional tours of the island's interior. The guests included powerful figures in industry and commerce, chiefly American but British and European as well, a number of Latin American aristocrats who owned villas in La Hispaniola, and bankers and businessmen, many of whom engaged in trade with the Republic of Los Lemures. Officers of local and foreign sugar and tobacco corporations were usually in evidence, as well as the omnipresent military advisers, confreres and cohorts of the autocrat. For all of them, an invitation by Falsalfa, and especially one to dinner at Casa Bonita, was a visible sign of election, a tangible reward for diligence and devotion in supporting not only Falsalfa but the right and authority of his autocratic rule.

It was during one of these dinners, a blaze of display in the great dining hall, twin ranks of a dozen guests each flanking the main table, Falsalfa posted at its head, that Fabian found his glance returning to a guest, a woman sitting diagonally across from him. She was in her early twenties, with an obvious, intense Latin beauty. Unlike the other women who so often

decorated Falsalfa's table during his weekends at Casa
Bonita, she was dressed simply, more by necessity than
by choice, Fabian gleaned, a wedding band being her
only jewelry, and something still of the teen-ager remaining in the charming but slight unripeness of her
manner. Fabian doubted that she would have detained
him had it not been for her eyes: large and expressive,
they commanded her entire countenance. Since protocol at Casa Bonita determined that dinner guests were
usually presented only to the host and seldom introduced to each other, Fabian did not know who she
was.

After dinner, he followed her as guests moved from
the dining room to have coffee and liqueur on the
moonlit terrace overlooking the gardens of the villa
and the sea. He had started to introduce himself when
she turned with a smile of affection toward an older
man who approached them.

"Francisco de Tormes," the man announced formally, bowing slightly to Fabian, "and my wife, Elena."

Fabian recognized the name immediately: Francisco
de Tormes, the republic's most controversial political
columnist, was critical of Falsalfa and his one-man
regime. When various international coalitions had
threatened Los Lemures with economic reprisals in
response to what they saw as excesses of Falsalfa's
power, El Benefactor permitted the strictures of de
Tormes to serve as a proof of the country's freedom of
the press.

De Tormes was conscious of the public awareness of
his precarious political status; he observed casually but
pointedly how much pleasure he and his wife took in
the beauty of Casa Bonita, particularly in view of their
imminent departure from Los Lemures. He explained
that he had accepted the invitation of a notable American school of journalism to join its faculty for a year as
a visiting fellow, and within a few weeks, he and his
wife of only four months would be leaving for North
America.

As he spoke, Elena de Tormes stood close to her
husband, her elbow brushing his hip. She was little

more than a third his age, but she seemed to have a rare maturity of spirit, a deep attachment to her husband, a unique engagement with his nature and being.

The charm of Elena de Tormes was contagious, and as Fabian felt himself succumbing to it, the cluster of guests parted discreetly, revealing the presence of Falsalfa, imperial in the white splendor of his uniform as the Generalissimo. As he bore down on Fabian and de Tormes, he extended his arm, greeting the columnist in embrace first, then in full view of the watching guests, kissing the hand of his wife.

"So here you are," Falsalfa called out heartily, "and conspiring against me no doubt!" He finished, the joke heavy, as he clapped Fabian on the shoulder.

"Indeed we are, Excellency," Fabian agreed, trying to maintain the levity while de Tormes smiled uneasily and his wife busied herself with her fan. "I was just thinking of inviting Señor and Señora de Tormes to go with me on a trip to the interior, to visit on horseback some of the less accessible settlements of Cacata."

At Fabian's proposal, de Tormes made a gesture of dissent. "In my work, I don't have much chance to practice riding, and as a student, neither does Elena," he said deferentially. "We might only be a burden, Mr. Fabian."

Fabian, sensing his apprehension, was about to propose another diversion, when Falsalfa curbed him with a smile.

"Come, now. It's a splendid idea," Falsalfa said. "What a pity that I can't join you." He turned his eyes on de Tormes, a veiled displeasure behind his joviality. "But is our famous de Tormes still interested in the primitive villages of his own country, which he is about to abandon for the big-town comforts of the United States?" Falsalfa's bitterness toward political fugitives from Los Lemures who opposed him from the safety of the United States was notorious, and de Tormes flushed at the public chiding.

Elena de Tormes broke in apprehensively, her fan slicing the air. "Please remember, Excellency, we will only be visiting the United States for a year. It is my first journey abroad, the honeymoon trip Francisco promised me."

"I won't forget, my dear, I won't forget," Falsalfa assured her, his manner softening. When his glance returned to de Tormes, he was again the essence of suavity and charm. "It's settled, then," he announced decisively. "Surely, de Tormes, you and your delightful wife must see Cacata before you go." He turned to Fabian. "Order the best horses dispatched, at once. My helicopter will be at your disposal early tomorrow." Falsalfa closed the incident with a lordly gesture, dismissing de Tormes and his wife, reaching out again to clasp Fabian's shoulder. "Meanwhile, we have our polo to plan for," he announced so expansively he could not fail to be heard. "Let us retreat to the library," he concluded, guiding Fabian firmly through the dividing crowd.

Trailed by bodyguards, Falsalfa pulled Fabian toward him with an air of mischievous conspiracy.

"Aren't you even going to thank me for what I have done for you?" he whispered in his thick English.

"For what you have done, Excellency?" Fabian stammered. "I'm afraid I don't understand."

Falsalfa stopped and pinched him gently on the cheek. "I am old enough to be your father, Fabian. You have no secrets from me." He quivered with laughter. "I saw you exchanging glances with the pretty wife of that sly fox de Tormes." Falsalfa chuckled with amorous speculation.

"I met Señora de Tormes for the first time at dinner tonight," Fabian protested. "I can assure you, Excellency, there hasn't been anything between us."

"Don't say anything yet, Fabian," Falsalfa interrupted, suddenly sober. "I have no right to pry into your feelings." The amiability returned. "In any case," he continued, "I'm glad you'll be on this trip with a woman you want. Let's hope you'll find a moment to be alone with her in Cacata."

Fabian attempted to disengage himself from Falsalfa's romantic illusion. "But Señor de Tormes is going with us, Excellency," he began. "And I don't hope, I wasn't really planning—" Falsalfa's eruption of laughter made him break off in embarrassment. They had arrived at the door of the library.

"Have a good trip, Fabian," Falsalfa said indulgently. "And when you make love to Elena in the jungle, watch out for our famous tarantulas—otherwise de Tormes might find one for you." The gusty insinuation of his laughter dissolved into the library, followed by the mute parade of Falsalfa's bodyguards gliding past Fabian. He was left before a closed door.

Fabian made the preparations for the trip as Falsalfa had ordered. He was told that horses had been dispatched by an army horse van to the place he had selected for the departure point, along with two guides whose services he had often made use of on other trips to the interior. His plan was to accompany the de Tormeses on the helicopter from Casa Bonita and to rendezvous with the guides and the horses at the site agreed upon. Two to three hours of steady horseback travel would be required to reach one of the oldest and most isolated settlements perched high above the river's rocky bank. They would have a picnic lunch there, and a helicopter would come for them in time to return to Casa Bonita for late afternoon tea.

On the following day, Fabian was up at dawn, the sun still a hazy dazzle on the glassy surface of the sea.

He and the couple met for breakfast on one of the villa's small terraces, the motionless air and limpid sky heralding a day of tropical heat. Elena de Tormes, in the sturdy twill and khaki the trip called for, was radiant with anticipation. Her husband, dressed, like Fabian, in heavy boots, double-padded cotton breeches worn under chaps, and the thick, soft shirt he would need for protection against jungle insects, might have been a prosperous Latin landowner setting out to inspect his cattle.

At breakfast, Fabian showed Francisco de Tormes a map of the terrain they would be covering, pointing out the route the helicopter would take to the outpost at which the horses awaited them, then the small Indian settlement deep in the jungle that was Fabian's goal for their excursion.

A powerful clatter of sound from a military helicopter descending on an adjacent stretch of grass broke the morning calm. The standard it bore identified it as the helicopter reserved for Falsalfa's private use. The pilot, an air force captain Fabian had not previously met, wore the special insignia of the palace brigade, the crack troops Falsalfa maintained solely to guard his person.

Fabian and the couple boarded quickly, and the helicopter rose in a sweeping arc, the guards at the gates waving it on cheerfully, the deep brick colors of Casa Bonita, its terraces and roofs, dropping away beneath them.

Soon the brilliant patchwork of villas and hotels of La Hispaniola yielded to endless stretches of thickly massed fields of sugar cane, slashed symmetrically by access routes and the single-line railroad that connected the fields with the sugar mill. On rude dirt paths leading to the railroad, they saw huge carts of sugar cane moving slowly behind six or eight oxen, but even these glimpses of life gradually ceased.

The helicopter tracked the jungle, dense with greenery, studded with explosions of rock erupting from the bristling green mat. It hovered low over a river, where alligators idled on a sandy bar, then it skimmed a clearing in the brush, tawny with sun, where a herd of wild goats scampered at the roar of the machine, and a startled boar staggered from its haunt in the bush, angry with menace, then vanished into the thicket. Soon the machine prepared to descend on a pad of red clay that jutted out from the end of a strip of dirt path slicing through the wilderness. Fabian saw horses and the shapes of the guides waiting below. The helicopter quivered to a halt. The pilot verified the exact location and the precise time at which the helicopter was to arrive at the Indian settlement to collect passengers for the trip back, then, touching his cap in salute, shook hands with Fabian. As Fabian led Elena and Francisco onto the patch of brick earth, the helicopter took off, a shower of clay and dust veiling it from their sight.

Fabian expected to find the two guides he had requested. Now he was startled to be faced by two men new to him, each squat, with thick, wiry hair, a sheathed machete at his waist, and a submachine gun over his shoulder.

One of the guides explained that they needed their guns for protection when, at the close of the excursion, after the helicopter collected Fabian and his guests from the Indian settlement to return them to Casa Bonita, the two of them would have to ride back through the jungle, with valuable horses in their keeping.

The guides moved about briskly, adjusting stirrup leathers and tightening girth straps, as Fabian inspected the horses and the tack, as well as the provisions in each saddlebag—the food that had been prepared for their picnic lunch and medical packs for an emergency.

Mounted on the waiting horses, the group started into the jungle, one guide at the head of the column, Elena behind, Fabian trailing Francisco, and the second guide bringing up the rear.

After two hours at a fast, steady pace, they veered onto a narrow path high along the banks of the Yuma. The trail had ended. The river here was at its widest, in full flood, swarms of wild birds nesting in the marshes, indifferent to the passing cavalcade.

With only the sinewy back of Francisco shielding him from a glimpse of Elena, Fabian was brought back to Falsalfa's jovially insistent insinuations about the columnist's wife. He was aware that, even though he did not intend to pursue her in any way, he was drawn to her nonetheless, and the source of that attraction was the visible force of the devotion she exhibited toward her husband.

Peering around Francisco, Fabian continued to watch Elena, in splinters and shafts of movement, now swaying lightly in the saddle, her hair caught briefly by the occasional sun, one hand slack on the reins, the contour of a hip.

The heat lulling about them, in fantasy he saw Elena de Tormes as one of the models in the adult sex entertainment centers commonly found in any large city. There would be booths, a girl to each booth, a booth to a customer, a man and a woman isolated on either side of a transparent glass partition that was immovable, and over the glass, a curtain that automatically rose for a brief interval each time the customer dropped a coin into a slot on the wall of the booth. The coin also set in motion a system, a grille of sound, through which the customer could ask the girl, in the safety of their separation from each other, to perform a suggestive act, or he might ask that she initiate one. To keep the customer aroused, and the curtain up, and to sustain the current of coins, the girl would resort to various forms of provocative undress, posing, prompting him with language aimed at arousing him even more.

In the booth containing the man and the woman, separated by the impregnable glass—the sight of each other and the exchange of their voices, the sole language of their contract—the woman, perhaps naked, might press her breasts against the cold surface, her nipples flattening, her flesh leaving a steamy blot, her tongue trailing a thread of moisture. The man, inflamed by her, by her voice and words, at the mercy of his own need, would continue to drop the coins, his passion congealing, locked away from the flame that had ignited it and from the source of release that summoned it.

On this trackless path, the jungle their booth, Elena's marriage and her husband the partition, the reverie flowed over Fabian. He imagined how it might have been had he met her in the city, in the anonymity of a booth, Elena on one side of the glass, he on the other, two strangers trapped in their silent contempla-

tion of each other. What would he tell her to do or ask
of her, what might he want her to say to him, ask him
to do? What would he tell her about himself, about
her? Would he be coarse and carnal with her to the
brink of abasement, and would he enjoy the spectacle
of a charming, sensitive woman incited, driven to language and action so lewd that they seemed to violate
the mouth and body that offered them? Would the
presence of that glass partition urge him to excess or
restraint?

The trees, motionless about them, were no longer a
shelter from the jungle heat. The narrow path rose,
twisting through hills of rock and clay; the horses,
hesitant and unsure, pawed the stones, shying at the
tangle of weeds and vines, slipping, threatening to
fall.

Fabian realized that the horses, though Casa Bonita's choicest, unsurpassed on the flat and open planes
of the polo field or the predictable vistas of the stable
grounds, were baffled at the unusually precipitous terrain on which they found themselves. Yet he was
anxious to reach the settlement at Cacata before the
blaze of noon, and he had said as much to the forward
guide, who was prodding his own horse to a swifter
ascent. It soon became apparent that Elena, though
uncomfortable on a horse and apprehensive at the
hazards of the climb, was still in command of her
mount, while Francisco was tiring rapidly, his legs
dangling, his horse not properly mastered, bucking,
fighting the bit in defiance. By now, the excursion had
become an ordeal, the jungle closing about them like a
tunnel, the staircase of rock they were ascending jagged and lacerating, shelves of stone notched and
gouged by time like petrified lava.

Looking for a shelter where they could dismount
and rest, Fabian was scanning the foliage when a loud
tumult erupted at the head of the column. The guide's
horse had lost its footing, its hind legs foundering, veer-

ing to one side, as the man, reins still in hand, jumped clear, at an angle, stumbling into the bush, his curses invading the heat.

The other horses panicked and dodged on the narrow precipice, rearing in desperation at the treacherous ground they could no longer trust. Fabian and Elena managed to remain in the saddle, hauling their mounts to steadiness, but Francisco, weakened by the punishing trail and the jungle heat, toppled out of his saddle, onto the sheer face of rock at their right, rolling onto the sharp knuckles of stone clawing at his shirt, gashing his arm. In fright, his horse heaved back into the brush, then, stung by the bristling foliage, charged forward, splaying out on the rocks. Fabian managed to catch its reins, noticing as he struggled to restrain the frantic animal that the fall had ripped a patch of skin from its hip.

The mishap forced them to stop directly in the path, the horses sidling and bucking about them. Elena and Fabian bandaged Francisco's wound, then, even though the journalist was shaken and tired, his clothes drenched with sweat, they were compelled to continue the climb. Without a place for them to bivouac, the laborious ascent continued for another two hours—an hour more than Fabian had thought it would take— before they broke out into the spaciousness of the plateau; they took the last stretch toward Cacata in a loping canter.

The region of Cacata was a wedge, a peninsula of level land carved out of the jungle, a wooded, dry shoal jutting thousands of feet above the river that snaked through the valley at its base. As the party approached one of the first settlements, the stir of the horses echoing in the silent lassitude of midday, hutches and shanties of clapboard opened on both sides of the road, and a pack of mangy dogs shot out to herald their arrival. The rutted, dusty strip widened before them as they made their way through the village. A swarm of children, naked and barefoot, abandoned the shelter of palm trees and joined the dogs in a squalling welcome. The village was routed from its siesta, as men and women of every age appeared in the shadow of the hutches, some naked or with only a knot of cloth around their bodies, a few crawling, a stray pig or goat nosing about the fringes of the commotion.

The riders pulled up and dismounted at a shabby wooden barracks, an old trading post, now disused, that seemed to be the center of the village, serving for infrequent and vaguely official government sanitary missions.

The guides hitched the horses, releasing the saddles, as Fabian and Elena settled Francisco on blankets outside the barracks. When the guides served the sandwiches and drinks they had brought, the huddle of villagers made a silent circle around the visitors, straining to see, intent on every flicker and move.

Some of the younger, bolder men gathered in a knot to one side, assessing Elena; she flushed at their open staring and moved closer to Francisco. Others, their interest riveted on weapons, surrounded the guides, posted warily against the wall of the barracks. Still others hovered about the horses, marveling at their sleekness, height and the intricacy of their tack.

To distract the attention of the crowd and to manifest a sense of ease and command in this strangeness, Fabian strolled leisurely around the village, a straggling cluster of watchful children in his wake.

Passing a shamble of huts, he startled a woman with a baby on her arm; before she retreated within, alarm for her own safety and that of her child broke through her impassive face. From behind a shutter, an emaciated old man smiled toothlessly. In the distance a group of young women closed in on a scampering pig, their naked breasts still shapely and firm, patches of bright cotton shielding their hips.

Fabian had reached the edge of the village, the highest point of the plateau. He felt dizzy from the sun and the altitude; below him he could see the sheer drop of foliage and bush, the distant river, a muddy trough of yellow stirring, dissolving into the mossy green of land stretched out endlessly. He checked his watch: the helicopter had been scheduled to come for them shortly. He found himself straining for the sound of its engine, but the dome of sky was silent.

He felt a twinge of anxiety. He began to realize how far inland they were, how remote from any town or village with police or a military outpost that could arrange their transportation to La Hispaniola. He returned to the barracks, where he found the crowd undiminished, still vigilant, still mute; Elena was sleeping on a blanket, Francisco's head in her lap.

The afternoon was receding. The natives began slowly to drift away to their shanties; only a few stray children and three or four young men still prowled around. The guides dozed in a stupor, guns cradled in their laps.

Fabian sat down on a blanket and watched Elena. Her blouse, undone at the throat, revealed the whiteness of her neck and breast, a contrast with the black of her hair.

The sun began to glide toward the crest of the palm trees; the helicopter still had not come. Fabian became alarmed. He roused the others, pointing out to them that there were dozens of small settlements like the one they were in scattered throughout thousands of square miles of jungle in the Cacata region and that the pilot might have misunderstood the directions. The guides admitted that they had tracked their path to the village only by calculating the position of the sun in relation to the river.

Fabian underscored the urgency of their situation while trying not to alarm Elena and Francisco. He pointed out that, in the casual atmosphere of Casa Bonita, their absence could easily go unnoticed for a day or two. And they had neither the stamina nor the resources to ride all the way back to La Hispaniola, a venture which would take days. He proposed that the guide who knew best the perilous way down to the river should go there, taking the horses with him so that, alternating his mounts, he could reach in a day the military post that had dispatched the truck with their horses to the place of rendezvous. Then he would notify the authorities to summon a helicopter. Surly with reluctance but afraid to disobey Fabian, the man left the village for the descent to the river.

The remaining guide began to prepare for the night. He selected the largest hut in the village and, without explanation, ordered the natives to evacuate it.

They left, a procession of men, women and children, as well as a scrambling array of dogs, cats and pigs, driven to find other shelter for the night. While the guide started a fire outside to cook a meal, Fabian removed soiled mattresses and blankets from the bunks, leaving them in the yard for the night.

In the evening stillness outside the hut, Fabian joined Elena and Francisco, watching the guide roast a small pig. From the bushes around the hut, the sudden rustle of a branch, a sneeze, a cough, laughter betrayed the presence of natives huddling and squatting, alert in their scrutiny of the visitors.

During the meal, each time Francisco reached for a piece of meat, a spasm of pain from his fall contorted his face. The guide took a share of food but kept his distance, the submachine gun always at his shoulder. Occasionally he would glance with undisguised hostility at Francisco, but toward Fabian, whom he knew to be a friend of El Benefactor, he maintained his usual servile manner.

After the meal, the guide prepared a pungent fruit punch. He passed it around in pineapple husks. The punch was exhilarating, and Francisco, Elena and Fabian returned to it three or four times.

It was not long before Fabian, exuberant with the punch and the intimacy of the night, told the guide to distribute what remained of the roast pig to the watching natives. The man called out, and soon a swarm of figures emerged from the darkness, stopping on the other side of the fire, hands burnished by the flames as they reached greedily for the food.

Some of the natives were already boisterous with

liquor; others moved into the circle of firelight, chant-
ing and starting to dance, first as if in exhibition for
their visitors, then with mounting intensity for themselves. At first the guide kept them at a distance, but
when a few of the men approached him with a jug and
gestured toward the visitors, indicating they wanted to
return the gift of the meat with a fruit drink of their
own making, he brought them over and whispered to
Fabian that it would be unwise to refuse. Reluctantly,
but caught up in the sensual flush, Fabian took a swig
of the searing juice, then passed it on to Elena and
Francisco; they drank it under the watchful eye of the
villagers.

The dancing was now a rite, the fire a beacon
against the sky. There were moments when Fabian felt
vehemently alert to color and shape; at other moments
he lapsed into a stupor of sliding sensation. Once, he
looked up into the mob and thought he saw Elena de
Tormes swaying in front of him, her hands at her
blouse, twisting it toward her hips, taunting him to tear
it off; then he felt his body weightless, empty of feeling,
cut loose, floating up from the ground toward her. Still
later, he saw Francisco rushing at him with a machete,
one that Fabian remembered the guide had used to
split the roast pig. The machete gleamed as it split the
table between them, Francisco's voice a distant scream.
Fabian's head streamed with terror and exaltation. He
reeled headlong toward de Tormes, but was snared
suddenly by a figure he could not make out. He felt
himself being carried inside the hut and placed there
next to Elena.

He dreamed that although she seemed to be
sprawled on the dirt floor next to him, her blouse open,
boots discarded, her riding breeches pulled down, she
was really behind a glass partition, lying next to another man; Fabian, from his exile in this hut, was
linked to her by thought only, his longing as translucent as the spill of a jungle cataract.

He felt himself being lifted, a tree uprooted, borne
by an undertow, a spume of greedy mouth, a spindrift

of venomous white froth, without respite. Elena was no longer far away, but moving beneath him, the stream that bore his vagrant tree, her mouth on his, their tongues folding, her hands prompting him to take her. He rose, leaning over her, taking her; then with her astride him, he took her again.

What he remembered at the last was a multitude of heads, nests and hives of faces he did not know, hovering over him, over Elena, intent on the two of them at love, as if witnessing the combat of insects locked in deadly embrace on the mud floor of the hut.

Fabian awoke slowly, pain splitting his temples, piercing his eyeballs, his joints stiff. In panic, he looked around.

He was lying on a bunk, daylight glinting through the thatched ceiling of grass above him, his naked body covered with a rough blanket, his clothes on the floor. Near him lay Elena, still asleep, covered with a blanket. In the farthest corner of the hut, masked by shadow, he saw Francisco slumped on the floor.

Fabian got up, stumbling as the bunk seemed to buckle under him and the roof skim low over his head. Shaking, he dressed himself and made his way out into the scalding sun.

A group of natives, gesturing with animation, stood around the guide. At the sight of Fabian, they fell silent and broke ranks; like a soldier on guard, the guide greeted him with a salute.

A patch of barren clay opened before Fabian. At its center, he saw a spider, black-bodied, as large as his two hands with fingers outthrust, its hairy legs motionless, the gray belly mashed. The spider was dead, but so real in its poised menace that Fabian stepped back involuntarily.

"This is the one which killed Señor de Tormes," the guide said.

In his stupor and revulsion Fabian assumed it was Francisco who had killed the spider, but the expression on the guide's face alarmed him.

"Who killed what?" he asked.

"A true tarantula," the guide said, nudging the spider with the tip of his boot. "It bit Señor de Tormes when he went out and lay down on the ground. Señora Elena, when she found out he was dead, drank a whole bottle of this"—he gestured toward what was left of the natives' punch—"so she wouldn't feel the pain."

Retching as the acid liquid volleyed out of his throat, Fabian staggered back from the spider and ran into the hut.

Francisco's body was still huddled in the dark corner. Gliding with horror, Fabian knelt by the dead man and raised the blanket that shrouded him, trying to prop up the slipping shoulders, the head that bobbed to one side. He laid one hand along the dead man's cheek. Francisco's face was white, the sunburned glow of the day before already erased, the eyes open, fixed somewhere beyond Fabian, one eyebrow raised, the mouth slightly agape as if in an expression of wonder.

Fabian covered the body and crossed over to Elena. In her sleep she was serene. He stroked her hand; she did not respond.

Outside, he ordered the guide to store the dead tarantula for the police and to take down the names of the natives who, by the guide's account, had witnessed the night's events. Then, on an impulse, Fabian drew the guide to one side, away from the villagers.

"Where were you when the tarantula bit Señor de Tormes?" he asked.

The guide hesitated. "I was—I was guarding you in the hut," he said. "I helped to undress you and keep you down, Señor Fabian. You were—you were sleepy from the drink," he blurted out. "Then I stayed with you so Señor de Tormes would not come at you again."

Fabian avoided his eyes. "I don't remember anything," he said brusquely. "Why would Señor de Tormes want to hurt me?"

The guide smiled knowingly. "He was drunk, Señor

Fabian, and he was jealous when he saw you touch his wife. He grabbed my machete and wanted to kill you."

Unable to challenge the man's account, Fabian shifted his inquiry. "Who was the first to see Señor de Tormes dead?" he asked.

"I was," the guard replied. "I also told Señora Elena what happened." He lowered his voice. "Señora Elena started to scream. She said things she shouldn't say, ugly things."

"What did she say?" Fabian asked.

The guide moved closer, until he was almost at Fabian's ear. "She said that someone might have put this tarantula under Señor de Tormes."

"But who would want to do that?" Fabian persisted.

The guide nodded in confirmation. "That's what I asked her. But she was drunk and kept saying that it might be"—he was whispering now—"El Benefactor himself who was responsible." He looked toward the hut sullenly. "She also accused me of it—of putting this tarantula under Señor de Tormes."

"Why you?"

"Because I work for El Benefactor. But you, Señor Fabian, you know that I couldn't do it." The guide was stressing each word, carving it as though with a machete. "You know best of all, because you must remember that I was with you, guarding you all the time. All the time," he repeated.

The roar of an approaching helicopter rushed in on them. The craft came in low over the trees and quivered to a halt in a storm of dust. Natives started to spill out of huts and bushes, running toward it, shouting with fascination and fear. The pilot stepped out, saw Fabian and explained tersely that he had had mechanical trouble the day before and had been unable to come for them after dark. He then joined Fabian and the guide in rounding up enough of the natives to carry the body of de Tormes and the sleeping Elena into the cabin.

During the short flight to Casa Bonita, Elena did not

wake up. Fabian got out, and the helicopter with Elena and the guide accompanying Francisco's body continued on to the capital.

At Casa Bonita, Fabian went directly to Falsalfa's quarters. He impressed the secretary with the urgency of his visit and was promptly ushered into the library, where he found Falsalfa in a hammock.

"I know about the accident. The pilot radioed us from Cacata," Falsalfa announced calmly. "What a sad case," he added, "de Tormes at the peak of his career, a young wife—all to end with the bite of a tarantula." He continued to sway in the hammock.

"De Tormes was murdered, Your Excellency," Fabian said evenly. "A tarantula big enough to catch a chicken is not found in Cacata. It was the assassin's best weapon."

"If there was an assassin, my dear Fabian, then it had to be you," Falsalfa said with emphasis.

"Why me?" Fabian asked boldly.

Falsalfa had stopped swaying, but the smile remained. "You were the only one with a motive to kill him— Elena."

"That's an ugly conjecture, Your Excellency," Fabian replied.

"That's an ugly crime." Falsalfa spoke with patience. "There are witnesses: practically the whole village saw you and Elena thrashing around on the floor, right under their eyes—and under the eyes of her drunken husband."

Fabian's body went as hot with sweat as his voice was cold. "I don't remember any of that," he said. "We were all drunk—or drugged."

"Others do remember," Falsalfa said. "When you and Elena became too obvious, Francisco almost killed you with a machete. It was the guide, a man in my service, sober fortunately, who disarmed him and saved your life. It was he who guarded you in the hut while Francisco raved outside." Falsalfa paused for emphasis. "And it was during the night that poor de

Tormes, so tired, so drunk, and so angry, sat down in the yard—right on a tarantula taking its midnight walk there."

"I'm certain de Tormes was murdered," said Fabian.

The smile was no longer on Falsalfa's lips. His hammock stopped swaying. "Would you like me to instruct my prosecutor to open a formal inquiry into the death of Francisco de Tormes?" He spoke brutally. "To tell the public what took place between you and Elena in that village of Cacata? Remember, Fabian, you are not in the United States. Here, what chance would you have for an acquittal?" Falsalfa's composure had returned. "The fact is, neither Francisco nor the tarantula can testify, but as for the guide, the villagers—show me one man or woman who wouldn't believe it was you who conveniently arranged that meeting between de Tormes and the tarantula."

Fabian stood silent as the hammock resumed its rhythm. He saw himself on a witness stand in a country whose language he barely spoke, many of whose customs were alien to him. In Los Lemures, where the whim of Falsalfa was the final court, a protracted trial would be his and Elena's downfall.

"What will happen to Señora de Tormes?" he asked abruptly, the change in his thought reflected in his voice.

Falsalfa recovered his smile. "Now, that is the concern of a reasonable man," he sighed. "All you really care about is—Elena." He considered the matter. "She is free to do whatever she pleases. But with Francisco gone, it will be a bit harder for her. Like him, she comes from a poor family, and all de Tormes left her are debts." He brightened at a statesmanlike solution. "Why don't you give Elena a call and invite her to Casa Bonita for a few days?" Falsalfa looked directly at Fabian, the smile broadening. "Better yet, Fabian, why don't I ask my personal secretary to invite her in my name? After all, Elena is the widow of my old friend, de Tormes, and the mistress of Fabian, my polo pal. What do you say?"

Fabian spoke in a voice harsh with rage. "I say, Your Excellency, that it is you who seized our trip to Cacata as the occasion to murder Francisco de Tormes. That's why I intend to leave Los Lemures on the first plane, unless I, too, happen to be bitten by a tarantula before I get on that plane."

Falsalfa measured Fabian with absolute certainty. "You're just a one-on-one amateur in whatever you do, Fabian. You will always be just an amateur. Nobody in Los Lemures would bother to waste a good tarantula on you!" He gestured toward the door. The hammock was still swaying as Fabian walked out of the room.

Years later, with Falsalfa no longer in power, Fabian had been a referee at a polo meet, with some of his friends playing on each side. The game passed with a few penalty shots, but otherwise without incident. That evening Eugene Stanhope had given a dinner party for Fabian at a local cabaret. It was crowded with tourists, and Fabian's table, at the center of the room, was the largest and most boisterous, with a dozen of his friends and polo colleagues celebrating.

Toward the end of the dinner, the lights in the room dimmed. Waiters suddenly appeared, bearing aloft an embossed salver with a large ice-cream cake resting in a pool of brandy and studded with a coronet of gleaming sparklers instead of the usual birthday candles. They placed the elaborate tribute in front of Fabian, and just at the moment the headwaiter put a match to the brandy around the cake, a trio of nightclub minstrels began to serenade Fabian in thickly flavored English. His friends joined in, and tourists around the room picked up the chorus. In pleasure and surprise, Fabian rose, tilting the salver, and, as he did so, a stream of flaming brandy slid down the front of his shirt over his jacket and trousers. He was on fire.

People applauded wildly, under the impression that the flames and Fabian were part of the entertainment. His clothes ablaze, he plunged through the room, stumbling by tables of still-cheering patrons, toward a side door opening on a verandah above the gardens. He vaulted over its railing, into the lush foliage below, blindly rolling over and over on the dewy ground to put out the flames. When, dazed, he sat up, his white suit hung in charred strips, his chest and thighs showing through the scorched cloth.

Fabian knew he had to do something about his burns at once. He went around to the back door of the cabaret to tell his friends that he was going home. A guard, looking at his disheveled state, took him for a drunk or vagrant, and rudely pushed him aside. Fabian then went to the main entrance, where couples in formal dress waited for admission to the cabaret. Once again, a guard shoved him away.

Fabian's pain was intensifying; he slipped back through the gardens to the verandah and climbed onto it again, returning to the restaurant by the same door he had left.

As he approached the table, Fabian met with a volley of greetings and laughter from his friends and people at nearby tables. Taking his appearance as a prank, they promptly opened a magnum of champagne. With faultless aim, they doused Fabian and his burns in the sparkling fountain.

Only at the table did Fabian recall that the guard who had pushed him so rudely at the door was the same man who was once with him in Cacata, the one accused by Elena of murdering Francisco de Tormes.

In times of calm, Fabian would yield to the ministry of nature, never intrusive. It came to him in the spreading reach of a forest, the pine scent, the shallow scrub bristling the rim of a lake, the vanishing ruts of a dirt road.

In times that were febrile and hectic, the city was his nurse, always on call, faithfully dispensing to him music that would heal, a theater, pensive, compact with figures that could abort or compel his energy and thought, cinemas blinking their colors and images, the kindling of burlesque, the tease of a live sex show.

In the city, Fabian inched his VanHome along the streets, scanning the sidewalks, alleys and benches for the figure of a woman alone. He could become as aroused by a lock of hair tucked behind a girl's ear, a certain contour of her hip or leg, as he might be by the sound of her voice, by what she said or how she responded to something in him. She would be young, tall, slender, long-legged, with large eyes and thick hair, a wide mouth, conscious of the impact her body and her walk made on men.

She had to acknowledge that he could offer no more than the union of the night, the courtship of a weekend or the intimacy of a few evenings. A man of the field and of country spaces, a man whose pattern of life was marked by abrupt change, by travel, Fabian could not permit himself to be detained too long by the solaces and distractions of a city or large town. He found himself selecting, isolating, soliciting partners as transient and avid as himself, as ready to initiate, as willing to discard.

One evening in a bar, Fabian came upon a sometime acquaintance, a well-known television sports commentator, who occasionally invited him to appear on his program to discuss various polo and horsemanship tournaments. Stephen Gordon-Smith was in his early fifties, handsome, with that virility of voice, gesture and looks, that easy directness of manner that was the hallmark of his profession. The two men were settling down for a drink when Fabian suddenly caught a glimpse, in a far corner of the bar, of two young women he had met earlier in the year. Employed by a clothing manufacturer, they were models working out of New York.

Fabian signaled them to come to the table and, when they did, he introduced them to Gordon-Smith. Both women were of Latin descent, in their early twenties, dark-haired, feminine and vivacious, with thick but well-drawn features and expressive eyes; tall and slender, they were proud of their well-defined breasts, narrow waists and firm buttocks.

Gordon-Smith made no effort to conceal his pleasure with the girls, particularly Diana, the bolder of the two, who flirted with him more openly. Fabian noticed that his friend's fascination with Diana was growing and when her companion got up to leave for an appointment, Fabian left too.

Three or four weeks later, after an interview about the importance of the Eugene Stanhope Polo Tournament, Gordon-Smith took Fabian to dinner and freely confided that he had been seeing Diana almost constantly and that he was considering taking a leave of absence from the network—as well as from his wife— to be able to travel and live with Diana.

Fabian, who knew how strict and conventional the

major TV networks were in insisting that their most visible spokesmen—among whom Gordon-Smith had to be counted—maintain irreproachable conduct in private as well as public life, was astonished by his friend's decision. It seemed to him especially bizarre in light of the affectionate intimacy he had observed between Gordon-Smith and Emily, his wife of over twenty years, whom Fabian had met once when she and their two daughters accompanied Gordon-Smith to an intercollegiate polo championship at an Ivy League college during Fabian's brief tenure there as polo coach.

"How well do you know Diana?" Fabian asked cautiously.

"As well as a man ever knows a woman." Gordon-Smith smiled expansively, with his easy air of male camaraderie.

"Has she told you much about her life?"

"There isn't much to tell," Gordon-Smith said. "Remember, she's only twenty-four."

"What was her life like?" Fabian maintained his casual tone.

"Didn't she tell you?" Gordon-Smith shrugged. He was not much interested in Diana's past.

"When I introduced you to her," Fabian said, "there was no time to tell family histories."

"Well, Diana left Ecuador—or was it Nicaragua?—just before one of those government upheavals they had down there. That's when her family lost everything, and she emigrated here to live with an aunt," Gordon-Smith explained patiently. "With a little private tutoring, she picked up the language, then worked in a couple of fancy beauty parlors. Then she did something in the fashion business, as a coordinator or, you know, a model—" He broke off, happy to change the subject, and reached eagerly for his briefcase. A file of glossy, neatly mounted fashion photographs slid before Fabian's eyes. He saw Diana glowing up at him in color and in black and white.

"Isn't she stunning!" Gordon-Smith announced with elation, spreading out the photos.

"She is," Fabian said. "What a beautiful woman she has become."

Gordon-Smith leaned across the table. "I've had my share of women, but"—his voice dropped even lower —"no woman has ever given me what I get from her." He laid a hand, commanding, on the photographs of Diana.

"She understands you?" Fabian suggested.

"Sexually—there's nothing she doesn't know about me. Nothing!" He finished his drink and reached for another that the waiter had just put before him. "We're so open with each other, so uninhibited."

Fabian shifted in his chair uneasily. "How long do you plan to stay with Diana?" he asked.

"Diana has made me realize what a conventional life I've been living all along," Gordon-Smith said forcefully. "I want to change it now." He stopped, the glance he threw at Fabian a challenge and also a quest for reassurance. "Even if it means breaking away from my past."

"What about your family?" Fabian asked.

Gordon-Smith waved the question aside. "The girls are grown up," he said. "As for Emily—" he hesitated. "Emily is as free to be herself as I am."

"And the job?"

Gordon-Smith chafed under Fabian's probing. "The job has nothing to do with my life—as long as I keep it private."

Fabian felt he should no longer withhold what he knew. "Diana is an extravagant character," he volunteered.

Gordon-Smith smiled indulgently. "She loves to go places, to travel. Last week she took me all the way to Miami so she could get a tan to show off, and I guess I've been to about every disco there is." Laughing, he raised his eyes and saw Fabian's expression. "Is there something you know about Diana that you're keeping from me, Fabian?" he asked, suddenly sharp.

"She's a transsexual, a man," Fabian said calmly.

Gordon-Smith wrapped both his hands around Fabian's wrists.

"She's what?" he shouted hoarsely, the familiar resonance of his voice spilling round the restaurant. "What did you just say?"

"Diana is a transsexual—a man who became a woman," Fabian said. He kept his voice steady as he released his wrists from Gordon-Smith's grip.

Gordon-Smith had turned sallow. "You're making that up," he muttered sullenly. "You've got to be. I know Diana. I've had sex with her. I ought to know a woman when I'm inside one."

"Diana was operated on some time ago," Fabian said, "and the operation altered her appearance and her sexual organs. She can perform sexually as a woman."

"Why do you know what I don't?"

"Where I met her, most of her friends didn't bother to hide what she was," Fabian retorted, "and that's a place I don't think you'd like to find yourself."

Gordon-Smith's movements were slack, tired. He suddenly looked his age. "Why didn't you tell me this when you introduced me to her?" he asked resentfully.

Fabian softened his tone. "It wouldn't have been fair. When you met her, she had been a woman, psychologically as well as physically, for years—convincing to herself, to people like me and apparently to you."

"Then what makes you think it's fair to tell me now?"

Fabian wished he could pinpoint his motive as accurately as he could strike a polo ball. "Perhaps it isn't. But most of those who enforce our sex laws run you down by snooping and denouncing, by informing on you. You're linked to a woman who, under some of the vagrancy statutes in this country, could be arrested, fined, even jailed as a TV, a transvestite, though she's not. I thought you should know that."

Gordon-Smith broke the long silence. "I can just see the headlines: 'TV Anchorman Anchored to a TV.'" He thought for a moment. "Tell me, Fabian," he questioned, "because I enjoyed myself so much with

Diana—does that mean I'm queer?" He asked the question with almost a professional detachment.

Fabian looked at his friend across the table. "I doubt there's ever been a judicial decision about what is meant by the concepts 'male' and 'female,' " he said gently. "When not even the law has defined the sexes, why should you?"

Some transsexuals—those men irreversibly altered into often beautiful women—knew the intimacy of Fabian's VanHome: one eager to test on him her newly acquired womanhood; one to reinforce her exaggerated femininity by offering to share it in lovemaking with both Fabian and another man; one testing herself by arranging to share Fabian in her encounter with a biological woman.

Manuela was among them. Whenever Fabian saw her, beguiled by her beauty and his own reaction to it, he experienced a sense of tumult, not unlike what he imagined Gordon-Smith must have felt when the truth about Diana's life forced him to question his own.

Manuela had come into Fabian's life within the orbit of the transsexual world—she was the friend of another transsexual, who had already gone the road of full conversion and who asked Fabian to accompany her while she received her regular hormone injection. Introducing Manuela to Fabian, his friend told him that, unlike herself, Manuela was only a half-change; her breasts enlarged by hormone treatment and surgery, the protruding Adam's apple elided, skin depilated to smoothness. Yet, she was still unwilling or unready to undergo the final passage to full conversion. Manuela blushed, stammered her name and, shifting uneasily, silently permitted Fabian's assessment of her sensual face and smooth neck, girlish breasts, and a waist, hips and legs of consummate shapeliness.

She was in her mid-twenties and worked in a large pharmacy owned by her father and mother. Since adolescence, she had lived as a female, an arrangement to

which her parents consented; it was for her sake, to
preserve her secret, that they moved to another city,
where Manuela would be known only as a young
woman. There were long intervals in her life, Manuela
told Fabian, when her anatomy tormented her, its
maleness a fraud; then she considered the prospect of
total surgical conversion. Yet, though she existed as a
woman and desired sexual relations solely with hetero-
sexual men, Manuela insisted that only by retaining her
male organ would she be able to experience desire and
orgasm. She felt that most of the fully converted transsexuals she knew suffered weakened sex drives; seldom, if ever, able to achieve orgasm, they became
sexually dormant.

Manuela told Fabian how, with a man who, not
aware of her duality, was captivated by her as a
woman or who captivated her, she was compelled to
maintain a maze of deceptions and theatrical ingenui-
ties to conceal her true identity. With the help of
adhesives and tapes, even with corsets, she constricted
her organ, folding and pressing it tightly against her
body; during lovemaking, the affirmation of her femininity and beauty, she invented elaborate strategies and
ruses, menstrual cramps as an instance, to prevent herself from having to undress fully before her partner;
then, when he was drunk or high on pot, she might
offer him her breasts, her mouth, any other mode of
love, so that he would be led to think he had possessed
her entirely.

She admitted that such exchanges were exciting,
flattering, and reinforced her sense of herself as female,
but she also acknowledged that sexually they often left
her unfulfilled, feverish with barren stimulation.

Manuela's predicament rang true to Fabian in mir-
roring the ambivalence he recognized in any relationship, however brief, that he entered into with a transsexual woman. He vacillated between having a lover
who had undergone the final transformation, though at
the cost of diminished desire, and having one who, like
Manuela, retained the force of desire, at the price of

forgoing the reality of the other gender she desperately lay claim to.

Fabian probed his fascination with Manuela. What seemed to him its source was a fuse and musk of charged femininity: her features and the shape of her body, her voice, her makeup and dress—all her being strove to enhance her reality as a woman. He was riveted by a youthful sensuality, always flagrant, in alliance with an expression of that sensuality, always studied—femininity on the make. Hinting at a revelation of what was vulnerable and soft in him, Manuela promised a discovery of sensation that was unexposed, untapped and all the more ripe for exploration. But at no time did her assumed womanhood, the authority of her femininity, obscure for him the physical fact of her maleness, and at no time did he find her duality troubling. In his VanHome, in a private chamber of his private fort, he was free to pursue, to assess and to meditate on the enigma of his own being—an outlaw at war with the league of crusaders, inquisitors and censors of sexual conduct.

On his way to the city, Fabian would call Manuela, and she would arrange to take time off from the pharmacy. When he arrived, he would leave his Van-Home close to a park; the next day, Manuela, who enjoyed riding, would join him when he exercised his ponies there.

That evening, carrying an overnight case, she would visit him. Her appearance in the VanHome's narrow doorway was always an event: a rustle and slip of grace, accomplished and knowing, like a ballerina entering from the wings or a model poised at a fashion show. It became their habit, before going up to the alcove, to linger over drinks in the VanHome's living room. Manuela was unquiet, even fretful during those interludes, wandering about as they spoke, flipping through one of the horse and rider magazines on his bookshelves, then discarding it. Occasionally, the brass fixtures in the room or the mirror on the wall would give her back her reflection: instantly, one hand would rise to the arrangement of her hair; she would examine her makeup, adjust the flow of the blouse draping her neck and shoulders. She always wanted to impress Fabian with the progress she had made as a woman, the perfecting of her beauty and femininity. Her presence was a ferment in the room: a sultry spirit, she would toss back and forth, as if bothered by the loosened knot of her lush hair, her shoulders and hips seething beneath her clothes. Outside, all was still, the city, the trees, his VanHome abolished in the tide of darkness. At its farthest fringe, a thread of burning orange, the lights of the city, held the park in its taut noose.

Soon Fabian would ask Manuela to go with him to the alcove. She would get up and prepare another drink, reassure herself for the last time in the mirror, and take the lead. Behind her on the stairs, watching the faultless line of her leg, the polished curving of a hip ascending before him, he would grasp in himself, once again, the inescapable knot of his need, the raveled mesh of what it was that he wanted from her.

In the alcove, Manuela would sit on the bed's edge, preening her legs, monitoring his scrutiny of their uncommon length in proportion to her rib cage. She would unleash her thick hair, to fan about her neck; when he reached out to touch it, some recognition in the circuit of his thought would affirm that hair, like skin or tooth or nail, knew no sex; it lent its beauty of texture, shape and color to female and male equally.

Now, as in the past, she would prolong this phase of their meeting, making the beauty of her face accessible, obedient in her will to please him, while the rest of her would remain concealed within her clothes, teasing, insinuating, conscious that he could not know whether the excitement that grew on her face was matched by her body's own response.

He could have her, he would tell himself, in this fashion, on terms that were arranged, by her, to satisfy and to please him—a man, one of those beings from whom she now saw herself estranged by her femininity, the spirit of her own world. He was aware that for her to offer him more of herself, to lay open to him her entire body, would be to give him less of what she perceived as her essential self, would make her betray what in herself she loved most.

Yet if he was aroused by her beauty, the texture, shape and fragrance of her womanhood, it was because he longed for a signal that she wanted to be taken, to give herself to him, and finally, no longer passive, spurred by his excitement, she wanted to take him.

Consciously, then, he would make known his yearning for that stirring in her, a signal that the narrow slip of cloth, now a mere leaf against the promise of her body, was the only frontier that separated her from him, the tape binding her flesh, the last prison of her being. She would respond with a request that he dim the lights in the alcove, denying the mirror there the power to bear witness to her nakedness, and, hesitantly, she would remove the narrow band of cloth and peel off the tape. She was naked before Fabian now, but still reluctant to permit herself to become aroused, the check on her body taut, in thrall to that image of herself that, even though she was naked, impelled her to keep herself clothed, hidden from herself. She still refused to let even her hand, the hand of the woman, scout the realm of what was man in her, still feared that the wakening of her own excitement would banish the woman in her. Instead, she volunteered to enhance Fabian's pleasure with her touch, to post herself in mediation between him and his own desire, even as she declined to obtain it from her own flesh.

Slowly, in her contemplation of Fabian and of his pleasure in being with her, Manuela succumbed to a realization that if he was not threatened by the form and shape of her pleasure, it need not pose a barrier to her. She came to see that she was, in her need of feeling and of arousal, no less a woman than, in his answering need, he was a man; that, by reaching with him the shores that confined the body's pleasure, she would only affirm her condition as a woman, consolidate her reality.

In this joint traffic of pleasure, a cycle of what was

given, what taken, Fabian's passion her only guide, Manuela would rise to the satiety of her own pleasure. Fabian was made conscious of possessing her, was free to stake claim to her body, free to impel her to her own revelation. He hovered over her, in awe of a body that had no fault, that seemed to incarnate the secret of who he was: at her mouth and breast, he was a boy necking with a girl; entwined with her, entering her, he was a man taking his woman; arousing her with his hand, he was a boy at play with a man; straddling her as she lay helpless beneath him, he was a man toying with a boy; inert, pinioned by her, he was a man at the mercy of a boy.

Now they lay together, the shudder of flesh waking them to its meaning, desire a stream between them, a chasm that only flesh could bridge. Neither lost to the pleasure of the other, they seemed two instruments shaped from one mold, to one end, each an embodiment of the other's quest.

Just as Manuela was no longer the contrivance of their first encounter, an icon of cosmetics and dress, of shapes and gestures, so Fabian, submissive to his own desire, ceased to be a tissue of his memory, of circumstance and the moment's decor. Dancers passing beyond the dance, music abandoned, movement and the stage obliterated, the two of them were now equally lovers, a habitat of flesh, bound to the revelation of that flesh through each other, assenting to its mercy.

Afterward, Manuela would slip quickly from the bed and disappear into the bathroom. When she returned, moist and cool from the bath, her hair combed, her face freshly made up, her nightdress wrapping her body in a mist of gauze, she would ask Fabian to turn on all the lights and then would sit beside him, gently guiding his gaze toward the alcove's mirror, making the two of them twins of contemplation. He would watch her adoration of her reflected self, as if she were a man discreetly admiring a young girl, her eyes pausing on her face, brushing her mouth, descending to fondle her breasts, glide over her belly, avoiding the slight blur of the narrow slip of cloth, then slide along her legs, returning once more to her face, once more to her breasts. The canvas of her eyes readily prompted her hands to a new life; aroused again, her eyes caught at the mirror, she would reach out to Fabian, stroking his flesh. But when he sought to interrupt that rumination, to bring her mouth back to his, she would succumb to him reluctantly, unwilling to abandon the mirror's seduction.

When bantering, he would ask her what was it that she saw; she would turn to him with a smile so artless that it restored him to the memory of the moment when he first surprised her in her engagement with the mirror. It was then, she said, that she had fallen in love with the beautiful woman in the mirror, a love, she went on dreamily, in which she was not alone. How could it be, she asked, that the woman arrested in the mirror, so sensuous and so complete, the woman now returning their gaze, should not be the object of their love, an artifact of their own devising, the murmur of her reflection rising from herself to enfold him, then passing on to something beyond the rapture of their dual fascination.

On occasion, Fabian would invite into his VanHome a new companion, one of the girls or young women whom he had met at a recent horse show and who was now to be alone with him for the first time. Earlier he would have arranged for Manuela to join them, and when she arrived, her allure would be in full glow, her sexuality fired by the challenge of another woman.

She would wait while Fabian took the girl on a tour of the VanHome. In the intimate quarters of the tack room, in the stalls next to the horses, those animals for whom the girl had professed her tenderness and devotion when she had first met him, Fabian had a chance to put her at ease, to establish between the two of them their shared love for horses.

He would walk next to her through the narrow spaces, then let her take the lead, his shoulder or hip brushing hers as they navigated, sniffing the scent of leather drifting about the tack room, listening to the rustle of horses nuzzling alfalfa in the stalls.

Back in the living room, busying himself with drinks and food, he would ask Manuela to show their guest his sleeping alcove and the bath. When they came back some while later, flushed with laughter, their glasses empty, he would observe, with some complacency, that the girl was already far more familiar with Manuela than with him. He would watch covertly how Manuela planted in their guest the conviction that, for their evening together to be transformed into an adventure, with something of the exhilaration of the chase, they must abandon themselves to the world much as they would to the wayward impulses of a horse on track or trail; for the three of them, the two women and Fabian, their friendship was now the stuff of that world, the swift laying hold of the moment, their private hunt.

Later, in a sensuous lull of the evening, when the initial reserves, defenses and barriers had been breached, the girl would confess to Manuela that, if she were ever to be intimate with another woman, beauty of face and promise of personality having exerted their magnetism, the breasts of that other woman would be the most alluring element. Avid to test her prowess still further, Manuela would now find a pretext to reveal the contours of her breasts, enticing under her thin blouse, the nonchalance of her movements masking the guile of the act.

Fabian would then leave the two of them in the room, withdraw to the alcove, change into a robe and wait. Soon, on a pretext of exchanging some mysteries of makeup or dress, Manuela would bring their guest to the alcove; absorbed in Manuela, the girl would barely notice that Fabian was wearing only a robe. The two women would proceed to mull over each other in the mirror, applying eye shadow, blusher, lip gloss, putting up their hair only to let it tumble in disarray over their shoulders, sharing that liberty of touch of those who share a common purpose. Manuela's mood would change. Acknowledging Fabian's presence with her eyes, she would become more openly seductive, permitting herself to fondle and kiss the girl, first on the cheek and then the neck; then, while dabbing perfume on the girl's temples, she would lean forward and kiss her lips, the movement fleeting still, the intent disguised. Manuela might then suggest that, to enhance her freshly made-up face and to transform her appearance even more dramatically, the girl ought to try on some of the clothes Manuela had brought with her. Intoxicated by the spirit of the exchange, mesmerized by the possibilities of her face and body, and the impact she might have, the girl would assent greedily.

Watching from the bed, Fabian still retained his post of detachment. Heedless of her own nudity, the girl was preoccupied only with Manuela's hands that slipped about her, undressing and dressing again, no longer stealthy in their search, brushing her nipples, skimming over her thighs, brief but insistent in their return, hesitant no more at her mound of flesh.

Extravagant in her adulation of the girl, Manuela would murmur in tribute to the subtleties of beauty enhanced by the new makeup, the teasing fantasy of the antique Victorian gown, its waist cinched, its ribbons and laces dangling in pretty disorder. She would embrace the girl, as if solicited only by the artifice of the paint and dress before her, and then, even more abruptly, kiss her on the mouth, the caprice of her own theatricality a license for the bluntness of the need.

Manuela's spell was now complete. Unmoored from the bonds of time outside the alcove, adrift in the sensation and possibilities that Manuela had forged for all three of them, the girl was free to interpret the events in the alcove as moments without reference to an external world of cause and consequence, a dream gathering passion unto itself, a destiny plundered. She, who had never been aroused by a woman before, was aroused by Manuela, although she glanced constantly at Fabian to reassure herself that he was part of what was taking place. The girl still allowed Manuela the freedom to undress her, but when Manuela helped her to emerge from the gown, the fantasy of lace and satin and velvet, it was now the girl who would reach out to her. Manuela disrobed and, masked only by the narrow strip of cloth that trapped her hips, lowered herself onto the bed, bringing the girl with her, the two of them kissing and caressing as they fondled each other, makeup smudging their cheeks, hands and shoulders.

Thrashing in their union, the girl would thrust her breasts against Manuela's, her mouth searching the mouth of the other, her hands fretting with the nipples, teasing at the brink of descent, threatening to move down, to tear at the narrow strip of cloth that still estranged Manuela from her. Then Fabian would place himself between Manuela and the girl, claiming the girl for himself, offering himself to her. Manuela would recede in response, her body dissolving from the space between the man and the girl, only her face an intermittent invader of the seal of their kiss, the third party in the triptych of their embrace. The girl, now as abandoned with Fabian as she had been with Manuela, finally gave herself up to her own sensation and ambivalent quest to touch and taste the flesh of either, avid to receive the badge of her adventure. The contagion of her need prompted Fabian to probe her deeper, with more force, while Manuela wedged in between them, offering her mouth to kiss and to be kissed, eager to know that the girl loved her as a woman and that the presence of Fabian—of any man—could not alter that infatuation.

Later, Fabian would let his curiosity play about Manuela and the girl. Retreating, he wondered whether Manuela's need to be a woman could remain more urgent than the need for fulfillment that would compel her to take off the narrow strip of cloth and reveal herself; whether she might choose to turn to Fabian for still another homage to her feminine power, now that he had seen her triumph in so exacting an arena of accomplishments; or whether she might reach her fulfillment later, alone, beguiled by the memory of herself with the girl, one woman loving another. He also wondered whether, with Manuela naked and aroused,

the girl's passion would prevail over the sudden muta-
tion, in an image more ideal, more persuasive, more
complete in its power to please than the one that
Manuela offered; whether the girl could accept, as
easily as he did, this mode of loving for what it was, a
quest for beauty, for its expression, in whatever form
or image or manifestation of touch, a love no different
in kind, at root, from that in the appreciative eye of a
horseman for a stallion, a mare or a gelding.

With his legs thrust wide, Fabian would sprawl on
his back, then slowly pull the girl onto him, her body a
firm blanket covering him, her back against his chest,
her head, the face upturned, tucked between his neck
and shoulder, his knees and calves bracing her legs,
urging her wide, fastening her to himself, her buttocks
straddling him, his flesh planted, settling deeper in her,
his hands snaring her wrists, binding her more tightly
to him, then scooping her arms wide, lapping her
breasts outward, her belly flat, her thighs forked,
tempting Manuela with the locked and coiling rhythm
of their bodies. From behind the girl's head he could
not see Manuela crouched at their feet, but within the
instant, he felt the warmth of her touch on his flesh. A
shiver ran through the length of the girl's body; lying,
still bound to her, he became the monitor of her
passion, of her every moment, as she let herself be
opened to the touch of the other woman while remaining open to his.

Straining as he thrust into the girl, he waited for
Manuela to respond; then, as he heard the girl's moan,
felt her taut above him, he was aware of Manuela's
weight upon them, a man entering the girl from above,
just as he had entered her, as if she were a boy, from
below. Now all was tightness and tension within the
girl's body, a substance thrashing between him and
Manuela, aware no longer, caring no more who it was
that brought her the sensation she could barely con-
tain.

Fabian began to chart his own sensations. The girl
had ceased to be a space sundering him from Manuela;
he felt Manuela as a tide within his own flesh, he

within hers, the girl only a veil or tissue uniting them, yielding to their common pulse and surge, an agent of communion, avid to transmit sensation from one to the other at the pitch of unaltered intensity she herself knew in the receiving and the recording.

Fabian's thoughts drowned in the onslaught of pleasure. Lost on a periphery of knowledge, he let himself vault into the midst and flight of his dream, the scope of his fantasy the vastness of a polo field, the grass fragrant and dewy, a blue dome of sky, the morning heat a rising mist, he on a horse, mallet in hand, the ball ahead.

In the seduction of a perfect shot, charging at the gallop, his legs prompting and gripping, he was set on the ball, his thigh against the saddle, his weight gathered in his foot, digging into the stirrup, his toes clawing; then, bending his body forward, his eye and thought strained to the target, he swung his mallet, striking faultlessly the center of the ball. A crest of feeling broke above him, elation at his feat. Just then the straps that fastened his saddle to the horse tore under his weight. Instantly his saddle gave way, keeling with him to the side. As his pony veered off, he pitched, then, plunging dreamily, free at last from the reins, the dew splashing him like cold sweat, he rolled through the grass, yielding to this jet and spume that seemed to rise not from the grass but from his being, making him one with his own flesh.

Neither polo nor ponies were fashioned for the stony wastes of high plains without horizon, the thin air, the snow drifting in thick billows of silence. And so Fabian always made for the hot, marshy lowlands, steering his VanHome to gentle ground where he and his ponies could wander at will, play, take their pleasure without rein. He shunned the featureless lure of the sleek turnpike and expressway, the heedless thruway, preferring the fellowship of the backwoods spilling before him, the intimacy and promise of the rural bypath, narrow, alert with surprise.

On warm nights, his VanHome parked deep in some wood, he might sleep wrapped in a blanket in the moist grass under a bush or in a juniper grove, perhaps sheltered by a stack of grain or hay. He would listen to the whiffs of wind, trees in their rustling, the swift rush of birds. When the last echo subsided and life hung suspended, the night air would flicker with sound, distant, sharp, close: a stranger, uncertain, timorous, sidling by his VanHome; lovers whispering, in search of a retreat; a dog tracking the pungent smell of Big Lick and Gaited Amble; the meowing of a stray cat.

In that solitude, Fabian did not envy other people their thronged existence. They appeared to him, most of them, to have consented to the manufacture of their lives at some common mint, each day struck from the master mold, without change, a duplicate of what had gone before and was yet to come. Only some accident could bring to pass upheaval in the unchallenged round of their lives.

It was not contempt he felt for them, merely regret that they had allowed the die of life to be cast so early and so finally. He preferred individuals whose singularity gave him insight into himself. He reasoned that, if in the course of his adult life, he chanced upon no more than perhaps twenty or twenty-five men and women, each of whom mattered to him as friend or lover, he would still be faithful to his calling. If this was true for him as a polo player, ever on the move, it would have been no less true for him as a lawyer, businessman, artist or politician.

For Fabian, nature offered a spectacle absolute in scope. In his parade of admiration for it, the barter of his wandering, he seemed to himself an explorer in quest of a vantage point from which he could more fairly contemplate himself.

He would leave his VanHome in a wood or field and ride his ponies in tandem, catapulting in play from one to the other, companioned by a wind that tossed bits of grain in his face and mouth or whipped him across desolate reaches of stubble. He might trot Big Lick or Gaited Amble under the slender trees of Idaho, still in their summer uniform, or race the horses through the supple grasses of Wyoming or over Utah flats blazing in a shower.

Sometimes, as he cantered through dry moss in Arizona or Nevada, the skeleton of some old mining town, a relic of boom-and-bust, would loom in the ghostly space before him. A church spire pierced the unanswering sky; the shells of long-deserted houses lay about him. Far away, a coyote howled, its long sour moan pricking Fabian's ponies to prance uneasily. Enthralled by so measureless a domain, he would race his horses at the rim of the desert, stampeding the whitish gardens of borax, vaulting the silver furrows that slit the salt fields, refreshing his steaming ponies in the tepid green of the pupfish marshes, stalking the hollow cages of sagebrush scudding over the broken mud flats.

Here, in this burning void, this landscape of heat and light and space as pure and luminous as a cube of metal or a shard of mineral so crystalline that no pool of rain water could impose on it a reflection, Fabian felt that he was nature's own conscience. Without him to see it, the natural world would remain unseen, unknown, a thing unto itself, radiance in a galaxy strewn with distant light.

The shelves on the walls of his compact living area were densely packed with books. When in his voyaging he came upon a large bookshop, a rare occasion in the country, rarer than some of the wildlife he encountered —whose survival was protected by law—he would browse among the counters and shelves for hours. He had to be discriminating: in his VanHome, space was tight, and to make room for a new book, he would have to relinquish one he already had, dropping it off at a community library along his way.

What survived his scrutiny in the bookshop, the books he took back with him to his VanHome, promised a landscape his imagination had not yet explored and could not scan in advance.

When he was in pain—bruised, or suffering the wounds of a rough game, apprehensive and restless, reminded of the vulnerability of his condition—it was to one of those books that he would turn, and always a novel. A private trailer for his mind, that novel would take him where his VanHome could not, permitting him travels to a reality outside the dominion of nature, a fusion of what the present was becoming with a history of what the past might have been, a weightless passing through time and place and thought, coasting with a freedom unmatched by any spaceship. At any point in such a voyage, Fabian would find himself no longer the solitary passenger of his VanHome, but a fugitive from an exhausted view of himself, a displaced person in an uncharted landscape, an émigré to the frontier beyond the scope of his transit.

Fabian shared with many Americans of his generation a dual past. The years of his childhood and youth had been spent in the stony, rural life of one of those marginal "old countries," their borders and boundaries forgotten now, during a decade of wars, of political and social upheavals that ravaged them every so often like a natural calamity.

The simple farmer who brought him up in a small village was blessed, or burdened, with too many children of his own; but, encouraged by the local priest to placate a not easily placated God, he took in Fabian, a refugee from the city where, for the time of yet another war, his parents chose to remain without him. The farmer had the grudging hope, the expectation, that the boy's advent would be the forerunner of more tangible gifts of favor and grace. When it was not, the farmer decided to make use of him, even though he was still a boy, as a farmhand, and the days of his childhood were spent in tending to horses, pigs, goats and poultry.

The horse was an inescapable presence in Fabian's early life, as inevitable and taken for granted as the car would become in the years of his maturity.

In the village, horses were used to pull plows, as well as to haul carts and carriages; they were treated no differently from other domestic animals, herded and penned in, their labor long and exhausting, their time at pasture brief. The whip was used to speed them up; at the first sign of illness, they were killed for meat.

As an outsider, Fabian was often sport for bands of other children, first in play, occasionally in fight, when they would turn on him in the bond and unity of their family kinship. It was during one of these games, threatening at any moment to erupt into combat, that, for the first time, Fabian found himself riding bareback.

A volatile stallion, taunted by a sheepdog lunging and snapping at it, thrashed about its enclosure; heaving against the bars, on the verge of breaking out. Fabian was tending a flock of geese when a group of boys seized him from behind, pinioning his arms, and heaved him onto the stallion's back. Caught off guard by the sudden ballast, the stallion halted; instinctively, in the moment before the horse reared, Fabian grabbed its mane. His legs flanking the ribs, he careened on its back, fighting desperately to keep from sliding off. The dog renewed its attack, and the stallion broke its bounds, kicking the gate aslant, picking up speed as it shot toward the open field, leaving the snapping, hapless dog and the raucous boys far behind.

Freed from the restrictions of its pen, the stallion bolted into frantic, unchecked flight, crossing a wide, pitted road in one leap, dashing into the hedges, its hoofs spraying the soft, sandy loam, the sharp branches of a cedar flogging Fabian's legs as the animal plunged through it heedlessly.

In a quiver of time swift as light, Fabian saw a fly attached to the horse's neck, perched just behind one ear, persisting, undisturbed by the pounding of the huge, sweaty mass that was ferrying it through the brush. He knew that, like the fly, his hope depended on clinging fast to the horse's neck, that if he were to fall, he would be pitched onto the ground with a force that could injure or kill him.

He edged himself up, his hands tangling in the stallion's mane, centering his chest and stomach to cradle in the niche of its back, no choice open to him other than to yield to the motion of the animal. And there he remained, the horse's head a shield against the branches as he moved through time, calm as the fly.

The barn that quartered horses had also been the pen of much of Fabian's boyhood. It was a lair of intimacy he often shared with them, and the scene of his initiation into the lore of sex and birth long before he could decipher the world around him, the world of men and women, girls and other boys.

A horse bristled and shook off another, bit and kicked at it in retaliation when nudged, tried to ignore it. Then the horse changed, became so gentle that Fabian at first worried that it was sick. But then, when it nuzzled and nudged the other horse, the sight stirred Fabian. It was a mare rubbing against a stallion. Her ears were now erect, vibrating to the stallion's breath and pulse, prickling when he snorted, alert to his every move, yet she stood passive, primed for the assault of all his weight. The stallion, too, was changed, his sex engorged, his moods seesawing between playfulness and violence; sometimes he mounted the mare as if determined to pierce her entrails, to wound her before she could escape his dominion. Yet what appeared to the boy a tide of violence, the mare's submission first to her own heat, then to the assault of the stallion, did not seem a breach in the cycle of nature. From the moment of their coupling, nature hoarded the time needed for new life to emerge from the moist enigma of the mare's insides.

The door of the stable, like one sovereign arm of an invisible clock, opened to admit the flush of summer and the chaff and thistle of fall, closed to shut out the onslaught of snow, opened again to acknowledge the moist scent of spring, a prelude to summer's return. The mare slumped, restless, then lurched, uncertain whether it should trust its belly or legs for support, panic in its eyes and movements.

Soon it lay down, reluctant, even unable, to get up again. A massive shudder ran through its body, and swiftly, between the mare's raised hind legs, the narrow muzzle of a foal appeared, its two forelegs a frame in a heaving sac of glistening filament, pliant, almost translucent.

Fabian had been ordered to tear the sac if it had not broken open while moving through the mare, and he touched the mysterious fiber in awe at this envelope that delivered new life. But the sac had already been split by the pelvis, and he saw the foal's legs protruding without obstruction, ready for further delivery.

The mare, exhausted, waited to muster more strength; the foal, most of it still huddled inside the sphere that had formed it, attempted to move on its own, already another presence in the world that would soon claim all of it.

Fascinated and afraid, Fabian moved closer. As if responding to his gaze, the foal, prodded by the mare, pushed itself forward, sloughing off the rest of the sac, eager to leave the home that was not large enough for it anymore, even though, once it was outside the mare, the foal was still bound to it by the umbilical cord, a pulse of blood.

Fabian waited a few minutes, carefully guiding the foal away from the heaving body of the mare, then, even though he was fearful that he might be cutting a source of life, he severed the umbilical cord boldly. The foal was on its own now.

Trembling to its feet within minutes, shaking but steady enough to keep its balance, it staggered about, oblivious of Fabian; confused, the foal broke into its first walk around the mare, then, exhausted, lay quietly at its side, waiting. In the morning, Fabian would run to his master's house to bring the news of the new life in his barn.

Later, with the mare resting and the foal surprised by its first sleep outside the womb, Fabian would lie in the straw, pondering the birth he had just witnessed. With a rush of envy and apprehension, he thought about the place that the foal had so heedlessly abandoned in the mare, its stall of warmth and safety, now bartered for the hazard of the whip.

He warmed at the thought of the mare and how he would have liked to nest inside it, alone there, well fed, its flanks his walls, its withers and croup his roof, its legs absorbing the shock of uneven terrain, and how he would be free to peek out at the hostile world merely by lifting the mare's tail, a curtain he might raise or lower on an uncertain stage.

It was then, when still a boy, that Fabian saw a horse die. The animal might have been grazing at pasture or hauling a plow or even resting in the barn. He remembered how, stirring to a portent of menace that seemed an alien odor invading its muzzle, the horse bolted, its head erect, its eyes hurtling to and fro, desperate to locate the lurking terror.

Unable to make out its enemy, to move swiftly from the threat, powerless to flee its sense of foreboding, confused, the animal faltered in a spasm of panic and pain, betrayed by its own body, its breathing easy no

more, its heartbeat, once so measured, broken now,
erratic. It heaved its head about, instinctively searching
out the presence of a herd, for others like itself, who,
in this last moment of life, would offer a confirmation
of continuing existence, copious and teeming.

But there was no herd within its field of vision, no
others to offer support, to draw sustenance from.
Dread fusing with pain, the animal, for whom earth had
been a field over which to range and race, found that it
could move no more, its muscles, tendons, ligaments
withered, refusing to answer the summons of life that
still nettled in its brain. It nodded instead to another
signal, the drifting call of gravity, nature's last.

Fabian watched as the great bridge of the horse
buckled, the useless pillars of its legs slipped sideways,
the boom of its neck twisted, the head, an empty
bucket, pitching down.

In a moment, the horse's power to breathe and to
run, the license to continue in life, had been snatched
from it, a merciless abolishment as arbitrary as the
generosity with which life had been offered once to
that newborn foal quivering under Fabian's eyes. Now
he saw that the body, which only a little while before
had commanded the earth with matchless speed and
endurance, was a heap of bone and meat, wrapped still
and again, as at the beginning, in a steaming sac of
skin.

In life, the horse had always appeared to Fabian
fleet and airborne, almost weightless as it skimmed the
ground, gracefully springing back from the surface
with the ricochet of its hoofs. Now, in death, it lay
slack, the plane of its flank level with the earth, dense
and resistant, dragged at the end of a thick chain by a
sluggish ox, the horse's legs floundering each time its
body passed over a freshly plowed furrow.

It was often Fabian's task to gut the dead horse. In
the barn, an ax handy, his knives sharpened on a
whetstone, he would start by cutting open the main

arteries, letting the blood from the severed vessels drip into a heap of desiccated hay. He then opened the base of the stomach, its entrails still hot, and started to disembowel the horse, piece by piece, organ after organ, mindful not to discard the edible delicacies of liver, heart, kidneys and tripe, or to soil them with the noxious colon and bloated cecum; unlike the rabbits, sheep and pigs he had often gutted, a horse had no gall bladder that, when carelessly cut, would spill its bile. He would then dump the offal and carrion into a corroded barrel and roll it down a small hill toward a pit he had dug, leaving the barrel open there, a feast for crows, dogs and rats.

If the work did not sicken him, the poring over the spongy mass, his hands and clothes bloodied, the mingled smells of blood, excrement and half-digested food, it was because he would always think of the supple grace and fluent perfection of the horse in motion, its muscles surging to pull a cart, flexing in a walk, stretching and thrusting at a gallop.

The flesh was gone now, the choicest hunks of meat hacked out by the farmer and stored in the icy pits under the main house. Only the skeleton remained before Fabian, its bones soon to be smashed and scattered at the edge of the forest, far from the pasture and fields that had been the horse's domain. Above all other abandoned, useless and decaying parts of the dead horse's body, the skeleton bothered Fabian most. Unlike the animal's skin or blood, the intestines, lungs, nerves or muscles, each a forge of moisture and heat, a furnace of life, the skeleton, with its two hundred and more bones that Fabian had once counted, seemed no more complex than the crude pillars, posts, joints and frames that made up the barn—and no more mysterious.

If the skeleton was the bony soul, the hardened essence of the horse, it appeared, when juxtaposed with the living mass of the animal, rather as its opposite, a caricature supplanting pliancy with rigor, fluency with brittleness, motion with stillness. What would have happened to the horse, Fabian wondered, if, throughout its life, instead of relying on its instinct, the animal had sought support only from its skeleton?

Later in life, domesticated in his VanHome, Fabian would pass at random across the border of California and Nevada, stopping, when the impulse took him, at Dante's View, a point of observation from which his gaze could sweep out over the panorama of Death Valley, a shallow, arid basin of rocks and flats, the floor of the continent he traveled incessantly, that rose at its farthest rim to the snowy drifts of Mt. Whitney, climbing the grizzled slopes until it came to rest on the peak needling the sky.

Posted above that parched and hazy sheet of Death Valley, he would marvel at the tolerance of nature, its indifferent generosity that permitted springs and streams, a lake and swamp, fish and other creatures native only to this measureless vacancy, in the midst of heat sometimes unmatched by any other on earth.

Having left his VanHome miles away in the safety of a motel parking lot, he would descend into the valley, then take refuge on an islet in a sudden grove, an oasis of surprise, bending, marshy rushes fringing the edge of its trickling stream. There he would lie down, the sandy heat kneading his back, Big Lick and Gaited Amble nuzzling him or heaving to rest at his side, the shield of his eyes a screen for dreams and thought, the film of his imagining broken only by a need as rude as thirst or hunger.

In the ceaseless rhythm of the stream, the darting flicker of a snake, the visit of a suddenly startled heron, the brooding of his horses at the shallow dunes, Fabian saw his solitude and his flight beyond the boundaries of time known and time yet to be forayed, testament, to his joy and his lamentation, harbingers of a voyage whose destination he could not ever know.

It was here, riding one day, that Fabian saw, far away on the flats, a herd of wild horses, their spotted hides a camouflage, their run kicking a screen of dust against the darkened hills and mountains.

He started to follow the herd, prompting Gaited Amble into a smooth gallop, and when she began to pant, spent with heat, he vaulted easily to Big Lick, the horses' gait unbroken. Soon he was close enough to make out the wild mustangs cantering loosely in a moving heap. Several mounted men chased the herd, hooting and slapping their thighs, slashing their whips at the slower horses, while a dozen or so dogs darted round the flanks of the mustangs, nipping at them.

Fabian followed the dusty, pounding blur. A massive corral suddenly loomed in the distance, row upon row of trenches scooped deeply out of the crumbling soil like open scars in the parched landscape, waiting to heal. Perched high above the corral, he watched, binoculars magnifying the sight, as the men and dogs tightened their trap around the herd, the wild ponies still frenzied though buckling in the surge of sun and sand and their sweating multitude. He heard the first shot ring out, and then the volley of rifles, mixed with the faint neighing of the panicked horses as the mounted men steered the herd toward the ditches. Some animals collapsed where they stood, others were dragged down by the force of their own speed and weight, keeling into the trenches, their necks and heads straining high in terror, gouging their last breath of air in the valley of death, halting abruptly as they rammed into each other, muzzles smashing against ribs as they tripped and toppled, heaving to stay erect, some trampled already, others clawing from below, rearing from under the stampeding herd, only to be felled by a bullet or by the melee about them, sliding back into the ditch, a few still struggling hopelessly to leap out.

The onslaught subsided; the ditches began to swell with the seething mass of horses, their neighing a distant tide in the vastness of sand and rock. Soon only a few mares were left to roam the corral aimlessly. Now the mounted men abandoned the easy pleasures of the gun for the challenge of lasso and the illusion of the hunt. Mad with terror, the mustangs hurtled through the net of their trappers, yet one by one, the whirling noose of rope brought each mare down, strangling it into submission, to be dragged headlong toward the swollen trenches, the dogs howling, the mounts of the men, inflamed with blood and death, now as terrified as the animals they hauled.

Fabian watched as the riders searched the horizon intently, to ensure that they had felled all the wild horses; then they made a last tour of the heaving trenches, huddled flesh still quivering and steaming in the great open gashes of earth. He noticed how quick, almost furtive, the men were about it, aware that the grassy plain they had cleared of wild mustangs was public land. The prosperous ranchers they worked for would soon bring their private cattle there to graze, the scarcity of grass no longer a threat. With the dogs in yapping pursuit, the men galloped away from the corral, heading toward their bunkhouses, their reward, chili, beans and beer. Slowly, Fabian descended to the plain, Big Lick's nostrils twitching, quick with apprehension as it picked its way toward the mass graves, Gaited Amble reluctant to follow, sniffing the air, its head tossing.

A curtain of dust hung in the air, drifting lightly over the valley, masking the rocks and flats with a grainy film. At Fabian's approach, a thin, whistling moan rose from the ditches, a sigh of desolation. Panicked, Big Lick thrust sideways, almost unseating Fabian and jerking Gaited Amble at the end of the lead rope. Fabian calmed the animals with his voice and hand, and the three of them continued to make their way along the ditches.

The tableau of massacre opened before him in all its grotesque composition. Cramped in heaps in the narrow furrows of the mass graves, most of the animals were dead; some twitched, a last flicker of life. Settled at the brink of the spilling trough, Fabian saw the mound of dead and dying mustangs as an infernal creation: meshed and intersecting heads, shoulders, hocks, erupting muzzles, ribs and tails, twisting coils of a monstrous snake that burrowed greedily through the stony ground of the valley, its scattered eyes blinking, its venomous mouth open, ready to strike, indicting earth and sky.

Suddenly, Big Lick gave out a vast neigh, all its power and strength of life in the cry, sundering the deathly calm of the valley. Before it could rebound in echo, from one of the ditches came an answering shriek, muted yet still firm, the last voice of life calling to life. But before it dissolved into echo, Gaited Amble called out, a third cry shivering the sky, the voice of a temporary victor in the battle of life, rallying the vanquished.

As if at a signal, Fabian tightened his legs and threw Big Lick into a gallop. With Gaited Amble abreast, the curtain of dust veiling them still, he moved past the corral, across the mesa, through the plains and peaks, the valleys of Nevada.

Early in the fall, after he had been idling on the road for about a week, he crossed into Arkansas and reached the Double Bridle Stables in Totemfield. As he drove up, the late afternoon sun was cresting over a string of spindly pine trees, their pointy tips like wooden arrows shafting the air, poised against the sky. Through the tracery of wood, the shell of an old mill hulked like a skull. Tiny cones of hemlock and spruce, a tangle of roots, littered his path. A drowsing melancholy invaded Fabian. Time always altered, rarely improved: the place looked shabby, not as he remembered it. He wondered if, in the intervening years, he had aged as gracelessly. He felt degraded by his poverty, which had brought him here now, for the second time; he wondered at the obsession that had once driven him here for the first. The obsession had been Vanessa.

He remembered her, a student in his riding class, waiting for him at the paddock or riding off with him into the woods. The place had been filled with young riders, parents, instructors—a confusion of horses, cars and bicycles. Because of her, in their midst he had seen himself as a figure of charm, authority and influence. Then he had thought that one day he would return to claim her; now, the more he looked around, the more uncertain he was of himself and of her.

What remained for him was the short walk to the office, where he would confront another woman from his past—but not to claim her.

He parked his VanHome just beyond the main buildings, near the pond, where, sheltered by trees, it would not obstruct a view of the stables. As he swung down from the cab of the VanHome, he caught sight of three Hackney foals gamboling in the paddock, whinnying in the quiet.

Fabian found Stella in the office. She looked well, the dash of her riding breeches a sweep of black, setting off the burnished gilt of her softly coiling hair, her skin even creamier than he had remembered. She had known when to expect him—he had telephoned a few hours earlier—but even so, he could not discern whether her allure was intended for him or for others.

Face to face with her, Fabian felt a rush of withered emotion; he could not plagiarize a past self, was unwilling to pretend that the sight of her touched him.

He took off his jacket and sat across the desk from Stella. A handwritten calendar hung on one dirty wall, a schedule of riding classes scribbled all over it in red pencil, and tacked above it were a row of yellowing photographs: Stella jumping bareback, Stella on the cover of *The Tennessee Walking Horse,* Stella exhibiting a two-year-old stallion, a champion of the Spring Jubilee, Stella with members of the Walking Horse Breeders Association at Shelbyville, Stella accepting an award from the American Legion Saddle Club. In one snapshot, Stella, poised against a graceful black mare, was visibly in her teens. The picture could have served for a poster of a Southern belle posing with her favorite Tennessee Walker. Had the photographer moved his camera one inch to the right, the snapshot would have included Fabian, for the picture had been taken only a few days after Fabian met Stella for the first time, after she had attended his horsemanship classes.

Now, as then, it was common for him to be at a horse show, as a spectator, or judging a competition, and suddenly hear his name called out: he would turn and face a young woman, vibrant, fresh and lovely, one of his former students. As she threw her arms about his neck, reminded him of who she was, where they had met, what had happened, how well she remembered what he had taught her and the stories he used to tell her, Fabian registered the force of her transformed presence, her command of age and time. Yet he was trapped by uncertainty, what to say or do, conscious of the crossroads before which he stood, his dilemma sometimes observed by the young boyfriend, manly and handsome, whom the woman had discreetly left in the background. In her embrace, the return of her voice, Fabian sought the outline of the young girl he had once known, tempted to know if she might consent to a fresh bond he could devise for the two of them. But he was aware that the same process of time that had carried her to maturity had made of him a man in midlife.

Closing in on youth—a young woman, a girl—Fabian could not resist its spell; he was compelled, his instinct honed by anguish. He would fix with an intensity almost clinical, bordering on obsession, on the sheen of a girl's eyes, the deep color that washed pupil and iris, each filament of hair that streamed from her head, the taut yet resilient skin that blanketed her bones and veins, the buoyancy of her flesh, its scent and feel not yet probed by another. All these were for him counters to the steady waste of time and age that raced between them. In that relentless flow, his age a constant subtraction, Fabian saw himself as the heir of time, an unransomable hostage to a past that was the only gift at his command. He saw himself appearing in a girl's life as time's agent, unbidden, indifferent to the drama of her destiny. He contemplated aligning himself next to her, unyoking their bodies to all that was spontaneous, involuntary—his flesh rising, erect, hers hardening, enfolding him as he sundered it, seed in its flood.

Fabian was convinced that in first love, a young girl sought the dream of love; later in life, love merely sought her. But he knew that just as he should not expect a pony to bend to the curb, to the rein and the spur without prior schooling and cultivation, neither should he expect a young woman, healthy and beautiful, to come to him, a man more than twice her age, his home the road, his house a thing on wheels, a man of undistinguished looks and without obvious charm, with no riches to seduce, no particular skill to enthrall, and no profession that enhanced—above all, a man outside of permanence, able to offer only a few hours, days, weeks of his presence. For this reason, he had to find a girl while she was still susceptible to a man of his experience, a mentor, even if he could offer her no more than adventure in place of advice, weariness instead of wisdom. Usually the girl would still be in high school, still be living with her parents. In singling her out, cultivating her, arranging their first encounter alone, Fabian wished to initiate her, to keep a hold on her will and emotions, to leave his brand.

He could not meet with the girl too many times without attracting unwanted attention, the notice of her fellow students, the teachers and staff of her school, often her parents. To avoid collision with the caprices of local laws, he would arrange no more than four or five meetings with the girl, some at public events, others in his VanHome. He saw to it that each meeting was intense enough to leave its mark for good.

In every town or sprawling suburb, pastoral outpost or even city where he gave lessons in horsemanship, lectured sometimes or took part in various horse shows or polo meets, Fabian kept a watch for two or three girls who would, he hoped, yield to him without mistrust.

Sometimes as he watched a young girl off in the corner of a stable, wholly absorbed in the patient ritual of waxing, flexing, polishing, buffing the riding gear and tack that lay clustered about her, he understood that horses were often an embodiment of the dolls the girls had coddled and chided in their childhood, the vulnerable babies they had nurtured in their adolescent fantasies. To horses they brought devotion and a passionate loyalty that did not falter. They cosseted them, were sensitive to their needs, anointed lovingly their lesions and sores. In the routine of grooming—the combing, soaping, brushing—they took a quiet pleasure, almost domestic. He understood, also, that with conventions of family and school weakened or discarded, myths and traditions of physical weakness and submission challenged, a girl riding at hunt or dressage, taking a jump, revealed and claimed her power to master, direct, and bend to her will a horse, a living creature so much larger and more powerful than herself.

Quickening to ripeness more swiftly than boys of the same age, girls revealed a more balanced temperament, coordination whetted to a tauter pitch. They often seemed to Fabian a curious union of ballet dancer and gymnast, and in his classes he found that he could treat them as his equals, independent, responsible, alert, complete. He responded to their persistence, their strong motivation, a certain competitive heat. Many of them had been bred on banal tales of life in the Old West, romantic fictions and fantasies of adventures in the saddle, and they projected themselves into the roles of those pulp heroines or heroes. They were determined to attract notice: fame was the spur, and they rode to win.

Sometimes, after the initiation had been successfully accomplished, the inoculation had taken, the brand burned indelibly, Fabian's interest in a girl began to wane. He might have considered her a bad prospect for a future relationship, unimaginative, the life of her fantasy already depleted. Rather than waste his time arranging future meetings with the girl, or sustain her belief that he was going to see her again, he would break with her. He was wary, though, never to reject her too abruptly or with too visible finality. This he had learned shortly after the publication of his first book on equitation.

The book, a novelty in its time, had been a considerable success; it won him a small reputation, as well as a steady flow of invitations to lecture or teach at various riding schools and academies. Among the first invitations he accepted was a request to join a house party—at which, of course, Fabian would be expected to show off his polo skill—at the Florida estate of a rich and powerful businessman, who had made his fortune in turnstiles and was celebrated for the horses he bred to race, as well as for the formidable array of breeds he maintained for polo and pleasure riding. Enclosed with the invitation was a gracious note from the millionaire, expressing the hope that Fabian would feel free to remain at the estate for several weeks as his guest.

To adjust to changes in climate, which often affected his health and his riding performance, Fabian was in the habit of arriving for any assignment at least a day or two before he was expected. On this occasion, still in the grip of a bad cold, he had left the Northeast a week earlier to escape the height of a brutal winter.

In Florida, when he stepped off the plane, released from the pressure of its claustrophobic cabin, soporific with the medicine he had been taking, he felt dazed by the wash of heat, the hypnotic lull of the palms, the distant glare of sand. He knew he should go directly to one of the small motels nearby, but, weak and lightheaded, decided to inquire first at a horse and tack supply shop about renting a horse challenging enough for the few days' workout he felt he would need before showing up—and showing off—at the millionaire's estate.

The shop was cramped, a bit forlorn, but even in his distracted state, Fabian was pleasantly surprised to find his book displayed on a counter, near a blaring portable radio. He was leafing through the book when a salesgirl came out from a back room. Impulsively, he held up the book, with his photograph on the back jacket next to his face, and asked about local stables. The girl had no visible reaction to his four eyes contemplating her, but simply told him, with routine politeness, that the owner was on vacation, that she herself had only started this job a few weeks before and that she knew nothing about horses or stables or where he might make any arrangements. Swept by a sudden vertigo, Fabian slumped against the counter still clutching his book; the medicine he had been taking, the plane trip, the onslaught of Southern heat had taken their toll. The girl hurried around to him and helped him to a chair.

She was in her twenties, short and plump, with an open face. Her waist melted heavily into her hips. Her breasts, large and shapeless, seemed too heavy for her torso, and they shifted with every movement she made, pouring from side to side, slapping against her ribs, sloping down when she leaned over.

She offered to call a taxi to take him to his motel, but when he told her he had not yet arranged for one, with floating neutrality she suggested that he come to her place, where he could wait until he felt well enough to move on.

Fabian agreed. She quickly fixed the portable radio on a shoulder strap, closed the shop, brought her car around, and heaved his luggage into it. With Fabian lying on the back seat, she drove off.

The girl lived in a one-room apartment in a housing development divided from the beach by a stretch of highway. In his feverish daze, Fabian did not object when she told him to go straight to bed, the only bed in the room, a slab of white in one corner. He undressed and climbed between cool sheets.

He woke to a damp weight on his forehead, jolted into consciousness, unfamiliar with the place in which he found himself. The glare of a bedside lamp filtering through a plastic shade was raw on his eyes.

Sitting beside him, the girl was impassively attentive, a blurred remembrance from that afternoon. As he stirred, she leaned forward and replaced the moist, tepid band on his forehead with the icy, welcome shock of a fresh cloth.

"I had to wake you up," she said, her voice without any Southern flavor. "You seem to have a fever, and you need to drink something. I found these pills in one of your suitcases." She pointed to a small bottle on the bedside table and then, like a nurse, drew him toward her as she plumped up the pillow behind his head, brushing his face with her shoulder. He was dimly surprised to notice that his suitcases had been unpacked, the shirts stacked on a shelf, his suits, jackets, riding breeches and tuxedo all hung on a pole bracketed below the shelf.

She brought him a cup of soup, and he drank it slowly. She watched as he washed down the pills with a large glass of orange juice. When he was finished, she turned off the light by the bed. "Now you go back to sleep," she said.

"Where will you sleep?" he asked.

"Over there." She pointed to another corner of the room. "I've got a sleeping bag."

In the dim light from the room's single window, he drowsed, drifting on a skim of sensation: the taste of oranges and tea and some kind of broth, an egg trembling in a cup, deep tides of sleep, the murmur of words, doors opening and shutting, a sudden bark of traffic. Dreams obliterated the shapes and contours of the room he was in. Sometimes he would become aware that a stranger was lying somewhere on the floor, near him.

Abruptly, in blackness, he awoke; alert, instantly sober, he knew at once the fever had gone. Thirsty, he got up and silently picked his way toward the kitchenette, past the girl lying curled on top of the sleeping bag, a blanket over her shapeless bulk. As the weak light of the refrigerator trickled across the room, she sat bolt upright; then, standing, trying to cover her breasts with the blanket, she plaintively urged him to go back to bed. When he refused, greedily draining the jug of orange juice he had taken from the refrigerator, she fell to coaxing and cajoling, her hand dragging on his arm. As he shook her off, the blanket slipped from her grasp and rustled to the floor. She stood before Fabian, naked, her body softly nurturing. Unreasoning, he reached for her, drawing her close, her breasts pressing against his chest, her thighs parting. He pulled her across the room, and they fell on the bed, her hands pressing him into her belly. He took her rapidly, almost forcefully, overwhelmed by her opulence, her body unfolding to him in pleats, absorbing his weight.

In the days that followed, Fabian, her patient, was also her lover. He was not yet strong enough to ride; instead, he would have breakfast with her before she left for the shop, then stroll down to the beach and doze in the shade, waking to sunbathe for a while, then withdrawing to the shadow of an umbrella to sleep again.

The girl would bring lunch to the beach, her radio slung over her shoulder, and when they had finished eating, sit beside him, sometimes tossing an orange from hand to hand in mindless rhythm, sometimes reeling and unreeling a yo-yo, watching its motion in fascination. She seemed to wear no clothes other than a bleached denim jacket and shapeless pants. For these beach excursions, she was topped with an old Royal Canadian Mountie's hat, its strap undone and trailing behind her shoulder. As she plodded across the sand, her face under that incongruous hat, Fabian thought of her as a refugee from some nameless war, forgotten, still in futile wandering, searching for a place she might call her own.

She always stayed fully clothed on the beach. Fabian guessed that, conscious of her body, of its fat creasing in layers, she would not undress. He watched her covertly when small packs of teen-agers, their bodies lithe and tanned, easy in the sun, surfboards under their arms, passed by, giggling and snickering at the two of them. The girl pretended to ignore the mockery, but Fabian, wincing at their adolescent cruelty, felt uncomfortable and angered.

She told her story neutrally, from a distance, almost

as if reciting the history of someone else. She had been born in the slums of San Francisco, the bastard child of white parents whom she never knew. A Japanese-American family had boarded her as a foster child, but they had no interest in the education of girls and let her drop out of high school. Soon afterward, exasperated at the government's many years of refusal to compensate them for their internment in a concentration camp during World War II, her foster parents decided to go back to Japan with their natural children. Alone, the girl drifted around the country, hitchhiking, taking occasional odd jobs, picking up stray bits of lore and skill, always migrant. She had arrived in Florida only recently, and in her tiny apartment Fabian could detect almost no testimony to her being —the Mountie's hat, a large map of the United States, folded and smudged with use, the yo-yo, stubs of food stamps. In the bathroom, a plastic puppet suspended from a hook bobbed when he brushed past it. Paperback books, shiny and untouched, were lined up neatly on a shelf. The books—all practical, Fabian noticed, in the "how-to" vein, with nothing in common, and among them not a novel, a single work of reflection, an anthology of poems—were guarded by twin toy flags. A little sticker—"The Stars and Stripes Forever"—ran across one flag, while the other showed the rising sun of Japan on a cube of murky white.

A bulky television set, incongruous in the cell of the girl's apartment, claimed one wall wholly to itself. For the girl, after the routine of the shop, the drowse of lunch on the beach, the ritual of supper, it was her own rising sun, the reward at the end of the Canadian Mountie's trail. She would hurry through washing the dishes each night—Fabian could not recollect her hurrying through anything else—and then she would settle down on cushions on the floor in front of it. Eating or yawning, she rose only to change a channel of which she was inexplicably tired or to replenish the plate of cookies that kept her company, the plastic dish of ice cream that seemed never empty, never full. She was not indifferent to Fabian, but merely unable to recognize that he might not share her delight and fascination with television, that its deafening sound and turbulent images ruled out any notice the two of them could take of each other's presence or wishes.

Fabian saw her as television's faithful babysitter, standing watch over a child that never offered her an unruly face, never encroached on her world, never imposed on her energy. She did not resent that it lived a life so much more crowded, eventful and frenetic than her own. She seemed to take reassurance from its world without rank; its ordered rhythm; its slots of time; the steady punctuation of cheering commercials that reminded her of life's arsenal of unrealized needs and wants but did not rebuke her failure to set out after them, that promised relief from pain; the unceasing parade of stars, their deaths never final; life's mysteries exposed by lovers who marry or divorce; villains murdering or being killed; diseases that consumed or were cured; wars that began and quickly ended, planets lost and regained.

Under the girl's care, Fabian recovered, restored to the fitness he would require for the pleasures of the millionaire's house party, if not for the demands of team polo there. The girl knew where he was going— he had told her of the invitation, asking about the route that led to the estate—but in his last day or two, whenever the subject surfaced, she would nod impassively and turn back toward the television set, the yo-yo unspooling between her fingers.

On the morning Fabian had set for his departure, she drove him to a car rental agency, where, her breasts jiggling under the shabby jacket, she helped him to carry his luggage from her car to the one he had just rented.

At the curb, after he embraced her, Fabian made no promises to see her again, to visit, to keep in touch; he could not tell whether she was resentful at his leaving. The Mountie's hat shielded her eyes. The cackle of country and western music spilling from her radio was in Fabian's ears as he drove away, her features already fading in his memory.

Installed in a guesthouse at the millionaire's sprawling estate, Fabian succumbed readily to luxury. Each day, after breakfast—sometimes at the pool, usually in his own quarters—he watched as two of his host's many helicopters rose from a nearby field, hovered briefly in the morning haze, then began to ply their rounds, bringing guests from airport to estate. Other guests came in chauffered limousines and in cars of every vintage and make, racing drivers sometimes at the wheel; and guests arrived by yacht or private plane or even an occasional motorcycle, no place unfilled at the day's end, the grounds a pleasure garden where the rich withdrew to consider providence, the powerful to manipulate simplicity, the industrious to manufacture leisure, the idle to play at occupation.

In the stables and paddocks, where Fabian was most at home, horsemen trailing Olympic glory mingled with polo players and matchless jockeys who had ridden their host's Thoroughbreds to victory. At the pool, they socialized with wizards of industry and finance, designers from Malibu and Big Sur, political impresarios and their cronies from Washington and New York, the sharks of Palm Beach bridge and backgammon tournaments. In the evening, nightclub performers, released from their Miami engagements, dropped by to hold court, perhaps to entertain, often staying over to lend their glamour to a game of golf or tennis.

In the lounges of the main house and on tables beside the pool, several copies of Fabian's book on equitation had been placed. Its presence was a consequence of two or three complimentary references Fabian had made in it to his host's achievements in international polo as well as to his splendid stable of Argentinean ponies. To a number of guests in the party, those references became a token of Fabian's intimacy with their host, and Fabian soon found himself, at drinks or dinner or while he was watching a game, the friendly target of those who had read, or merely seen, his book and now wanted to talk to him about polo, riding or horses.

It was here, in the seductive atmosphere of easy

acclaim, that Fabian met Eugene Stanhope, who initiated their friendship with that sudden whim of the very rich, so that, before Fabian quite knew what was happening, he found himself enlisted as a friend and working as a polo partner of a man he hardly knew.

Soon after Fabian's arrival, the host gave a supper party around the pool, to celebrate the birthday of another guest, an elegant young Texan socialite, a divorcée who had settled in for a leisurely stay. Her interest in Fabian was evident—she had asked him to inscribe a copy of his book to her as a birthday present—and Fabian was just about to ask her to dance when a small group of polo enthusiasts detained him on a fine point of technique. Impatient, he lingered with them for a few moments and was edging toward his Texan quarry when a servant approached and drew him aside, whispering that a young lady had just arrived, claiming to be a friend of Fabian's.

Baffled, Fabian followed him through the halls to a small drawing room. There he saw her, his unexpected visitor, the girl who had nursed him through his fever, awkward amid the ghostly network of rattan, the billow of cushions, a forlorn blur against the paintings.

Still in the denim jacket and baggy pants, but without her radio, the girl saw him and ran forward, bobbing on her short legs, the Mountie's hat bouncing down her back. "I missed you. I had to come to see you," she said, reaching up to embrace him. The servant, his task accomplished, withdrew discreetly. Fabian gently sat her down on one of the love seats.

"You should have called first," he said, kindly but firmly, sitting next to her.

"Your voice isn't enough. I miss you," she replied.

Unnerved, Fabian glanced about. Through the French windows of the drawing room, thrown open to the night languor, he could see across to the terrace, with its steady promenade of guests, couples gliding between the manicured hedges of the garden, lingering at the carved iron benches strewn about the lawn, the cool white or black jackets of the men, the women in their drifts of chiffon, trailing Spanish shawls. He was acutely aware that at any moment someone might enter the room and come upon him and his guest. Caught in alliance with a girl whose very existence elicited condescension and incredulity, he would have to introduce her; he was afraid, also, that she might subject him to further humiliation by naively volunteering her reasons for having come in search of him.

"Why do you miss me?" he asked impatiently.

"I just do," she said, smiling, her breasts, under the jacket, pressing against him. "Have you missed me?"

Fabian's irritation grew as he remembered that, by the pool or in the gardens, the divorcée might be talking to another man; he had no time to lose.

"I remember you," he said sternly. "But I haven't missed you—at least not yet," he added, to soften the impact of his words.

"Can I stay here with you?"

He could not hide his annoyance. "Stay with me—here?"

"Yes. Until you have to leave. I took a week off from my job."

He was angry now. "No, you can't," he said coldly. "You haven't been invited."

A couple from the garden appeared in the doorway. They glanced at the paintings across the room and were about to move in to look at some photographs when they saw Fabian and the girl. Fabian shifted in the love seat, turning his back to the couple. Smiling wanly, they left.

The girl refused to notice the implications of his manner. "You can invite me now," she said. "I can stay with you in your room."

"You can't and won't. I don't want you here!" Fabian said decisively, standing up. "You're going home, and you're leaving now."

She sat there, lumpish. "But why? I can help with the horses," she said, convinced that what she wanted would come to pass.

"You're going home. Now," Fabian announced,

reaching down to take her by the arm. But she still made no move, and instinctively he pulled at her, suddenly rough. She winced at the pressure and stood up.

"Please let me stay," she said. "I want to see you. I want to see you ride."

"Home. Go." He dragged her by one arm toward the door. Reluctant, her pants flapping, she followed. Outside, he steered her toward the front gates, until he remembered that he might come face to face with other strolling guests. He quickly guided her to a service road reserved for deliveries.

"I brought my sleeping bag with me. I could sleep in the woods and just see you during the day." There was a note of stubborn pleading in her voice. She attempted once again to embrace him; once again, he pushed her away.

"You're going home," he insisted. As he pulled her remorselessly forward, the bobbing of her Mountie's hat kept time with their steps.

They reached the gate of the service road. In the haze of the solitary lamp, he saw the sullen resignation on her face. He pushed her firmly through the gate and, without a backward glance, quickly returned to the main house. The divorcée was where he had left her, graceful, draped along a lounge chair beside the pool, one finger idling in his book. But she was practiced in resistance, a challenge that soon helped Fabian erase the girl from his mind.

The next morning, at stick-and-ball practice with several of the other guests, Fabian was riding along the field when a spot of familiar shape and color blinked out at him from the spectators in the stands: the Royal Canadian Mountie's hat and a shabby jacket. In a flush of rage, he reined his horse in sharply, wheeling, then drove it straight at the stands. The girl clumped down the wooden planks toward him, eager, her sandals clapping against the wood, her shoulders plunging, coming at him, the landscape of her chest bouncing.

Fabian loomed over her, his pony snorting, his mallet erect, almost poised to strike. A few women in the stands looked down, murmuring, amused at the mismated pair. Fabian kept his voice low.

"What are you doing here?" he asked.

She came closer, her face next to the horse's muzzle. From it, a trickle of saliva dribbled onto the bulge under her jacket. She did not seem to notice; her eyes were on him.

"I came to see you," she said smiling. "I miss you."

"I told you to go home," he said. He prodded her with the mallet.

"I slept in the woods," she said. "It was nice. I liked waiting for you like that."

He was aware that their encounter was being observed on the field. From a distant corner, two players started to ride in his direction. "You have to go home!" he hissed.

"I'll wait for you over there," the girl said evenly, pointing at the woods beyond the limits of the field. "Please come."

"You're going home," he said. Bristling uneasily, his pony was quicker to pick up his agitation than the girl. She looked up at him again. When Fabian saw her smile, he knew his words had passed over her mind like yet another image from television.

"In the woods," she said again, as if confirming instructions. "Right behind the cactuses." Her smile was gentle, a homage. She grasped nothing of his anger. "But if you can't come, don't worry; I'll wait anyhow."

"Do what you want." His voice was savage. "I won't be coming." He kicked the pony into a sudden turn, spraying her with dirt as he took off across the field.

After practice, a picnic lunch was served in the meadow next to the polo field. The guests lounged on a brilliant patchwork of cloths and pillows on the grass while waiters in white jackets dispensed the generosity of the household. A flurry of sprouting champagne corks ruffled a flock of pheasants from their roost in the distant tall grasses; in pluming alarm, they streaked toward the woods.

Fabian sauntered away from the picnic, crossing the fragrant meadow. Flushed with champagne and the exertions of the morning, he stumbled slightly at a break in the ground. The meadow gave way to a stretch of cactus plants, and he carefully began to pick his way through the shaggy blanket of prickles. In the midday blaze, a cadaverous breath rose from the plants' spiny branches, their corpselike stems.

He came to the end of the cactus field and followed a narrow path that led him to a bower deep within a wooded thicket. There he saw the girl, framed in bramble. She was humming a song, waiting. When she saw him, she heaved herself up, pushing her way through a maze of wild hops.

"I knew you'd come," she said. "I just knew."

As her arms reached toward him, the heat thick about them, Fabian submitted to a tide of rage and shoved her away with such force that she fell backward, tumbling into a bed of blackthorn.

"Why did you do that, Fabian, why?" she asked, puzzled, without fear, clumsily getting up. "All I want is to see you. Please let me."

She was on her feet now, again moving toward him, her hair and jacket strewn with brambles and crushed white petals.

"You are going home!" he screamed. A bird, cawing, took flight at the echoing sound. The pitiful look of entreaty on her face, her stubbornness, enraged him more.

He began to hit her, the palm of his hand slapping one cheek, then the other, the back of his hand tearing across her face. He was screaming, "You're going home, you're going home." The girl swayed, her breasts pouring from side to side with each blow, then she stumbled to her knees, her eyes misted with tears. She covered her face with her hands. "But why, Fabian, why?" she moaned, unleashing another crest of fury within him.

Abruptly lucid, he stopped, drained, the rage spent. He raised a quivering hand to his parched mouth. Drawing breath in quick gasps, he looked down at her, prone at his feet, grass bending dreamily over her.

"Why, Fabian, why?" It was a whimper.

"Because I don't want you here. That's why! Do you understand?" Trembling, he tried to regain his steadiness. She rose slowly, small forking reeds sticking to her face.

"Without you, my life just isn't much," she mumbled through her tears.

"If it's not much without me, it's not much with me," Fabian said.

"All I want is to see you." The refrain was unrelenting. "To be near you, where you are. All I have is you."

As quickly as it had fled, the fury took him again. He grabbed the girl by her hair and, twisting her head, brought his face close to hers. Her hair was sweaty and matted in his hand, her pale, freckled skin already swelling from his blows.

"All I want is to see you, to be near you," he mimicked, her hair still clutched in one of his hands as the other ripped open her jacket, spilling her breasts. He went on, ripping the suspenders that held up her pants, then pulling at the pants until they fell in a heap about her ankles, revealing gray shorts underneath. "I'm not your TV, you can't turn me on when you want to!" he shouted, shoving her away. She tumbled, trying helplessly to stop her breasts from slapping about her rib cage, her fleshy thighs a rash of reddish insect bites. "Not your TV!" he screamed. "You have nothing but yourself," he went on shouting, "and do you ever think about yourself? See yourself? Listen to yourself? You haven't read one book, done one thing that would force you to find out what it is you want from life or what it is life still might give you." He could hear his voice raging in the silent grove. "You think of nothing, you see nothing, you understand nothing." He was breathless, but he went on. "You've got nothing to give, nothing to share. Your emotions are as crude as your body, your mind as slow as your ass, your life as empty as your feelings. Your TV deserves your company—I don't."

She sat up, turning toward him, brushing the grass from her face. "Maybe one day you won't mind me." He heard her burp suddenly, like a child.

" 'One day' is a long time away. Too long for me."

He started to move toward the path. She scrambled to her feet, hiking up her pants, her hair rumpled with the debris of the woods, her skin mottled and livid.

"I know you're alone, there's no one to look after you," she stammered. "I'll wait for you. I'll be here."

Thought abandoned him. He stopped at the edge of the grove, turned back and walked over to her. Seizing her shoulders, he began to shake her, her head careening, her eyes lifeless, her body pulpy, jerking, her breasts bobbing as if they would break loose from her body.

"Don't bother!" he screamed. "Don't bother to wait! I'll be on another channel!" He pushed her and saw her thud to the ground.

Sweat glazed his forehead and neck. Without feeling, his heart pounding, he looked at the blur that lay sprawled on the ground, snuffling and sobbing quietly into the grass. He leaned against a tree for support, his thoughts as shapeless and undefined as the girl on the grass.

He turned again into the forest, dragging greedily, in gasping relief, on the air that flowed back over him. He plunged along the narrow path, crushing berries beneath his feet, staining his boots, the tangled burrs and knifing weeds pulling at him.

Trembling still, he stopped every few moments to get his bearings, his mind a vortex of sensation: fury at the girl, a rankling resentment that he had succumbed to such a flood of obliterating vehemence. As he approached the cactus plants, a flock of birds broke cover, sallying back to the dense safety of the thicket. A brood of tiny plover, hovering, agitated, marked his passage through their covert.

At the guesthouse, Fabian found a note, from the divorcée, slipped under the door of his suite. She hoped that he might be free, after breakfast the following day, to instruct her in polo. He made himself a strong drink and ran a hot bath, savoring the promise and intimacy of the note. As his eyes returned to the fluent elegance of the note rustling between his fingers, Fabian resolved with a certain grim finality that, whatever he might lack in magnetism or glamour, in the resonance of family or name, in money or fame, he would never again permit himself to be made the puppet of a creature so maddeningly pathetic as that girl he had just left in the woods. After his bath, he fell asleep, and the lump of the girl kept slipping into his dreams of the divorcée. Drained by the incident in the forest, he slept all afternoon and had dinner in his room, then went back to bed.

The following morning he awoke alert, swept clean. In sanguine high spirits, he rose and dressed with meticulous care for his encounter with the divorcée. At the stables, he picked out a string of ponies for their stick-and-ball practice. He was just about to mount one of the ponies when he heard a man, scuttling along in an electric golf cart, calling out his name. Fabian, unable to place him securely in memory, stopped, with a vague tug of recollection. The man, nondescript in dress, left his cart and came toward Fabian, poised at his horse.

"Excuse me, sir. It was I who brought to you the young lady the other night," he explained, cap in hand, a touch of halting servility in his voice.

"Yes, you did indeed," Fabian said. He was convinced the man had come to announce her return. "Has she sent you to me again?" he asked coldly. He briskly checked the tension of the straps in the pony's bridle.

The man hesitated. He would not meet Fabian's eyes. "In a way, yes." His reply was a mumble.

"Then you can tell her I'm busy," Fabian said, vaulting onto his pony. He looked down from the saddle. "And that I won't see her." He pivoted his pony in front of the man as the animal frisked, eager to break away.

"I'm afraid I won't be able to do that," the man said, his voice firm.

"I think you will," Fabian insisted. "Just tell her I asked you to deliver that message."

His manner stern, the servant raised his eyes to Fabian. "That's a message I can't deliver," he said.

Fabian shifted uneasily in the saddle as the apprehension rose within him that the girl once again might ruin a tryst with the divorcée.

"All right, then," he said angrily. "Just tell me where I can find her."

The man lowered his gaze. "She is at the service gate," he said.

Fabian squeezed the pony with his legs and cantered off along the path that circled the stables, leading to the kitchen wing.

At the gate, he saw the morning sun blinking on chrome: two police cars, a huddle of black men and women about them. As he dismounted, faces turned toward him. He strode to the gate, noting almost mechanically the odd angle at which some of the field hands held their hats, as if in tribute. His eyes swept the crowd, grimly expecting the Canadian Mountie's hat. He finally saw it, settled neatly on a picket fence nearby. Then he saw the girl's familiar shape.

Heart pounding, his throat gone rigid, mouth caked, knees braced only by his boots, the polo mallet trembling in his grasp, he moved along the road toward the fence, toward her. The small crowd, silent, parted for him. From the boundary post that marked the limit of the fence, the girl's body swayed. He stared at the coarse, dun-colored rope that furrowed her neck, the thick wooden column climbing above her head, the empty fruit basket, yellowing straw, its load of grapefruit strewn about, kicked away when she did not want its support anymore. He saw the familiar jacket, its buttons ripped off, hanging open, the dull flesh of her breasts, her baggy pants, their suspenders drooping around her hips, the sandals, their straps cracking, their heels worn down.

His eyes returned to her face, which had been wrenched by the drag of the rope to one side, tilted upward, her mouth open, the tongue frozen upon a lip as if to cover a scar. A butterfly, a shimmer of amber, flickering, tremulous, hovered in descent on a glassy eye that could not blink it away, defenseless before the assaulting sun. He saw the marks and bruises his mauling hands had left on her cheeks, the scratches on her breasts, the reddish patch on her thigh.

A hand on his shoulder scalded him. He turned to face one of the policemen.

"We're told she came here to see you," the policeman said in a matter-of-fact voice as he gestured toward the body with an open notebook in his hand.

"That's what she told me," Fabian replied. He tried to measure his tone against the other man's.

"And what did you tell her?" the policeman asked.

"I told her," Fabian began to stammer, "I told her to go home."

The policeman looked up from his notebook. "What else did you tell her?"

"I told her—to leave me alone."

The policeman scribbled something in his notebook. "What else?"

"To leave me alone. Not to bother me anymore," Fabian said.

"That's all?"

"That's all." Fabian stood silent.

The policeman snapped shut his notebook. "I guess she took your advice," he said.

For a long time, Fabian had been in the habit of leafing through *The Saddle Bride,* a trade journal of the horse world that also chronicled the social milieus of tournament, turf, stable and show. Each month, he would examine the feature "Ladies of Horse: Who's Who Under Seventeen," columns between advertisements for riding apparel and gear, notices of forthcoming meets, trivia of the track. The glossy pages would slide through his fingers: photographs of young horsewomen—jumping, at the paddock, in full show regalia, in ball gowns or riding breeches—accompanied by brief accounts of their rich and usually prominent families, the medals and competitive standings the girls had received, their parties, their aspirations and engagements, their homes, the stables they frequented, their favorite mounts. Fabian would thoughtfully sift through an issue of *The Saddle Bride,* selecting young women, his intention to approach each subtly and to engage in an intimate partnership.

One summer, at the onset of school vacation, Fabian arrived in Shelbyville with a solitary polo pony in his VanHome's stall, a Morgan acquired for a third of its value because the brown stallion had no proof of ancestry. Fabian had been hired by a group of prominent Tennessee horse breeders to conduct a series of lectures for young teachers of horsemanship, in which he would explore developments and revivals in riding and jumping. He had accepted the job because, some months earlier, he had been drawn to a photograph of Stella, in *The Saddle Bride,* receiving her award as champion of the Plantation Pleasure competition; the caption went on to cite her accomplishments in numerous other amateur shows of the Walking Horse Breeders Association, as well as in the Breeder's Futurity event for young riders.

Anxious to meet her, Fabian telephoned Stella at the nearby boarding school from which she had just graduated with honors; he had read that she would be staying on there throughout the summer to continue training her horse, at a stable in the vicinity, for the annual Walking Horse Show. He invited her to attend his lecture series as his guest. She was hesitant at first, but finally consented. At his opening lecture, Fabian saw her slip in, alone, and sit on a bench at the back of the hall, apart from the others.

Stella was fashioned in the classic American mold, the pearly oval of her face lighted by topaz eyes, spaced wide, her blonde hair sweeping easily about her neck and brushing her sensually protrusive jaws. The high arch of her cheekbones framed a small nose, its tip flattened, and lips, oddly thick, in which Fabian caught a flicker of insolence. Yet he noticed as well her shyness, a holding back.

It was only after Fabian had spent several brief interludes with her, having coffee, discussing horses, that Stella began to warm to him, to speak of herself, of her family. Her parents had been divorced when she was still a child, and each had remarried. Far removed, to New York and New England, happy with a new wife, a new husband, preoccupied with the children of these unions, they had scant time for Stella, their first daughter, now grown, on the brink of womanhood.

Several days later, Stella invited Fabian to visit her at the stable where she kept her horse, Ebony's Ebony, her favorite possession.

Fabian found her dressed in a rough leather blouse, leather chaps sheathing her jeans, which stressed her well-defined, jutting buttocks. The tough, supple hide threw into sharp relief the fragile, lambent glow of her neck. She was trotting Ebony's Ebony around the paddock, carefully guiding the horse, the heavy chains attached to its forelegs—the action-inducing devices used in training gaited horses—clanging harshly.

Ebony's Ebony, a Tennessee Walking horse, was descended from the old plantation walking horse, which had carried planters and their overseers. Like most Southern owners of the breed, Stella kept the mare in constant training, refining and perfecting the horse's three gaits: a flat-footed walk, a fluid canter and the high-breaking running walk of four even beats, each foot striking the ground separately, that was its hallmark.

Fabian watched as Stella monitored the time and intervals of each of the horse's hoofs as it struck the ground beating out a diagonal sequence. Intermittently, the horse lost rhythm, breaking into a mosaic of disjointed fragments—its heaving chest and front strained to the running walk, its haunches, buckling under Stella, still at a trot, the extravagant licking of the forelegs hesitant and askew.

Discouraged, Stella dismounted and took the horse to her workroom, at the rear of the stable. Jars of ointment, lubricants, a gallery of weights, hoof wedges, pads and chains of every size and thickness, crowded its shelves. Stella guided Ebony's Ebony carefully to a space at the center of the room and, after tying the animal between two posts, she dismantled the armory of chains crusted around its forelegs. The horse, un-yoked, pawed the ground in quickening anticipation, heaving slightly, eyes alert.

Just above the hoofs of Ebony's Ebony, Fabian saw a mass of sores, some healing, others suppurating, striated, an inflamed cincture like a decoration around the horse's pasterns. Stella took a jar and a pair of rubber gloves from one of the shelves; hunching down, she began patiently to smear the ulcerated beds on the mare's forelegs with a viscous paste. She explained to Fabian that, like so many other owners of Tennessee Walkers, she was forming a "sore lick"—an open sore in the flesh that pressure from a chain or a weighted boot would keep raw and sensitive. To alleviate the pain, the horse was driven to distort its prance and spring, an alteration that permitted the animal to develop what its breeders claimed to be its predisposition for the running walk.

Stella went on explaining that most commercial preparations for such soring treatment did not satisfy her. Some were too potent and cauterizing, others too bland. Therefore, she had concocted her own blends of soring paste, ranging from one so volatile that it almost singed the flesh when crammed under the boots or chains just before or during a ride, to another so subtle that one could leave it on the horse's foreleg overnight or even for a day, confident that it would slowly raise the sore one desired. She hoped that all her efforts would be rewarded at summer's end, permitting her to qualify Ebony's Ebony for the National Celebration in

Shelbyville, the country's most spectacular exhibition of Tennessee Walking horses, and thus to transform Ebony's Ebony from a local blue-ribbon horse into a national prizewinner.

With each new layering of the paste, a quiver ran through Ebony's Ebony. Tied between the posts, the mare seemed locked between warring impulses: rebelling against this distortion of its being yet willing to bend to a plan beyond questioning. The animal seemed to sense that the treatment meted out to its legs was part of a larger, more intricate and subtle design—one in which reward or fault had no part—than the random, fleeting flick of a whip on its rump, or a spur's sudden nudge against its sides.

Stella entered upon a celebration of Ebony's Ebony. There was a lover's tenderness in her voice. "I used to watch Tennessee Walkers when I was a little girl. They have a harmony no other breed has." Ebony's Ebony shuddered slightly as Stella's gloved fingers smoothed the paste. She flexed the horse's foreleg for Fabian's inspection. Ebony's Ebony flinched, but Stella's grasp was confident, secure. She looked up at Fabian for a moment, her eyes innocent and serene, her neck velvety. "I like to think of Ebony's Ebony as my partner —all that power, yet without me the horse wouldn't be able to show what it can do," she said. She shifted around Ebony's Ebony to begin her labors on the other leg.

"To get the horse to do that running walk, that nodding of its head in rhythm, that big lick, aren't you crippling it?" Fabian asked.

She passed over his question with a smile. "Crippling? Its running walk is important—you can't get a horse to do a smoother gait!"

Fabian was unconvinced. "I've ridden horses in Latin America, the Paso Finos, that perform their inborn gaits without any training, with no special boots. If your Tennessee Walker has natural gaits, why do you have to sore its legs and force it to wear those boots and chains?"

Stella shrugged. "The natural tendency to do its

special gaits has to be brought out," she explained patiently. "It has to be shaped, improved, enhanced by training, just as you have to train a Thoroughbred, to bring out its potential for racing or jumping."

"To train, yes, but not by burning its flesh, by burdening it with weights and boots and chains!"

"It's not that different from what trainers do to other breeds." Stella's voice grew sharp, but she was still gentle as she smoothed soring paste on the horse's foreleg. "How much training does it take to get a Thoroughbred to strain beyond its limits on a race course? To leap over six-foot-high fences and seven-foot-wide triple bars at a jumping competition? Jumping isn't natural to a horse; even when it's hungry, it won't jump over a fence or a ditch to reach food." She glanced at Fabian with a look of mild irony.

"And what about that Morgan locked in your trailer? What did it have to endure to become fit for polo? And what does a polo pony go through during the game?"

"Leaping and chasing, the sheer spirit of running, are part of the horse's nature," Fabian said. "Sores and chains and boots aren't."

"Neither is the bridle or the whip, the spur or the saddle—even the rider," she flared back. Then she shifted into a new, soberly impersonal key. "I don't manipulate Ebony's Ebony into any tricks or stunts that nature didn't make possible in the first place. I merely guide the horse in discovering its essence. How can that possibly harm it?"

"Some time ago," Fabian said gently, "I was one of the members of the American Horse Protection Association who testified in Congress on behalf of the Horse Protection Act." Stella listened, her expression guarded, unchanging, as Fabian went on. "That act outlawed soring as well as overbooting. It prohibits the use of any substance or device for the purpose of affecting a horse's gaits. It also outlaws any practices that might cause the horse physical pain or distress or inflammation, or bring on lameness. What if Ebony's Ebony should be disqualified before the National Celebration because of what you've done to it—and what if the inspectors should prosecute you?"

Unperturbed, Stella stood up. "Ebony's Ebony is just one of thousands of Tennessee Walkers and American Saddle horses being trained. There are only about two dozen federal inspectors—they could hardly check the condition of every horse!"

"But do you want to break the law?"

"What law? That Horse Protection Act was put through by people who don't know anything about the South, anything about our Tennessee Walker. They still can't tell the difference between soring and lubricating, between padding and overbooting—so they want to ban it all!" Stella wiped paste from her gloved fingers as methodically as she had applied it to Ebony's Ebony.

"What if all this talk about the horse's essence is only a myth, just a convenient excuse to justify training practices that enable the animal to compete more strongly on the open market against other breeds, some of them better endowed by nature?" said Fabian, patting the horse on its muzzle. "What if what you do to these horses is just a derivative of what the Southern masters used to do to their slaves?"

Stella ripped off the gloves and tossed them into a corner. "That's nonsense," she said decisively. "Our horses are the result of careful breeding, and our training methods bring out inherited genetic characteristics that have been scientifically proven to exist. The Horse Protection Act threatens to make these Southern breeds extinct—to wipe out a whole industry. Hundreds of thousands of people who love, breed, trade and exhibit these horses, our whole way of life down here—all that would go."

She started to release Ebony's Ebony from the bonds that had immobilized it. "In any case," she said with a mischievous glance, "under that Horse Protection Act so dear to you, no incident of soring or overbooting has ever come to trial—and I kind of doubt that one ever will." She smiled at him guilelessly.

Ebony's Ebony champed and stretched in its new freedom. Fabian remained silent, and Stella, her tone casual, said that, after the National Celebration, she would attend a college in Kentucky. It was the only one in the country that allowed its students to major in horsemanship and stable management; she wanted to study new methods of training the Tennessee Walking horse.

There was a spirit and resolve in her manner that sharpened Fabian's interest. Yet simultaneously, the disquieting awareness came to him that he had not been able to break her equanimity, that without bolder action on his part during what remained of summer, he would soon be forced to relinquish Stella to the demands of her new calling. She had declined all invitations to visit him in his VanHome, resisted or averted his other solicitations to intimacy. Her privacy challenged him, piqued his curiosity to know whether she was involved with another man. The gathering force of his fascination drew him increasingly to the stable at which she worked.

Fabian wondered what means he would have to use to seduce Stella. The slightest details of her manner, her demeanor, the texture of her daily life possessed him. He watched for any sign of weakness, a rent in the fabric. He found none. Her ability to reconcile her love of Ebony's Ebony with the knowledge of the pain her training caused the animal only deepened her mystery for him.

He came to suspect that for Stella the simple act of sexual taking, the ruptured tissue, would mean less than her memory of the expectation of it. Before he could take her, she would have to imagine herself as his willing partner, she would have to prepare the path of her surrender to him. Once she had done this, she would be his whenever he wanted her.

And so, at a future time, if he wished to, he could return to her, the lover unannounced, and take her, a girl no longer, now a woman, perhaps engaged, perhaps married, perhaps bearing or having borne the children of another man. On that day, Fabian hoped to be paid in coinage that memory alone had minted, and only for him.

One morning at the stable, while Stella was fastening even more cumbersome chains to the horse's forelegs, Fabian, on an impulse, leaned over to assist her. His head, bending in the apparition of an embrace, brushed her hair.

At that moment, an old black man, one of the stable's hired hands, abruptly turned the corner of a stall and came upon them. The stable door slammed shut too late to announce his arrival. Startled, Fabian moved quickly away from Stella, disturbed at the invasion of their intimacy, reluctant to have his abortive embrace observed.

Wordless, unsmiling, the black man looked first at Fabian, then at Stella; his eyes rested on her a moment longer. Stella returned the black man's stare, the balance between them poised, their gaze an equation. Fabian, at Stella's side, felt a swift rush of instinct, like a horse vividly alert to a new reality. The space between Stella and the black man vibrated with her fright, glints of which showed in her eyes. The black man snapped the tension as abruptly as he had created it. Dropping his glance, pretending that he wanted something he could not find in the stable, he wandered about, then left. As the door closed behind him, Stella, her terror banished, turned calmly again to Ebony's Ebony and the weights. But she did not look at Fabian.

Later that day, lying in the alcove of his VanHome, Fabian played over and over in his mind the scene of Stella and the black man. It brought into focus several odd aspects of Stella's conduct. He remembered her discomfort before a group of black boys who watched from behind the stable fence when she rode Ebony's Ebony, her expression of love for the South and her hate of the ghetto-ridden North, her exaggerated air of the Southern belle. And there was her reluctance to discuss her parents, her cryptic remark that they were too involved with their respective second families to visit her at school.

The next day, after Stella had finished at the stable

and was about to board the school's minibus, to go back to her dormitory, Fabian offered to drive her there. She smiled but said she could not go with him.

"Why not?" he asked, stepping down from the door of his VanHome.

"I told you," she said, demurely polite. "You're just not my type. Not yet, anyhow." She turned away.

Fabian caught her arm. "Not your type?" he said. "Is it," he hesitated, "is it because I'm white?"

An invisible hand arrested her at half-turn. Suddenly a figure in a pantomime, she wheeled to face him. A dusky flush mounted her neck, stained her face. Against her suddenly swarthy skin, her eyes stood out in ghostly relief.

"I don't understand," she stammered, her gaze fixing him. "Why would I mind your being white?"

"You know why," Fabian said. He was convinced that he had arrived at the truth.

She swallowed rapidly, her throat pulsing. Adamant still, she held him off, a note of menace in her voice. "I don't know why."

"You do," Fabian said. "You do because even though everyone takes you for white, under that snowy skin, all that blonde, blonde hair, you're black, ebony black, just as black as Ebony's Ebony, that mare you love so much. Some people might call you a white Negress; other places, you'd be a beautiful albino. But you're a full-blooded black, Stella, as black as those parents of yours nobody's ever seen, as black as I imagine the rest of your whole family is, as black as that old man down in the stable. He knows it, and I know it."

She glanced around, panic in her movement and eyes at the danger of someone overhearing. Her teeth locked; for a moment she was beyond speech. Then she whispered, "Nobody knows it. Nobody. That old man just looks at me as if he knew something. He knows nothing. Nobody knows. Nobody."

"Let's go," Fabian said. "I'll walk you to the bus."

Stella looked at him, her lips tremulous. Her eyes

brimmed with tears. "I don't want to be alone," she said. "Can I stay with you for a while?" The tears spilled over, streaking her cheeks.

"You can. But whether you stay or you don't, what I know will stay with me. Only with me," he said, putting an arm around her.

Inside his VanHome her sobs relented, but Fabian was still aware of her punished eyes streaked with tears. In the few moments that had elapsed since Stella's acknowledgment, she had changed. Her aloof manner, the languid rise and fall of her speech, her gracious condescension had withered, dissolved. A wound had opened in their place; fear had yielded to sorrow, the newer vulnerability of her being.

"How did you find out?" she asked. Her question was a conspiracy. Slowly, uncertain, a wary child, she took his hand and clutched it in her lap. "Who told you?"

Fabian could feel the heat of her body through her skirt. "No one told me. I just sensed your fear. You were holding something back. Then I saw your face, what happened to you when that old black man looked at you."

"But I'm white." There was weariness in her voice. "My parents, all my kin are black. With my white skin, my hair and my eyes, there was no place for me in their world. I had to leave them, go somewhere where nobody could know who I was. No white person has ever guessed the truth before. How did you?"

"Maybe because as a child I too lived among people to whom I was an outcast," Fabian said. "And here I am, foreign born, still an outsider."

Stella continued to cling tightly to his hand. The flush had gone from her eyes; she looked down. "But until now, you didn't know I was black. Yet you were after me."

"I was drawn to you," Fabian said. "Now I want to know you even more."

Releasing his hand from her grip, he reached for her with both arms, his hands cradling her ribs, his thumbs deeply invading her breasts. Again a dusky blush suffused her face, spreading to her neck and shoulders. He released his grip on her and pulled her hair back from her face with one hand, exposing her forehead and ears, while gliding the rough skin of his other hand, in a mock threat, along her cheeks, then down, brushing her nipple more harshly than he intended. She recoiled, suddenly tense with alarm.

"Ever since my parents sent me away to live as white," she whispered, "I don't know who I am."

"Do you want to know?" Fabian asked.

"I do." Stella was silent, her arms locked across her breasts.

He dropped his hands to her hips and brought her closer. She swayed against his chest, chastened, broken and obedient, clinging to him. There was fear in the silent touch with which she brushed his lips. "I want to go through it with you," she whispered. "I am myself. Finally myself." She glanced about at the VanHome's interior, suddenly conscious of where she was and what enveloped her.

Fabian's VanHome now became the sanctuary for the rites of their intimacy. Stella entered an uncharted world of knowing and being known; with every step, with every movement, she retained the freedom to leave and return, to voyage at her will to an unmarked solitary goal or back to the point she had abandoned. Stella's freedom was the ground of Fabian's acts: without it, she would be but the captive of his will; with it, she was the captive of her own need. Silence was their sound, an echoless chamber. Gesture, touch, pressure, stroke composed their only language, a vocabulary of such variety and plenitude that it restored the dominion of a power usurped by speech. In their hours together, sensation was unsullied by thought, thought impervious to feeling.

In movement—an eye, his head, a hand, a foot—in gestures as simple as the flicking of a light switch, now on, now off, with the steady pressure of any part of his body, he would have her strip off an article of her dress.

Dressed or naked, or wearing only his riding boots, his spurs a steady threat to her skin, he would follow a sequence as incidental as each item of clothing itself. He might begin with a shoe or with her blouse; he would leave her clothed or in a state of partial undress. Sometimes he would start with her naked and then have her dress herself again; perhaps he would signal to her that she should stand or kneel or lie down—on the staircase, in the lounge, the alcove, the bathroom, the tack room, over the wooden horse, even next to his pony. He would keep her neither bent nor straight, here supple, there braced, perhaps seated, lying, her suspension between those states only another state, to last as long as he would not alter it.

He would bring his hand to her face time and again, pausing to offer the moment of aversion, of election, and when she did not seize it, again use that hand, then stop, then continue using it, perhaps on one side only or alternating side to side, until her submission would overwhelm her. He would stop then and bring her back to the present by grasping her hair, letting her head drop low between her knees. When she looked up at him, her head at his arm's length, he read in her gaze that she had reclaimed awareness of her self.

He might give notice that he was uncertain whether to stay with the surfaces of her, watching the scoring of his hands, his teeth, his feet, on the landscape of her body, the mutations imposed by the strategies of his hip, a knee, sometimes a shoulder. When her movement or expression declined to reveal what inhabited her most inward self, he would elect to thrust within her, in quest of that withheld annunciation. He might guide her, his knee or spur the goad, to a corner, steadying and bracing her against a pole or a shelf, the burden of him heavy on her until, pressed to the last border, she would go limp, undone, in readiness for the moment when she would regain awareness by herself or he would choose to breathe it into her; it might pass that, at her first deep heave of renewal, that first lolling nod, he would continue with her as he had begun.

He might employ her face, clasped between her thighs, his knees a weight upon her hair, as yet another neutral pad of flesh, another buttock or hip, without reflex of its own; or he might squat downward along her body finally quiescent, her head mobile, her face watchful.

Sometimes, under his grip, a realm of her body would take on a darkening hue, bluish, then a sullen red. He saw in these the emblems of the fusion of their entities, as he did in another response to his touch: that moment, flowing in slow motion, when blood would seep through the skin that had split open at his stroke, the touch of his spur, and, hesitant, would trickle earthward through the folds of her flesh. In such stigmata he read her response to him.

He might have her with her eyes closed, as if in darkness, or staring at him or at the wall, through the window or at the clustered thickets steeped in the murky fog of a summer evening. Perhaps he would permit her to know that she was the object of his gaze; or, contemplating her without her knowledge or the complicity of her eyes, as trapped by her blindness as she by his stare, he would give himself to be tasted, or he would taste her, or he would have her taste herself at his mouth.

Sometimes, when he was with her, when she expected to be taken to the alcove or to leave it, perhaps even in the act of having her there, he would rise and motion for her to follow him. In silence, he would lead her to the stall with the horse in it. There, simply, wordlessly, he would gesture toward a pile of magazines, glossy, profuse in their graphic visual and verbal celebration of the erotic pleasures of the saddle and the mount, their pages curling in the humidity given off by the hay and the horse.

She would move toward the magazines, hesitant, as if once she went, there were no retreat. She would pause before them, then select one at random, a ticket to a lottery she had elected to play. Resting against the shelves, she would start to turn the pages, rapidly at first, as if eager to know in advance what were the stakes in her lottery, then slowly, deliberately returning to the page that had first compelled her. Undistracted, her eyes intent on a drawing or a photograph, she would examine it as if detained by what she recognized as her own or captivated by what she had never yet seen or imagined. She would linger over a fragment of text, then turn the damp page, then return to it, as if to verify that she remembered all that had streamed before her eyes.

He waited for her, the chambered silence of the stall breached only by the noises of the horse, its warm, gusting breath, one hoof pawing impatiently, overstepping the other, a sudden bristling as it tugged at the rope that bound its collar to a ring fixed in the wall.

She would lay the magazine aside, her eyes averted, her posture a signal that she was now accessible, no movement too ungainly, no region too confining to restrict her freedom to offer herself.

There were now the three of them, a stall their bed. The animal that had come between the man and the woman was no longer excluded, the bareness of their bodies made each of them aware that the animal was always naked, muzzle and flanks, haunches and loins, the heat of its parts without disguise, always present to smell and sight and touch.

Stella would lean against the metal hayrack, its rails imprinting her thighs, her arms limp, her hands dangling on the rack, her fingers uncoiled, a sign that she would not clasp it if asked to step away.

He would then reach for her and, guiding her gently by her hair, as if deferring the touch of her skin, move her next to the animal. The surfaces met: one white, dry, smooth and cool, the other dark, hairy, moist with heat. The woman's hair would ripple over her shoulders, drift onto the neck of the horse, blend with its mane.

He would brace her back against the animal's ribs, ranging her arms along them, shoulder to hip; her head would rest between withers and loins, at the place where the saddle lies, and his body would press on hers, the horse laving her with its heat; he would guide her slowly toward the croup, her arms down, her head grazing the animal's hip, her back molded by its flank, supported by it; he would lean into her, spreading her against the hind leg, the hock rough, the bone a constant menace, his knee tracing the frame of her thighs, feeling her flesh open and moist.

He would then move her behind the horse, her face toward its croup, her arms on its flanks, her hands stretched out toward the mane, the animal's tail a shawl draping her breast and belly, flowing smoothly between her thighs, fusing with her own hair. His weight impelling her forward, framing her around the animal's rear, he would take her from behind, the stallion patient and still, a silent partner in their silent play.

Slowly then, he would fit her and hold her beneath the animal, its eyes turning to survey the woman who, trusting its shape, curved under and submitted to the hulk of its body, her face fronting its flanks, where she would remain, tucked and coiled between its forelegs and hocks, its chest a humid dome to the breathing cavern. To Fabian, the horse was no longer a thing apart, a wall of heat to thrust against, but another region of his own being.

At times, when she could no longer master herself, her body arching, the silence ruptured by the chiming within her of a remote moan mounting to a shriek that might become a word, a scream that might break into speech, he would gently pull her forth from under the animal. As the horse, surprised at the fountain of warmth suddenly withdrawn, bent its head again to look at the two of them, Fabian would bring her to her feet. Steadying her, he would guide her past the pony, out of the heat of the stall, through the passage to the tack room. There it was cool, the pungent musk of leather, rope and metal stinging the air.

To prepare an arena for Stella and himself, he

would push back to the wall the revolving rack, its arms weighted with saddles heaped on each other like dead birds, their denuded wings forlornly down. A swarm of bridles and webs, of headstalls, cheekpieces, throatlatches waited in the corners of the room. On the open floor, he would throw pads of felt and saddle blankets plush with mohair, then lower her onto them, her body unresisting, falling as if into a shoreless pool. Near her feet, a welter of nosebands and reins spilled and jutted like the roots, suddenly bare, of a huge, stricken tree. Above her, trays mounted the wall, their overflow a shimmer of bits and metal equipage, snaffles, curbs, rein loops and mouthpieces, alien jewelry of stud and mare. From hooks on another wall, stirrup straps and girths, collars, breastplates, martingales and halters were coiled like snakes frozen in their twining. In the stillness, she seemed at one with these objects, but made of a more lustrous and pliant substance.

Careful not to bruise her skin or jar the articulation of her body, he would match her hands and shoulders, her wrists, her ankles, knees, hips, to some of those objects that, in their variety of forms, seemed to have been contrived just for her; one by one, he would place them upon her, harnessing and rigging her with them, fastening, tightening, knotting and buckling, rope and mesh and coil, until she was made taut, yoked and girdled, a swaddling of metal, leather, hemp, no limb unchecked in whatever impulse might stir it to reclaim a power of movement she had surrendered, none exempt from restraint that might upset her composure. He would, at times, bind her with straps to a saddle, the softest he owned, her thighs forked over it, its seat sealing her from him, her feet in stirrups bound together beneath the saddle, her hands tied to the stirrups, her position forcing her breasts down, to divide over the seat's pommel, inclining her head forward over her knees, in a bow. He would then harness her with a breast collar, compressing her breasts until the narrow neck strap slipped to fit over her head; then he would run the girth in a noose over her neck, cinching it tight under the saddle, bringing her face down over one knee, blocking access to her mouth. Lying on her side, bound to herself, she was sealed from him, and he would drape her with a large woolen blanket, to keep her warm.

He would leave her in the tack room, making his way to the alcove or the lounge, where he would wait, permitting her time for the lulling of her own thought, free from his touch.

Sometime later, he would come back. He would expose her and with deliberation commence the ceremony of unbridling her, releasing, in a sequence of disburdenment, the grip of straps, loops, bands, the truss of latches, girths, halters, thongs, reins, unshackling them, discarding them, until she lay before him as nude, as unadorned as when he had brought her there from the stall.

Now free to move, she could not. Her body, joint and nerve and muscle, still felt the harness. As though bound, she would remain constricted, her head down, her thighs straddling the saddle, her breasts smothered by it. Slowly he would wedge himself behind her in the saddle, pushing it down as he took her onto himself, keeping her taut, without flex.

To invade her, he would stretch her flesh, pulling on it, squeezing it with all his strength, biting into it. To probe her, he laid her down, then raised her; brought her belly, then her rump to face him; wheeled her about so swiftly that when he halted her she would not know; twisted her so slowly that she thought he had stopped though he still turned her; braced her ever tighter, denying limit beyond limit, pushing her further, coming at her from above, rising toward her from below.

Sometimes, the tide of challenge would rise within her, and she would shift. Accepting the challenge, he would refuse to blindfold her, permitting the weight of her stare upon him to track his every move, to measure the density and conviction of his zeal, the cycles of his will, the nature of his want. Her eyes, steadfast, announced the fullness of her compliance with his design, her surrender of still another zone of her being to his appropriation.

Each time Stella left the VanHome, on her own, her clothes masking discolored skin, or weak and wasted, aided by Fabian—who would dress her and drive her, in silence, to her dormitory—Fabian wondered whether she would return. She always did.

Ebony's Ebony failed to qualify for the National Celebration. Disenchanted and depressed, Stella was inconsolable; just before her departure for college she put the mare up for sale at a large public auction. For Stella, to be rebuffed at the celebration was painful enough, and to part with her mare the final anguish: she stayed away from the auction. But Fabian went and, by bartering his Morgan, and with the money saved from Eugene Stanhope's gift, as well as from various one-on-one encounters, was able to outbid all others for Ebony's Ebony, acquiring, also, another loser, the five-gaited American Saddle horse, celebrated for its amble, a broken slow pace, as well as for its rack, a very fast, evenly spaced one. After collecting the money for her horse, Stella saw Fabian in his VanHome one last time, their parting as silent as all their meetings.

Within months, Fabian, now owner of his own portable stable and ready for classes and demonstrations in equitation, had succeeded in retraining both mares for polo. He decided to rechristen them, and they went with him from that time on as Big Lick and Gaited Amble.

A few years later, a Kentucky stable owner who had known Stella told Fabian that after graduation from college she had married. Her husband was a young black lawyer; once a civil-rights activist, he was now a member of a prominent Washington law firm. The couple did not have children.

Soon afterward, Fabian, driving across Virginia, found himself within a few hours of Washington. He thought of Stella, and he called her. She was surprised to hear from him and asked about Ebony's Ebony. Then she invited Fabian to come by and meet her husband.

Fabian arrived in Washington the next day, at mid-morning. The city bustled with expectation; his Van-Home, patiently navigating its course through the packed streets, was surrounded by a small flotilla of cars and buses with license plates from every state in the union. Tourists paraded at leisure, cameras hanging from their necks, guidebooks in their hands. He passed the East Potomac Park, a polo field favorite with the diplomatic corps and the scene of many one-on-one encounters from his past. As he approached the White House, his VanHome ground heavily to a stop in traffic. A dozen cars flanked both sides of the street, their roof lights wheeling and blinking.

In Lafayette Park, fronting the White House, was a colony of Indian tepees, wigwams by the hundred, their pyramids of hide, vivid paint and leather thongs incongruous in the official city. Fabian gathered from signs and banners fluttering from their crests that they had been erected as part of a demonstration, the Longest Walk, a coalition of American Indian tribes that had been descending on Washington for the last several days. He had inadvertently timed his arrival to coincide with the peaceable uprising of the first Americans.

Many of the Indians he saw were old, but just as many led or carried small children. They were holding up posters and signs denouncing legislation enacted against them by a Congress of white men; they demanded an end to a program for sterilization of Indian women supported by federal funds; they insisted on compensation for land they claimed had been illegally taken from them by the United States government.

From his cab high above the roofs of other cars, Fabian could tell that a vanguard of Indians, mostly young and boisterous, must have come too close to the gates of the White House. They were soon face to face with a solid wall of heavily armed riot police.

The police made the first move, rushing forward, their clubs in full swing. The Indians swayed under the assault, but stood their ground; then, propelled by the crowd behind them, they reluctantly started to forge ahead. The police, fearful, intensified their violence, and the first Indians fell to the ground under their clubs. The heaving tide pressed on, a rush of feathers and motley blankets, some faces streaked and splashed with dye, the honking of cars punctuated with the screams and howls of those beaten and those in danger of being trampled. A woman, the blood on her face almost indistinguishable from its paint, raised her squalling baby above the crowd; arms reached out for it, receiving it, passing the live parcel from hand to hand. Others followed, children swept along by raised hands and arms, toward the refuge of the tepees and wigwams.

Stella and her husband lived in a comfortable apartment in a sprawling complex. When she opened the door, Fabian saw a figure that was less girlish than the one he had known so intimately, her beauty fuller, more womanly, graceful. Stella's husband was a handsome young man of easy manner, with the brisk air of one on the move.

Over drinks, Stella recalled various amusing incidents from the time when she was at school and went to Fabian's lectures. Fabian discerned nothing unusual in the pleasant interest of her husband's response.

The three of them dined together that night. Stella's husband mentioned that he had to leave the next morning on a business trip to New York, and that from there he was scheduled to fly directly to Europe for a week. In his presence, Stella asked Fabian whether he could stay in Washington for a day or two. She was anxious, she said, to help him find a stable around Washington where he could exercise his ponies; she wanted to ride Ebony's Ebony again. When Stella's husband joined her in the invitation, Fabian decided to stay.

On the following day, diffidently, with a vague rustle of curiosity, Fabian went to see Stella. He did not know what to expect; nothing in her manner, no inflection of her voice, no inclination of her body betrayed the memory of what once had taken place between the two of them.

She greeted him alone. A thickly embroidered caftan covered her from neck to ankle. She served coffee, mentioning, as if in confirmation, that her husband had left as scheduled; she was glad, she said, to be with Fabian again, but she spoke in a tone so empty of feeling, of emotion, that Fabian, startled, looked up to catch her expression. She was staring at him as she had during that summer, each time she was about to enter his VanHome, in her eyes that onslaught of feeling that he had once come to know. She was still waiting for a sign, in its absence unwilling to take one step toward him or to move away.

Fabian did not ask; he got up and walked slowly across the living room, to the bedroom. The thick carpet muffled his steps—and those of Stella, following in his wake.

He closed the bedroom door behind them. The shutters were drawn, the faint attempts of morning light defeated by the darkened chamber. He sat down on Stella's bed, recalling the bed in his VanHome and the rites enacted there. In wonder at the laws of darkness that kept their sway over him and Stella, he began to undress. Stella stood motionless, awaiting his signal; Fabian gave it with one hand. As if heaved on a reef, she foundered, sinking in a smooth, unraveling curve to his feet. Another sign, and she uncoiled, the brilliance of the caftan, a tapestry of snakes and leaves and birds, spilling onto the carpet. Once more, a sign.

He looked for a note of hesitation, but time had not
eroded the meaning of his gesture. It came to him
vividly that he must know how far she would go with
him; he remembered too well that the brand of his
hands, of his body upon her skin had marked her for
days; only with time had the marks disappeared. She
was free to act however she chose; he would no more
curtail her than he would impose a restraint upon
himself.

After a long while Fabian heard a sound, a man's
voice, strong, buoyant, carrying. A moment later, Stella heard it too. "It's me, honey! Had to come back!"
The space of the room contracted as Stella rushed to
the door—her first movement not governed by a sign
from Fabian—but before she reached it, her husband's
figure filled the space.

Framed in the light of the hallway, he fumbled at
the wall and turned on the switch. "Stella, are you
here?" he asked, just as his eyes, blinking in the rush
of brightness, wandered across the savaged field of the
room. He saw Fabian standing by the bed; then his
glance slid to the pillows and sheets. He turned finally
to Stella, his eyes stopping at her breasts, belly, thighs,
gliding over the patches of blue, the freshets of wetness
that were too recent to have dried. In an unbroken
stare he took in the man and the woman, then he left
as quickly as he had appeared.

In his permanent state of transience, Fabian rarely
quit his mobile world for the confinements of a room
or house, places that made him feel disembodied, a
pony without a field. With no address or family ties, he
was accessible only by chance or when he initiated the
connection: to renew a friendship, to bridge an absence, he had to make the first move.

He could not recollect, then, whether it was at a
polo tournament or at one of the horse shows he

occasionally scouted that he heard that Stella's husband had divorced her and that she had moved to Totemfield, in Arkansas. She had not remarried, the report went, but with the money from her divorce settlement had taken over an old, dilapidated stable, the Double Bridle, where some years before Fabian had given a series of riding classes. Fabian remembered having told her about the place, urging her to visit it.

In his roamings, Fabian lost track of her again; and now, in her presence, he felt the unmoored weariness of the void, the fugitive, the revenant.

He stared at her across the shabby, cluttered desk. There was Stella, whose every apparition, on the field or the trail, in the paddock or a coffee shop, and, finally, in the wordless chamber of his VanHome, had once roused in him an anguish, a surge of possession that shorted out the steady currents of pleasure and pain. He was left with a rush of slipping images from the past; his imagination declined to conjure new ones.

Waiting, Stella returned his scrutiny. He avoided the conventional inquiries. "Would you have anything for me to do here?" he asked in a low voice.

"How about reading a book?"

Without shifting her gaze from him, Stella pointed at a shelf heaped with books on horsemanship that she used for her riding classes. Fabian got up and went to the shelf, to look at the books. The glossy jackets of the three he pulled out—his—were hardly thumbed.

"Down here they don't buy your books," Stella said. "They complain there are no pictures, not even drawings. And they get upset by what you write about riding."

Fabian shrugged. He wrote only about what seemed to him self-evident, yet always he found himself having to defend his books.

"Why don't you write something easier to take?" she continued. "Why bring up all those accidents, those traumas?"

"Because horses are not living-room pets, Stella, as

smart as cats or as faithful as dogs. Sports on horse-back are dangerous. You and I and a lot of horse people know that. But many don't, and many get injured or crippled or killed."

"Well, they still won't read your books."

"So what? Neither will eight hundred million Chinese. Still, what I know about riding is the only truth I feel I must share." Abruptly Fabian replaced the books on the shelf, ready to change the subject.

"How do you make a living these days?"

"Certainly not from my books. That's why I need a job. Would you have one for me?"

Stella fidgeted. "Not really," she sighed. "Totemfield is not what it used to be when you taught here. Breeding and showing Tennessee Walkers and Saddle horses is all big business now—too late for me to catch up." She glanced around the walls of her office. "This place will probably fall apart soon."

She saw that she made him uncomfortable. "But don't worry," she said, smiling. "It's all set for you. On weekday mornings you can have the whole field and our arena for stick-and-ball and a little jumping to keep yourself and your ponies in shape." She paused. "But make sure the ball doesn't hit the windows, or you the dust." She looked at her calendar as if recalling something that had troubled her.

Fabian was aware that they were marking time. He sat down, waiting for her to allude to their past mute sharing, but she did not. Nor did she speak of her life in Washington that had ended so abruptly.

"What kind of job do you have in mind?" she asked.

He stretched in the chair. "Well, maybe teaching a rich Southern kid a little polo?"

She looked at him in mock surprise. "Polo? In Totemfield? This is our fabled Old South, Fabian. This is where your gaited horses come from!"

"Anybody can ride a gaited horse, but they have to learn polo."

"If they're rich, they learn it at Retama Polo Center,

Boca Raton, Oak Brook, Fairfield, anywhere but here."

"Then, could you fix me up with a one-on-one polo match?"

"One-on-one?"

"Not so long ago, polo used to be played one-on-one. Now, it's a rodeo of the rich. How do you think I make a living these days?"

"I didn't know rich people still played games like that." There was a break in Stella's composure.

"Maybe they don't. But I do."

"Why would anybody rich want to play one-on-one polo with you?" she asked.

"Why do the rich play anything? For fun, for money, to show off."

She continued to bait him. "Around here, polo isn't exactly a big deal, you know. At your age, neither are you. Why don't you switch to golf—polo without a pony? Or, how about bicycle-polo? Or, better yet, water-polo—just to keep you afloat?"

There was a time when *Polo Magazine* had called Fabian a low-flying, self-created centaur, whose polo playing had become better known than that of any other player in American history, and when *Equus*, the nation's best horse magazine, praised him as a philosopher-polo player whose books did not permit the reader to sentimentalize the experience of horsemanship. But now, only a decade later, no hardcover bookstore ever carried more than one or two copies of each of Fabian's books, few of which, he discovered to his sorrow whenever he stopped in a city or large town, ever seemed to sell. When at times he had questioned the managers of bookstores about his slow sales, they replied with some hesitation that what the general public seemed to want on the subject of horsemanship were illustrated guides to riding, books that portrayed it as an easy diversion, as fun; what the public did not seem to want were reflections on the state of equitation, without illustrations or photographs. Fabian's books failed as mass-market tributes to the pleasures and rewards of riding.

Because he mistrusted pictorial representation, Fabian would not permit his publishers to include illustrations in his books. He felt that an excessive appeal to the sense of sight was insidious and debilitating, a specious claim to the reproduction of the world as it really was. He resisted the lulling implication that knowledge was above all what was to be seen, and refused the passive luxury of the spectator's chair, the flattening of reality, time arrested in one angle of vision. He suspected that to submit to that vision would be to clog the active play of images that were fluent and mobile within each person, fantasy and emotion that written language alone could quicken.

The Runaway, Fabian's first book, concentrated on the trauma an accident had on riders, and it won particular praise, even though it disturbed many critics and book reviewers by what they labeled as Fabian's mistrust of the established principles of horsemanship. *Obstacles* was his second work, a detached rehearsal of the still more complex variety of potential mishaps that might ensue within the riding arena. The audacity of its technique was widely acclaimed, and even though *Obstacles* was singled out for the prestigious National Horse Lovers Award, the book further alienated a large number of critics, who chose to ignore the wisdom of its warnings to unseasoned riders, electing instead to warn unseasoned readers of the unwisdom of exposing themselves to such a foreboding book. The pattern continued with his subsequent books, the critics disowning his conception of the equestrian art as too bleak, a brutal excess of case histories written by a man without generosity, with a splinter of ice in his heart.

One bookstore owner, an educated man and a fine rider, who counted himself among Fabian's fans, had been particularly upset by the failure of Fabian's books to attract a larger readership. While passing through town one day, Fabian stopped by the store to see him and to inquire how *Prone to Fall*, his latest book, was selling. As Fabian entered the store, he noticed a handsome, well-dressed woman in her thirties who was preparing to pay for two books she had selected; *Prone to Fall* was one of the two.

At the sight of Fabian, the owner lighted up, happy that, for once, the sale of a book by one of his favorite authors would take place in front of the author himself. Quivering with pleasure at such a coincidence, expanding with smiling grace, the owner bent deferentially toward the woman just as she set both books before him.

"Forgive me, madam," he began, and when she raised her eyes quizzically, he flourished a hand at Fabian. "This gentleman is Mr. Fabian, the author of one of the books that you're buying." He lifted *Prone to Fall* from the counter, turning it over, a precious stone offered for her scrutiny, and triumphantly revealed the photograph of Fabian on the book's reverse.

"That's Mr. Fabian, the author himself," he repeated, waiting for her to rejoice with him in this favor of chance. Her calm unruffled, the woman raised her eyes from the photograph to look at Fabian. Her glance rested on him a moment, returned once more to his photograph on the book, then rose again to his face. The owner still hovered, his face a flowering smile, anticipating her admiration.

"I don't think I'll take this one," the woman said, evenly meeting the owner's astonished gaze as she decisively set Fabian's book to one side. There was no discourtesy in her manner, no attempt to offend. The owner was stunned. He began to stammer, unable to release his distress in words. Fabian quieted him with a gesture. Unperturbed, the incident behind her, the woman paid for the other book and, with a slight nod of farewell addressed to both men, left the shop.

Fabian did not look at Stella as he spoke, fixing his gaze instead on a large wall poster of the Tennessee Walking horse, a kind of scientific diagram of variations in the skeletal measurement and angles of articulation in the breed. From the web of captions he gathered the poster sought to prove that anatomy enabled the Tennessee Walker to perform the running walk.

He turned to confront Stella directly. "I need a job," he repeated sharply, almost urgently.

"You're supposed to be the one with the connections," she said. Then, softening: "What about that rich polo-playing friend of yours—what was his name? The one who helped you to get your VanHome."

Fabian shifted his eyes to the diagram of the Tennessee Walking horse. "Stanhope," he said curtly. "Eugene Stanhope. He died in an accident." His tone closed the subject.

"Stanhope." Stella was unwilling to abandon it. "Stanhope, Stanhope," she murmured, tapping the desk pensively. Then she cocked her head almost provocatively. "I think I may have a little job for you."

"How little?"

"One of our riding students, Betsy Weirstone, is giving a party tonight for Vanessa Stanhope, one of her boarding-school friends. Would Vanessa be related to that Eugene?"

Fabian gave no sign that he knew Vanessa. "I don't know. There are a lot of Stanhopes all over the place." He steered her back to the goal. "Do I get to go to this party?"

"Not quite. But you can be part of the fun."

"How?"

"Betsy is planning a surprise for the evening. She wants a mysterious stranger, dressed in white and on a white horse, to appear unannounced at twilight on the lawn in front of her house. Vanessa and all the other guests will already be there, nobody expecting anything. My helper, Tommy, was supposed to play this masked rider, but his wife is sick and he can't make it."

"What else?" Fabian was guarded, noncommittal.

"I'll give you Trekky, our white Paso Fino. It was a police parade horse before I bought it." Stella hesitated, looking at him with no trace of emotion. "You used to be fond of Pasos, of their inborn gaits that never call for any training." She checked the fragment of her memory, then went on. "First, you'll circle in the shadows. Then you'll ride closer, let Trekky show off its classy gaits, then gallop toward the crowd of guests, stop just short of them, rise in your saddle to salute Vanessa, your beloved Dulcinea, the belle of the night, and—gently—throw a rose at her."

She gave him an appraising glance. "White will suit you fine. I've already gotten all the stuff from a school theater here. White pants, a cape, a golden mask, a hat with a plume, a sword, boots, gloves—you name it. You'll be the real thing, Fabian—a knight errant on your Rocinante." She was provoked out of her usual impassivity into an indulgent laughter.

Fabian ignored her laughter. "I'll do it. In return, you'll have my horses groomed and fed. Tomorrow morning I'd like to give them a workout in the paddock."

She looked at the clock and got up. "Get yourself some rest and be ready by seven, all in white. I'll be there on the dot with Trekky."

Back in his VanHome, he opened the case Stella had given him, the costume for his night ride. A tumble of white spilled out, the pungent sting of camphor and bleach flooding the alcove. He fondled the oversized gauntlets, the boots of soft white leather, the cape which swung in a bold flare; they showed no signs of wear. The plume in the tricorne was a shade scrawny, hanging limply as he cocked the hat in front of a mirror. He laid the costume out, an array of white, on one side of his bed, and stretched out on the other, finally free to think of Vanessa.

Pain raked across his shoulders, near his neck—a strained muscle or a warning of arthritis.

At the time Fabian had begun to teach at the Double Bridle Stables, he was invited to deliver a lecture on horsemanship at the private school Vanessa Stanhope then attended. The headmistress, an older woman he had seen occasionally among the spectators watching dressage or jump sessions, greeted him on arrival, flanked by student representatives of the lecture committee, Vanessa among them. He noted that Vanessa's school uniform, a blazer and pleated skirt, concealed the shape of her body, a body he knew well. In his role as her riding instructor, he greeted her; in her role as his pupil, she answered, astonishing him with her poise, with her ability to hide how well the two of them had already known one another. He was reminded again sharply of Vanessa's age, and of his, as he watched her among other girls of her own time and place, the sound and freshness of their laughter engulfing him as they took him on an impromptu tour of the school.

They paused at one classroom, where an instructor was showing a film on biology. Fabian observed the serenity and knowingness on the faces of the girls as the screen disclosed a sequence of images of life's processes: lovers linking hands, a kiss, an embrace, then the unstoppable flow of embryo and fetus and birth.

The tour continued, and Fabian passed the school's video center—banked with rows of television sets and screens, film and television cameras, monitoring instruments—then another room, dense with computers, a gleaming arsenal of technology, behind each computer a girl sometimes half Vanessa's age. His tour guides in knee socks spoke easily to him about a computer's retrieval system.

He had pondered often what it was that separated him, a man already in the middle of his life, from these girls, and why the conventional barriers of time and age and physical strength seemed to play so negligible a role either in the initial attraction or ultimately in the impassable gulf he knew to exist.

Certainly, he was aware of the superior stamina and resilience of these young women, their capacity to ignore fatigue, to function with little rest or sleep, to thrive on indifferent food—all powers he could not hope to match, yet in his relation with them of no particular consequence. He enjoyed seeing the unmarred freshness of even the simplest girl's face, her lithe and supple body, the tautness of her skin when contrasted with his own condition, the proof of his mortality. He regarded the qualities of youth merely as signs and symbols, even symptoms, of life as a spectacle of beauty and not as a venture in experience and knowledge. But still, beautiful or not, the girl to whom he chose to offer the intimacy of his VanHome usually held a view of herself, of him, of the two of them in the world, a view that was essentially at one with his own, a sensitivity and perception agreeable to his. What, then, determined the gulf in these attractions— of what was the barrier composed?

Fabian thought that it was memory.

When he contemplated his past, scanned or traveled its corridors, each emerging from an interval of years, even decades, he saw not one fixed and continuous being, but multiple selves, skins that he had shed, phases of the body and the mind now exhausted, abandoned, though alive in memory. His past, then, was a storehouse of what had chastened, enhanced or maimed him while he was in the process of living it.

What eluded him was his childhood. Memory faltered there, the storehouse plundered. He saw only a sequence of fading cameos of himself as a child, without connection to his present reality, snapshots in a stranger's family album.

When reaching to her own past, however, Vanessa or any other girl who was once Fabian's youthful companion could confront only one form of her past: the pristine image of herself as a child. Her present with Fabian was the only adulthood she had ever known.

He got up and prepared for his new adventure, shaving, showering. The tunic, cinched with a golden belt, fitted him well; the breeches were perhaps a bit tight; the boots a trifle loose. With a rakish swagger, he hiked the cape over his shoulders. In full costume, he took his measure in the mirror: the radiant horseman amused him. All in white, he seemed younger, the hat's enormous brim shadowing his face, the sword completing the image of a swashbuckler.

Stella drove up to his VanHome and honked twice. He stepped out into the dwindling afternoon, hoping that no one would see him. He climbed up beside her in the trailer's cab and eased himself into the seat, careful not to wrinkle his costume.

"Not bad," Stella said. "If I met you at night on a lonely road, I guess I could fall for you." A rose wrapped in cellophane lay between them on the seat. From the partition behind them, the horse snorted in its stall.

"Is Trekky as ready for the show as I am?" he asked.

"All white, ready and eager."

Stella drove the trailer onto the highway and threw him a searching glance. "We'll stop behind the fence," she said. "Just before the guests go inside to dinner, Betsy will change from rock to country music. That's your signal, and you'll start out on Trekky, swirling your cape around, but still keeping to the bushes. Then the music will change to Chopin, and as the Chopin plays, you approach the lawn at a gallop, you stop, salute, and throw the rose to Vanessa—and make sure she can catch it!"

"How will I know her?" he asked, attempting to sound offhand.

"She'll be the tall one, all in white, just like you. Slender, but with that luscious hair men love! You can't miss her. After she gets her rose, you salute again and, mysterious stranger that you are, you disappear into the night, never to return to her again. That means you'll deliver yourself and Trekky back to me."

"That's it?"

"That's it. I'll take Trekky home and on the way drop you at your pony express."

They swerved onto the country road, and Stella gradually slowed the trailer to a more stately, deliberate pace, as if in homage to the princely houses and estates guarded behind moats of trees and plush, clipped shrubbery. The road was narrowing to a dead end when Stella pulled to the side and switched off the engine. They had been driving for barely ten minutes.

"Here we are," she said. "You can get a peek at the house from here if the fence isn't too high."

Fabian stepped down from the cab. Twilight hovered, a slight chill brushed the air, dew lapped the ground. Moving cautiously so as not to snag his clothes on the underbrush, he slipped through the trees until the house stood revealed before him.

It was a sprawling place, the windows great sheets of glass, with terraces stacked on every level. Clusters of guests of every age—Fabian thought there must be about a hundred—were drinking and talking on the front lawn, a few dancing to the throb of rock music.

Stella moved over to him, taking in the scene. "You can't see Vanessa from here," she said. "But once you're close, you won't miss her." Fabian followed her as she walked back to the trailer, dropped its tailgate and guided Trekky out.

In the unfamiliar surroundings, Trekky whinnied and shied. While Stella calmed the horse, Fabian adjusted the stirrup leathers.

"We still have some time," Stella murmured, glancing at her watch. "When we hear country music, you'd better be ready."

Fabian mounted Trekky, and the horse dodged and fidgeted. He held it in check, calming it, testing its gaits. Trekky began to perform, lifting its forelegs high and rolling them to the side at the top of the stride, arching its neck, ready to go into the fine step for which the breed was famous.

"It's time for the mask and flower," Stella said, unwrapping the rose from its cellophane. Fabian fastened the mask on his face and tucked the flower in his belt. He saw himself in the trailer's chrome coating: a silver ghost from a silent film looked back at him.

He prompted Trekky to circle and prance around the trailer, to feel his weight and obey him. He began to rehearse mentally his appearance out of the gathering twilight: a crest of white emerging from a horizon of somber green.

Stella was intent, listening for the change of music. "Any minute now," she said. "And remember, you're the knight-errant, in love."

Fabian shifted alertly in the saddle. The pounding rock seemed to swell, then abruptly stopped; country music followed.

That was his first cue. Immediately, Fabian backed up the horse, then spurred it forward. Within a few paces, the trees gave way to dense shrubbery, then underbrush. Trekky bolted and nervously broke through the bushes. Dew invaded the slits of Fabian's mask, splashing against his skin and mouth, slipping down his chin, dampening his chest.

The guests noticed him quickly, one after another pointing to him with their drinks. He guided the horse past the bushes, teasing the crowd by keeping to the far reaches of the lawn. As the music continued, he pivoted· Trekky on its haunches, edging closer. The guests stared in his direction. He rode in a broken line along the deepening shadows of the trees, pivoting the mare again and again, trotting in a serpentine pattern. There was a shaft of silence, interrupted only by murmuring laughter from the guests, as the country music halted.

Fabian heard the opening bars of the Chopin, his final cue, rippling across the dappled lawn, and he spurred Trekky forward.

Suddenly light showered down from one of the terraces, illuminating the guests. Fabian calculated quickly that the hosts must have wanted to make his task of finding Vanessa easier, but they had not: Trekky, jarred by the glare and the sudden turbulence among the guests, panicked and veered sideways. Fabian reined the horse in sharply, gentling it into a trot, guiding it straight at the group. Trekky pranced in a flat walk, deliberate, as they headed directly toward the center of the circle of light, the gleaming guests. Fabian finally saw Vanessa. He recognized her instantly, first by the sudden rapid pace of his heartbeat, then by her hair drawn up high on her head, the slender curve of her neck rising from a column of white chiffon. She was alone, somewhat to the front of the other guests, one hand shielding her eyes from the glare. She searched the lawn as though hoping to decipher clues to the masked rider's identity. Fabian put Trekky through its show paces, its step smooth and elegant; swiftly and fluidly the horse passed first into the fast walk that absorbed all roughness of movement, then into the broken pace, neither a fast trot nor a canter. He reined Trekky to a halt directly before the closest group of guests; their faces upturned, they fixed on him in astonishment. Only Vanessa, as if alerted by something familiar in his figure, stepped forward, straining to see him more clearly.

Fabian rose in the stirrups, dropping the reins, his gloved hand touching his plumed tricorne at a full salute. One of the guests raised a camera and clicked the shutter button; the electronic blaze blinded the horse. Trekky reared back, jerking its head in fright, then plunged and shied. Fabian grabbed the reins as other camera flashes shot out of the party in quick succession. Trekky, now frantic, heaved and bucked desperately, apparently determined to throw Fabian off. A sudden lurch pitched him forward. Unprepared, accustomed to his own well-behaved ponies, which never rebelled, Fabian lost the stirrups and with them his balance, tumbling sideways onto the grass, his hat flying, the sword dangling at his thigh like a useless mallet. A roar of laughter swept the crowd. Still clinging tightly to Trekky's reins, Fabian was for a moment so startled at the ease with which he had fallen that he lost all sense of place. Other cameras still flashed, but Trekky had turned away and dropped her head to champ the cropped grass. Picking up his hat, its plume quite bedraggled now, Fabian got up. He pulled Trekky over to him and quickly remounted.

The crowd was still laughing, with obvious good

nature. They seemed to think his fall had been shrewd-
ly staged for their diversion. Fabian saw that Vanessa,
too, was laughing. A stray lock of her hair dangled
over her shoulder. All in white, engulfed in the pool of
light, she might have been a little girl enthralled by a
parade. Yet she appeared taller now than when he had
last seen her. It might be the cut of her gown, he
thought, or she might be wearing high-heeled shoes, or
perhaps she had simply changed from the girl he had
known to a woman. He gently tossed the rose to her.
She reached out and caught it easily. The guests
started to applaud. Fabian raised his hat in salute and
bowed. Spurring Trekky vehemently, he took off at a
full gallop.

At the trailer, he dismounted, and threw Trekky's
reins over the hitching hook near the tailgate. Stella
examined Fabian with her flashlight, then began to
maneuver the horse into its stall.

"That was some fall you took," she said quietly.
"Did your Dulcinea get her rose?"

"She got her rose, and somebody got a picture of me
falling off my horse. My reputation as a knight-errant
is ruined."

"Your reputation doesn't matter, your back does.
Did you strain it?"

Fabian tested the small of his back with his hands,
stretching, then inclining forward. "A bit, I think. I fell
so suddenly."

Stella closed the tailgate of the trailer. "You once
taught me that, when I'm about to fall off a horse, I
should look away from the line of the fall to avoid
injury. Did you remember your own lesson?"

"I forgot. I looked at Vanessa—in the direction of
my fall."

"Too bad. Did you at least get a good look at
her?"

"I did," he said. "Might want to meet her again."

"She's not for you. She's rich. Young. Tender."

"Now that she's of age, I just might like to drop
another flower in her lap, that's all. What car does she
drive?"

Stella laughed. "I thought all you did was stick-and-ball!"

"What car, Stella?"

"A yellow convertible. Can't miss it. The only one in Totemfield." Stella got behind the wheel. "Let's go, my cavalier of the rose," she called out. "I'll take you home."

"Home? I thought we were going to join the Weirstones. After all, the night is young."

"The night is. You are not." She started the engine.

T hey left each other at his VanHome. Stella promised to have Big Lick and Gaited Amble groomed and to return the outfit the following morning.

He slowly took off each item of his white costume, now soiled and crushed, and sank into a scalding bath. In spite of the heat of the water, the familiar painful spasms in his back began, the inevitable result of his fall.

It was a pain to which he had become accustomed, but familiarity offered no relief; constant or spasmodic, the pain slid down along his thigh and leg, stiffening the ankle and foot, or shifted across his lower back, immobilizing it. If the inflammation were to get any worse, he knew he would be unable to make his way about his VanHome, to follow the daily routine of mucking out the soiled litter of wheat straw, wood shavings and sawdust from his ponies' stall. He might be left wholly to the kindness of Stella and the local druggist and delivery boy. He was particularly careful not to sneeze or cough; any movement of the leg, any tilting of the pelvis or rotation of the hip intensified the pain.

Fabian knew there was no cure for his condition other than rest, carefully controlled exercise, and the partial relief provided by the support of an elastic brace. Over the years, doctors had given him drugs to mute the pain, but the drugs usually brought on violent stomach upheaval or gastric bleeding; they also left him spiritless, in a stupor. And he was wary of submitting himself to the obliteration of a narcotic. Pain imprisoned, inertia consumed, yet Fabian saw benefits in his distress: it offered him an occasion to observe his own responses; it also stimulated his quest for distraction, for the company of others. Drugs, no matter how heady, isolated him equally from himself and from others. Fabian had made choices: it was one thing to live in a VanHome, quite another to be its prisoner. Pain awakened him.

Fabian recalled with amusement an incident some years back, when he had accepted an offer to conduct a seminar at an Ivy League university that prided itself on its long tradition of polo and horsemanship. The dean left Fabian to choose his subject, and he settled on the title Riding Through Life. Even though the seminar could accommodate only twenty students, more than a hundred undergraduates bred on movie and television images of cowboys applied to take the course. To thin the herd, Fabian arranged for an introductory session.

Standing before the applicants in his most elegant riding apparel, he announced that the title of the seminar was merely a metaphor for its real subject, which was the fertile role of pain, illness and age in the human condition. Students who were accepted would examine the philosophical and emotional as well as the corporeal aspects of suffering, aging and dying. To induce a profound comprehension of the subject, Fabian continued, maintaining a straight face, the students would be confronted during the course of the seminar with the various manifestations of pain: how it is given, how received, by participating in experiments on various animals—a dog, a cat, a mouse, a squirrel, perhaps a horse. They would also be required to visit and to participate in the workings of a hospital, an asylum, the town morgue, the autopsy laboratory of the police department, and a cemetery. Fabian said he was particularly pleased to announce that an undesignated member of Suicides Anonymous had volunteered to spend the last moments of his or her life with the seminar and, in its presence, perform the rite of death.

With a smiling flourish, Fabian reassured them that their Suicides Anonymous one-way guest would not be an alumnus of their distinguished university; they need not fear, he told them, that the school's good name would suffer because of the suicide. Also, in accordance with the university's strict fire and weapons regulations, the visitor, in his final act, would have recourse to some means other than a torch or gun.

The students listened to Fabian in stunned silence; here and there, from the rising tiers of seats, came a nervous cough or sudden sneeze. Someone raised a handkerchief to his mouth; no one was willing to get up and leave the auditorium openly, yet everyone squirmed in agony, waiting for the end. Fabian finished; a frantic scampering to every exit broke out. Only a few candidates for Riding Through Life were left.

No longer a knight on a white charger, Fabian stepped out of the bath and dried and dressed himself. Though his back pain persisted, he left his VanHome. The night was cool, the stars shining with almost tropical brightness.

He followed one of the country lanes, becoming a target for fireflies and overhanging branches, aware that he was walking toward the house where the party had been held. He refused to ask himself what it was that he sought. The image of Vanessa gracefully catching the rose dissolved into his memory; he thought of her small breasts and narrow waist, slightly muscular thighs, feet that seemed at least one size too large for her body. And he remembered her face: exaggerated features and expressive eyes, smooth skin, the white teeth that showed when she laughed, the thickened lip—and the scar.

At the Weirstones' house spotlights still commanded the lawn. Through the large windows, Fabian saw the guests seated at clusters of tables in the living room or carrying laden plates to other rooms or out to one of the terraces.

He circled the house and went to the parking area. He saw a yellow convertible with a dark top, headed straight toward it and opened the door. Two tennis rackets lay on the back seat, next to a container of tennis balls and a pullover. He reached inside and picked up the sweater; the soft wool gave off a musky perfume mingled with perspiration. He put it back, shut the car door and lay down on the grass behind the bushes that marked off the parking area. From the pond across the road, night sounds—hooting, croaking —lulled him, and, despite the aching in his back, he dozed off. He awoke sharply to the brittle patter and flurry of guests leaving the house, heading for their cars. As more people moved toward the parking area, he hid in the bushes. The scramble and rush of farewells soon died down. Only a half-dozen cars were left now.

Fabian saw Vanessa and two young men walk out of the house. She had draped a white shawl over her shoulders and still carried the rose he had tossed to her. The three stopped by a large sedan parked next to her convertible.

"That's just so sweet of you, Stuart, really. But you'd better start for town before it gets any later. I can drive home alone—it's only a couple of miles, you know." Vanessa's voice was as unaffected as he had remembered it.

"Wednesday, then? I'll see you in town?" It was one of the men.

"I don't know yet," she answered. "I'll let you know." The two young men got into the sedan, and one of them called out good-night through the open window before they drove off. Vanessa opened her car door, and tension gripped Fabian. He was about to speak to her when she hesitated, threw the rose on the dashboard and, with an air of distraction, as though she had forgotten something, walked quickly back to the house. Suddenly unsure of himself, of her, Fabian resisted calling after her. He watched her disappear inside the house. Waiting, he became afraid that she might return with someone to take her home. He got up, brushed wet grass and leaves from his pants, and, unwilling to ponder the consequences of what he was about to do, slipped quickly into the back of her car, drawing up his legs and clutching his arms around them, concealing himself behind the high headrests of the car's contoured front seats.

More than sensations, images stirred and sustained desire. Now, huddled in Vanessa's car, waiting, Fabian wanted to reappear to her as a new presence, a fresh image to erase the familiar one. He heard her opening the car door, slipping into the driver's seat, pulling the door closed. In the shadowed light filtering through the car's rear window, Fabian caught only the wreath of her auburn hair above the headrest of her seat. The drift of her perfume broke over him as he heard her insert the key to turn on the ignition. The car jerked, moved forward, then swerved so abruptly that, in order to remain undetected, Fabian had to grab the seat. They passed the house, its light slashing through the car's interior in staccato flares. She shifted again and, veering the car, picked up speed. The darkness outside told Fabian they were on a country road, and he assumed she would soon reach the main highway. Lifting his body slightly and leaning to one side, he looked between the front seats and discerned in the greenish glow of the dashboard the ghostly shells of her hands resting on the wheel.

He could not decide what to do. How could he reveal himself without frightening her? If she panicked, they might crash. What if she were to pull a gun from the glove compartment and shoot him?

He tried to decipher the darkness. Woods seemed to border both sides of the road, its surface rough. Vanessa was now driving warily, with a slowness that would lessen the chance of an accident if he frightened her. He would wait no more. Inclining to the right, he inched toward the front passenger seat. She had depressed the clutch and was about to shift when he loomed over her.

She opened her mouth in terror, gasping, but no sound came; she slumped over the wheel. The car rolled forward, still in neutral. Her right hand clutched the gearshift, and her left gripped the steering wheel before her. Fabian could not tell whether she found the brake pedal by instinct or consciously, but he pitched forward as the car skidded to a halt. Only then did Vanessa scream; it was a scream that seemed to pierce the windshield.

The headlights flooded trees; the car was pointing off the road. The oil indicator light on the panel glowed red. Fabian lunged between the seats, throwing his left hand over Vanessa's mouth and switching off the ignition and lights with his right. Vanessa struggled under his hand, unable to turn her face toward him. He eased his grip slightly, but kept her mouth sealed. His middle finger sought the scar on her upper lip, sliding into the deep groove; involuntarily, he further eased his grip, as if fearful of opening an old wound.

Vanessa was trembling; a wave of heat came from her body, her sweat wetting Fabian's hand.

"I won't harm you," he whispered tensely at her ear. "I won't, I won't," he repeated, his hand loosening against her mouth.

She nodded, the muscles of her chin unclenching beneath his fingers. He took his hand away from her face.

Clinging to the steering wheel, she seemed about to collapse. Slowly, she pushed herself up and turned toward him. Her mouth opened in recognition, but she remained speechless. He moved closer, placing his arm around her. She was still trembling.

"I gave you that, Vanessa," he said, pointing at the rose on the dashboard.

"Fabian!" She coughed, gagging as she cleared her throat, her voice hoarse and uncertain. "You frightened me so!" She threw her arms around him, then she pulled back, studying him intently. "You haven't changed, not at all!" In the greenish light, Fabian saw how her scar broke the line of the lip, cutting into one nostril.

Vanessa Stanhope had first entered Fabian's life smiling up at him from the pages of an issue of *The Saddle Bride*.

He had focused on her not only because she was a Stanhope, a name that stopped him instantly, but because of the note of seduction the photograph had arrested in her: the expressive eyes, high cheekbones, lush hair, the wide mouth, even teeth—all that exerted a command on him. Accenting her mouth was a deep cleft in her upper lip, a scar that invited speculation about her. The caption under the photograph extolled her as "a fresh and vibrant beauty, an honor student, an accomplished rider." It also informed the reader that Vanessa Stanhope lived with her parents in Totemfield. So it was that, as Stella had earlier prompted his trip to Shelbyville, Vanessa now became the chief cause behind Fabian's selection of the Double Bridle Stables in Totemfield. Soon after receiving Fabian's letter of inquiry, the owner of the Double Bridle Stables hired him as a riding instructor.

Once settled in, with his classes in horsemanship well attended, Fabian telephoned Vanessa. He complimented her on her riding accomplishments cited in *The Saddle Bride* and, casually alluding to his own expertise and distinction, invited her to join one of his classes.

Flattered by his phone call, Vanessa exclaimed that she had read all his books on equitation. The following

219

morning, with the approval of her parents and her school's headmistress, she appeared for Fabian's class. When he saw her, the full force of his obsession—a longing to own her—frightened him.

She became his pupil. Watched by friends and parents of some of the other students in his classes, she would enter the arena, riding one of her family's horses. Fabian could hear murmurs of approval, or surprise, from the spectators. He would follow Vanessa on one of the stable horses, the two of them cantering in circles, half-turns and serpentines. Years later, the image remained with him of her sloping forward in taut breeches, her thighs and buttocks pressed into the saddle or rising in a trot; he remembered her burst of laughter when he caught in midair like a polo ball in flight the training helmet that had flown off her head during a jump.

He instructed her in how she was to follow the movement of the horse with the propulsion of her loins and back, her pelvic bone pushing now sideways, now forward or back in starting, turning, halting or backing up the animal. Sometimes he stood close to her, his hands correcting her foot and heel, then, while checking her seat, brushing the inside of her thigh; his fingers lightly kneaded the cloth of her breeches, inches away from her groin.

Once, under a pretext of correcting her position in a canter, Fabian took Vanessa out along the stable's bridle path. Alone in that private wooded track, they were cantering easily when he suddenly brought his horse close to hers and, seizing her reins, teamed the horses, startling them into a full gallop. Bluntly Fabian reached out and slid his hand, knuckles down, between the pommel and Vanessa's seat, digging deep into her breeches, until he could feel her every move.

She turned to him, staring, her mouth open, the scar pale against the color staining her face. Fabian slowed the horses and swerved them deeper into the woods. He dismounted; Vanessa, vaulting off her horse, followed. He tied up the horses, then without a word went to her. He took off her helmet and dropped it on the grass. For a moment, they looked at each other; then, lifting a hand, he laid his fingers on her mouth, delicately tracing the scar. She began to lap his fingers with her tongue, licking his thumb, sucking his fingers into her mouth. Her tongue between his fingers, the palm of his hand warming against her mouth, he began to kiss her neck, then buried his face in her hair. She trembled, her teeth kneading his fingers, her body resisting, pulling away from him. He held her fast, searching the fragile shell of her ear with his tongue, coaxing it deeper, licking and darting, her heat mingling with his own breath. She no longer tried to pull away, her breath, in short spurts of fervor, breaking over the palm of his hand.

Aroused, he wanted to take her, but his purpose was stronger than desire. He knew that if Vanessa were to come to him as he willed, it must be to imprint him in her memory; like a colt, she was to be schooled, he at the lead, she following at liberty, without rigs, harness, reins. A fresh tide of heat surged through her clothes, warming his chest. As her orgasm burst forth, Vanessa slid to the grass, her head against his thighs; he had yet to kiss her mouth, to touch her naked body, to enter her flesh.

Sometimes, during class, Fabian would reprimand Vanessa openly in the presence of other students, citing a defect or carelessness in her riding. Signaling to her in a code of brow and smile, he would observe aloud that she did not settle deeply enough into the saddle or thrust her heels sufficiently down, or that her calves had slipped back and her elbows jutted out.

He would demonstrate her errors in readying her horse for a jump: how, by straightening her legs too rigidly and releasing the grip of her calves, she permitted the animal to come too close to the fence, denying it space to gather momentum for its spring. Then he would suggest that Vanessa needed to practice in a larger area than that offered by the cramped arena, and he would schedule a private lesson on one of the bridle paths that webbed and threaded the sprawling woods around the estates of Totemfield. It amused him, at times, to announce boldly in front of others that he would be waiting for her at a certain time, the place confirmed, his own ponies at the ready, the lesson planned. At other times, he and Vanessa rode out together openly, taking the stable horses past the indifferent gaze of instructors with their students.

Many of the bridle paths, once a pleasure of the hunt, were now narrow and disused, their jumping obstacles—a pile of timber, a fence, the barricade of a fallen tree—collapsed, or mottled with patches of grass and moss, ragged bushes shoring them up like bats with outspread wings. In serried ranks along the paths, monumental firs, their shaggy peaks heavy with cones, bowed.

Soon Fabian would signal to Vanessa to turn off the path and, guiding their horses through the clawing underbrush, they would wander over the parched beds of streams, cantering along banks of sand that had caved in, past wasted trees felled by lightning. Roots dragged at the hoofs of their mounts as they lingered at the brink of humid gullies.

Spent, drained of strength by the exhilaration of the chase, Fabian and Vanessa would dismount and lie down. Enfolding each other, heady with the dew of ferns, the scent of cold resin, they would talk of those hazards of the mind exposed to none until this, an intimacy as limpid and inevitable as a forest brook.

Through these exchanges of desires and confession, Fabian came to know Vanessa as he felt he had never known another. In the wisdom with which she set aside conventions, however binding or plausible their force, in the candor with which she saw herself, she never ceased to be, for him, sovereign in her possession of a flame of life.

There were times when Fabian was immobilized with the old pain in his back, unable to ride or to teach, confined to bed in his VanHome. After her classes let out, Vanessa would go to him, having told her family that she was studying with friends. She would prepare a meal for him and, when he had eaten, she would smooth bed sheets, plump the pillows around him. Tenderness displacing passion, she girded him with a steady flow of patience, to ensure that, as he moved, no limb would be wrenched, no nerve strained. Under her hands, he would turn onto his stomach, and she would straddle his back, her weight on her knees, her hands kneading and easing his shoulder blades, pressing into his muscles until the last knot of rigidity was gone.

The sole grace of his age, his ability to suffer quietly, he found himself contemplating whether his longing for her was the lost thread of some primordial quest of the child in him, of his need for a mother, the solace of her touch.

After Vanessa had tended him, she never forgot to feed, water and groom his ponies. Drowsy with the pleasant rustle of her moving about the tack room or kitchen or alcove, he would fall asleep, a last balm the certainty that, when he woke, there would be tucked under his pillow or waiting next to his bed a note of love from her.

As long as Fabian taught riding at the Double Bridle Stables, he and Vanessa saw each other regularly. Under some excuse—having the suspension of his Van-Home checked or a tailgate light fixed—Fabian would leave the stables and take a winding country road to a clearing in the woods beyond Totemfield. Vanessa, alert not to be followed, would ride her bicycle toward the same retreat. She would enter his VanHome, dragging her bicycle behind, dropping it with the indifference of a child abandoning a toy, then rush to embrace him.

Fabian would then steer the VanHome onto one of the state highways around Totemfield and drive until he reached one of the areas at the side of the road. There, among trucks and other trailers, his VanHome would not be noticed.

With the muted whirring of traffic the only intrusion of an alien world, he and Vanessa would be undisturbed, secure in the midst of his polo gear, among his books, Big Lick and Gaited Amble standing guard. Fabian knew that, because Vanessa was legally a minor, in so small a town as Totemfield the two of them had to consider the possibility of surveillance—by her parents or the staff of her school—as well as the curiosity of her friends and the nosiness of local authorities. His VanHome was not impregnable; the prospect of a sudden invasion was never to be overlooked.

In imagining the possible circumstances of such an invasion, Fabian always considered the caprices and peculiarities of the laws regarding sexual relations with minors. His behavior itself, he was aware, would be sufficient to support a conviction on the charge of statutory rape if it could be demonstrated that, "by circumstances and surroundings" alone, his acts had been indulged in with intent to arouse his passion; the consent, passion and sexual desire of his alleged victim were a matter of legal irrelevance.

Moreover, the law drew little if any distinction between direct evidence and that which was purely circumstantial. Even if the girl had not been a virgin at the time she had first met him, for Fabian to be found guilty, medical authority merely had to establish that a lustful act had been accomplished with her by the accused, once only or many times, not solely at the time in question, but at any time in the past, however remote.

In addition, Fabian knew that although a charge against him might designate Vanessa, his mature but legally underage companion, as "prosecutrix," the law could excuse her, as a minor, from the obligation to testify should he be brought to trial. Nor could she be compelled to submit herself to cross-examination. In no scrupulous fashion, therefore, could Fabian effectively challenge charges brought against him.

Vanessa's hymen became in their encounters a focus of allure, of exaltation; to break its seal was the only taboo. Their lovemaking found license in the existence of that intimate veil. In accommodating both her virginity and their desire, they refined pleasure, amplified excitement.

Sitting at Vanessa's side, Fabian would bring her close. He might begin with his teeth to fret her neck, his fingers stroking its nape; she would arch up, her breath rasping. Gently he would lay her down, his fingers fumbling with the buttons of her blouse; quickly she would brush his hand away and undo the blouse herself, yet leave it on, almost as if afraid to part with him for even a moment. He would unclasp her brassiere. However girlish its presence, the contours of Vanessa's body were rounded and womanly; her breasts seemed small in proportion to her hips, her buttocks too full. His fingers would capture the nipples, twisting them gently, teasing, pulling, rolling them, until they hardened. He would move his mouth from one nipple to the other, then back again, sucking and pulling, until she started to squirm and moan, her head thrown back.

When Fabian would begin to loosen her skirt, Vanessa would raise herself slightly, to help him slip the skirt off. He would spread her calves with one hand, the other between her thighs, stroking in rhythm, exciting her; his hand would quicken, his fingers sliding over the filmy fabric of her panties, feeling the crease, the mat of her hair; slowly he would stretch the fabric, revealing the flesh beneath, until, his lips swept by the heat she gave off, he would boldly bend his mouth to her flesh.

It was broad and extended, long in shape, its outer lips spacious palms that were the mark of its beauty, lithe, fanning and outstretched, the shaft of the flesh a crest of frenzy surging under a hood. Fabian was intrigued by the bold protrusion of her inner lips, elliptical, yielding wafers, wet with her fluid. He remarked that one lip was distinctly longer than the other; she told him it was, like her harelip, a birth defect.

Her hands splayed wide on Fabian's bed, her legs flexed outward, the calves gently pinioned by his hands, her back lifting, Vanessa would rise lightly, as if to offer her inmost self to him. He would touch her breasts again, then gather them in a caress. In haste, listing to one side, Vanessa would shed her panties, impelling herself against his mouth and chin, her pelvis in spasm. He would kiss her, the long lap and lick of his tongue blending his own moist heat with hers. What began as a moan would swell in volume as his head bent to her, the flick of his tongue prodding the hood, in quest of the firm gland, then snaring it, letting go ... moving lower, wedging between the inner lips that parted before him. As she plummeted to orgasm, she would open the wholeness of her flesh even wider to him, his tongue infusing her, unrelenting, until it arrived at her hymen, moving over the taut shield, then withdrawing to the chamber of her inner lips.

N ow, in her car, Fabian placed his forefinger gently on her lip, tracing lightly the furrow of the scar.

"You frightened me so!" Vanessa said again. She glanced at him, and he caught the change in her mood; she brought her hands tentatively to her face, as if testing it for traces of Fabian's hand. She lifted her arms and blotted the sweat on her face with the billowing sleeves of her dress. She touched a slight swelling by her mouth, then smiled. "Your left hand is a bit strong for making passes, Mr. Fabian. You haven't become left-handed, have you?"

"Left-handed? A southpaw can't play team polo! You've forgotten all about me, Vanessa," he said in mock grief.

Her hair tumbled in auburn disarray as she slumped against the door. "It's been so long, Fabian! You used to tell me that you wanted to adopt me and be my make-believe father. You said we'd share our own special bond, a bond to be free, to surprise each other with freedom, which blood fathers and daughters don't have." She was pensive, her eyes on the darkness outside. "I felt such freedom only with you." Slowly she turned and rested a hand on Fabian's shoulder. "Will you promise, Fabian?"

"Promise what?"

"That you'll surprise me."

"Surprise you with what?"

The pressure of her hand increased, then she removed it. Abruptly, she started the engine. "You'll think of something. Since I saw you last, you must have done more than pitch flowers to young ladies."

She shifted into gear, backed the car onto the road, and drove it slowly forward.

She pulled up at his VanHome. He waited for her to say that she wanted to go inside with him, but she said nothing. The thought that this might be their last meeting, that she might not want him, gripped him, and suddenly he did not know what to say, how to tell her that since he had left her, he had had too little money to return to her and that now he had not expected to find her still in Totemfield instead of away at college. They sat in silence for a few moments, then, just as he was about to get out of the car, she again placed her hand on his shoulder; the hand rose to his neck, resting there, not committed to a full embrace.

"Why don't you take me with you?" she asked.

Her scar was a saber cut in the night glow. He reached out and touched it; moisture tipped his finger.

"Take you where?"

"You used to say that one day, when I'd be free to go places, you'd return to take me with you. I'm not that little girl that visited you in your VanHome. I'm old enough, and free to go with you. To be led by you." As she withdrew her hand from his shoulder, the aluminum panels of his VanHome, reflecting the headlights of her car, silvered her face, her hair.

"I've thought of you often," she said quietly. "At times, I believed you were my only reason to grow older, to mature. I'm glad you came back to give me a rose at my party."

He stepped out of the car and shut the door. "Tomorrow night?" he asked.

She nodded, and the car began to crawl away.

It was almost midnight. Fabian steered his Van-Home through the city's teeming, narrow heart, crowds spilling from its sidewalks into streets narrowed by double-parked cars. Policemen threaded between the cars, methodically fixing parking tickets to windshields. As he waited for a traffic light to change, Fabian reflected that, only a short distance outside this packed zone of energy, the rest of the city, muffled, was caught in the inertia of the night.

Vanessa stretched lazily at his side and looked at him. He returned her gaze. In the stream of passing light, now sharp, then blurred, her eyes on him, the scar gleaming on her lip, she seemed tranquil, almost voluptuously at ease. Fabian sensed that, like her, he could readily succumb to the seduction of passivity, let himself flow toward her.

He chose to rupture the mood. "How do you feel?"

Her answer surfaced through the weight of her lassitude. "It would be nice to go swimming," she murmured. "That would feel good."

"A swimming pool?"

"Yes, a pool with lots of cool water." She was musing; her hair tumbled over the headrest.

They had reached a park and were driving into its leafy blackness. The VanHome's headlights slipped over police cars drawn up discreetly along the pathways, picked out a solitary cyclist, the bloodshot eye of the bicycle's tail light winking back at them, then a sudden flurry in the underbrush, a scramble of small animals. At the fringe of the park, they passed two men, dim shapes on a bench, tucked into each other. The VanHome glided out of the park.

"You've never told me anything about your life," Vanessa said.

"What do you want to know?"

"Why don't you ever use your first name?"

"Most people can't pronounce it. 'Fabian' is so much easier."

"Were you ever married?"

"My wife died while you were still a child."

"How long were you married?"

"Six years."

"That long?"

"Six years seems long only to someone your age."

"Did you love her?"

"I was attached to her."

"Any children?"

"No. We never wanted any."

"And your family? Where are they?" she kept prodding.

"I have no family."

"How come?"

"My relatives died in a fire."

"All of them?" She turned sharply to look at him, incredulous.

"Except my parents. It was arson. One of the biggest fires ever."

"Is that why you won't settle down under one roof?" She was pouting slightly, the scar a sullen blemish.

"Roofs catch fire," Fabian said.

"Whom do you miss most from your past?"

"My father."

"Why?"

"Because he loved me most. Ever since he died, I regretted that I told him so little about myself."

"Why didn't you tell him more?"

"The truth would have hurt him; I loved him too much to cause him that grief."

"What was the truth?" The languor in her voice had dissolved.

"When I was about your age," Fabian said, "my family shared an old house with two other families and a single girl. She lived across the corridor from the two rooms we had, in a single room of her own. She was a factory worker, plain, ordinary, withdrawn. In the evening, after work, she went to night school, and she wasn't around the house much. But often, when she came home and my parents were asleep, I'd sneak over to her room. We were both lonely; what we lacked in passion we made up for in urge. Usually I'd stay with her all night and leave just before dawn.

"One morning, when I got back to my room, I found my father—he was a professor of classical drama—in his pajamas and robe waiting for me. I was barefoot and had nothing on under my raincoat. My shoes and my clothes were near my bed. I was convinced that my father knew where I'd been, so I said nothing. What was there to say? But then he reached out to hug me, and he kept looking at me through his thick glasses, looking at me anxiously. I bent down to kiss him on the forehead, and he patted my hair, as if he wanted to find out whether it was wet; of course, it was dry. 'Thank God it isn't raining,' he said. He brought my head closer until my face was next to his. I could feel the stubble on his cheek. He said, 'On a night like this, you went out only in a raincoat? Not even a hat and scarf?' Then he saw my bare hands, but he didn't notice my bare feet. 'Not even gloves? That's asking for pneumonia!' But he wasn't angry—he just patted my head and trotted out in his old slippers. All my father saw was what he wanted to see. That's how he was."

Vanessa was silent. His eyes on the road, Fabian felt her stare. He pulled his VanHome up short and, swerving, drove into a crowded parking lot. Outside, in the humid air, Vanessa watched him while he attached to each side of the VanHome the QUARANTINED signs. He took her arm and led her across the street to an imposing building. At Fabian's ring, the door, a slab of heavy stainless steel, glided open.

A young man stood squarely before them, the powerful muscles of his upper arms and shoulders outlined in a black T-shirt announcing, in gold script, the legend DREAM EXCHANGE. He stepped back and directed them to a desk, where a young woman, in a DREAM EXCHANGE T-shirt so snug that her nipples threatened to pierce it, asked Fabian to pay the admission price and gave him a card to sign. When he complied, she pressed a button, allowing Fabian and Vanessa to pass through a turnstile. They went past black-padded, vinyl walls rimmed in gilt, down a carpeted staircase. Iridescent panels of mottled glass, mosaics of glittering pebbles, peacock-hued and lighted from behind in subtly suggestive shapes, threw a rippling, splintered glow on their path.

"Who's allowed in here?" Vanessa murmured.

Fabian held up the membership card and read the small print aloud: "Valid for any man and woman of legal age who enter as a couple, contingent on the payment, in cash or by credit card, of the full price of admission. Initial admission fee confirms membership in DREAM EXCHANGE for a period of six weeks and permits members subsequent admissions at reduced rate."

"If it's open to anyone, why the membership?"

"As a club, DREAM EXCHANGE is free from most regulations that govern places serving the general public."

"What do you get for your membership?"

"Free drinks, free food—and of course, the free use of other areas set aside as meeting places for consenting couples."

"Consenting to what?"

"To a certain way of being with other men and women."

They stood at the brink of a steamy cavern, the air beating with an urgent disco sound. The cloying odor of marijuana, mingled with vaporish trails of cigarette smoke, hung over a raised oval dance platform, where a crush of men and women jounced under strobe lights.

Almost half the dancers were naked and barefoot; others wore briefs or swimming trunks or towels; only a few danced in street clothes. At the edge of the platform, two women moved in a steady rhythm, each twining her arms about the other's neck, their bare breasts in contact, their mouths joined in a kiss. Near them, another woman, her hips bucking, reached down and, without losing the beat, clasped her naked partner's organ, gently twisting and tugging it, then crouched, burying her mouth in the wiry hair on his underbelly, nuzzling the insides of his thighs.

Other people, many of them naked, lolled on sofas or stood leaning against the mirrors that framed the room, watching the dancers. A man wearing a towel tucked around his waist snapped his fingers to the music while his partner, a naked girl, observing herself impassively in a side mirror, cupped her hands under her breasts, lifting them, pinching and squeezing the nipples. A young man, cradled between the knees of another, rubbed himself in long, slow strokes. From a couch, a woman glanced at the men, then trailed her hands up and down her thighs, along dimpled fat; the muscles of her stomach contracted; lost in sensation, she closed her eyes as she slid one hand between her thighs. Her gesture was beautiful, though the woman was not; and Fabian admired it.

Shifting in surprise and fascination, Vanessa moved closer to Fabian. A streak of cobalt light, bluish, flared on the whites of her eyes, veiling the pupils; rebuked by the mystery of her face, it illumined only her body.

"Who are these people?" she asked.

"Just people, their appetites traveling without break between desire and gratification," Fabian said. "When DREAM EXCHANGE first opened in New York, television and the papers announced that it was the most infamous orgy palace since the last days of Pompeii. Thanks to their coverage, it quickly became more famous, and soon DREAM EXCHANGE opened up branches all over the country."

He led her past bodies glistening with sweat on couches, bodies stretched on mattresses or pillows banked against the walls, bodies kneeling or curving beside each other, bending, moving above or beneath one another, sliding from kiss to embrace, lips to groin a damp circuit of voyage and return in the misty air.

"My friends would never believe me if I told them what people do here in public," Vanessa said.

"When we disbelieve what others could do, we end up disbelieving what we could do ourselves. That's how we're punished for our failure to imagine."

"Have you been here before?"

"I have," Fabian replied.

She spoke after a long silence. "Have you ever made love in this place?"

"I have." There was simple declaration in his voice.

"Did you ever share a woman here?"

He nodded.

"A woman you brought here?"

He nodded again.

"What made you come here with her?"

"A need to change," Fabian said evenly. "I felt stagnant, a tired actor in a dull play—every night the same entrance, same lines, same stage. Here, at least, the stage was different."

DREAM EXCHANGE had entered Fabian's life some years back. One night, the owner of a well-known stable on the East Coast, a generous and expansive host, invited him to the benefit performance of a singing star, once legendary, whose recordings now no longer led the charts and who had not appeared in public for years.

When Fabian and his fellow guests took their seats, toward the front of the auditorium, he was curious to note the presence of a broad cyclorama, a bandage of white across the stage. Suddenly the hall darkened, and the cyclorama was swept with a wash of color and light, a film that splashed images of the star in an unrelenting tumble: the star in close-up or at Olympian distance, as an infant in her mother's arms, a child in school, a nymphet, a leather-clad teen-ager—advancing seductively, retreating provocatively, frozen in gesture or careening in speeded-up movement—her bust for drugs, her arrest and conviction, her imprisonment, her release, her marriages, her divorces, her children, her record hits, her movie roles, her figure filling the screen, an icon above audience and stage, then diminishing to a magnetic, throbbing dot as her voice rose from a whisper, gathering volume, swelling, magnified by the sound system almost beyond the audience's endurance. Fabian felt invaded—his clothes, nostrils, skin—and bound, not only by the strip of images, but by the intersecting beams of light that remolded color, shape, sound into a whirl of sensations.

When the star herself finally appeared on stage, she seemed to Fabian to have been born of and from and into the images that had preceded her, a Venus rising from the foam of technology. Now, her voice and her songs hardly mattered: she was as triumphant as the images that had heralded her.

From the orgiastic turbulence of that spectacle, in the heat of that frenzied, stampeding audience all roused to a pitch of exaltation and surrender by an elaborate strategy of invasion and manipulation—an impact that no single effect or device, however powerful, could have achieved—Fabian drew back.

He understood the radical mutations that techniques of light, sound and projection had wrought upon her performance. He realized that, against the drama brought about by technology, the contours of his life had gone flat, the secret pulse of his energy and quest slack, without spirit.

Not long afterward, Fabian arrived at the reality of the sex clubs, the elaborate fraternity of health spas and massage parlors and baths. DREAM EXCHANGE was only one of them, a link in a network of establishments, national in scope, that were opening in response to changes in habits of intimacy. For some time, within the familiar domestic boundaries of living rooms and bedrooms, men and women had had access to a prodigality of images, first in various pictorial guides to the joy of sex and unabridged "how-to" manuals of lovemaking, in a book or on a video tape, ordered through the mail, then on cable and even regular commercial TV, in films that once had been confined to the movie houses and peep shows of the aggressive, even lawless, sexual combat zones in a few large cities. At newsstands, in drugstores, at airports and bus stations, any adult person could now buy magazines—slick or pulp, chic or gross, expensive or cheap—on every aspect and variation of sexuality. In the torrent of images, no possibility went unexamined.

The sex clubs offered the next stage for the exploration—and exploitation—of the new intimacy. Fabian was among the first to accept the offer.

When, at dinner or a party, in a riding competition or during one of his seminars, usually among friends but not always, Fabian came upon a woman who attracted him, he would invite her to the theater or a movie, to dine with him or have supper. Later in the evening, he would propose that she accompany him to DREAM EXCHANGE or a club like it. Possibly because his invitation was always extended with decorum and detachment, in language and manner divested of palpable sexual intimation, it was seldom refused.

Inside the club, Fabian would take his companion first to the locker room which adjoined the dance floor. There, against rows of regimental gray, the metallic bark of metal snapping open and shut around them, he would suggest that they disrobe and go out in towels only. Though they were surrounded by men and women who were naked or half-naked—adjusting their towels or preening in DREAM EXCHANGE T-shirts—the woman often held back, shy, reluctant. Fabian would point out that she should expect to feel uneasy about undressing for the first time in a public place, but that her nudity in the club, among other nude people, would not leave her uncomfortable: the mode of dress there was undress. In a world of panties and socks, of jock straps and brassieres, men and women, fresh from the showers, stood drying themselves, confirmation of the truth of Fabian's observations. The woman would usually begin to disrobe—her first commitment to abandon herself to the situation.

Then, the two of them in towels, Fabian would guide her through the club. From the first, she would witness sexual play at its most unhampered and extravagant: men and women, singly, paired or in groups, investing their intimacies with the ease they would bring to social gatherings in their own living rooms.

Soon the woman would be lulled by the climate of mundane assumption, her need for privacy ratified by the sense of enclosure. She would risk permitting herself the exploration of touch with a stranger, often a woman, who seemed less threatening than a man. Sometimes her discovery of her own nature, of her own curiosity, would proceed in the anonymity of a nest of bodies, female and male, sequestered in one of the club's more isolated rooms. Fabian might watch these stages in her revelation, or she might signal that she wished him to leave and wait for her, reserving to herself the scenario of her abandonment.

Then, the fluent persuasion of circumstance having enforced its own code, the woman made herself accessible to Fabian, her response natural now, an expectation fulfilled, an inevitable compliance with the mood of the time and the place. What the two of them shared was a covert knowledge of each other seldom if ever conceded to a possessive lover or the complacent partner in marriage, the knowledge of sensation alone, conveyed by sexual acts perhaps never to be repeated, never even alluded to outside that sexual arena.

Music still throbbed as Fabian guided Vanessa down a long channel of stairs, the passage narrowing, the darkness deepening, to yet another floor of DREAM EXCHANGE.

"Would you ever want the two of us to make love among other people here, strangers?" Vanessa asked abruptly. "To share me with other women?" She hesitated. "Other men?"

"Only if you and I would want to share and be shared. Would you?" he asked gently.

"One can share only what one possesses," Vanessa said distantly, looking at him, a thin smile flickering about her mouth, teasing the scar.

Silent at her side, careful not to brush against her with his body, every touch a signal, Fabian pondered the realm into which Vanessa was guiding him, unsure still whether he should reveal to her a truth he had felt ever since those afternoons in his VanHome, his face next to hers, one hand buried in her hair, his mouth at her ear and neck, breathing in the scent of her body: that as long as they were lovers, she must be free to want and to experience life without his mediation, that her need for another lover, a man or a woman she had already known as a lover or would want to know in love, could never alter her place in his life. He wanted to tell her that he would never be jealous of her freedom or desire to experience herself in lovemaking with others, privately or with him as a witness or partner, because the two of them would not be relinquishing their essence to others, but, rather, absorbing others into it.

The others would be merely transient evidence of an extraneous world, a gift belonging neither to him nor to her, yet open at any moment to possession by either or by both in concert, a gift of vision, a glimpse at fragments of oneself with others, shafts of light thrown on that outer world, reflecting back on one's own.

Fabian gently pushed Vanessa forward, and they moved through corridors opening onto saunas and steam rooms. They passed a couch on which a girl lay, staring at the ceiling, her eyes glazed, her body bare. A crew of men, runtish and sweaty, their towels on the floor, took turns probing her limp frame, determined with sullen resentment to invade her entire being. With each of their thrusts the back of the couch struck the wall, rhythmically marking their progress.

Nearby, in the ruddy glow of overhead lamps, a naked couple reclined on lounges. The man, short and stocky, his scant hair receding from a mottled forehead, closed his eyes, his mouth half open. The woman, tall, her hair a gray mat, her thighs veined and wasted, cuddled against him, stroking his flesh, while she watched a couple pushing fiercely against each other on the floor. The woman saw Vanessa and smiled at her.

"You're so pretty!" she called out. "Why don't you undress?"

One eye now opened, the man glanced at Vanessa. "Why don't you?" he chimed in. Then he noticed Fabian. "Come and join us, you two," he mumbled, his eyes closed again.

Fabian and Vanessa arrived at a large area housing pool tables and rippling with the light and jangle of pinball machines. Vanessa slipped off her shoes and dropped onto one of the floor pillows. She gently pulled Fabian down beside her and laid her head on his thighs.

Uncertain of what she might expect from him, he wanted to bring his mouth to her hair, to undress her, to stroke her, to caress her breasts, to turn his gaze on her body with the same ease he had had when assessing the bodies of so many others that evening. Her warmth was on him, but he could not see her eyes. She might have drifted into sleep.

The intensity of his emotions bewildered him. In his years away from her, he had registered Vanessa's reality only hazily; now, close to her, he was sharply aware of every shade of his feeling that she evoked. Now, as in his past with her, he took in her every expression, every gesture, every move. But the pattern of what he felt came in fragments; he could not determine what absorbed him most—her presence or his own need.

Before them, a man, shedding his towel, dropped onto a floor mat, tumbling with him a woman wearing only white stockings with garters around them, and white high-heeled shoes. They were both in their twenties, the man dark and compact, the woman blonde and well-shaped. Giggling, they lay back, the woman reaching out for the man, throwing open her legs. The man moved between her thighs and rammed into her again and again, his hands squeezing her breasts, his torso pinning her down. She twisted, her hands pushing against his shoulders. The man slid down, his face between the woman's thighs, his tongue inside her, her legs a vise about his head.

Nearby, in shadow, a little bald man watched the couple. Darting quick glances around, he crawled closer to the couple, a howl stifled in his toothless mouth, his naked body blotched, his face bruised, his eyes bulging with lust. A dim, wily smirk came over his face as he saw Vanessa and Fabian. Quickly, as if loosening a too-tight collar, the little man turned back to the couple on the floor. There, the woman moaned as her lover slipped his hands under her buttocks, bringing her flesh closer to his mouth. She wriggled, her breath in gasps, a shudder coiling through her body.

The little man jerked his shoulders and neck, swiveling his head sideways; his forehead wrinkled in concentration as he began to milk his flesh, squatting, his knees apart. Absorbed in each other, the couple had not noticed him, and he inched forward until his flesh was above the woman's face. As if bracing for a heroic act, smirking, sucking his lips, the little man touched the woman's chin with his flesh. Involuntarily, avid for fulfillment, she opened her mouth and wrapped her lips around his outthrust organ. Shaking, shivering, muttering to himself, lifting his shoulders, breathing swiftly, he strained, ejaculating. Her body quaking under her lover's touch, her eyes closed, the woman swallowed, licking her lips, collecting each drop. Like a boy delighted by his own mischief, snickering, his eyes now vacant, the little man scuttled away.

"Everyone here seems so eager, greedy," said Vanessa.

"They're consumers of passion in search of bargains," Fabian said, scanning the room. "Here, at the dime-a-dance ballroom of sex, bargains are often damaged goods in disguise. Some of these women are really escorts or prostitutes that men hire to pose as their wives or girlfriends, to be swapped for the girlfriends and wives of other men. And a lot of the men are pimps or rough trade in search of new business. Others are tourists who might have been in a whorehouse in Tijuana or Hong Kong yesterday; tonight, fresh off the jet, they dump at DREAM EXCHANGE germs they didn't check through customs! Then there are the clean and innocent Ivy League first-timers, lured by the promise of free sex—and sex for free."

"Don't these people ever worry about infection or disease?"

"They probably do. Most of them wouldn't share their toothbrushes. But here. . . ."

He broke off as another couple brushed by them, the man guiding the woman toward the nearest mattress. He was slender, with a lean, alert face; she was frail, her beauty touched with that blend of innocence and carnality Fabian had often observed in fashion models. Her manner and expression were demure; she stiffened with reluctance as, sitting down next to her, her partner undid her towel, leaving her naked. In an instant, he was on her, kissing her mouth and neck, licking her nipples, her underarms; aroused already, he was determined to arouse her.

Unquiet, Vanessa stirred on Fabian's thighs. She sat up and put her shoes on again, a gesture Fabian read as a signal that she wanted to move on. He took her past another area—where clusters of men in towels huddled like schoolboys before lighted squares of electronic games—and into the bar.

Among naked people and those in towels were several men wearing dark suits; a few women gathered the long sweeps of their dresses about them. One couple seemed to have come fresh from a society dance, the woman's gold lamé gown winking against the starchy white tie and tails of her escort. At one end of the bar, next to platters of cold cuts, stood a group of Oriental men, all in towels, the gold rims of their eyeglasses glinting in the light. Vanessa remarked that they seemed to go into conference. Fabian smiled, then pointed out the presence of their American call-girl companions, bare-breasted above jeans or shorts.

One of the girls, a stunning redhead with cropped hair, high cheekbones and wide-set eyes, glanced at Vanessa, then at Fabian, and walked over to them.

"I'm Cheyenne," she said, assured and at ease. Then, appraising Vanessa as an escort hired by Fabian for the evening, she turned to her. "Why don't you let me know when you're free," she said. "Jackie"—she pointed out one of the girls—"doesn't feel too hot and would like to go home, and you could take her place for the rest of the night. Since this club requires members to leave in couples, she could leave with your gentleman."

"How do you know we're not married?" Vanessa asked, taking Fabian by the hand.

The girl gave Fabian a long, seductive look before answering Vanessa. "If he pays you to say that the two of you are married, it's fine with me. At his age men pay for all kinds of tricks. But these guys—" Gesturing with her head at the Oriental men, she lowered her voice. "They'll pay you better than anybody, because paying is *all* they do better." She grinned. "They're all little Toyotas, you know. You'd be surprised what kinds of stiffeners, extension rings and battery-operated gadgets they keep under their towels. It's like screwing a hardware store." Chuckling, she went back to join her group.

Aware of the glances of a few drinkers standing nearby, Vanessa grew uneasy. Her hand tugged at Fabian, and he took her away.

They passed a sales counter, its glass shelves outlined in rhinestones and heaped with fluorescent plastic replicas of the male and female sexual organs, batteries to make them vibrate, sexual toys and whimsies, pendants and rings, playing cards, curiosities of leather and chrome and brass. A special shelf held vials and pellets of a chemical, the inhalation of which, their labels claimed, caused the blood vessels to dilate and the heartbeat to accelerate, deranging the perception of time and inducing an illusion of prolonged orgasm. Behind the counter a tall platinum blonde, in a garter belt and net stockings, teetered on high-heeled shoes, the tight lacing of a Victorian corset pushing up her breasts, their skin coarse and mottled, slick with sweat.

Near the counter, on a stained mattress, two bodies, white on black, interlocked. A black girl in pigtails, her blouse crumpled round her naked buttocks, socks drooping over her low-heeled shoes, lay pinned underneath an old white man with a gray crew cut. Over the man's bony shoulder, the girl caught Vanessa's stare.

"This is the only place we've got to be alone," she explained, with the freshness of a school-girl on her first date.

A tall, handsome man hit Vanessa with his elbow in passing and smiled an apology; she turned to him, only to start in confusion: the man's stiffened organ served as a hanger for his towel. Just then, a woman, her hair tied back, her expression coquettish, approached him. Without warning, she lifted the towel and tenderly kissed the tip of the flesh. Then, smiling, she paraded on.

At the whirlpool, a man crawled out of the mist toward a woman and gripped her buttocks tight against him. As he rocked her back and forth, another man dug sharply into her from the front, his large belly slapping against her jutting hipbones.

Attracted by the scene, a woman slid out of the pool and came at the trio. Two other bodies that had been paddling in the water joined the tableau, as did a frail-looking boy with freckled shoulders. The bathers and those idling at the whirlpool watched the more active group with casual interest.

A young man, naked, his towel in hand, his hair slicked down, eyes magnified by glasses, fixed his stare on Vanessa. Next to him, two naked women, his companions, their copper skin sheened by the vapor from the pool, balanced uneasily on spike-heeled shoes. The man turned sharply to Fabian as if resuming an interrupted conversation.

"Pelvic constrictors," he announced jauntily, pointing at the golden two. "Illegal entries from way down south. Good for anything except speaking English."

The women smiled, sensing that they were being spoken of.

"Swap one, swap all," the man went on.

"I'd rather not," Fabian said.

The man was not deterred. "Or let the *señoritas* chip her." He eyed Vanessa, but he spoke only to Fabian. "Or, better yet, how about chipping into her with me?"

Vanessa pointed a finger at herself. "Why don't you ask her? *Her* speak English," she said evenly.

The man changed his tactics, but continued to focus on Fabian. "Have you had any experience with men?" he asked him emphatically.

"Yes," Fabian said, "we were in the army together."

Discouraged, the man wandered off, his companions trotting obediently behind.

A couple, both in their late sixties, their bodies

pendulous over spindly legs, stumbled out of the whirlpool, a trail of wet footprints their signatures.

Fabian and Vanessa picked their way through a
labyrinth of small lounges, then approached a large
room, its walls clear Plexiglas. They saw dozens of
men and women, all bare, lying and squatting, kneeling, crouching, standing, tumbling, toppled, massed, on
mattresses and pillows. All bonds slipped; the men and
women copulated, couples alone, or in nests and knots
of three and five and more, hands straying over bodies
and breasts, heavy, pliant, fragrant, withered, fingers
making their way into inner recesses, yielding or rigid,
lax, furrowed, the invasion obliterating, a choreogra-
phy of touch, the withdrawal, rising, converging, the
shift of partners, the run of positions, thrust and pull
and strain, an army, voracious, remorseless in its advance over a terrain of flesh.

From the huddle, a couple got up. The man was in
his late fifties, his gray hair disordered, a medallion
resting on the damp hair on his chest. The woman was
young and shapely. The man guided her toward the
exit, along a path between the bodies, her walk the
practiced confident strut of a seasoned nightclub strip-
per. Outside the room, they slumped into a double
lounge chair. Proud of her looks, the woman spread
her thighs. Fabian was about to turn away when a
flicker in her movement detained him: from the shape
of her well-defined inner lips, he recognized that the
woman had once been a man.

Silent, Vanessa followed Fabian through a zone of
cubicles, some shut, some with their doors ajar. From
behind the thin walls came whispers, chuckling, the
slap of flesh on flesh, a body thudding against the
floor, the moan of a woman, a man whimpering, broken words and phrases stillborn. Vanessa turned
sharply, almost colliding with a door barring entry to
another section of the club. Uncertain, she pushed
open the door and, clutching Fabian's hand, went in.

They were alone in a room containing a large swimming pool, enclosed on all sides by a ledge of polished
tile, and a sauna at the far end. A diaphanous film of

steam hung suspended over the water, the play of green lights skimming its surface, revealing the contours of the pool's floor. Its quiet unbroken, the room might have been in a private home.

"It's all yours," Fabian said with a smile as Vanessa released his hand in happy astonishment. "Just what you wanted. Cool water, and lots of it." He lay down on an ornate bench at the side of the pool.

Vanessa took off her shoes and, lifting her skirt, sat down, on the tile ledge, her legs playfully disturbing the water, her back toward Fabian.

Suddenly, without a word, she pulled off her sweater and tossed it to him. She stood up, removed her skirt and panties, and came toward the bench, dropping them beside him. Her belly passed near his head. He was not yet aroused; his mouth felt dry.

Fabian looked up at her, catching sight of her groin. She opened herself to his exploration, moving one foot ahead of the other, her gaze fixed on him. Aroused, he was silent and motionless.

Vanessa returned to the pool and plunged in, her clean strokes those of a trained swimmer cutting easily through the water, scarcely rippling its calm. After a few laps, she climbed out of the pool, her hair slicked back.

Fabian threw her a towel. She sat down at the pool's edge, and as she swathed herself, shielding her breasts and hips, he was tempted to go to her but he remained seated.

The door opened, and a tumble of laughter and strong, loud voices spilled into the room as four men and two women, all black, in their mid-thirties, burst in. Glancing at Vanessa and Fabian, they shed their towels; one after another, they dived into the pool. The women, short, with high breasts, their hips broad on stocky thighs, dabbled in the shallows, squatting, gently plying the water; the men, thick and massive through the shoulders and middle, struck off powerfully for the far end of the pool, dashing spurts of foam at one another, clowning for their women.

One of the men surfaced in front of Vanessa, careful

not to splash her. He looked up, smiling, and then ducked mischievously, making no secret of his curiosity about what her towel concealed. Vanessa smiled back, and the man swam closer; his fingers brushed her toes.

"Would you like to celebrate our meeting with a bang or a swim, baby?" he asked, his head bobbing at her feet.

"I'm too cold for either one," Vanessa came back. Her voice was low but not hesitant.

"You don't look cold to me, beautiful," he announced exuberantly.

"But you do to me," Vanessa replied promptly, her smile steady. She was growing bolder. "Cold or not, though, you're still the longest I've ever seen!"

The other men in the pool, hearing the byplay, started to swim closer, their laughter rippling with the waves they made.

"The longest? No kidding?" The man was pleased, then puzzled.

"I said the longest." Vanessa was bantering with him now, flicking water in his face with her feet. "If you don't believe me, ask my father." She pointed to Fabian.

"Your father?" The man jerked back with astonishment, shaking the water out of his eyes. "You brought your dad here?"

"What makes you think my dad didn't bring *me* here?" Vanessa asked. The men and women in the pool turned to see how Fabian would take this.

"If my pet says it's the longest," Fabian drawled from his bench, "it must be the longest. She's done enough petting in school to know what's long."

The two women, not wanting to be left out, had drifted over from the shallow end.

"Haven't seen anything yet, honey," one woman sighed loudly, between giggles. "Now, you leave the young lady alone," she said to her man, her mock scolding coated with affection; then she turned to look up at Vanessa.

"Honey, by now all my man can do is remember what's long, not how to make it last long," she went on, setting off a fresh tide of laughter. Her man began to swim closer, his face pretending outrage. She moved out of his reach with a vigorous splash.

The game had run its course; the black men and women began to climb out of the pool. Picking up their towels, they waved to Fabian and Vanessa and piled out the door.

The room was silent again; the surface of the pool subsiding, the water translucent then opaque with the dappled play of light. Vanessa got up and went over to the bench where Fabian reclined, one hand propping his head. She perched on its edge; she seemed to be waiting for him to speak. She shivered briefly, not looking at him.

"Well, you've had your pool," he said. He reached beside him for another towel and tenderly cloaked her shoulders with it. She slid against him, pressing. He asked, in playful imitation of the black man, "Is there anything else I can do for you, beautiful?"

"Yes, there is—Father," she said quietly.

"Then tell me, what is it, my child?" He remained playful.

"I'm still a virgin, Fabian," she whispered. She slipped from his grasp, rising. He stood up to bring her closer; the towel slid from her neck and shoulders, and she trembled, his arm about her waist. She turned finally to look at him, her face lifted to brush his mouth, her lips cold and dry. "I don't want to be anymore."

He wondered if she were telling him this so that he would go with her to one of the rooms they had passed, thick with couples in the act of lovemaking. He imagined her in the clasp of another man, a nameless body.

Fabian released Vanessa and stepped back. Instinctively, she reached out and touched his cheek.

"I don't want it, Fabian," she said.

"What do you want?" he asked, his voice neutral.

"You," she whispered, her eyes serene, her arms folding across her breasts. She retreated to the bench and lay down on it.

For a moment, he hovered above her, then eased himself to the ground before her, guarded, afraid to touch her. He wondered if for her, as for him, memory had begun to act as a courier, bearing images of their inviolate exchanges in his VanHome.

"I'm often attracted to young women," Fabian said warily. "I'm drawn to those who'll give me a second look, and also to those who won't. There are girls I want to stir me up, and others I want to stir up. But always, before, when I wanted a woman, the faster she passed through my life, the more exciting I found her. But you—you were never one of them. I've always been afraid of losing you. I'm afraid now."

He stopped, reluctant to name what he felt. Now, when she was willing to resume what he had initiated so long ago, to receive the finality of his mark, to embrace the long arc of his design for her, he saw himself caught in that design.

"The first time I saw you," he went on, "beyond anything else I felt that whatever might happen between us, I could never have you, that the day might come when you would outgrow your memory of me, and I would become, for you, a pathetic figure from your riding days."

She gave no sign of registering his intensity. Her eyes remained serene; her arms still enclosed her body.

"I thought of you when I was alone and when I was with others," he continued, "and the thought always brought with it the same regret—that, as your father, I would have been at least the one who shaped your past, but as a lover, nothing I could ever do, no force of my will breaking in on your life, could ever change it." In his vehemence, he had drawn closer to her, his shoulder brushing her thigh. "I've loved you all along, Vanessa."

Vanessa did not respond; he laid his head in her lap. She reached up to his face and touched his mouth with her hands. A door slammed, a distant sound. Vanessa removed her hands, bringing one of his to the scar on her lip.

"Then love me now," she said simply.

They rose. Fabian led Vanessa, who was carrying her clothes, toward the sauna. Opening the door before her, he switched on the light. A smell of shavings and dry bark spilled over them; the benches, bleached and plain, offered spare comfort.

Vanessa went toward the benches, her towel abandoned, and deliberately put her clothes on the top bench. Then she sat on the one beneath waiting for him.

He began to undress, placing each item of his clothing beside the small mound Vanessa had made on the top bench. To find the freedom that had been his with her before, he willed himself to remember images of afternoons in his VanHome, of Vanessa undressing before him, carefully placing her clothes within reach in case they might be interrupted and she would have to dress quickly. He realized that then, in the conspiracy of his VanHome, it had been he who took her, a mere girl, for his lover, putting at stake the only security he knew, containing his need for her, restraining the impulse to break the seal that bound her to herself. Now it was she who was taking him for her lover, bidding him to come, inviting him to break that seal.

Naked, his body was not yet responsive. He sat down next to her, his shoulder lingering at her back, the scent of her hair mingling with the pungent smell of wood, his mouth on her neck, his lips grazing the soft mound behind her ear, soft as it had been when he had first kissed it. His hands slid over her breasts, and the stir that rose in her quickened him, but his knees did not urge her to part her legs. A disquiet that he might soon cause her pain grew in him. He wondered whether she was also apprehensive.

He slipped a hand between her thighs, skimming her flesh, brushing its folds; his fingers, deeper still, found her moist. Slowly, unresisted, his hand invaded; a force within her, he drew her to his side, her eyes on him, her arms swaddling him. Memory and thought drowned in a touch he could no longer flee, as if the knowledge of who he was lay within her, and only by claiming her could he discover it.

He bent her gently to the wooden plank, her head back, her legs spread, one angled to rest a foot on the floor, one snaring his hip as he lowered himself, his hand braced to ease his weight on her, the other hand guiding the crest of his flesh along her crease, still reluctant to sink into flesh that had abandoned resistance, the tautness in his groin rising. She arched both legs, girdling his hips, and impaled herself on him, and he yielded, his flesh sinking into her, wedging her flesh until it found its obstacle, a limit of tension which seemed at one with his own urgency. He sensed the straining of her neck; her eyes, hooded, defied his scrutiny. He bore down, her nails knifing his skin, until he pierced her, breaking through to the spasm of her brief, harsh cry, the signal that he was free now to enter her deeper, to gather himself in her, swift in his motion, to reach her where she had never been reached before. Her face was distorted in a grimace, at once that of a young girl on the brink of tears and that of a woman in labor. Her hand commanding his hips, she began to thrust at Fabian, her body springing back as the tip of his flesh met her womb.

Above the sound of their breathing, Fabian heard the rasping of her teeth, a wailing from her closed mouth, its lower lip tightly bound against the other, as if to cover the scar. His hands were under her buttocks, lifting her, his flesh breaching her still further, each stroke a summons to her womb. Pushing her shoulders sideways, she curved her belly to him, her hands above her head, fingers clawing the wood as if to scrawl on it, her body sundered, waiting for him to keel into her, offering herself to a deeper quest.

He felt a warm trickle on his thigh, and he knew it to be her blood. Yet he did not lift his eyes from her face. Fusion with a body that had become his, a port of incessant entry and departure, left him uncertain whether with each step he was binding her closer to

himself or setting her adrift, to shores and reaches of
her own.

Moving within her, he recalled the Vanessa he had
first known: a slender girl on a horse next to him, his
eyes trapped by her thighs, the shape of her breasts,
the flex of a knee, the space that, with every movement
of the horse, opened between her and the saddle. He
looked at her now, his vision clouded by the thought of
her, of time yet to come, the inert burden of life
without her, a space brackish with the tedium of himself as a mere consequence of that life and no longer
the sire of it. In the blood that dabbled his thighs, he
knew he had drawn forth proof that something
uniquely hers marked him indelibly, pronounced him
as the first lover to touch her womb.

Vanessa seemed remote, her face contorted, the rasp
of her teeth more audible, her hands clenched. As if by
instinct, whether to be free of her or of himself, he
could not tell, he lifted his body in a vague threat of
partition and his hand moved down, fingers prodding,
searching for her flesh, capturing it. She moaned at his
touch, and, withdrawing his hand, he pushed back into
her. Her womb contracted, her hips and belly falling
back. Erupting, her body pounded against the wood,
her face shielded by her arms, her mouth agape, torn
apart by the moan, the scar of her lip protruding,
reluctant to remain hidden any longer, the stiffened
nipples of her breasts strong with desire on the palms
of his hands, her legs, bloody, unlocking from around
his hips.

He framed her head with his arms, his thighs cleaving hers, his chest over her, the shuddering calves of
her legs now over his shoulders, her feet above his
head. He watched the tide of blood his every thrust
spilled. In a sudden urge to share it with her, he withdrew his flesh, a column of blood, and stroked her face
with it, each stroke leaving a track of red; he repeated
this, bearing into her and pulling out again, returning
to her prodigal with blood, brazing her forehead, mark-

ing her cheeks, brimming her mouth, obliterating her
scar. Then, his face to hers, he licked the blood from
her forehead, her cheeks and neck, his tongue gathering it to her mouth. Caressing her lips, cajoling, he
kissed her, kisses she returned, tasting the gift of blood
he brought to her from her own depth. As she plunged
beneath him, her eyes staring, her mouth trapping a
scream, he moved into her again, a reeling of ebb and
flow pulling her apart, buckling her in quivers of desire.

The landscape of her, riven, swells and fissures overwhelmed him. His thirst unappeasable, he bent his
mouth to her mound, his tongue where his flesh had
been, a pilot in the wake of her blood, tasting her flow,
receiving it, tasting her again, his tongue fluttering, the
last pulse of his energy spending itself to absorb her
every drop, greedy for all that had once been hers.

Gathering her in or letting her out, idle or tense,
sliding into her or taking root, he held her to him until
she was beyond strength, energy, feeling, her mind
open no more to the sensations her body insisted on
bringing to flood.

From that peak, she toppled. To open her again, to
make her conscious of her freedom to withdraw, to
stay inviolate, he knelt over her, poised in the space
that divided them, his hands thrust back, his body
erect, the cone of his flesh close to her face, ready to
brush her cheeks or lips, her chin, her neck. She
gathered him in, avid to make fast her hold on him, to
strip him of the freedom that was his, to force him to
surrender to his own flesh and, by that act, reveal that
when he was with her, like her, he was powerless
against sensation. With his hands still thrust back, he
started slowly pushing into her, moving, swaying, then
plunging, filling her, swelling. Her head tilted back, she
fought for air, but in her freedom chose to retain him,
drowning as she sought to swallow, her eyes open, her
feet drumming against the bench. Her arms, suppliant
in defense, then arrested by will, stopped in midair,

reluctant to initiate an assault or to surrender to him. As her eyes closed and her arms dropped back, he receded, leaving her mouth open to the flush of air, but with her first deep breath, she once again reached toward him in silence, empty now of all but their shared need. The drumming of her feet subsided, a dwindling echo in the small wood hutch.

Fabian looked down at her face. She had waited for him to return; now she would wait for him no more. She was beyond waiting, beyond the deed she had once imagined. She was finally free of him, free of herself.

In the late autumn Fabian found himself on the road again, moving from stable to stable and giving lectures, always in search of work. On his way to Massachusetts, he detoured to New York, his destination the National Horse Show at Madison Square Garden, a venerable annual event drawing horses and riders from all over the world.

Even though the show had been in progress for almost a week, Fabian was curious to see the remaining events. And there was another reason; during their recent encounter, Vanessa had told him that Captain Ahab, her stallion, a present from her father, had qualified at the Garden for the Stanhope Cup international open puissance class, a jumping event in which the score rested on the horse's performance, power and endurance in clearing a number of large obstacles. The prize—a silver cup and a substantial purse—had been established by Vanessa's grandfather, Commodore Ernest Tenet Stanhope, and was the grandest the show could confer on a horse.

When Fabian had talked to Vanessa last, she had been almost certain that she and her parents would not be in New York for the show, and she had been pleased to learn that Fabian would be there to see her horse perform.

The Stanhope Cup was one of the major events of the show's closing days, and as Fabian walked into the

Garden, he caught the stir of anticipation, its excitement overcoming his distrust of competition.

Men in black tie or tails and top hat, their ladies nests of jewels and heavy, trailing furs, crowded onto escalators and moved along the round stairwells and huge corridors that spiraled the auditorium. The flame of scarlet hunt coats blazed wherever Fabian looked.

The vaulting auditorium was filled and seething with activity. Attendants put the last touches to the ring and the course; judges checked the distance between obstacles; television crews set up their cameras and lights; photographers leaned over the barrier around the show ring, trying out the most favorable angles to catch jumps.

Dizzied by all that splendor and feverish preparation, Fabian left the auditorium and walked behind the main arena, to the paddock, an area set aside for practice riding, for stabling the horses and housing the equipment, tack and supplies. There, at the Stanhope tent and stalls, he hoped to catch a glimpse of Captain Ahab, familiar to him from several local competitions in Totemfield. Because the area was not open to the general public and required a pass for admittance, Fabian had taken along the jacket of his book *Prone to Fall* and presented it to the guard as his credentials. Impressed with Fabian's photograph on the back cover, and his equestrian accomplishments listed on its flap, the guard let him in without a pass.

In the paddock, a more orderly life reigned. Fabian passed the rank of tents and stalls housing major national and foreign equestrian teams, their horses bearing insignia of the most renowned stables. He saw breeders and owners with their families, fleets of trainers and coaches, riders practicing and dressing for one event while their fellow competitors recovered from another, grooms currying and saddling and unbridling the mounts.

At the far end of the passage, he found the Stanhope Stables tent and stalls. The baroque family coat of arms stood out boldly against the deep blue stain of the stalls, the red fabric of the tent, the yellow wool of the horse blankets and hoods.

Fabian came upon the head groom, a man who remembered him from a time when Fabian had taught his young son at the Double Bridle Stables in Totemfield. The man, crippled in his youth by a fall from a horse, hobbled among the horses and tack with the aid of two canes.

The head groom told Fabian that Captain Ahab was already in the practice ring adjacent to the entry to the main arena, being warmed up there by Stuart Hayward, a young man from a prominent Southern family who had frequently ridden the stallion for the Stanhopes, working his way up through novice, junior and open events until he had qualified for major competitions. Riding Captain Ahab to victory in the puissance class at the Garden would be the culmination of all his efforts.

Inside the warm-up ring—unusually small in proportion to the number and height of the obstacles erected around it—Fabian saw that, in preparation for the main event that was to start in half an hour, several riders had already begun to pace their mounts at an even rhythm over the practice jumps. Next to the ring, he noticed the spectacular silhouette of Captain Ahab, an American Thoroughbred of impeccable lineage and breeding. At his side, the rider was in the process of adjusting the horse's tack.

Fabian walked briskly over to Hayward. The young man was slightly taller than Fabian, with strong thrusting legs, blond hair falling with unruly charm over his forehead. Fabian could see him on a college football team or behind a tennis net.

"I'm Fabian," he said, extending his hand.

Hayward shook Fabian's hand with the well-bred deference of the young toward those twice their age and accomplishment. "So you're the polo player who once taught riding in Totemfield?"

"Right," said Fabian. "A long time ago," he added.

"Vanessa always says that you gave her more than

any other teacher, Mr. Fabian," Hayward said, a tinge of admiration coloring his voice.

"I'm glad Miss Stanhope thinks so," Fabian said.

Hayward kept looking at him, as if Fabian's presence were a source of reassurance. Fabian felt a spontaneous warmth toward this young man, so forthright in his manner and bearing.

It was only after Hayward returned to the adjustment of Captain Ahab's tack that Fabian noticed how pale the young man was. Even though the warm-up ring was cool and he had not yet been riding, Hayward's forehead and upper lip were filmed with perspiration. His hands were trembling at the saddle. Sensing Fabian's scrutiny, Hayward suddenly mustered bravado.

"C'mon, Ahab," he called out, joking as he mounted the stallion, "let's go after our white whale!"

Circling the warm-up ring twice, his posture faultless, Hayward posted to a slow trot, then held firmly in the saddle during the canter, with Captain Ahab prancing a bit, still uncertain of the new environment as Hayward approached the first fence. His shoulders and hands forward, toes up, heels down, he kept his eyes ahead, maintaining his seat well in the saddle, his calves and the inner curve of his legs in intimate contact with the horse. As the animal cleared the obstacle, the line of the reins from the horse's bit to Hayward's elbow remained unbroken, a fluent stream through his fingers, permitting the horse the scope it needed. In the descent, Hayward smoothly sank back into the saddle, his ankles flexed, his knees absorbing the shock of the landing, the reins taut once more, the connection between the rider's hand and the horse's bit unruffled.

It was a perfect jump. Fabian, pleased for the younger rider, was about to leave the warm-up ring when he saw Hayward suddenly tilt sideways in the saddle, losing his balance. Jarred by a sudden tug of the reins, Captain Ahab refused to take the next jump, braking in panic before it, hind legs digging into the sawdust. Hayward quickly regained his seat and pulled out of the line, allowing other riders to continue their practice. Swaying in the saddle, he rode over toward Fabian, and when he pulled Captain Ahab to a halt, he almost toppled to the ground. Fabian reached up and grasped him by the elbow, to help him dismount. The young man's face was sallow, beaded with sweat. He looked ill.

"What happened?" Fabian asked calmly.

Hayward looked at him with unfocused eyes. "I don't know," he mumbled. "I feel—I feel strange." He kept swallowing as if his mouth were parched.

"What is it?" Fabian insisted, leaning him against the ring's wall, undoing the stock at his throat, loosening the starched noose of his collar and unbuttoning his jacket.

"I took some pills before," Hayward muttered thickly.

"What pills?"

Hayward's eyes were shut; he seemed close to fainting. "To steady my stomach through all this," he stammered. He gestured forlornly toward the main arena.

"How do you feel now?" Fabian asked.

Hayward slumped against the wall; he tried to drag himself up, but could not stand erect. "I don't think I can ride." His hand smeared dust as it wandered over his face. "Maybe I should try anyhow."

"A bad fall might finish off both you and Captain Ahab," Fabian said.

"What do I do, Mr. Fabian? Should I ride?" Hayward's eyes flickered blearily as he tried to stretch in the tight riding clothes.

"You're ill," Fabian said. "You won't have leg control, you can't keep your balance."

"There's nobody else to take my place. It's too late—Captain Ahab was announced, and everybody expects him to jump."

"A lot of riders withdraw at the last minute," Fabian said. A slow vision of what he was about to do, of what he had to do, started to unfold, the knowledge gathering momentum like a polo ball rolling inexorably toward the goal posts. "In any case, I'll ride Captain Ahab," he said, the ball through the goal posts, his vision now complete.

Hayward looked at him in disbelief. "You, Mr. Fabian?"

"Why not?" Fabian said. "That's the least you and I can do for the Stanhopes," he added forcefully.

"Would you really?" Hayward mumbled, his doubt dispelled.

"Let's go," Fabian said. "I need your clothes."

"Maybe I should go and tell Vanessa that you'll ride Captain Ahab for her," Hayward murmured, almost to himself.

"Vanessa?" Fabian asked.

"She was here with her family and their guests only a few minutes ago. They went to their box," Hayward said.

Fabian's first impulse was to go and see Vanessa, even to glance at her from afar, unseen. Then it dawned on him that if he rode Captain Ahab, Vanessa would soon be watching him, his every move under the spotlights of the arena. For a moment he panicked: he might discredit himself in her eyes and in the eyes of her family and guests; he was no longer certain whether he should ride Captain Ahab. But he quickly reassured himself that just as riding Captain Ahab was an event in his life, the judgment others passed on him was an event in theirs.

He looked at the clock. The puissance class was scheduled to begin in fifteen minutes. Swiftly, he tied Captain Ahab to a post.

Hayward was about to collapse, his sickness and the anguish of his helplessness blotting out his awareness of what was happening. The object of curious stares from the other riders, Hayward submitted to being steered by Fabian back to the Stanhope tent, where Fabian slid him onto a cot.

With panic in his eyes, the head groom listened as Fabian told him he intended to ride the stallion. "I'll have to tell Miss Vanessa," he said, hobbling about frantically on his canes.

Fabian cut him off abruptly. "There's no time. Call a doctor, then notify the show secretary that, as an emergency substitute, I'll be riding Captain Ahab; they know who I am." He started to pull off Hayward's riding boots as the head groom lurched out of the tent.

On the cot, Hayward was in a stupor, his breath heaving. Fabian stripped him of his riding clothes and briskly slipped on the breeches and the jacket. The boots were most important, and they fit, despite a light pressure on his insteps. He fastened Hayward's entry number around the jacket and, seizing the hat, whip and gloves, bolted from the tent.

Captain Ahab was still tethered to the post, its eyes sidling with only slight apprehension as Fabian began to adjust the stirrups. The warm-up ring was emptying, the other contestants allowing their mounts a brief respite before the event. Fabian mounted the stallion and started to walk it slowly around the ring, testing the horse's mood—and his own.

He reviewed the elements of the competition: how the horse and rider would be confronted at the start with six obstacles, two of those eliminated at the completion of each round of jumps, and the remaining obstacles raised progressively for the next round. The course took its toll gradually, as mounts and riders, failing to clear the fences, were eliminated. Finally, only two formidable obstacles would remain, a spread of double rustic gates and a massive wall that, in its progressive elevation, could exceed seven feet.

He could not keep the terror back, recognizing that as a horseman he would soon face the fiercest demand of his life: performing on a mount he had never ridden before, in a realm of horsemanship in which he had never excelled and was not sufficiently practiced. The lowest obstacle in the Stanhope Cup was among the highest he had ever negotiated; the highest was one he had never even contemplated. He dared not permit himself to think that, in the presence of thousands of spectators and fans, most of them passionate followers of the sport, he and Captain Ahab would be competing against horses possessing exceptional jumping power, ridden by seasoned veterans with scores of championships to their credit, their names burnished with the celebrity of national trophies, world cups, Olympic medals. He could not know whether the audience would take his attempt as gallantry or insult, if they would be vocal in their anger and displeasure with the arrogance of a horseman flaunting his ineptitude on such a formidable national stage.

For himself, he knew that his zeal of the moment, his bravery in jumping Captain Ahab, might be punished by a fall that could cripple or kill him. He was also aware of the danger to the horse: what he did with Captain Ahab might affect permanently the condition of a valuable jumper, in great demand as a sire. And he would be riding the stallion without the permission of its owner, the one to whom the animal was most precious, the one whose happiness Fabian saw as his custody—Vanessa.

Soon he would have to enter the theater of his ultimate challenge. Terror twisted him in a fresh assault, and he gagged, but he managed to keep down the bile. There was no opportunity for those rituals with which he had always harnessed his fear—no voiding of his body, no honing and healing it in a warm bath, no music to rally his fortitude while he shaped out of cloth and polo gear a figure with which to sustain himself during the contest.

Afraid to put the stallion, or himself, to the first trial, Fabian circled the warm-up ring and willed himself to one vision: that of himself, a rider a few strides away from the fence, bearing down on it at an even pace, embarked on a strategy that allowed no chance or change.

A loudspeaker called for the first entrant, a member of the Irish Equestrian Team, wearing the uniform of an officer of the Irish Army. As the rider left the paddock area and entered the arena, applause from the auditorium broke the tense hush of the paddock. The other contestants, all mounted, lined up near the entrance to the arena, gauging the Irishman's performance.

Fabian resisted the temptation of joining them. He had glanced at the setup of the course, the nature and size of the obstacles, when he arrived at the Garden. Watching the first rider take the obstacles would be time subtracted from the preparation he needed for his own performance. He had to focus his concentration, rely on his feeling and sense of Captain Ahab, on his ability to convey to his mount a state of tension, of collection and the impulsion to jump.

He prompted Captain Ahab with his legs, and the animal, alert, instantly responded; then he tightened the reins slightly and let himself sink in the saddle; collected, the stallion responded again. The man had sounded the first words of the silent language between rider and mount, the communion they alone knew; it was time to test this communion.

Fabian approached the first of several practice fences at an even pace and threw the stallion into a canter. Captain Ahab rose toward the obstacle and cleared it, a harmony of balance and movement, taking the hurdle so smoothly that Fabian was barely conscious of the slight jolt of landing. Spirited in manner, without a perceptible trace of fear or hesitation, the horse maintained its pace over the next fence, then over the others, breasting them with security and ease, its neck extended, forelegs tucked in high.

The Irish officer returned, his exit from the auditorium accompanied by bravos; over the loudspeaker, the steady voice of the announcer cited his score. It was an adequate one, although his horse had been penalized for faults. The second entrant was announced, an American, a young woman, a member of the U.S. Equestrian Team, riding a powerful Thoroughbred gelding, at least a hand taller than Captain Ahab; her appearance in the auditorium was recognized with a tumult of applause, homage to her standing as one of the finest jumpers in the country.

Fabian circled the warm-up ring for the last time, and again Captain Ahab seemed to know exactly what was expected, executing the variety of jumps with a unique suavity and fluent cadence. The horse's composure his tutor, Fabian thought of possible strategies he might employ in the arena. He knew he might keep the animal tautly in hand, his legs tight, pacing its steering before each obstacle, whetting the horse to become a springboard of propulsion that would impel it over the obstacle, the parabola of its leap sculpted by the rider. usurping the animal's own scope and impulse at the very moment when the safety of the animal itself was as much at stake as that of its rider.

Or he might pace his mount in a smooth run, the sequence from obstacle to obstacle, no matter what the height or position, uninterrupted, confirmation of his supreme trust in the horse, intimation that he had surrendered the speed of the course to the animal's own instinct to control the condensed power of its hocks in the jump and the extension of its neck over the barrier; nature and training would guide the horse in tucking in its forelegs and raising its hind legs sufficiently to crest the obstacle at a proper height.

Fabian thought of photographs he had seen in riding manuals, grim mementos of horse and rider come to grief in open jumping competitions—a horse crashing head on with a wall, the rider tossed over it like a wooden doll; a horse vaulting, its forelegs already on the ground, its hind legs almost vertical, still gouging the air, the rider's feet trapped in the stirrups, reins in hand, but his body toppling already over the animal's neck a second before the heaving weight of the horse would bury him under its loins, the horse's neck broken, the rider squashed like an insect by the impact of the mount. Fabian knew those images to be abstracts of fugitive time, irreversible, deadly intervals in the lives of other men, irrelevant to his own specter of himself spilling under Captain Ahab.

He saw himself falling, with the horse or from it, his hands, arms and shoulders reaching down to protect himself from the ground, a natural reaction though a wrong one, leading to a sprained wrist, a broken arm or a head injury. He reminded himself that he must avert his gaze from the line of a fall, because his hands and arms would follow his gaze and turn him away from the ground, making the back of his shoulder absorb the impact.

The American rider returned, openly delighted, enjoying the volley of applause that followed her from the arena, her mount backing up excitedly as she guided it through the paddock. Fabian heard the announcement—a perfect score.

The next contestant was a member of the Belgian Equestrian Team, an Olympic medalist. Fabian watched the magisterial containment of rider and mount as they passed into the arena, the Belgian's mare an Anglo-Arab, splendid in confrontation, at the very peak of collection, the rider a master of its urge to spring, an awesome instance of human ingenuity and persistence imposed on animal force.

Fabian was to go next. He rode out of the warm-up ring and brought Captain Ahab to a halt near the entrance to the arena, still reluctant to face the blaze of display, the murmuring tide of expectation that waited there, ahead of him. Once again, he rehearsed mentally the layout of the obstacle course, honing freshly his awareness that he must not let his concentration stray from the network and progression of the jumps, that he must keep his eyes always fixed on the jump ahead.

He heard a storm of applause, then silence, then another volley of encouragement spilling over the audience in gusts, then another. There was silence again. Fabian moved to the entrance and looked out into the arena. He saw the Belgian's horse curl toward the big wall, then trip and keel over it. A low moan from the audience reached the paddock before the din of the crash; Fabian saw the rider, shaken, leading his horse away.

Fabian watched as the crew restored the wall, in prelude to his entrance. Suddenly, with a volume and clarity that startled him, he heard the loudspeaker announce his name and number as the substitute rider on Captain Ahab.

The paddock master gave him the signal, and Fabian prompted Captain Ahab through the opening into the arena. As he moved forward, instinct overtook fear and thought, and he found himself at the brink of a field of yellow sawdust, the obstacles looming shapes of darkness before him, tiers of balconies ascending the arching dome of light and depth, walls of collective scrutiny closing about him.

He entered the ring, Captain Ahab at a walk; a flurry of scattered applause was distant in his ears, his sense of proportion assailed by the magnitude of the auditorium, by some buried impulse censoring any reminder that he was a target of curiosity for Vanessa, for her family, for so many others, subverting any challenge to his conviction that now, on this stage of scattered obstacles, he and his horse were alone, the world divested of all reality but that of one man, one mount, of their fusion—and of his solitude.

He broke into a slow trot, Captain Ahab as peaceful and unruffled as it had been in the paddock only moments before, moving slowly to the right, toward the far side of the arena and the first obstacle, a post-and-rails, close to the spectators. But before he was able to reach the line that would take him there, he accelerated the trot, his body in a rhythm of rise and fall, then slowing down again, then picking up speed in a rocking canter as he circled the line of jumps. He decided to let Captain Ahab take the first jump with reins almost loose, his legs barely prompting the animal, his manner implying security and confidence. The horse went over the rails as readily as it had done in the paddock, landing without a jar, continuing just as readily toward and over the triple bars, the second obstacle. At the curving end of the arena Fabian slackened the horse and turned right, into the center of the ring, toward the double rustic gates. This time, his legs firm against the ribs, he guided Captain Ahab toward the obstacle, but still let the animal pace itself in front of the jump. As the horse took off into the air, Fabian, detecting no hesitation, kept the reins taut, inches from its neck, to signal, but not to curb; his own body was supple and thrust forward slightly above the saddle. He discerned no faltering when, to an eruption of applause that momentarily invaded his concentration, the stallion cleared the obstacle.

Fabian turned to the left side of the arena, toward the fourth obstacle, a brush-and-rails. Captain Ahab sprang forward at a canter and, as if spurred by the lure of the hunt, cleared it with at least a foot to spare, then went straight ahead at a double oxer, a wide spread. Fabian prompted Captain Ahab to a smooth canter, and the horse cleared the fifth obstacle evenly. Applause swelled around the auditorium again, but Fabian rigidly shut out the distraction. He continued across the arena, steering Captain Ahab to the left, advancing back into the center of the ring, toward the final jump, a wall over six feet tall, its wooden blocks painted to resemble reddish brick, its top curved. As he lifted his eyes toward it, he reminded himself that he was not running the course under a time limit and that there was no need for haste; he slackened Captain Ahab to a slow trot just before making a turn toward the wall.

Alert to the tension gathering in his mount, Fabian chose not to dispel it and, binding himself even tighter to the body of the horse, he signaled with the lock of his thighs that it was time to start for a jump. Captain Ahab obeyed instantly, moving at a collected trot, almost prancing. As Fabian braced himself, inclining forward in the saddle, the horse, now in the rhythm of the accelerated stride, sprang up from its hocks to vault the wall. In the stillness of the auditorium, Fabian, still in midair, heard the ominous bark of its hind legs, insufficiently raised, as they rapped the wooden surface of the obstacle. Instinctively Fabian leaned further forward to unload its back, but by then, Captain Ahab had already cleared the wall, landing with its habitual smoothness, to the accompaniment of tumultuous applause. Slowing to a trot, then a walk, prancing gracefully, the horse carried Fabian out of the light, into the darker enclosure of the paddock.

There he was assailed by his name and number announced over the loudspeaker. Only four riders remained to compete in the second run, and Fabian was among them. He felt the urgency of composing himself, and hoped Vanessa would not visit him in the paddock, but would remain with her parents and friends, in the audience, waiting for the outcome. Even she, and his sense of her, seemed severed now from the single reality that engulfed him: the sheer pressure of the necessity that he hold his seat on Captain Ahab and conduct the horse through this second run. The course would be shorter by two obstacles, but that advantage was offset by the new challenge of the remaining four, which had been substantially elevated. He knew he had to keep Captain Ahab as unhampered and fluent as it had been in the first run, yet sufficiently in check to hurdle obstacles, particularly the wall.

Fabian withdrew into the vigilance of readiness; a tide of applause, then a long silence remained at the margin of his awareness. He was called to full alertness only at the announcement of his name, and he entered the arena, oblivious to the applause that greeted him.

He kept his eyes fixed on the first obstacle, the post-and-rails, during the approach; the reins and his legs tight, he forced the mount to coil in anticipation. Then, just before the obstacle, he let the reins flow like a rope being played out to an anchor. Collected, Captain Ahab jumped forward, breasting the fence as cleanly as it had in the first run. The next two obstacles, the brush-and-rails and the double oxer, the stallion cleared with no effort.

Fabian moved Captain Ahab toward the wall. Its height was now considerable, because blocks several inches thick had been added to it. Once more Fabian registered the animal's apprehension, and rather than take the jump as an extension of the driving stride, he decided to pivot the mount toward a spot that was as far away from the wall as the wall was high, a strategy that would prompt the stallion to slow down before taking off from its hocks. But when he sent a surge of pressure through his legs and alerted Captain Ahab to go, the animal refused the command, prancing instead where it stood. Fabian once again gave the cue for the horse to take off, but still Captain Ahab would not move.

Fabian did not know the habits of Captain Ahab, and he was reluctant to use the whip or to spur the horse too painfully; moreover, the animal's refusal did not appear to him to be the obstinate defiance of a sulky horse. Pressing with his legs, bracing the muscles of his back, Fabian made a final effort to rally the stallion for the jump. But instead of moving forward, Captain Ahab defiantly stepped back. A ripple of laughter ruffled the audience. Still patient and calm, refraining from punishment, trying to decipher the instinct that dictated the horse's behavior, Fabian pulled the reins to swerve Captain Ahab away from the wall. When the animal obeyed, Fabian assumed the horse felt more secure in taking the wall as it had in the first run, by approaching at a faster pace.

He put the stallion into a trot and, circling, turned it evenly toward the wall, increasing the pressure of his legs, releasing the bit, goading the horse, driving hard and straight at the wall, aware of the dangers of too early a takeoff at a fast pace, which, by extending the length of the jump, would lower its arc. He readied himself for his mount's sudden refusal, which could unseat him; he also knew that, if pressed too strongly, the horse might hurl itself into the obstacle, not over it.

Its haunches bunching, Captain Ahab began to approach the wall, its strides now shorter, gathering force, then, with its hocks fully extended, its head down, its crest curving, it catapulted forward and up, clearing the wall in a gliding motion, coming down to yet another gentle landing, sprightly and composed.

With applause pursuing him, Fabian rode back to the paddock, past the other entrants awaiting their turns, and steered Captain Ahab toward the farthest corner of the warm-up ring, away from the commotion. Now, alone, in order to block the sudden onrush of images of fall and defeat, of this pitch of time and what lay beyond it, he thought of Vanessa. He let himself wonder where she was in the audience—sitting with her parents and guests, people he had never met and could not even envisage.

The clamor of triumph and defeat spilled around him again as the remaining contestants ran the course. He tried to stop a wave of apprehension when he saw the last of them return, spent, to the paddock. Then he heard his name again, loud, and that of the young American woman from the U.S. Equestrian Team, who had followed the Irish officer at the opening of the event. She and Fabian were the finalists for first and second places.

She looked across the paddock at Fabian, her competitor. She was young, her hair neatly drawn into a snood beneath her riding hat, her hunt jacket and skintight breeches well-cut. There was a quiet confidence about her; in his ill-fitting costume, Fabian felt awkward. As she rode into the arena, her entrance brought the wildest applause yet.

Fabian listened to the applause, aware that he was not seduced by the allure of competition, by the promise of celebrity. All that had mattered to him from the outset of the event was his own safety and that of Captain Ahab. He resented the thrill of danger that audiences seemed to demand.

A riot of exhilaration in the auditorium told him, even before it was announced over the loudspeaker, that the young woman had run the course faultlessly. At best, Fabian could match her performance, but he dreaded the possibility of a jump-off, with the obstacles raised even higher, approaching a mark that few horses were strong and masterful enough to clear.

He heard his name; he was being summoned. Responding mechanically, he left the warm-up ring, emerging from the paddock slowly, almost sluggishly, into the bright arena.

The audience was silent. Fabian cantered smoothly into the line of the jump, toward the double oxer. He sensed that to clear the spread, now substantially raised, Captain Ahab needed a fast pace for takeoff. His legs and seat closely gripping the animal, he signaled his readings to go for the jump.

Once again, Fabian allowed Captain Ahab to select its own place for the takeoff, and once again, gathering its hocks, the horse gauged it, its ears pricked up, head and neck extended. Impelled into the air, the animal seemed to float over the width of the spread, its forelegs no longer tucked in under the belly, but this time instinctively unfolded, raised and stretched out as if to better absorb the longer sweep of the jump, the hoofs level with the muzzle. For landing, the horse raised its head, its forelegs reaching out; its croup was high, the hind legs retreating to the ground to absorb their share of the shock the forelegs had already registered; its head and neck low again, the horse was ready to resume the run.

Applause carried Fabian and Captain Ahab at a fast pace to the wall, now over seven feet, looming over the horse's head, a hulk of awesome challenge. Fabian could not leave this jump to the instinct of the animal. To prompt it over the obstacle with not a finger of space in excess between its hoofs and the wall, he had to guide the horse, even at the risk of another refusal, to take the jump not as an extension of a long driving stride, but, rather, as a leap from no more than three or four paces, surprisingly close to the base of the wall.

Not a whisper disturbed the audience. Fabian steered Captain Ahab toward the wall, his body at one with the stallion's, his breath even, his eyes on the obstacle.

The horse obeyed, moving at a smooth pace. Almost at the spot from which Fabian wanted it to leap, he tightened his calves, bracing himself and the animal for their supreme effort. Again, the horse followed his command, gathering in its hocks all its energy, readying itself to spring up for the takeoff. With its haunches well under its belly, Captain Ahab pushed off, its hocks about to straighten, its crest arching, head lowered, when, from the audience at ringside, at Fabian's right, a loud shout of "Take it, Fabian, take it now!"

pierced the silence. Unwittingly, Fabian turned his head for an instant to the source of the voice that was so familiar, catching a glimpse of Alexandra Stahlberg, her tunic tight and golden, leaning out of her seat, beside Michael Stockey.

Curved like a dolphin, Captain Ahab already had cleared the wall with its forelegs; its hoofs were now higher than its belly, its croup rising, its head descending. In the glimmer of time that Fabian glanced at Alexandra, his body inclined backward, his weight shifted over the animal's hind legs, hampering their passage over the wall; the delicate balance of control snapped. Off-balance in its descent, Captain Ahab twisted jarringly, hooking the top of the wall with its hocks. A moan rose from the audience as the horse, its head up, sank onto its forelegs, a section of the wall brushing the animal's croup and toppling behind it. Momentarily unseated, about to fall over the horse's mane, Fabian regained his balance with a reflex that placed him back firm in the saddle; simultaneously, just as the animal was about to fall, he curbed it, pulling the reins to lift the horse's head even higher and unweight its forelegs. Steadied by Fabian, its hocks absorbing the full impact of the landing, Captain Ahab rebounded and continued to run, returning its rider for the last time to the shelter of the paddock.

There Fabian heard his name announced again, a final summons to the arena, where Captain Ahab would be awarded second prize. Fabian was startled, as he rode toward the judges, to see Vanessa in their company: it was she who had been appointed to present the prizes that bore her family name. He removed his hat and put it under his arm, leaning forward to look at her when she pinned the rosette to Captain Ahab's bridle. She looked up to him, and he took her hand; he saw her eyes wet with tears, her lips framing the words "I love you," soundless, perceptible only to him. He experienced the same pain of separation he had felt each time she had left him in his VanHome. It was as if—with the judges, their retinue, the reporters and photographers, her family and friends all around—no longer tangible, she was a mere extension of points of space and time she occupied in his memory. He put his hat back on and, backstepping Captain Ahab, turned and trotted away.

In the paddock he delivered the horse to the head groom, who, excited by the success of the stallion, almost forgot to tell Fabian that Hayward, already attended to by a doctor, was now asleep, and there was no need for further concern.

Fabian changed quickly back into his clothes. Anxious to avoid a meeting with Vanessa's family and another confrontation with Alexandra, he merged with the departing crowd and sneaked away from the sprawl and tumult of the Garden. He was soon lost in the throng of the city and before long arrived at his Van-Home, its signs, SELF-REACTOR: AUTHORIZED PERSON-NEL ONLY, an effective deterrent to the lawful and lawless alike.

Fabian was on the last stretch of a trip to Palm Beach, curious to see Wellington, the resort designed and built as an enclave for polo, its stables and fields a lavish habitat for the player, his ponies and his game. There, at the Palm Beach Polo and Country Club, he hoped to find those willing to play him.

He was entering the expressway; he had paid the turnpike toll, met and matched the stare of the attendant assessing the splendor of his VanHome, and started to pull into the center lane, building up speed, when he noticed a state police car passing him, the trooper waving to flag him to a stop.

He slowed down, pulled over to the shoulder of the road, and lowered the window at his side. The signs on the sides of his VanHome read INTERSTATE STAGE-COACH and he did not expect any trouble with the law about them. His driver's license and VanHome registration were in order; he had not exceeded the speed limit.

The trooper came over to the cab and looked up, smiling. "Sorry to stop you, sir," he said, "but if you're Mr. Fabian, the owner of this"—he paused and leaned forward to read the sign—"of this stagecoach, then we have an urgent message for you."

"I am," Fabian said. "But from whom?"

The trooper reached into his shirt pocket and pulled out a telegram, which he handed to Fabian. "From the State Continental Bank, Palm Beach branch," he said.

"They expected you to come this way and asked us as a courtesy to flag you down at a turnpike booth."

Fabian opened the envelope and glanced at the telegram; it asked him to come to see the branch manager at his earliest convenience.

"How did they know I'd be coming this way?" he asked. "Even I wasn't sure I'd be making the trip."

The trooper adjusted his sunglasses. "Is there anything these banks don't know?" he asked.

To Fabian, whose dealings with money had been mostly a reality of cash in hand, the negligible income from his books attended to by remote agencies, banks seemed an impenetrable geometry of computing and calculation, negotiated by people caged behind counters and Formica desks, people so programmed to be efficient, civil, ready with a practiced smile, that the very juices of life had been leached from their bodies. Like the cash machines that were posted in bank lobbies, transacting the lives, on approval, of the sentient creatures in their presence, delivering or withholding money in accordance with some higher wisdom, the men and women who worked in banks were to Fabian as functional as currency itself, at once as abstract as the hieroglyphics of mathematics and as concrete as the cash without which he could not feed his ponies or move his VanHome from one place to another.

He became increasingly apprehensive as the expressway opened onto the suburbs of West Palm Beach, row upon row of trailers, now permanent homes, fenced in neat cubes of arid space, a solitary palm tree or hedge the only relief. He could not remember who might be aware of his presence in Florida or interested in his whereabouts. He had mentioned his destination to only a few people—the manager of the stable where Big Lick had been freshly shod, the mechanic who had checked the brakes of his VanHome, the barman or waiter in a restaurant he had stopped at. Yet none of them knew him sufficiently to care where he had been or to take note of where he was going. Then it occurred to him that perhaps Stockey or someone else at Grail Industries would think of enlisting the aid of a bank to track him down, since Florida was a plausible region for a polo player to visit during the winter.

He arrived at the center of Palm Beach. The State Continental Bank had a private parking lot, an open-air showroom of limousines, with chauffeurs lounging at the wheels of precious curiosities refurbished to eccentricities, of lavish cars built to order. Some chauffeurs looked up from their newspapers to stare at Fabian's VanHome.

Inside the bank, a middle-aged woman in spectacles and a pastel linen suit listened to his request to be taken to the manager. She made no attempt to conceal her disapproval of his jeans and work shirt, but after a brief consultation in another office, returned to usher him in.

The bank's manager, a slender man about Fabian's age, was cool and skeptical, his Palm Beach elegance frosted with financial propriety. He was more candid than the woman in his baffled appraisal of Fabian, and he directed Fabian to an adjacent conference room, an intimate retreat reserved for the bank's important patrons.

Fabian took a lounge chair, and the manager settled across from him in an armchair and opened a leather portfolio. He looked up with a smile intended to undercut the tedium of the bureaucratic protocol he had to follow.

"So you are Mr. Fabian," he announced briskly and then continued as if no reply were in order. "Is all this information correct?" he inquired pleasantly, handing Fabian an index card with typing on it.

Fabian read the card: his full name, place and date of birth, the names of his parents, his Social Security number, the address of his publisher. All were correct, neatly typed.

"It looks all right," he replied, "but I still don't know why you've asked me to come here."

The manager spread his hands in a gesture of apology. "I do hope this hasn't caused you any inconvenience, Mr. Fabian, but there was just no other way to let you know that we had been authorized to take temporary custody of your property until you could be located." He removed a letter from the portfolio; Fabian could see that the letter was typed and had an envelope attached.

The anxiety stung him that some past negligence, a failure, perhaps, to meet a payment on his VanHome, had resulted now, so many years later, in a claim on his property, a demand initiated by someone using the bank as an intermediary. Instantly, he put himself on the defense.

"I am sole owner of everything I have," he said evenly. "I have not authorized anyone to take charge of my property."

The manager lifted one hand in apologetic explanation. "Of course you haven't. I'm afraid I haven't made myself clear, Mr. Fabian." He placed the letter and the envelope ceremoniously on the small table next to Fabian. "We were entrusted with the title of this gift, with most specific instructions from both the donor and the officers of the donor's original trust that notification of the gift be made to you expressly, in person."

Fabian glanced at the letter without reading it and saw a space at the bottom still to be signed. He felt no less apprehensive, no more enlightened, than he had before.

"And what are my obligations if I choose to claim this gift?"

The bank manager brought his hands together, fingers tapping against each other. "None," he said, "of course, none." Then he corrected himself. "That is, none short of signing this letter of acceptance for the check that has been made out in your name." He leaned forward, and with the tip of one finger, smoothly prodded the letter and envelope toward Fabian.

Still mistrustful and hesitant, Fabian reached for the

envelope. It was unsealed. He opened it, his touch uneasy, and withdrew the large blue check that was inside.

He looked at the check, the name of the bank, its logo in thick print at the top, the date of issue a few days earlier. He saw his name, the letters typed in capitals, stretching along one line, the first and middle names he never used striking him as incongruous, occupying too much of the check's limited space. Then his eyes moved to the line of letters, capital again, spelling out in words the full amount, the line long, again the space spilling over with words. Yet he could not get it in focus, his eyes reeling above it to the right, the figures visible and neat in their accustomed space, the dollar sign clear, then the figures blurring, the sequence of zeros a confusion. He went back to the dollar sign, its serpentine shape curiously at odds with the directness of the figures, the number in the box reserved for dollars, the progression of zeros, those preceding the division of the comma, then those before the next comma, and finally, the two following the period in the small box, the cents.

The figures wavered, and he began again, trying to decipher them, the number and the zeros parading one after another; and only after he had taken all the steps, nine figures in all, two of which, slightly apart, stood for cents, was he able to register the magnitude of the sum. Heat started to build up under his shirt, a flush at his neck and face, as he returned to the words he had abandoned, the line now clear to him. He let his eyes move toward the bottom of the check, the flourish of official signatures, stamps and symbols of authority, the imprint of validity.

"I don't understand," he managed to stammer, the check adrift in his hands, raising his eyes to the manager, sweat on his forehead beading an eyebrow before he stemmed it with a brush of his hand. "Why—why is this check made out to me?"

For a moment, the bank manager's eyes flickered in collaboration with Fabian's bewilderment. Then he said calmly, "This check represents an unconditional gift to you, Mr. Fabian, by Miss Vanessa Stanhope. As you must know, Miss Stanhope, the only daughter of Mr. Patrick Stanhope, and a granddaughter of Commodore Ernest Tenet Stanhope, inherited at birth a substantial interest in her grandfather's estate. She is also the sole benefactor of a trust established by him in her name. She has recently come of legal age and is therefore, as I am sure you realize, in a position to make a gift of cash." He trailed off at the sight of the check lying on the table, where Fabian had put it. "Even, shall we say, such a substantial one, though, quite likely, only a fraction of the estate itself." He continued. "It was at Miss Stanhope's urgent request, Mr. Fabian, that we intervened and had you paged, so to speak, thanks to the state police."

Even in his agitation, Fabian struggled to focus on the memory of Vanessa. He had not seen her for weeks, since the events at the Garden, although he spoke with her often on the telephone, each time from another highway booth, and she from that house he had never seen, in the midst of a family he had never met. Frantically, he sought to recall their last conversation, but then, as always, he had wanted simply to listen to her voice, imagine her movement and expression; he remembered, though, her asking casually about his next stop, and how he had recounted the itinerary that would take him to Wellington. He remembered, also, her remark that she wanted to be with him after Wellington, the two of them watching Captain Ahab competing on the Southern horse show circuit, and his promise that he would call her from Palm Beach.

The bank manager was waiting.

"I don't deserve such a gift," Fabian said. "I can't accept it."

The manager nodded patiently, a teacher confronting a student. "It is, of course, a gift, Mr. Fabian, an amount of cash voluntarily, gratuitously and with full awareness transferred by one person to another, with no expectation of compensation." He wanted to be certain that Fabian grasped the implication of what he was saying. "You may be confident that no issue of reciprocity, whether past, present or future, is a condition. And as the reasons for the gift are vested entirely in its donor, Miss Stanhope, in this instance, you, Mr. Fabian, as its recipient, should not want to belittle it." He waited for Fabian's response to his slight reproach. When it did not come, the manager slid the letter and the check closer to Fabian, as if to entice him with their presence.

"I can't accept this gift," Fabian said. "I just can't."

The manager rustled suddenly with irritation, but just as suddenly his composure returned, and he leaned toward Fabian, removing the typed letter of acceptance from beneath the check and presenting it for Fabian's scrutiny.

"If the taxes to be paid on such a gift are your concern, Mr. Fabian, you will see that, as this letter acknowledges, they have all been paid already in their entirety by the donor, Miss Stanhope." He reached over and with his finger drew an imaginary circle around the letter's paragraph about taxes.

The manager settled more comfortably into his chair, convinced that his obligations in the matter had been met. Visibly expansive, he flourished a fountain pen from the inner pocket of his jacket and set it on the table, next to the check.

"Since Miss Stanhope has deposited these funds for you with us, you might wish to have this"—he inclined gracefully toward the check—"transferred by us directly to your bank account." He hesitated, then made his suggestion, careful not to appear pushy. "Or you might think about opening an account with us here. In any instance, we—the bank and I—are at your disposal."

Fabian lowered his head, pretending to read the letter. Vanessa's check waited on the table beside him, an agent of transformation, and his thoughts unreeled the lucid image of himself, of his life and the shape of it. The reel accelerated, and he saw himself suddenly free from the chance and desperation of snaring a one-on-one game, the panic before the contest allayed, the tension of the game slackening, the easy drifting away of all that was absolute in him, all that defined the elusive order of his nature.

The reel shot forward in time, and he saw himself a resident at Palm Beach, the lavish spaciousness of a private villa the successor to his VanHome. There he would be, the celebrated polo player again, the renowned author, once more a key figure on the international polo circuit, not just with Big Lick and Gaited Amble, but with a string of prize ponies at his disposal and grooms to tend them in the polo club's own stables. Or perhaps he would return to Los Lemures—the shadow of Falsalfa gone, the dictator having been assassinated long ago—and make a princely residence in La Hispaniola, near Casa Bonita, a neighbor of the rich and powerful, his ponies always at the ready for a game or a trip to the mysteries of the interior.

He still saw his sieges of pain, his face in the mirror, the coming of old age, the time of crippling and waste, but knew that for him there would be clinics and spas, outposts of medical technology and healing, the attention of doctors, the solace of young nurses, the obliteration of pain through treatment, then the recovery, in the garden, on the terrace, at the gymnasium, health restored, age delayed.

And then he thought of Vanessa. The gift she had "voluntarily, gratuitously and with full awareness transferred with no expectation of compensation" was simply a gift of life, but of life to be lived in the fragile awareness that it came defined by the nature of the gift, the memory of the giver, and that his own life's every moment was no longer of his own devising.

He stood up, the letter and the check on the table. "I'm sorry, I can't—I won't accept Miss Stanhope's gift," he said, his voice sure again, the rhythm of his heartbeat and breath restored.

The manager rose in astonishment, unable to camouflage his shock. "The Stanhope family has always been one of this bank's most highly valued clients, Mr. Fabian. I trust we have done all we can to convince you that Miss Stanhope's gift was made in good faith—"

Fabian cut him off. "I'm certain Miss Stanhope will understand my reasons."

He extended his hand, and the manager shook it. They walked in silence to the door. As Fabian turned to leave, the manager reassured him that, in accordance with Miss Stanhope's instructions, her gift would be left at Fabian's disposal, in the bank, for an indefinite time, its use subject only to Fabian's acceptance and his signature confirming that he had received it in full.

At the wheel of his VanHome again, windows sealed against the heat and distraction of the world beyond, the receding lawns and estates, then the marshaled ranks of trailers, Fabian's eyes moved mechanically from the highway to the odometer, the odometer to the highway, with the obsessive constancy of a pendulum.

The reel was still turning in his head, merging with the road winding before him and the changing numbers of the odometer, the wheeling of the road and of his thought as one, all twining in a single thread racing toward the instruments of fate lying in wait at each turn.

He recalled, from his childhood, the fable with which his father had kept him enchanted and terrified—of the three sisters, invisible, and how they would always be near him, often when he least suspected, determining the span of his time. There was the youngest of the three, his father had told him, the most beautiful, whose task it was to survey and untangle the knot of life and recover from its maze the thread of each man's time. And then there was the second sister, the one you could always recognize by either of the masks she wore, the funny one or the sad one. It was she who bore the measure, took the thread and placidly went on spinning it, intent only on the turning wheel, indifferent to what pattern the thread would make. Finally, there was the oldest, so fond of her shears that she would never let them from her grasp, always eager to undo the labor and design of her sisters, to snip the thread at any time.

He thought he heard the whistling moan of the spindle, the turning wheel. He realized it was Big Lick and Gaited Amble pawing at their stalls, and he stopped reluctantly to feed them, pulling over to a rest space off the highway. The food he carried for them, the flaked maize and crushed oats, the boiled linseed, sugar-beet pulp, the forage of hay and soybean and corn, the timothy, ryegrass, clover and trefoil—all these seemed to him now an unreal substance whose only purpose was transformation into the bulk of meat, the heft of weight and strength the animal would become with time, the fuel that fed its glossy coat, the fleshed vault of its ribs and spine, the subdued prominence of its hindquarters.

Later, when noon had declined into a golden haze, Fabian stopped again, veering off the highway at the glimpse of a retreat, an unguarded field. There, stealthy as a horse thief about his rounds, he released his ponies to run, quick and urgent, steaming in sweat but never exhausted, the sole goal of the workout a translation of their weight and strength into the force and speed he would want from them in a game.

Still later, unable to focus on the road swallowed by night, he pulled to the side of an unfinished highway and, huddling in the lounge of the VanHome, napped, covering himself only with a blanket, too spent to change his clothes, unwilling to squander the time to walk up to his alcove, undress, sleep, bathe, dress again.

Fabian arrived at Totemfield toward dusk. The twilight stillness baffled him: he had not anticipated the closed fronts of shops and stores, and even the mall, always a small flurry of commerce, was abandoned. It was only after he passed an intersection and turned into the main street, sleepy and bare except for parked

cars on each side of it, that he realized he had intruded
on the close of a Totemfield Sunday. The morning stir
of church, the afternoon withdrawal to the intimacies
of family luncheon, the evening retreat to the seclusion
of home—all had subsided. An occasional car, Fabian's
VanHome in its wake, picked its way reluctantly
through the deserted streets, moving as if rebuked by
the spell of calm.

His reflex was to take the road to the Double Bridle
Stables, but he checked himself: it was not Stella he
wanted to see. Then the wry knowledge came to him
that even though he knew in which part of Totemfield
Vanessa's family lived, he had never driven past their
home, fearful that his VanHome might draw the attention of her family, servants or neighbors.

He took the Stanhope Hill Road, following its
spiral turns, guiding his VanHome away from im-
maculately trimmed borders. He passed through the
gate to the grounds, an ornate shield of iron, imposing
but open, the ancient guardhouse locked.

As the road widened, the VanHome moved onto a
smooth ribbon of fine white stone and sand, the corridor opening before him defined by neat hedges, not
one capricious twig marring the symmetry of their
shape.

The road forked. Far away, at the end of the drive,
he saw the commanding front of the house, the sentinels of its classic pillars guarding a reach of lawn
where two or three large shapes, sculptures of marble
and metal, loomed in the falling light. Several cars
were drawn up at the fringe of the garden, one of them
a yellow convertible.

Fabian turned his VanHome to the right, toward
what he took to be the service entrance, but as he
arrived at it, he hesitated and continued instead past
the garages, toward a row of stables and the paddocks.
A brace of colts gently nuzzled the bars of the paddock, and two or three ponies were feeding calmly. In
the back of his VanHome, Big Lick and Gaited Amble
began to frisk, quick on the scent of other horses and
the stable.

A middle-aged man in high rubber boots and plastic overalls came out of the stable. Fabian caught a swift glimpse of a suit under the overalls. The man moved with the air of an overseer on his day off, dropping by to assure himself that all was working well in his absence. Fabian stopped at the stable and stepped from the cab of his VanHome.

The man's eyes took in Fabian, then slid with annoyance toward the VanHome. "A delivery on Sunday?" he asked. "Can't you guys give yourselves and others a time for prayer?" His head bobbed in anger. "You'll have to wait with unloading. The stable boss and all the hands are off today. I'm just the guard here," he finished.

"My fault," Fabian said. "I thought it would take me longer to drive here."

"Nobody told me to expect new breeders or to make space for them! Nobody tells me anything anymore!" The man flapped his hands in mock despair. "How many did you bring this time?"

"Just two," Fabian said, moving back toward the cab of his VanHome. "But I can wait with them till tomorrow." He kept his tone conciliatory.

The man's voice softened in response. "That's real nice of you," he said. "I reckon till the boys get here, you have everything you need inside that coop of yours."

"I sure do," Fabian said. He was back in the cab now.

"Fine," the man replied as he shed his overalls and boots, ungainly in his dark blue suit and shined shoes. "I'll be in my house—over there on the grounds." He pointed to a small carriage house nestling in the woods. "When the boss comes back, ask him to sign your delivery papers," he called out as he moved away.

"Will do," Fabian answered, shutting the door of his VanHome. He stood for a moment in the lounge, then went to the alcove and opened one of its side windows. He lay on the bed, his head inclined toward the open window.

A wave of fresh air assailed him, a quickening of

autumn, a mixture of humid earth and dry wood, of leaves and grass, broken by a faint scent of horse and stable. A grove of oak trees separated the stables from the residence. He imagined that in one of the rooms of the main house, its windows open to the dusk, to the breeze that touched his shoulders and cooled his chest, was Vanessa.

A rustle of muted laughter and the sound of wheels slipping on gravel broke into his reverie. Abruptly he opened his eyes to darkness; outside the window, the trees were no longer visible.

Dazed, his body stiff with chill, Fabian forced himself to get up. For the first time in days, he took off his clothes, then eased himself with a hot bath, and shaved. He decided to wear his good suit, a relic of an earlier decade, made for him in London. The evening shirt was also an echo of other days: not the silk original that had been designed for him once in Rome, but cotton, a copy, one of several he had had inexpensively duplicated for him in La Romana, during his last polo tournament there with Eugene Stanhope.

Dressed, he went to the mirror. He flinched at the gaunt figure watching him, his pallor accentuated by his unfashionable outfit, so drastic a decline from the more youthful image he had of himself in polo or riding clothes, so different from that other time on a Totemfield lawn, only months ago, when he was a rider all in white, a rose in hand, a sword at his side, a plume in his hat.

At the door of his VanHome, he lingered, weary still from the traveling, torn between whether to let the moment pass unmolested by judgment or whether to judge it before it dissolved.

He went out into the cold evening air. The sense that only a brief walk through space and time had to be endured, whatever the consequence, before he might once again be with Vanessa, acted swiftly as an elating force, like the stir of mobilization that came on him before the challenge of a polo game, abolishing the shadowed void of his spirit, allaying even his wonder at the current of chance that had brought him here to Totemfield, at this time, on this night, once more to lurk in the darkness, alone, the interloper in a family.

He walked, uncomfortable in the tightness of dress shoes, through the grove of oak trees. The house was before him now, its light playing over the movement of his figure past the parked cars. He mounted the shallow marble steps at the entrance and pressed the embossed bell to his left.

The door swung open at the sound. A black servant in uniform smiled in welcome at the visitor framed in the doorway.

"Good evening, sir." The warmth of the smile reassured Fabian.

"Good evening," Fabian said. "Am I late?"

The servant grinned. "Never too late to enjoy yourself, sir."

Fabian touched him on the shoulder with the freedom of an old acquaintance. "You're Joseph, aren't you?" he asked.

"Brady, sir. Just Brady," the black man answered, responding to the new guest's interest.

"Tell me, Brady, where is everybody?"

"Mr. and Mrs. Stanhope and their guests are having drinks in the library."

"And Miss Vanessa?"

"Miss Vanessa is also in the library," Brady said.

Fabian took Brady by the arm and brought him close with an air of amiable conspiracy. "When Miss Vanessa called me, she said she wanted to talk to me alone before we join all the guests. Now, Brady, would you take me to her rooms, and then go and tell her that her old teacher is waiting for her there, but don't let on to anyone else, just keep it a secret between the three of us. Would you do that for her, Brady?"

"I sure will, sir," the servant said. "You just follow me." They passed too swiftly through the halls for Fabian to take in more than a shimmer of light and polished wood, his heels hard on the marble, then melting into carpets, a blaze of crystal from a chande-lier irradiating the furniture and the staircase.

They stepped aside to make room for several ser-vants, trays of drinks and food adroitly balanced in their hands.

Brady took him upstairs, toward the end of a long corridor, its walls a rich glow of portraits and draw-ings. A gust of laughter and voices from below fol-lowed their ascent.

The servant stopped in front of a door, rapped perfunctorily and then opened it, ushering Fabian into the foyer of a suite, a small carriage lamp on the wall its only light.

"You just make yourself at home, sir," Brady said, gesturing toward a sofa as he receded noiselessly through the door. "Miss Vanessa will be right with you."

Fabian moved through a study toward the entrance to Vanessa's bedroom. He trailed a hand across a chest of drawers, the pretty clutter of objects dotting the room, his eyes gliding over her bed. These were the realities of her intimate life and had been so before he entered it, would be so after his departure from it, things closer to her than any man.

He returned to the study. On the desk, another lamp revealed two large, framed photographs of him: in one, cut from the pages of *U.S. Horse and World Report* when the magazine had interviewed Fabian about the current state of horsemanship, he was mounted on a polo pony, the Fairfield club in the background; in the other, he was on Captain Ahab, accepting from Va-nessa the second-place prize at Madison Square Gar-den.

A stack of envelopes, all open, addressed to Vanes-sa, lay on the desk. He touched the thickness of the letters inside and glanced at the return address on the first envelope. It was from Stuart Hayward. In-stantly Fabian regretted that he had seen them. In his relationship with the world, whether of nature or of men, he took his cue only from what was a conse-quence of his own doing, from what, by confronting him directly, demanded an equally direct response from him. He would no more look through a keyhole, read the letters of someone else, go through someone else's possessions, than he would steal someone's money. An uninvited venture into the life of others carried, for Fabian, the risk of denying the unity of his own.

He turned toward the door at the sound of steps. The lamp in the foyer revealed Vanessa as she came in, the evening gown making her look nubile, more womanly.

She looked at the man in the room, searching his face in the obscure light; she stepped closer, and suddenly astonishment broke on her. Wordless, she went to him, put her arms about his neck, the gown flattening against his suit, her face against his, hands caressing his forehead and hair.

He disengaged himself. "Your gown, Vanessa," he said tenderly.

She turned on another light, and in its sweep he saw how radiant she was, lustrous, the beauty he had known always, makeup enhancing the symmetry of her mouth, the scar a reminder of her fragility.

"Finally, after all those times in your VanHome, you're my guest now," Vanessa said. She took in the formality of his clothes. "I've never seen you looking so—"

"Fatherly?" he suggested wryly.

"Fatherly," she agreed, laughing. Then he saw her eyes turn pensive, concerned, a mistress of the house. "When did you arrive?"

"A few hours ago. I took a nap in the VanHome."

"In the VanHome? Where is it?" she asked.

"Outside. At the stables."

Vanessa came closer, lifted one hand to graze the back of his head, then let it drift down, along his back. Her hip brushed his, then disarming the gesture with a teasing husk of laughter, she gathered his hand to her breast. "Why didn't you come straight here, to nap with me?" she murmured, her lips on his neck. "You're going to stay with me here, aren't you?"

He turned to her and tried to release himself. "You must listen to me—" he began.

"I won't listen to you. This is our home now, yours and mine." She stopped, distress clouding her face. "You upset me, Fabian, by leaving the bank without—" She broke off, and he could see it was difficult for her to speak. "Without claiming what's yours now." She was silent again, intent, her features tightened as if in pain. "No one has ever done more for me than you. You made me free with myself, with others. With my thoughts, my needs, my body. Free with my love for you: you can't turn down a gift of love—you must accept it." She brought her eyes to his. "You must because I love you, Fabian," she whispered.

He did not answer but held her, the two of them sealed in embrace, Vanessa's forehead bent to his shoulder, her hands clutching at his hips, his face eclipsed by her hair, her hands trailing the contours of his body.

"With that gift, you're free to do anything," she whispered, "free to go anywhere. Most of all, you're free to be with me."

He listened to her, his tenderness more that for a child confessing her secrets than for a woman who was his lover. He found himself, though, on the verge of telling her that he understood her, that he would never refuse anything of hers again, that all he wanted was to be with her, to have her at his side. But he remained silent.

She took him by the hand. "We shouldn't let the guests wait, should we?"

Suddenly, sharply, he was conscious that he was a stranger in her world. "But—your parents? I wasn't invited."

"You are now—it's my house, too."

Fabian followed her out into the corridor, and, as if to give him time to compose himself before they went to the library, Vanessa took his arm and drew him through some of the rooms. He felt confused by the easy splendor of antique furniture beneath bronze sconces, swelling porcelain vases, windows that were fretted networks of stained glass, the floors a mosaic of ebony and citron and boxwood, the doors sheets of mahogany, mantels of marble under paintings of landscapes, people and horses, their faithfulness of detail a challenge to nature.

From behind the door of the library, the rhythm of conversation, muted, filled Fabian with apprehension. Vanessa boldly opened the door and went in before him.

He saw the fireplace first, ten or twelve couples grouped before it, a few scattered on sofas, secure in conversation. Vanessa took Fabian's hand and walked straight toward a tall, rangy man, slightly balding, his face broad, the smile a flash of gums and large, uneven teeth. Fabian saw a resemblance to Eugene Stanhope.

The man was in conversation with an older couple when Vanessa tugged gently at his arm, and he bent indulgently toward her.

"I want you to meet someone very special, Father," she said.

With a vacant smile that was the reflex of a lifetime of social exchange, the residue of countless cocktail parties and receptions, Patrick Stanhope extended his hand to Fabian.

"Father, this is Fabian," Vanessa said. "He's just arrived to be with me."

Patrick Stanhope's hand was firm when Fabian shook it, but at Vanessa's introduction his smile narrowed, then vanished. Fabian observed with surprise that he was probably older than Stanhope.

"I'm glad you could come, Mr. Fabian," Stanhope said curtly. Then, conscious of Vanessa's watchful gaze and the curiosity of the older couple, he introduced Fabian. Vanessa's mother approached at that moment. She was in her forties, a handsome woman, with thick brown hair and a healthy complexion, her limber body announcing her ease in the world of sports.

"I'm Doris Stanhope, Vanessa's mother," she said pleasantly, "and you taught our girl to ride so well!"

At his daughter's side, Patrick Stanhope faced his

wife and Fabian. The older couple drifted away. "Eugene spoke often of you," Stanhope said to Fabian, his voice matter-of-fact.

"I apologize for coming without an invitation," Fabian said, on guard in what he knew was not neutral ground. "But I was eager to see Vanessa—and to meet you."

"No need to apologize, Mr. Fabian. We're glad you came," Doris Stanhope said, politely.

"Aren't you going to ask them for my hand?" Vanessa broke in, the playful child again. "He might as well." She turned abruptly, but laughing, to her mother. "He's already taken everything else!"

Patrick Stanhope looked around him, apprehensive that his daughter's remark might have been overheard. He maneuvered his wife to block a group of guests bearing down on them, then he moved closer to Fabian and spoke with a low, blunt urgency. "How long will you be in Totemfield, Mr. Fabian?"

"Fabian is staying with us for a while," Vanessa announced confidently.

Fabian was startled at the security of his voice as he took Vanessa's arm and replied to her father's question. "Unfortunately, I have to leave early in the morning."

A flush rose to Vanessa's face as she pulled back in dismay. "You can't, Fabian!" she whispered, pain on her face. Stanhope reached out instinctively to shield her shoulders.

Stuart Hayward walked across the room toward them; there was a smile of familiarity, an assurance of being welcome, in the way he wedged himself between Vanessa and Fabian.

"How have you been, Mr. Fabian?" He shook Fabian's hand. "I've never had a chance to thank you for what you did at the Garden for us." He paused. "For Vanessa and me. And for Captain Ahab, who's now in the big leagues."

"It was easy after all the great jumping you'd done with Captain Ahab so often," said Fabian.

Vanessa raised her eyes toward him. The stricken

expression was still on her face and, noticing it, Stuart bent toward her in concern.

"Are you visiting Totemfield for long, Mr. Fabian?" he asked. He was trying to slip his arm around Vanessa's waist, but, still distressed, she avoided him.

"Mr. Fabian is leaving tomorrow," Stanhope said, forcing the bonhomie.

Locked into uneasiness, his smile automatic and mirthless, he clapped Hayward on the shoulder with perfunctory heartiness. "Why don't you and Vanessa help her mother with the other guests, while Mr. Fabian and I take some time out in my study? We've got to have a little talk about this troublesome colt of mine." Before Vanessa could interrupt, he motioned Fabian toward a door off the library.

Stanhope led the way into his study, its stateliness hushed and curiously insulated from the stir in the library. Fabian took in the leather and mellow wood, the baroque desk in the corner. The only incongruous notes were a large video system to one side of the desk and a sleek array of telephones on its top, their ranks of buttons burnished in the light of the fireplace. For a moment, he remembered that other afternoon with a Stanhope, in another place, a drawing room, Eugene shouting from behind a hunt table, Alexandra at his side. Now, with Patrick Stanhope, a lush ruby spill of Persian carpet muffled their voices as well as their steps.

Patrick Stanhope gestured Fabian toward one of a pair of large red armchairs flanking the fire. When Fabian sat down, he looked up and caught the imperious mien of Commodore Ernest Tenet Stanhope, the family patriarch, whose massive portrait commanded the room.

The façade of a false bookcase swung open at Stanhope's touch, revealing a bar. After Fabian's refusal of a drink, he prepared one for himself and then sank into the armchair across from Fabian.

Stanhope's face was haggard with disquiet. "I can't quite bring myself to tell you what's on my mind, Fabian," he began. "Somehow, it just seems either too strong or not strong enough. First, let me assure you that I have never, never," he repeated emphatically, bringing his glass down on the arm of the chair, "held you responsible for my brother's death. It's true, Eugene and I had our differences. We didn't see much of each other, but I knew he and you were the best of friends. Of course, I also knew about your reputation as a tricky player. God knows, there was enough talk about it. Still, I'm convinced Eugene's death had to be an accident, an accident pure and simple." Stanhope was putting all his conviction into his voice. "And I hope you know that I was the one who asked Stockey to keep trying to get you as the host for our polo television series."

Fabian nodded.

Stanhope leaned back in the chair wearily, as if the burden of what he had to say was a physical weight on him. "But, frankly, Fabian, I wanted you to work for us partly because I also knew how much Vanessa worshiped you as her riding coach. I want you to know this, to show how much I appreciate what you did for my daughter."

Stanhope took a long, slow draught from his drink. "Vanessa is our only child, and with her deformity—" He broke off, suddenly desolate, then looked up.

"You mean her scar?" Fabian said gently.

"Her scar." Stanhope nodded. "The poor child went through all those operations to have it removed. The first one was just after she was born. Her mouth was so bad they could only do a little at a time, and soon there was another operation. When the Commodore, my father, up there," he said, raising his glass toward the portrait, "saw what she would have to go through, he made Vanessa the chief heir to his money. She was his only grandchild. He passed over his two sons, Eugene and me, for her." Stanhope was speaking vacantly now, dull with recollection.

"She was operated on again when she was seven, in New York. But nothing seemed to help. And that wasn't the end. When the scar still showed, and she was no longer a child, we took her to Switzerland, to a famous surgeon in a clinic in Sion. He corrected a lot of it, but—" Stanhope's voice faltered in resignation, but then he rallied himself, as if to underscore the importance of what he was about to say.

"Doris and I have always tried to be good parents to Vanessa," he said distantly, his eyes moving without expression over the richness of the room. "Because of what she'd had to go through, we've often let her have her own way," he went on, "even when we weren't sure it was a good thing. The doctors told us that all that surgery, all those operations, might have just as damaging an effect on her psychic life as the original deformation—such a violation, all that mauling of her mouth and face." Stanhope flinched at the memory. "They said a child who had to go through things like that could turn on herself or come to hate everything around her." He was suddenly more alert, still in pain, but measuring every word. "Or that she might become desperately anxious for love and terribly possessive about it when she found it, always afraid of losing it." He rose abruptly, the glass empty in his hand, and went to the bar. "Vanessa is such a possessive girl, Fabian. The money she gave you is part of her trust from the Commodore. This money is her only power." Stanhope was preparing another drink with the precision of a chemist. "She gave it to you not because she loves you—not *only* because she loves you," he corrected himself, "but because she wants to own you, to control you." As he finished, the glass rapped sharply on the counter. He returned to his post across from Fabian and sat down, his eyes tracing the design of the carpet.

"When Vanessa made up her mind to transfer this money to you," Stanhope continued, as if musing aloud to himself, "until she had arranged it all with her lawyers and bankers, it seemed as though she was afraid you might run away from her." His voice thickened not with bitterness but with a pain he could not stem. "That was when she told us she was going to marry you. Even when Doris and I pointed out that she was hardly out of school, that she still had college ahead of her, that she was——" he faltered, unwilling to wound, but gathering boldness from the sympathetic intentness of Fabian's presence, "that you were——that she would be marrying a man so advanced in age, in fact, a man older than her mother, older even than her father——she said age didn't make any difference, that she wanted you, and only you. She said that her gift would make you free and make others certain that you wouldn't be marrying her for her money."

Stanhope put his drink on the table before him. "But now that you've turned down Vanessa's gift, Fabian, everything's different. Do you think that marrying Vanessa would be the best thing for her? For the children she might want to have one day? The wisest thing for you?" In the play of light on the pale eyes confronting him, Fabian saw tears.

Fabian rose and crossed swiftly to the other man, his arm going out to touch Stanhope's shoulder. Vanessa's father accepted the gesture and its warmth.

"I love Vanessa," Fabian said. "I always have. She is a child I never had, a daughter I always wanted, the lover so much younger than I." The pressure of feeling tightened his grasp on Stanhope's shoulder. "Most of all I love the spirit that makes her as free as she is. I hope I've done nothing to confine her——and I won't now."

Gently he removed his hand, and spoke to the silence of the room, more than to Stanhope. "That's why I could never marry Vanessa or take her away with me. And that's why I'll be leaving tomorrow, leaving without her."

Patrick Stanhope stumbled slightly as he rose, and when Fabian steadied him, he felt the other man's rush of feeling, unstoppable, his arms closing in clumsy relief around Fabian.

"But remember," Stanhope said thickly, "she's easily hurt; don't make her feel rejected." He stepped back and looked at Fabian, stressing each word. "Try to make her know you're leaving her because you have to——because of a commitment," he faltered, "to your way of life."

"Vanessa knows me quite well," Fabian said. "She won't have to ask me why I am the way I am."

Stanhope was recovering now: the executive overtook the father. "I think Vanessa ought to leave Totemfield. With you gone, she won't stay here one day longer anyhow—the memories are all wrong." Action and decision had rallied him. "I'll arrange to have her flown to her aunt in Virginia tomorrow, then send her on a long trip abroad." He stretched his arm and led Fabian briskly to the door. "Time to get back to the party," he said, the automatic smile returning. "Somebody might think we've eloped."

In the library, Vanessa again attached herself to Fabian, at once basking submissively in his presence and yet radiant in her claim on him. But Fabian felt a decisive shift in the atmosphere. Warmth had supplanted Doris Stanhope's earlier amiability; Patrick Stanhope was almost effusive on several occasions, bringing Fabian forth as a family friend. Only Stuart Hayward kept his distance, ignoring Fabian with studied politeness.

Vanessa registered the altered mood of her family, puzzlement yielding slowly to resignation.

The Stanhopes were to attend, with others of their guests, a charity dinner later in the evening. As they prepared to leave, Patrick Stanhope insisted that, if Fabian were to depart on the following day, before they awoke, then he must return for another visit soon.

Stuart Hayward remained in the library, sullen, trying to arrange a moment alone with Vanessa. As she moved away in rebuff, Fabian went to her, whispering that he wanted to see her and would wait for her in his VanHome. She nodded.

He left the house and went out, back through the cluster of trees. Shafts of light from the main house threw the sculptures on the lawn into somber relief. From the side of an upstairs wing, cubes of brightness shone into the night.

At his VanHome, he left the door open, switched off all the lights and stretched out on the sofa in the lounge. He was waiting.

The image of her face returned, the surprise and hurt that had twisted her features when he said he would be leaving in the morning. He thought of Vanessa in the evening gown, the womanhood that was hers now, the assurance with which she had fended off young Hayward.

Fabian wondered how she would come this time. Would she slip out of the main house, through the darkness, the welcome fugitive noiselessly invading his VanHome, a small girl tempted by the game of hide-and-seek, perching somewhere in the lounge or the galley? Or, would she tiptoe up to the alcove or along the corridor to the tack room, lurking behind the wooden horse or in the stall with the ponies, signaling her presence with a first deliberate hint of sound, alerting him to the spell of the hunt?

"Why are you leaving me?" Vanessa's voice came at him as if from above, detached from a body that he could not see. He sat up and reached toward what he thought was its source, but she was not there. He was reaching out into vacant darkness, a blind man without his cane.

"Why are you leaving me?" The voice came again, below him now, as though muffled by the floor. He fell to his knees and crawled silently toward the sound, one arm extended, an antenna.

"Why are you leaving me?" Now her voice was muted, drifting from behind the galley or the bathroom. He began to move swiftly through his Van-Home, surprised at how well another might know it, even in the dark.

He reached the stairs to the alcove, certain that she was waiting for him in his bed. He was about to walk up the stairs when he was arrested by a sound; it came from a small cleft between the tack room and the stall, a secret area Fabian had turned into a sleeping berth, a hideaway that he had devised solely for Vanessa in those days when, insisting that they both be naked, she had rushed to be with him, and he had agreed to her demand, confident that the berth, opening into the tack room through a concealed door, would protect them and allow them time to dress or to stay hidden should anyone intrude.

He reached the tack room and pressed his face to the hideaway's door. Even before he heard her breathing, the sense of her presence came at him. He began slowly to open the door, but suddenly it was pulled open from within, and he was swept in. The light above him went on abruptly.

Vanessa was naked, her gown and shoes heaped on the shelf high above the berth. She did not repeat her question, but came to him avid for his touch, the heat of her mouth dry, her cheeks burning, her eyes seeking out the answer he had not given her.

To escape that scrutiny, to impel her back to herself, he laid her on the berth. Vanessa's gaze was still on him as, grounded between her thighs, he watched her, his face hovering above hers.

There was a moment when her tension alerted him, compressing and inciting her as it sought release, a force opposing his presence in her depths. Her breathing came in tidal spasms, the rhythm of each tide broken, now impetuous, then spacious, the beat of it persistent, her tongue sliding urgently along his fingers and the palm of his hand. Her nostrils distended, her only sound was a sigh, a spill of air warming his hand and face. As he raised his eyes to gauge her sense of him, she broke into a wrenching gust, a volatile pitch constrained no more, unbound, fusing in flight with the air about the body that had held it captive. Her stare slid over him, tears anointing her nose and lips, falling over her shoulders and breasts, a salty flow merging with the other remote fluids of her body.

Now the rhythm of sobs was unleashed, its pulse inconsistent, her breath imprisoned. He saw that her face, pale now, was no longer turned to him. She lifted herself, her feet and hands away from him, but just as he was about to reach out for her, to reclaim her to his touch, to her sense of him, she fell back, the sobbing gone, her breath fluent, tears in check.

"Why are you leaving me?" she murmured, his silence and his hand on her body the only answer she wanted when she fell asleep in his arms under his hand, a child tired after a long voyage.

At dawn, he attempted to wake her, to tell her that she would have to return to her own bed in her own house. But she refused to stir and bound herself tightly in his plaid blanket of coarse wool, only the hand that had drawn the blanket over her body and face resting limp on top.

Beyond sleep, Fabian sat next to her, guarding her rest, aware that, if compelled to relinquish that last moment at her side, driven to retract it in time, deny it in memory, he would rather have renounced what was left of his life.

He dressed and went to the cab. He sat down behind the steering wheel, a captain about to take again to the sea, switched on the ignition, and felt the warming engine send a tremor through his VanHome.

He opened the windows. The morning air blew Vanessa's scent from his face and body. He heard the muted snorting of his ponies, chafing at the long confinement in their stalls.

He shifted into gear; the massive trunk of the Van-Home shuddered and moved. He guided it quietly around the house, near the main entrance. He left the engine running while he went back through the lounge, the galley, the tack room, to the berth where Vanessa was still sleeping, just as he had left her, her hand on the blanket. He slipped his fingers between Vanessa's body and the sheets, wedging his hand under her, receiving her weight, lifting her gently. He brought her to his chest, and held the inert warmth of her body there a moment. She opened her eyes.

"It's time," Fabian said.

Knowledge of what he meant dawned on her, and

the two of them looked at each other, pain the only presence in her face. He put her down and reached for her clothes and shoes on the shelf above the berth. In silence, he held them, waiting for her.

"You won't come back to me anymore, will you?" Vanessa asked, huddling in the blanket.

Fabian avoided her eyes. He let his memory wander over her hair, her shoulders, her hands, the rough blanket that separated her from him: she had already gone beyond his reach. "No I won't, Vanessa."

Awkwardly, she gestured with the blanket cloaking her. "May I keep this?" she asked.

"You may."

She walked ahead of him, padding barefoot through his VanHome, her hands kneading the blanket. In the lounge, she waited, her eyes lingering for a moment on the staircase to the alcove.

Then she was at the door to the cab.

She turned to face him, her eyes a screen of tears. She caught her breath sharply, her teeth trapping her scar.

"Good-bye, Fabian," she whispered. She reached out blindly for her clothes, her shoes. The blanket opened on a shimmer of her breasts, then closed.

Suddenly, she was gone. At the door of the house, she did not turn to look back. The door closed behind her.

He drove through the streets of Totemfield, noting mechanically the road to the Double Bridle Stables and the other road, to Betsy Weirstone's, the deserted shopping mall, an occasional gas station intruding on the monotony of highway-and field. Finally, he turned into a road that took him past the abandoned railway station, past the garbage dump, deep into the woods.

The route he took now was familiar, still unpaved, a track of wilderness. He had traveled it often when he was teaching at the Double Bridle Stables. It led to a clearing in the woods, broad enough for his VanHome, the ground firm enough for its weight, a traction for its wheels, the brush and trees a ready camouflage. Now, again as he had done in the past, Fabian backed into the clearing, facing the road, ready to drive out as quickly as he had entered.

The clearing seemed unchanged since he had been here last. Beyond its shallow plain, the stretches of land were dappled with milkweed and mayapple, with spongy beds of cypress; from the stubby fields pungent with the tartness of autumn, the tide of memory, of waiting for Vanessa, broke over him, as he listened, even now, for the faint signal of the bell from her bicycle.

He wondered why, when he had come here for the first time, so many years ago, he had not paused to search himself as closely as he had searched this clearing; and whether, if he had, he might have foreseen that he would come back here time and again, that no matter what he sought, he would always find himself, alone in this clearing. Now as then he felt the inexorability of the past and was baffled by his failure to thwart its cycle of repetition.

The weight of memory, of his own thought and fatigue, overtook him. He dragged himself up to the alcove and onto the bed. He remembered his ponies, hungry and untended for so long, as he drifted into sleep.

Fabian woke at midday. In the bath, the reality assailed him, as scalding as the water on his body, that until now, whenever he had left Vanessa, she could be certain of his return. Now it was she who would be leaving, and he could be certain that, lost to her future, she would never return.

Time would no longer be the span that had passed since they had been together, and no more would he be the architect of time, devising a form to arrest its ceaseless motion. Chaos spilled in on him again, a tangled maze of action without intent, emotion, wanton and fugitive, closing over, sealing irrevocably the serene space of that morning at the Double Bridle Stables, when he had first seen her.

He wanted to speak with Vanessa once more, a last time, even though all that was to be said between them had already been said many times. What he longed to tell her, could say to her, eluded him in his solitude. He knew he would not want to say anything that might disturb or wound her.

He acknowledged the nature of his despair: confronted by the reality of her feelings for him, he could no longer sustain the image of himself as the heir to her time, the witness and sole chronicler of her history as a woman, the image of the two of them as the reef that divisive time, healing one wound and inflicting another, could not wear down. To give her the right to confront her life on her own, he had to unfasten the chain that bound her to him. The spring and hidden purpose of what he had done so many times, of what was now the only reality of his past binding him to his future, broke on him—how, at times, in the middle of the night, when he chanced upon a hospital, a home for the aged and abandoned, a warehouse for those whom the world had discarded, he would stop his VanHome, lock it, and go there.

Once inside such a place he would ask for the doctor in residence, a nurse in charge or a guard on duty. He would introduce himself as a man in transit, a horseman to be sure, but a writer too, a teller of tales, stories about people who ride horses, stories it would please him to give pleasure with, gladly tell to one who, at such a late hour, was lonely, could not sleep and was willing to listen. His credentials established, Fabian would be escorted through corridors and lobbies to a post between oxygen tanks, kidney machines, the grotesque armory of weapons in the defense of what was least defensible, most vulnerable—life, solitary in its evanescence, the flesh in decay, beyond healing, a cancer in the innards of time, death having already dispatched its calling card, the pungent scent of mortality.

Here was the regency of pain that imprisoned time, drugs that could numb and stupefy, its only challenge, television's images and sounds no longer a distraction, the presence and voice of a visitor a ritual in useless mime, one's own imagination the sole messenger of consolation. Intent on the shape before him, Fabian would address himself to a man or a woman, on occasion a child—not to be cured, but breathing still, thought alive—as a traveler, with time and inclination to spare, eager to meet one who was, like him, traveling, but merely on a different path. He would settle in a chair and begin to tell some fable of his own or of another, his VanHome once more on the trail of life, of time lived or time left behind or time still to come, of nature that exacted and then forgave, of man's greed and man's love. He would set the stage for the play of passion for one for whom passion was no longer a play, for whom it had lost fascination and allure, mystery and enigma. Always careful to keep his fantasy in check, so as to release the imagination of his listener, Fabian might explain the art of horsemanship, talk of strategies of combat to one for whom victory was beyond reach, chronicle the embraces of lovers to one who would embrace no more.

Fabian dressed quickly, snatched a handful of coins for the telephone and rushed to the stable at the back of his VanHome. He prodded Big Lick onto the path outside, saddling it in frantic haste, and, once mounted, threw it into a gallop, panic choking him at the thought that he might be too late, that Vanessa might already be on the plane.

The sandy road reeled past him, muffling the beat of the mare's hoofs, a track of dust rising from the earth to cloud and pursue him. He reached the telephone booth just as it began to glow in the afternoon sun. Now his panic encompassed fear that the telephone might not be working. He fumbled for a coin, found one, then, trembling, dropped it into the slot and dialed. The signal began, an electronic cadence, a long spill of sound sliced by silences that punctuated his anguished impatience; the phantom of the telephone in Vanessa's study materialized, the ringing piercing the quiet, Vanessa rushing, her hand reaching for the receiver.

But the signal continued. He could not bring himself to believe that she was gone, that he had missed her, that the words she had spoken in his VanHome were the last he would hear from her. He hung up abruptly, let the coin return and dialed again. Now he could not be shaken in his conviction that Vanessa had answered just at the moment he hung up and that the line would be busy.

The line was not busy. The signal went on—a moment, perhaps two, time an astringent on his heart, while outside, unperturbed, Big Lick nuzzled the glass wall of the booth. Standing with the receiver in his hand, hearing the insolence of its monotonous signal, Fabian knew that time had blocked his path, that it was too late to return to his VanHome and drive it to the airstrip. He bolted from the booth, mounted the horse and, cutting through the woods, raced for the airstrip. He took a shortcut, following the path that ran along the abandoned railway, a road he had taken only once before, frantic as he saw it narrow after a mile or two, clogged with empty barrels and abandoned, corroded cars. His only goal now was to go fast, faster still, straining Big Lick flat out to jump the barrels, careening through the hulking rubble, hoofs hacking at the skeletons of glass and metal.

The railway line ended in brush that was its frontier. Beyond, the airstrip spooled out, a shimmer of heat and asphalt. A small two-engine jet was the only plane on the strip. Readying for takeoff, it was slowly bearing down on Fabian, and even before the plane swung to turn, its colorful corporate symbol glinting on the silver bulk, Fabian knew its passenger. Now despair gave way to regret, and Fabian no longer thought of Vanessa: all that mattered was his horse, freed from the oppression of the brush, ready to race. He started along the runway, Big Lick unrestrained, whipping the withered grass to a fine dust. Fabian came abreast of the plane and glanced at the windows, a row of one-way mirrors. Its engines roaring, the plane started to roll for takeoff. As it wheeled past him, the mirrors of its windows winking, Fabian imagined the pilot turning to Vanessa, directing her gaze to the runway, relishing what he saw. "Take a look, Miss Stanhope! You don't see many of those anymore!" he would say. Vanessa, her forehead bent to the cool glass of the window, would catch sight of a man on a horse, streaming along the black strip of runway, the man's helmet, shirt and breeches all white, his horse black, the run of the horse unbroken, the rider tilting, as if charging with a lance, in combat with an enemy only he could see.

ON KOSINSKI

Jerzy Kosinski has lived through—and now makes use of—some of the strongest direct experience that this century has had to offer.

TIME

To appreciate the violent, ironic, suspenseful, morally demanding world of JERZY KOSINSKI's novels, one must first acknowledge the random succession of pain and joy, wealth and poverty, persecution and approbation that have made his own life often as eventful as those of his fictional creations.

He was born in Poland. When he was six, all but two members of his once numerous and distinguished family were lost in the Holocaust of World War II. Abandoned, suspected of being a Jew or a gypsy, he fled alone from village to village in Nazi-occupied eastern Europe, working as a farm hand, gaining his knowledge of nature, animal life, farming—and survival. At the age of nine, in a traumatic confrontation with a hostile peasant crowd he lost the power of speech, and was unable to talk for over five years. After the war, he was reunited with his ailing parents (his father was a scholar of ancient linguistics, his mother a pianist) and placed in a school for the handicapped. While on vacation, he regained his voice in a skiing accident, and with renewed self-reliance promptly worked his way through high school.

During his studies at the state-controlled Stalinist college and university he was suspended twice and often threatened with expulsion for his rejection of the official Marxist doctrine. While a Ph.D candidate in social psychology, he rose rapidly to become an associate professor and grantee of the Academy of Sciences, the state's highest research institution. Attempting to free himself from state-imposed collectivity, he would spend winters as a ski instructor in the Tatra Mountains, and summers as a social counselor at a Baltic sea resort.

Meanwhile, secretly, he plotted his escape. A confident master of bureaucratic judo, Kosinski pitted himself against the Establishment. In need of official sponsors, and reluctant to implicate his family, his friends and the academy staff, he created four distinguished—but fictitious—members of the Academy of Sciences to act in that capacity. As a member of the Academy's inner circle and a prize-winning photographer (with many one-man exhibitions to his credit), Kosinski had access to state printing plants, and he was able to furnish each academician with the appropriate official seals, rubber stamps and stationery. His punishment, had he been caught, would have been many years in prison. After two years of active correspondence between his fictitious sponsors and the various government agencies, Kosinski obtained an official passport allowing him to visit the United States under the auspices of an equally fictitious American "foundation." Waiting for his U.S. visa, expecting to be arrested at any time, Kosinski carried a foil-wrapped egg of cyanide in his pocket. "One way or another," he vowed, "they won't be able to keep me here against my will." But his plan worked. On December 20, 1957, Kosinski arrived in New York fluent in several languages though only with a rudimentary knowledge of English, following what he still considers the singular most creative act of his life. "I left behind being an inner emigré trapped in spiritual exile," he says. "America was to give shelter to my real self and I wanted to become its writer-in-residence." He was twenty-four years of age—his American odyssey was about to begin.

He started wandering widely in the United States as a truck driver, moonlighting as a parking lot attendant, a cinema projectionist, a portrait photographer, a limousine and racing-car driver for a black nightclub enterpreneur. "By working in Harlem as a white, uniformed chauffeur I broke a color barrier of the profession," he recalls. Studying English whenever he could in a year he learned it well enough to obtain a Ford Foundation fellowship. Two years later, as a student of social psychology, he wrote the first of his two nonfiction books on collective society. It became an instant bestseller, serialized by *The Saturday Evening Post*, condensed by *Reader's Digest*, and published in 18 languages. He was firmly set on a writing career.

After his publishing debut he met Mary Weir, the widow of a steel magnate from Pittsburgh. They dated for two years and were married after the publication of Kosinski's second nonfiction book.

During his 10 years with Mary Weir (which ended with her death) Kosinski moved with utmost familiarity in the world of heavy industry, big business and high society. He and Mary traveled a great deal—there was a private plane, a 17-crew boat, and houses in Pittsburgh, New York, Hobe Sound, Southampton, Paris, London and Florence. He led a life most novelists only invent in the pages of their novels.

"During my marriage, I had often thought that it was Stendhal or F. Scott Fitzgerald, both preoccupied with wealth they themselves did not have, who deserved to have had my experience. At first, I considered writing a novel about my immediate American experience, the dimension of wealth, power and high society that surrounded me, not the terror, poverty and privation I had seen and experienced so shortly before. But during my marriage I was too much a part of that world to extract from it the nucleus of what I felt. As a writer, I perceived fiction as the art of imaginative projection and so, instead, I decided to write my first novel about a homeless boy in war-torn Eastern Europe, an existence I'd once led and also one that was shared by millions of others like me, yet was still foreign to most Americans. This novel, *The Painted Bird,* was my gift to Mary, and to my new world."

His following novels—*Steps, Being There, The Devil Tree, Cockpit, Blind Date* and *Passion Play,* all links in an elaborate fictional cycle, were inspired by particular events of his life. He would often draw on the experience he had gained when, once a "Don Quixote of the turnpike," he had become a "Captain Ahab of billionaire's row." "Kosinski has enough technical virtuosity to outwrite almost any competitor," wrote *Los Angeles Herald Examiner,* "but few novelists have a personal background like his to draw on." Translated into most major languages, at first his novels have earned Kosinski the status of an international underground culture hero. Official recognition followed: for *The Painted Bird,* the French Best Foreign Book Award; for *Steps,* the National Book Award. He received a Guggenheim fellowship, the Award in Literature of the American Academy and the National Institute of Arts and Letters, as well as the Brith Sholom Humanitarian Freedom Award, and many others.

While Kosinski was constantly on the move, living and writing in various parts of the United States, Europe and Latin America, close calls with death persisted in his life.

On his way from Paris to the Beverly Hills home of his friend, film director Roman Polanski, and his wife, Sharon Tate, Kosinski's luggage was unloaded by mistake in New York. Unable to catch the connecting flight to Los Angeles, Kosinski reluctantly stayed overnight in New York. That very night in Polanski's household the Charles Manson Helter-Skelter gang murdered five people—among them Kosinski's closest friends, one of whom he financially assisted in leaving Europe and settling in the States.

For the next few years Kosinski taught English at Princeton and Yale. He left university life when he was elected president of American P.E.N., the international association of writers and editors. After serving the maximum two terms, he has remained active in various American human rights organizations. He is proud to have been responsible for freeing from prisons, helping financially, resettling or otherwise giving assistance to a great number of writers, political and religious dissidents and intellectuals all over the world, many of whom openly acknowledged his coming to their rescue.

Called by *America* "a spokesman for the human capacity to survive in a highly complex social system," Kosinski has been often labeled by the media an existential cowboy, a Horatio Alger of the nightmare, a penultimate gamesman, the utterly portable man and a mixture of adventurer and social reformer. In an interview for *Psychology Today*, Kosinski said: "And I have no habits that require maintaining—I don't even have a favorite menu—the only way for me to live is to be as close to other people as life allows. Not much else stimulates me—and nothing interests me more."

Traveling extensively, on an average Kosinski wakes up around 8 A.M. ready for the day. Four more hours of sleep in the afternoon allows him to remain mentally and physically active until the early dawn when he retires. This pattern, he claims, benefits his writing, his photography, and practicing of the sports he has favored for years—downhill skiing and polo, which, as an avid all-around horseman, he plays on a team—or one-on-one.

As a novelist and a screenplay writer (he adapted for the screen his novel, *Being There* which starred Peter Sellers, Shirley MacLaine, Melvyn Douglas and Jack Warden, for which he was nominated for the Golden Globe and won the Writers Guild of America Best Screenplay of the Year Award)—Kosinski is frequently interviewed by the press and appears often on television. Thus, he is apt to be recognized, and to obtain private access to public places he sometimes disguises himself; occasionally, he takes part-time employment in businesses and corporations that interest him.

A critic once said of Kosinski that he "writes his novels so sparsely as though they cost a thousand dollars a word, and a misplaced or misused locution would cost him his life." He was close to the truth: Kosinski takes almost three years to write a novel, and rewrites it a dozen times; later, in subsequence sets of proofs, he condenses the novel's text often by one-third. Kosinski said that "writing fiction is the essence of my life—whatever else I do revolves around a constant thought: could I—can I—would I—should I—use it in my next novel? As I have no children, no family, no relatives, no business or estate to speak of, my books are my only spiritual accomplishment."

"Learning from the best writing of every era—wrote *The Washington Post*—Kosinski develops his own style and technique. . . . in harmony with his need to express new things about our life and the world we do live in, to express the inexpressible. Giving to himself as well as to the reader the same chance for interpretation, he traces the truth in the deepest corners of our outdoor and indoor lives, of our outer appearance and our inner reality. He moves the borderline of writing to more remote, still invisible and untouchable poles, in cold and in darkness. Doing so, he enlarges the borders of the bearable."